This book is dedicated to Eve Watson, my partner in crime.

OUR
LITTLE
LIES

ALSO BY SUE WATSON

Love, Lies and Lemon Cake
Snow Angels, Secrets and Christmas Cake
Summer Flings and Dancing Dreams
Fat Girls and Fairy Cakes
Younger Thinner Blonder
Bella's Christmas Bake Off
We'll Always have Paris
The Christmas Cake Café
Ella's Ice Cream Summer
Curves, Kisses and Chocolate Ice Cream
Snowflakes, Iced Cakes and Second Chances
Love, Lies and Wedding Cake

OUR LITTLE LIES

SUE WATSON

Bookouture

Published by Bookouture in 2018

An imprint of StoryFire Ltd.
Carmelite House
50 Victoria Embankment
London EC4Y 0DZ

www.bookouture.com

ISBN: 978-1-78681-750-1
eBook ISBN: 978-1-78681-749-5

PROLOGUE

We watch the news coverage, horrified yet mesmerised. As if the body they're putting in the ambulance now isn't someone we know. But it is… it's someone we know very well.

CHAPTER ONE

It's the way he says her name that first alerts me. I'm buttering toast for the children when he says 'Caroline…' I don't hear the rest, just the way his mouth caresses *Caroline*.

It's hard to explain, but something tells me she's more than a colleague. Perhaps it's the way his tongue rolls languorously over the 'r', ending with a contented sigh on the 'ine'.

I run the knife slowly along the butter as I look up and see *her* in his eyes. I know, I know, I haven't a clue who this woman is and it's stupid of me to jump to conclusions. I need more evidence than the sound of his bloody voice. But then again I know. I just *know*. I've known for some time; she's been with us – with me – for a while. As yet undiagnosed, experience tells me these symptoms can't be ignored. I can't leave them to fester and bloom like cancer in my marriage. Picking up a fresh knife, I open the jar of marmalade and dig into the viscous amber stickiness. *Caroline*.

'Is she new?' I ask.

'What?' He feigns vagueness. 'Oh, Caroline Harker?' There it is again, the roll of the 'r', the sigh of the 'ine'. 'Err… no… she started in surgical before me.'

'Where's she from?' I'm now cracking an egg on the side of the bowl, trying not to imagine it's her head.

'Edinburgh. Very talented, only thirty-two…'

I'm overcome by a sharp wave of nausea and move away from the eggs, opaque and sickly yellow. Pulling my bathrobe around me to ward off the chill, I quickly jam the lid back on the marmalade jar, like something might escape. But it might already be too late. Wobbly and disorientated, I spritz the kitchen counter, covering any lingering odour with the zing of fresh lemons.

I move around briskly now, wiping all the surfaces. I don't stop at one, I can't – I must clean them all.

'I was thinking Elephant's Breath...?'

He looks up from his phone, puzzled, an undertow of irritation on his face.

'The paint shade for the sitting room... it's a sort of grey?' I explain.

He nods, absently. I'm talking about wall colours to remove Caroline from the kitchen, *my* kitchen, where *my* children are about to eat breakfast. I wipe harder at the kitchen surfaces, wishing it was as easy to wipe her away. I throw the cloth into the sink with unnecessary force and turn back to the task in hand. Breakfast.

Slicing the home-made wholemeal I baked at three this morning, I whip the raw eggs vigorously and pour freshly squeezed orange juice into three glasses. *That's better.*

The twins are yelling and thundering around upstairs and I glance at Simon, who rolls his eyes.

'Do they ever do anything quietly without trying to kill each other?'

'That would be boring.' I laugh, pulled out of my abyss as Sophie wafts in, a faraway look in her seventeen-year-old eyes.

I look at her and am filled with maternal love. I fell for her when I fell for Simon. He'd lost his wife, Sophie her mother. She was only seven and so lost and bewildered. I'll never forget the first time we met and she looked up at me and asked 'are you going to be my mummy now?' And in that moment I melted and knew I could love this child like my own. She needed me and I like to think that once I was in her life I made the world okay for her again. I can never replace her mother, but we're close – it's just been difficult since I had the boys to give her the time and attention she needs. I feel guilty about that. She adores her half-brothers, but they fill our lives with their boisterousness and noisy demands and I worry Sophie may feel a little pushed out sometimes. I try and snatch half an hour here and there with her, a bit of shopping, some lunch, and we laugh together like we used to, but it's rare, and recently she seems to have withdrawn again. I presume it's the sudden move here, or perhaps it's got nothing to do with home life and she's fallen in love? *Don't do it Sophie. Don't fall, you'll never get up again.*

'Can you shout the boys for me, darling?' I smile at her, using this as a chance to look into her face, to try and gauge the level of teenage hormones and happiness.

'Alfieeee, Charlieeee,' she yells loudly, virtually standing next to me.

I cover my ears playfully. 'I could have done *that*,' I say. 'What I *meant* was go to the bottom of the stairs and call them.' I'm now lifting a pile of wobbly golden eggs onto plates and putting them neatly down at each place. I smile indulgently at her through the steam.

'Sophie, do you have to yell like that? You're seventeen not bloody seven. Grow up!' The sudden sharpness in Simon's voice cuts through the warm, buttered-toast air.

He doesn't mean to be harsh, she just gave him a start. He's trying to concentrate and lashed out a little, something he rarely does with the children, which is why we're so surprised. I glance at Sophie and she seems to shrink before me. I look over to see if he's realised the effect his words have had on her, but he's still on his phone, already in work mode. In his absence, I'll put the plaster on her hurt feelings.

'Your eggs, Your Majesty,' I say, rolling one arm in an elaborately subservient manner while putting the plate in front of her. But it's too late, she's now sulkily slumping into a chair, her gossamer wings crumpled. If only he realised how much she loves him, how she so desperately wants his approval. Sophie's always been a daddy's girl, and I know he adores her, and would do anything for her, but her teenage insecurities overwhelm her sometimes and his insensitivity can sting. I ache for her but don't have time to try and bring her round now. It's already 8.15 and the twins are thundering down the stairs. They 'land' in the kitchen, arguing about who can do the loudest belch, and this is accompanied by vigorous and revolting demonstrations.

'Boys please, that's not nice,' I say wearily, but they continue to make disgusting noises from their mouths and there are serious threats that this may extend to their bottoms.

I look at Simon who smiles indulgently at them but gives me a disapproving look like it's me who's suggesting a bloody burping competition. I wait for him to either reprimand them or join them in their pursuit of the loudest belch, but instead he grabs his coffee, takes it through to the orangery and settles with his phone.

My identical six-year-olds both have thick dark hair like their dad and are completely wild. Charlie, at four minutes older, is the leader of the two, usually starts the fights and is obsessed with everything vile. What Alfie doesn't dare to do, Charlie will push him to it. They are now trying to smash their breakfast plates on each other's heads, which apparently is a new and innovative technique to test who has the strongest skull.

'It's a MEDICAL EXPERIMENT,' Charlie shouts in my face when I protest.

I speak quietly, hoping he'll match me, and gently suggest this isn't the time or the place for medical experiments and they must eat their eggs or they'll be late for school. Not surprisingly, this mention of school causes a quiet rebellion and Charlie gives one final whack to his brother's head in the name of neurological medicine.

'That's ENOUGH!' I shout, as Alfie clutches his head and starts screaming.

'Charlieeee just killed me.'

'No he hasn't *killed* you, but carry on like this and someone will – me!'

I attempt to console Alfie while reprimanding Charlie as Sophie turns the radio on to drown out the noise, which really doesn't help. I wonder how on earth Simon can concentrate on his damned phone with this cacophony going on through the open door into the orangery. But my husband has this amazing ability to shut everything – and everyone –out, like many men, if what I hear at the school gate is anything to go by. Mind you, in Simon's case, it's probably a good thing, given how important his work is. He's often on call, always checking his texts and emails 24/7 in case of any emergencies. As he says, being a surgeon isn't a job, it's a state of mind; it has to be, because so many people are relying on him. Someone in Simon's position can't just switch off and, consequently, he doesn't always have the time or energy for the minutiae of family life. But that's where I come in. I'm needed here in our life of crayoned pictures on the fridge, grazed knees, childish squabbles, rushed kisses in the morning and all the laughter, tears and chaos in between. I wouldn't have it any other way, although my friend Jen thinks I'm mad.

She's married to a wealthy man and has Juanita, her nanny, who drives like a drunk, screams at the kids and has various boyfriends over for the night. But Jen loves her, says she gave her back her life and she can do as she likes because she's worth her weight in gold. Jen would be lost without her, but I enjoy looking after the children. Jen isn't into kids, despite the fact she has three, but thanks to Juanita, she has lots of what she calls 'me time'. She's learning to dance, taking Italian lessons and is busy with all kinds of charities, but I'm not like her. I don't need 'me time', I just want to be with my kids, like a proper mum.

I once considered retraining, going back to art college and brushing up on new techniques, but, as Simon said, why? We don't need the money, he has a good salary, his mother died a couple of years ago leaving him a fortune, and besides, who'd look after the children? At seventeen, Sophie's pretty self-sufficient, but she needs me there as much as the boys do – just in a different way. It's good for her to have someone to talk to, especially since we moved and she had to say goodbye to her friends, but there are times I really have to stretch myself. My days are filled with cleaning the house, cooking, ferrying the boys around and preventing them from harming themselves, or anyone else within a five-mile radius.

Simon might be considered a little old-fashioned by some people, but he appreciates the traditional roles. When we met, he was a struggling junior surgeon and widower with a young daughter, his wife had died the previous year and life was hard for him, so I know how much he appreciates everything I do. He doesn't value me any less because he goes out to work while I stay at home and nurture our family, keep our home clean and welcoming.

'We're a team, Marianne,' he always says. 'Your job is no less important than mine. Without you I couldn't earn a living and give you all the things you want.'

To everyone else, he's Dr S. Wilson, the dashing and brilliant cardiac surgeon, but to me he's just Simon, my husband and father to the children. He's also one of the most intelligent people I've ever known – I don't even understand his job title, which includes a specialty in mitral valve repair, transcatheter aortic valve implantation and atrial fibrillation surgery (I learned that by heart to impress him, I just hope he never tests me on it!). I understand how stressful his work is and sometimes he brings that stress home, especially at the moment as he's hoping for a promotion to Senior Consultant Surgeon. He's working incredibly hard – we barely see him some days – but as he says, it will be worth it if he gets the post, and I have faith he will. My concern is that he's so driven, he puts huge demands on himself and bottles up his stress. Thing is, he can't really share it with me because I don't understand the intricacies and skills of heart surgery – who does? *Caroline does.*

'Darling, I can't even begin to explain to you what happened today because you wouldn't understand,' he said the other evening when I asked if he was okay. 'People's lives are in my hands... I'm permanently on high alert. I don't get coffee breaks and days off like some halfwit bean counter.' I think he was referring to Peter, Jen's husband, who's big in banking. Jen had invited us to their place in Cornwall for the weekend, but Simon couldn't get the time off and the kids and I were disappointed, which made him cross. He hated saying no to us and was angry with himself; Simon hated letting his kids down.

I should have just accepted this, but I pushed things, as usual, and pointed out that we'd been excited about spending the last weekend of summer in Cornwall with the Moretons. I made him feel terrible and we argued quite vigorously that night, but later, when the kids were in bed, I joined him on the sofa and it was soon forgotten. Even now, after being together for ten years, I still can't be cross with him for long, and one look into those eyes is all I need to remind myself that he's everything I ever wanted. And I'm so lucky.

I've always loved Simon, from the minute I saw him, and though we've had our problems I was just beginning to feel like we were back on an even keel when we moved here. But now there's the spectre of Caroline, a 'talented' thirty-something he spends his days with. I can't for a moment let him think I'm going down that road again though. So I will keep my unwelcome thoughts to myself, and try not to imagine them together in theatre, masked up, their eyes meeting over an open chest, flirting over a defibrillator. I feel the blood rising in my neck as I imagine her passing him his scalpel, long eyelashes batting, their gloved hands 'accidentally' touching. I hear his commanding, sexy voice instructing the team while working on a complex quadruple bypass, causing every woman present to go weak at the knees – I do, just thinking about it. Jealousy fills my stomach and chest until I'm so packed with it I want to vomit at this imagined tableau imprinted now on my brain. I feel faint and far away watching Alfie take his revenge on Charlie with a teaspoon to the ear. I do nothing.

As the boys scream and shout and hurt, I take a scouring brush and clean the sink, pushing away my stupid nightmare fantasies of Simon with another woman and turn my attention to the good stuff. I stop scrubbing for a moment and glimpse the children now eating their breakfast; seeing them always makes me feel better. Okay, so the boys are pushing their food inelegantly into their mouths while slurping down orange juice, but I feel that familiar rush. I feel the same watching Sophie nibble delicately on a small corner of toast, her big, blue eyes gazing ahead, probably dreaming of her prince, or whoever she's got a crush on in Year 13 this week. Then there's my gorgeous husband – who may or may not be contemplating an affair while sitting in our beautiful orangery, looking gorgeous, his thick, dark fringe over one eye as he drinks his coffee and gazes into his phone. It's all so Instagrammable – I want to capture it, to photograph them here in our beautiful home. #MyHome #MyLoves. The hidden message to any Carolines out there who think they might have a chance, the clue is in the pronoun – my, mine – NO ONE else's.

We've only been here since early spring, but I love this house, the beautiful big garden, the high-end German kitchen we put in as soon as we moved here. Simon says every woman should have a fabulous kitchen, and this was his gift to me, and it's perfect, except right now it feels like my perfect canvas has been stained. I watch the way the early morning sunshine slants through the huge windows, waiting for the calm to wash over me, but nothing's happening – it's Caroline's fault. I usually love the way the sun plays on 'Borrowed Light', turning Farrow and Ball's wonderful paint shade into the dreamiest cloudy grey on my wall. But this morning I'm not achieving 'calm', however deeply I look, and there's only so long a person can stare at a wall in a busy family kitchen before one of the kids asks, 'Has Mum gone funny again?'

Having learnt about Caroline's existence today, I'm on edge. *Damn you, Caroline, with your youth and talent and close working proximity to my husband.* It's positively primal the way my hairs stand on end when I so much as think of Simon with anyone else. Not that I do. Not a lot anyway.

Earlier this year when I thought Simon was having an affair with Julia, the kids' piano teacher, I completely resisted saying anything. I wanted to prove to myself that I could stay sane, and besides, it wasn't worth all the drama that would inevitably follow. Oh, and I had absolutely no proof, which wouldn't actually have helped if I'd wanted to confront him. And, as time passed, I eventually stopped believing it. I showed myself that I *can* control my irrational fears, I *can* keep a lid on those feelings that fill my tummy and chest until I can barely breathe and make me ill. My therapist at the time asked me if Simon is a man who puts his wife's needs and happiness before his own. I said, of course, I mean, look at my life – I have the beautiful home, I don't have to work for a living and my husband gives me everything my heart desires. And I asked myself, could a man who buys his wife flowers as often as Simon does really cheat on her? He shows his love in so many ways, but my regular bouquet from Simon is proof that even in his busy schedule of saving lives and running an operating theatre, he stops to think of me. The bouquet arrives once a fortnight, on a Tuesday, it's always white, seasonal, beautiful, expensive and a constant reminder that Simon loves me. And only me.

We've had a couple of rocky years, but things started to settle down once we'd moved to this new house last February. I've definitely calmed down after ten years of marriage. In the early days, when I was younger, passionate and more visceral, I was terrible. I was even more jealous than I am now and would face my ridiculous suspicions head on, regardless of the consequences. It caused so much trouble between us that Simon eventually threatened to leave, said I was making it hard for him to love me. So I promised I'd change and we went to couples counselling, but I couldn't even deal with that in a mature, lucid fashion.

'You can't keep doing this, Marianne,' he'd said, after I'd verbally attacked him in front of the counsellor, accusing him of all sorts.

'And *you* can't sleep around,' I'd snapped back, a little woozy from the medication I was taking. I saw the look pass between him and the therapist, and in my drugged-up state I knew what it meant. They were both silently acknowledging the fact that this was all in my head. He was a caring man, who wanted the best for his wife, who gently stroked her hair, even while she raged, and wouldn't dream of cheating, despite the fact she constantly accused him and embarrassed him in public on a regular basis. The look confirmed I was unhinged, crazy and deluded.

It took several weeks in hospital and a lot of therapy (not to mention patience from Simon) for me to accept that I was wrong and my anxiety levels had caused me to imagine things that never happened. And only then, when everyone was sure I wasn't a danger to myself or others, was I released.

'Eat slowly,' I murmur to the boys. 'Don't gulp...' I distract myself by cleaning the shelves inside the fridge, hoping the gulping noises behind me aren't a prelude to another belch-fest. I notice out of the corner of my eye that Sophie's eaten barely anything and is now gazing into her phone. I push Caroline aside to allow the increasingly familiar and unwelcome thoughts to reboot: *Is Sophie eating enough? Is she anorexic?* She's certainly become more insular than ever since we moved here.

Oh God, I have to stop.

Simon says she's perfectly healthy and if she wants to cut down on food there's nothing wrong with that. 'I've checked her BMI, she's fine,' he said when I brought it up. 'She probably just doesn't want to get fat or it'll ruin her tennis.'

I'm sure he's right, and I know he was trying to stop me from worrying. And, as he pointed out, he has so many real issues to deal with in his everyday life that me whingeing about one of the kids not eating their greens is just irritating. But Sophie looks thinner to me and I can't help but worry. I've seen photos of her mum, Simon's first wife, who was also very thin, so perhaps it's a genetic thing? In contrast, I have a tendency to gain weight if I'm not careful and Simon's always so supportive when I diet, talking me through calories and what my BMI should be. He certainly keeps me on my toes, but he doesn't like it when I mention his tummy, which sometimes protrudes over his trousers if he hasn't had chance to play tennis recently.

Anyway, I suppose as long as Sophie's healthy, it's okay, and she might be skinny but she exercises, which is good. Simon takes her to tennis with him as they are both members of the lovely club on the outskirts of town, says she has a strong backhand. It costs an arm and a leg to join the tennis club, but it's beautiful, with amazing outdoor courts and a lovely clubhouse with a bar. Simon keeps saying we should go one evening, but we haven't had chance yet as I'm too busy with the boys. We really must synchronise our diaries better though. I'd love to see Sophie play tennis, perhaps even enjoy a G&T in the clubhouse afterwards. Thinking about this makes me feel better. Like my therapist said, it's good to focus on positive things, stuff to look forward to.

'I think you've forgotten something,' I call as Sophie now runs to the door, rucksack on her back, heading off for the day. 'Sophie?' I say a little louder, and she turns in the doorway, the sun spinning her hair a million shades of caramel. She's tall like her dad, statuesque really – and I see a glimpse of the woman she'll become. I take a snapshot in my head, remembering the motherless little girl I'd fallen for and here she is now, almost a grown-up. I remember being Sophie's age. I catch my breath, and wish I was seventeen again…

'What?' she says impatiently.

I blow her a kiss. 'Bye.' Sophie says, softening and, rolling her eyes. She puckers her mouth, blowing a kiss back at me into the air before sticking her tongue out affectionately at her brothers. I catch the kiss and smile as she retreats through the door to be engulfed by her day.

Simon wanders back into the kitchen. 'I'll do the school run,' he says, handing me his dirty mug, compensating for this with a kiss on the forehead.

My heart sinks. I like taking the boys to school; it's one of the few things that is truly structured in my day. Besides, I had plans this morning. 'Thanks, but I think I may have mentioned I'm going for coffee with Jen.' I smile, folding a tea towel neatly, patting it and looking back at him.

'Jen?' He raises his eyebrow slightly, and my heart sinks.

'Yes.'

'But why? It's such an odd friendship. She's so not your type.'

'She's nice,' I say, not sure what he means. 'What's my *type* anyway?' I giggle to indicate this isn't meant in a confrontational way.

'Well, she's just *different* to you.'

'She's more fun, you mean?' I try not to sound hurt.

'No. Just different… very different.'

I wish he could see what I see in Jen, but he doesn't like her, never has. I think he finds her a little threatening, ever since she pounced on him at the school's summer barn dance. Him and about five other attractive dads, I might add. That's just her style.

'The plan is to meet in the playground when we drop the children off…' I say, hoping this will be enough to secure me a pass. I've been looking forward to catching up with my new friend; I still feel bad about letting her down on the weekend in Cornwall. I know it will take time to build our friendship, but the Cornwall thing didn't help, and we're always cut short by the school bell or an injured or angry child. A coffee and a chat away from all the distractions would be the equivalent of about a week in playground catch-ups. Jen's son Oliver plays rugby with the boys, which is how we met really – she's fun and popular and as we've only been in the area a few months I'm both flattered and grateful for her friendliness towards me.

'I pass the school to get to the hospital; I'll drop the boys off,' Simon is saying.

He clearly thinks she's a bad influence and will lead me astray. Chance would be a fine thing. Apart from anything, there simply isn't much you can do between the hours of 9 a.m. and 3 p.m.

'But I wanted to see Jen…' I start half-heartedly, knowing it's pointless to argue with him. *Pick your fights.*

'But what about those paint colours for the living room? You need to decide on those as soon as possible,' he says, like it's a career choice.

'I know, but Jen's expecting me to…'

'I'm sorry, Marianne, but let's face it, Jen's a mess with her brassy blonde hair and tight dresses, and she's so *loud*. I can't imagine why you'd want to spend time with someone like that. Let me save you – I'll see her when I do the drop-off, and explain that you're busy…' He walks towards me, slips both hands around my waist, his hips pushing against mine gently. He hasn't shown this kind of interest for a while, and I'm flushed with relief and pleasure. Perhaps he isn't contemplating an affair with this mystery Caroline girl after all? 'Darling,' he murmurs into my hair, 'I can't believe you'd rather sit in some dusty old coffee shop with loudmouth Jen than be here, in this beautiful house.' He gently pulls away, turns me around to face him. 'I wish I was as lucky as you and didn't have to leave here every morning…' He strokes my hair, lifting a strand and pushing it softly behind my ear. 'What I'd give to be here with you, just pottering about, cooking and gardening… I can't remember the last time I had the chance to just *be*.'

I look into his eyes, feeling guilty now. I think back to our first house together, the two of us excitedly choosing a new sofa and curtains, and know he'd love to stay here and go through paint swatches to help make our home even lovelier for our family. But the ungrateful bitch that I am, I'd rather sit drinking coffee and gossiping. He's only thinking of me – he's worried going for coffee with someone excitable like Jen will stress me out. And he's probably right, I should stay here where it's safe. Where *I'm* safe.

'And besides, darling, I don't mean to nag, but have you seen the state of this place? Didn't you say you wanted to give it a good clean once the kids were back at school?' He smiles and I feel bad. The whole house *is* pretty untidy after a summer of children and their friends: scuffed paintwork, toys everywhere and impromptu snacks and fruit juice now ingrained in the carpet. I suddenly feel all itchy and can't wait for him to leave so I can start scrubbing, erasing all the stains of summer. The sofa's wrecked. The living room carpet looks like a Jackson Pollock with splashes of blackcurrant and various unidentifiable marks whose origins I daren't begin to imagine. I don't know what I was thinking. Simon's right, how could I sit in a coffee shop listening to Jen moaning about her husband and gossiping about the other mothers when I could be here clearing up and making the house nice?

'Not to mention that I'm looking forward to a good dinner this evening.' Simon's now winking at me, suggesting a romantic meal together. Shit, I hadn't expected him to want a romantic dinner on the first day back at school; there's so much to think about already. What the hell can I make tonight that will keep him in this loving mood? There's no excuse. I have all day and I'm sure he's bored of the Jamie Oliver recipes I've thrown into a pot while refereeing wrestling matches and summer pirate invasions.

No, it's about time I gave something back and made my husband feel loved and appreciated. Tonight will be our opportunity to regroup, spend some time together and try and get back to where we were, once upon a time.

I'm now going through recipes in my head, one worry replacing another and another and another, like shuffling cards. I know a recipe isn't exactly 'a worry', but it's the way my mind works, and it's torture as Simon's a bit of a perfectionist, and he seems so affectionate. I want the mood to continue.

I think back to the early days when we first met. I vowed to myself that I'd be the perfect wife and mother to him and his little girl. I soon developed a close bond with Sophie – a grieving child who was fragile and vulnerable – and, along with Simon, provided the love and support she needed at a terrible time. In return, they both gave me such joy and Simon the love and security I'd longed for all my life. We all saved each other in a way. I took great delight in caring for Sophie, cooking nice dinners, keeping the house spotless. I took a sensual delight in ironing Simon's shirts, the faded scent of aftershave in the fabric re-awoken by the warmth of the iron, filling me with the thrill of him. I totally gave myself to this perfect little family who needed me as much as I needed them. Simon always appreciated what I did, but then life came along like a huge tidal wave, bringing all kinds of trouble, and these days I sometimes find it hard enough to do beans on toast, let alone provide a three-course gourmet meal for Simon. Unfortunately, I raised the bar all those years ago and he came to expect a warm kitchen, a calm wife and a cake cooling on the rack when he came home from work. On good days, I can still give the impression that I'm on top of things and might just make nomination for Wife and Mother of the Year. I may even have discovered a reawakening in the fragrant ironing of his thick, cotton shirts, if he hadn't said 'Caroline' the way he did.

I hand him his flask of coffee and sandwiches – French Brie on rye with my own home-made onion marmalade.

'So can we say you want me to tell that woman that you have far more important things to do than make inane small talk with her?' he says gently, still talking about my now-cancelled coffee with Jen while taking the brown paper bag from my hand.

'Yes… but don't put it quite like that.' I smile, concerned he'll offend her.

'Of course I won't. I'll be perfectly charming.' He smiles. 'And you can be sitting here in your beautiful kitchen face deep in shades of Farrow and Ball.'

I smile back. Simon can still make me smile when he wants to.

'If your interior decoration is as good as I think it's going to be, we could even think about doing Christmas drinks this year?' He raises his eyebrows, dangling this before me like a glittering bauble.

I grasp it. We don't entertain; he doesn't really like it. 'Oh, Simon, I'd love that,' I say. I want to make new friends, open our beautiful home and bring in the neighbours. Most of all I want to prove to Simon that I can still be what he wants me to be and he doesn't need anyone else.

Despite Christmas being almost four months away, my head's already filled with gleaming trays of canapés and fairy lights adorning every crevice. I see myself welcoming our guests in cocktail-length red velvet, standing by my handsome husband. I can hear them all now: 'The Wilsons, you know, the surgeon and his lovely wife.' I see them too, those women who steal glances, flirt with him and slip their phone numbers into his pocket when I'm not there. I know they wonder what he sees in me and amuse each other with stories about how I snared him, what tricks I pull to keep him, but they don't know. Christmas drinks would show them all. 'Oh so *that's* what he sees in her? She's a fabulous hostess, everything's just perfect and that red dress shows her curves. Her quiche and soft furnishings are to die for. Have you tasted her crab puffs? Oh, now I get it, *she* is the woman behind the man. He's gorgeous and successful and brilliant – yet nothing without her. Do you know she even chose the paint colours for the sitting room… why would he go anywhere else?' I glow at the prospect; already I'm writing the guest list in my head as I help gather the boys and their belongings together.

'Don't forget I need you to be out of school straight away today so I can get you to violin class on time, Charlie,' I warn. 'Oh, and Alfie, have you put your cello in my car yet? You're at Miss Pickering's at 5 p.m. and I don't want to have to drive back from school to fetch it like last term.' I glance over at Simon as I say this. He's always amazed at how I remember what each child is doing on each day, but he's suddenly miles away.

Simon's always been very keen that the children do after-school activities – his own parents didn't go in for that. His father died when he was young and his mother stuck to a rigid routine of school and home, and Simon wants his children to experience lots of different things. 'So many children come home from school and are plonked in front of a TV or PlayStation, but not here,' he always says, acknowledging all the running around I do. I love the look on his face when I reel off the children's schedules when he asks what they're doing. 'I don't know how you remember it all,' he says whenever it comes up. But as I always point out he has far more important stuff to remember than I do and in all honesty I've been known to turn up to collect Alfie from Miss Pickering's a whole hour early, but we don't tell Dad.

I suppose he's thinking now of his day ahead as I remind the boys of their week: 'French on Tuesday, film appreciation Wednesday and don't forget rugby training Thursday, martial arts Friday.' I stop at Friday; the weekend is a Rubik's Cube times three and even I'm sometimes confused about who should be where and at what time. It's so complex, I joke to Simon that I need to plot a grid and have little red dots where each child should be, but that's my job. I love it, and Simon loves me for doing it.

'Come on, guys,' he says now, corralling the boys. He turns and kisses me in his usual perfunctory way and heads for the door in a tidal wave of twins, and my heart sinks a little thinking how quickly they've grown and how I can't believe they are now about to start Year 3.

'Now be good today, boys. You have a new teacher, and a new classroom, so make sure you don't forget and go to last year's.' I kiss them both. Apart from wanting to meet up with Jen this morning I would have loved to see them into their new classroom. Every moment is special with your children, and a new term is a watershed, so I'm sad not to deliver them today. 'Are you sure you can take them, Simon, it won't be a problem for me?' I almost plead.

He looks at me quite sternly. 'Marianne, I thought we'd just talked about it.'

I nod – he's not budging on this, but it's nice for them to have their dad there instead and of course it gives me time to try and make headway on the house and tonight's meal.

'Busy day, darling?' I ask, indicating I've moved on, and he won't have any more trouble from me. I follow them all into the hallway, genuinely intrigued about my husband's day; a difficult operation might explain why he's been glued to his phone all weekend. He barely spoke to anyone at the barbecue on Saturday, and tea with his mother on Sunday was quite torturous as she'd looked disapprovingly at the boys pushing crustless finger sandwiches up their nostrils. Simon did nothing. But then why should he? She blames me for their behaviour. *And I blame her for Simon's.*

'Is everything... okay...?' I mumble now, not meeting his eyes as I pick up a comb from the hall table and comb Charlie's hair vigorously. He screeches his disapproval, putting my teeth on edge.

'Of course, why shouldn't it be?' he says, and I hear the snap in his voice. I'm asking about work, but I'm really looking for clues, a sign that something's not quite in place.

'You're fussing, Marianne,' he says.

'Yeah, stop fussing, Mum,' Charlie repeats, squirming from under my comb.

Given my previous 'difficulties', I don't want Simon to get wind of this, so keep my voice bright and breezy – which probably has the opposite effect. 'I'm sorry, I was just asking…'

'Well, for your information, Theatre 33 is booked out for the day, could be eight hours.' He sighs, and I nod, torn between wonder and envy. How amazing to work inside someone's body. My husband opens up chest cavities, reaches in and heals hearts, holding them in his hands, walking the tightrope between life and death. I can barely comprehend this. How I wish I could concentrate long enough to even contemplate it; I find it hard enough to sew a few pieces of fabric together – let alone a human body.

Within seconds, my family have disappeared to start their day and I close the front door as silence overwhelms me like a thick blanket. I'm left alone to worry about Sophie, the boys' first day in a new class – and the way my husband's mouth moved over the name 'Caroline'. I walk back into my beautiful kitchen and wonder if I'm right, or am I mad and have no real feeling or instinct any more? Has the Mirtazapine I take for my anxiety flattened me again, or has something else excised the throbbing life from my chest cavity? Perhaps, ironically, I need a surgeon to fix *my* heart and make me well again?

I put the juice glasses into the dishwasher one by one and gaze around at the kitchen, smiling at all I have. I'm so lucky. I still love my husband after all the years. I love him with a blind passion that has no reason, no sense, and I'm aware that there are times I should be stronger, but I'm irrational where Simon's concerned. As a child I'd never have dreamt a life like this could be mine and it's all thanks to him – without Simon I have nothing. I *am* nothing.

Which is why I'm so very worried about Caroline. *Young, talented Caroline.*

CHAPTER TWO

If you'd shown me a piece of video footage of the life I would live as an adult, I'd never have believed you. I grew up in a council house, the only child of a single mother who couldn't cope with life and handed me to social workers when I was three. My childhood was a montage of foster homes, care facilities, free school meals and being bullied by other girls. I never wanted the same for my own children, and when I met Simon I knew he could give me and any children we had the family life I'd craved. And despite what lies underneath, the itching under my skin, the quiet torment in my head, I think I might finally be pulling it off.

Our life is like an article from a Sunday supplement: the children are gorgeous, my husband is handsome and on a good day I'm an attractive mum of three. We live in this beautiful home, and five pairs of Barbour wellingtons stand in the hall, from tiny ones covered in ducks for the boys, to Sophie's florals to Simon's large green ones. The children have grown out of theirs now, but just seeing them lined up waiting to be filled with little feet gives me a warm feeling inside, especially on bad days.

I adore my family and throw myself into everything, from a walk in the park together to the kids' birthday parties. I make sure everyone is dressed for the occasion and the setting is perfect. The other day, me, Sophie and the boys went for a walk to the nearby village green to collect conkers and, being me, I turned it into a photo shoot. I insisted they wear their new matching Boden coats and scarves and when we bumped into a mum from school she smiled in awe. 'Look at you. Three kids and you always look so good, and the kids too – like one of those families you see in magazines,' she'd sighed, shaking her head in admiration.

I was delighted at the compliment, but as I waved goodbye, and we continued on for home, my heart dipped a little. If only she knew. Everything at Number 5 Garden Close, (described by the estate agents as 'a prestigious family home set amongst magnificent private parkland') is not all it seems. It's bloody hard work being effortless and appearing to have everything under control, and it doesn't come easy to me. There are days when I struggle with my own high expectations of myself. I can never really rest, never leave anything to chance, because for Simon everything has to be perfect. And who can blame him? As he points out, the last thing he needs when he walks through the door after a day from hell is to slip on a toy train, or be greeted by dirty, screaming kids and no dinner. I want everything in our home to be perfect and spent hours today just gazing at paint colours for the sitting room. I've found it really hard to focus but finally gone with the least controversial – House White. Apparently it's a clean off-white with a fresh, citrus feel, and it made me feel cleansed just reading about it. I love the idea of a new, fresh white canvas on the walls, to cover everything up; a whitewash I suppose? But left to my own devices, I'd fill the house with splashes of colour – a shocking pink wall, mismatched cushions in primary colours, velvets and silks and tassels. I smile to myself as I drive to school to collect the boys. I can only imagine Simon's reaction being faced with a bright pink wall; he'd say it was vulgar. He'd probably be right too. I used to be able to put colours together – my old art lecturer said I made colours 'sing' – but that was before I learned that Simon prefers a less-is-more approach. And one thing I've learned from therapy is that you have to compromise.

The mums in the playground are waiting for the kids and talking about holidays now as I stand on the periphery, slowly being accepted. As the children only started here in February, the middle of the school year, I'm still the new girl and will have to earn the privilege of automatic inclusion. It isn't like I can just invite them all round for a glass of wine after school. Nor can I accept an after-school invitation for drinks in their gardens while the kids play on the lawn. Imagine if I wasn't there when Simon came home? He'd be horrified, and even more so if he walked in on a gaggle of inebriated mothers and unleashed kids running wild in *our* garden. Since the boys started at the school I've received invites to charity coffee mornings, mums' nights out, book clubs, Prosecco nights and everything in between. I'd love to say yes, but I don't. It wouldn't be fair on Simon to leave him babysitting the kids after he's been at work all day. Besides, I'm not stupid – these women don't really *want* me at their 'girly evenings'. I'm sure they're just being polite and I'm only tolerated because of Simon. I'm the handsome surgeon's wife and in spite of my limited socialising outside the school gate, my status affords me slight inclusion into the group because they want us both at their evening soirees. Simon describes these women as 'pointless', and as they chatter about school fees and scented candles, I see he has a point. I smile and nod at what they say, but I'm not really with them. I'm looking for Jen.

'I saw your husband drop the children off this morning,' Francesca says, like he's some kind of rock star. She's the alpha, and just like teenagers at school her 'girls' are around her, motivated only by her approval. She would probably have bullied me at school, but not now I'm married to a man who counts. 'You are lucky, wish mine would give me a morning in bed,' she adds, and the others laugh, not because it's funny, but because she said it.

'I wasn't in bed, I was up baking bread at 6 a.m.,' I say defensively, worried I might appear less than I am. I don't want anyone to start thinking I'm ill again – not that they would know about the past. This is a new area; we're starting afresh. I hear Simon's voice: 'No one need ever know, Marianne, as long as you behave.'

So I continue to defend my no-show on the first morning of a new term. *Unforgivable.*

'Simon only dropped the boys off because he passes the school on his way...' I say, still desperate to make my point. *I am a good mother.*

'To the hospital... yes.' Francesca smiles, looking me up and down. She's wondering what he sees in me. She gave me the same look at her barbecue last term as she skewered raw meat and talked to Simon about Brexit. He loves to discuss politics, and world affairs, but it was laughable to watch Francesca's attempt to be knowledgeable as her lashes batted and her spatchcock sizzled. I don't even know why he agreed to go to her barbecue, but for once he said yes and effortlessly charmed everyone there.

I turn away, feeling exposed but then instantly relieved to see Jen teetering across the gravel, car keys in hand, waving and calling my name.

I want to run towards her, my salvation in this enclave of hard-edged, pink-lipsticked yummy mummies. Simon says the trouble with this school is the cliques of mothers, who seemingly all married well and behave like they won the lottery. 'You can't make a silk purse out of a sow's ear, Marianne. And believe me, those women are more sow than silk,' he said. Unfortunately, Sophie overheard him saying this and called him 'a fucking misogynist', which really pissed him off. He was so upset by her language he told her she couldn't go to her prom, and she cried and cried for days. Admittedly, he eventually gave in and let her go, but I think it took the shine off things for her and, in an attempt to make it up to her, he offered to pay all the cost of the shared limo. But this had the opposite effect and Sophie's response to his kind offer was to tell him he couldn't 'make everything better with money'. I stayed out of it, but I felt so sorry for him on the night of the prom when she flew off down the road on the back of a motorbike with one of the boys from her year. Simon adores his children and doesn't always get it right, but who does? Anyway, Jen told us she'd also gone to her prom on the back of a bike and it hadn't done her any harm. I doubted she had – and even though Simon's not her biggest fan it did the trick and seemed to placate him. Jen's good that way; she has this knack of making you feel good about yourself – she reassures me and make me laugh, even when I'm feeling low. The other mums aren't as much fun as Jen, but I'm sure once I've done my time and they accept me fully they will be fine, and Simon's comments about them will prove to be a little unfair. Anyway, he never says anything to their faces, thank God! In fact, as I recall, it wasn't just at her barbecue, but Simon didn't seem to have a problem with flirty Francesca when he was partnered with her on the tombola at the school's summer fete either. And I'll never forget the way she never took her eyes off his while thrusting her hand into the tombola to fish out the winning tickets.

'Hey, good to see you. Sorry you couldn't make coffee this morning.' Jen's now hugging me hard, filling my nostrils with Fracas, the expensive French scent she often wears. It's tuberose-based, sexy – very Jen. I haven't seen her since the school picnic at the end of July, so we've lots to catch up on.

'Yeah… sorry I couldn't make coffee Jen, I had stuff to do,' I say mysteriously, hoping it sounds like I have an exciting life and haven't been cleaning and studying paint swatches all day.

'Oh, it's okay, Simon explained you weren't feeling well, said you had a headache?'

'Oh… yes… I had a headache as well, but mostly I had stuff to do,' I added awkwardly. Why did he always say I was ill? Honestly, men just have no imagination when it comes to excuses. Only the weekend before last we'd been invited out for drinks round at a neighbour's. Sophie was going out so there was no one to sit with the boys, but instead of explaining this and declining the invitation, Simon insisted one of us go along, nominated himself and told them I was in bed with a terrible headache. I had no idea until I bumped into the couple walking their dog, whose opening gambit was 'goodness, should you even be out after being so poorly?' After last year, I don't want people thinking stuff about me again, and if this is a fresh start we both need to be honest about where I am. I know in the past Simon's used 'Marianne's headaches' as a cover-all. But I feel like everyone knew it was a euphemism. 'Marianne has a headache again' was, I'm sure, translated to 'Marianne's barking at the moon again.'

'How was your holiday?' I ask Jen, the usual September catch-up line. She and her husband Peter own about three properties: the almost-mansion they live in here, their weekend retreat in Cornwall and a farmhouse in France.

'Glorious. In France the kids spent three weeks in the water. They were also vile, made too much noise and swore a lot... some words I'd never even heard before.' Considering the youngest is only three, I feel this might be an exaggeration, but this is classic Jen. 'Peter was grumpy and disgusting as usual,' she goes on, 'but fortunately we only had to have marital relations twice, and I was drunk both times, so barely remember it.' She giggles.

Jen sometimes makes me gasp at the things she says and does, like when she sold the headmaster a kiss on Red Nose Day – and gave it to him – in more ways than one. It seems his wife wasn't too pleased when she'd heard that tongues were involved and he certainly got more for his 50p than he'd bargained for. I know Simon thinks she's vulgar, but I love Jen's confidence. I suppose it's because that's something I've never really had. She's also funny and warm and I love the way she includes me in intimate conversations like we've been friends forever.

She made a beeline for me last term when we first moved here and I didn't know anyone. 'Are you the surgeon's wife?' she'd asked, and I'd nodded, feeling a little frisson at the title, but at the same time a little embarrassed. Everyone notices Simon; it happens wherever we live. He just has this air about him. He's very handsome and charming and when people find out what he does for a living they're always impressed. We don't always accept the many proffered social invitations. After a mad week at work, Simon's often far too exhausted, but occasionally we'll say yes to a dinner party or charity event and I'll watch as other guests sit around the table in awe. Simon's dark hair falls over his left eye as he speaks, his passion for his subject filling the air, thrumming through the room. His stories of life and death and in between always enthral – particularly the women. The hostesses want him at their dinner parties and barbecues, loving his dramatic tales of blood and gore, those moments when life is hanging in the balance, and with one swift decision, a deft movement, he brings a person back to life.

The women shift in their seats at my amazing husband as he delights and horrifies them with his stories from theatre. I know what they're thinking, because I'm thinking the same. But I'm the lucky one… *he's coming home with me.*

The school bell rings and the mums disperse, but Jen's telling me about some horrific seafood poisoning they'd all suffered in Brittany.

'So there we are in bloody A & E… Oliver's vomiting blood all down my chambray dress… Why are you smiling, Marianne?' She looks puzzled. I just know she'd have been more concerned about her dress than the child bleeding in her arms and it amuses me.

'I… I'm not, I'm not smiling… I'm horrified,' I say, and she nods then continues and I feel bad. I'm keen to give her the reaction she desires, because I don't want her to think I'm bonkers, and I so want her to like me. I've known her a matter of months, but she's the closest thing I have to a best friend –someone to confide in and giggle with. I haven't been close to another woman for a long time. When you're married to a man like Simon you don't need loads of friends, and I've always been a little wary of making friends because so-called friends have let me down in the past. As Simon says, 'If they are a true friend, they'll accept you whatever,' so I guess those I thought cared about me didn't. But Jen's different. She's so wrapped up in her own life; she isn't trying to take a bite out of mine.

The weather's warm for September, with a summer hangover in the air, and Jen's making the most of it with a tight, mint linen dress. The pastel shade looks good on her, and the full bust and tanned décolletage is not missed by the few husbands waiting in the playground. She seems oblivious to the attention, flicking her blonde, Marilyn Monroe haircut and closing her big blue eyes in repulsion as she now recalls the recent memory of sex with her husband.

Caroline has suddenly come back to me with a jolt and thoughts of her have inexplicably now lodged in my brain. I fight them, willing them to leave, until eventually they ebb slightly and I am able to smile while nodding at Jen, hoping she hasn't noticed I slipped out for a moment and wasn't completely focused on what she was saying. I think I probably try a little too hard with Jen because I'm so keen to make a friend – but I find it difficult to be natural. Then again, I'm not sure what 'natural Marianne' is any more and I'm grateful when the school doors fly open and I don't have to pretend to be 'me' any more. I can fall seamlessly into 'Mum' mode and the kids will fill in my blanks.

After a few minutes, they all march out into the playground like little soldiers and my heart sinks – I wish they'd run and shout and hurl their bags down. But the school is very strict on discipline and they daren't step out of line. Simon says it's one of the things he likes about this school, and when I'd campaigned for a more artsy school for Alfie, who loves to draw, Simon argued that a school focusing on art allowed children to behave like savages. So here we are at Brownhills Prep, which is less art and more sports and military in its approach to discipline. Charlie's taken to it like a duck to water, and I'm sure Alfie will come round eventually, and it is good for them both to have some discipline. Sophie's in the sixth form – the same school but half a mile away -- and she hates it, but she didn't like her old school much either, and as her dad says, who ever *liked* school?

Jen and I greet the kids between snatches of seafood poisoning stories and her hilarious tales of sex avoidance with Peter, her older, wealthy husband. 'Makes my skin crawl.' She pulls her face and I giggle like a naughty schoolgirl, shocked and delighted at her irreverence.

We walk en masse with the kids to the car park, where Jen leans on her black Audi and talks non-stop for another fifteen minutes, covering pretty much her whole summer. During this time, the metaphorical straitjackets that have been imposed on the boys all day are gradually flung off until they default to their usual mode of wild animals. As Jen's son Oliver bashes Charlie over the head with his (quite heavy) bag, I cringe and try to listen to Jen's comprehensive account of her experience of French A & E and a particularly 'dishy doctor'. Oliver then attempts to kill Alfie by pushing him in front of a moving car, just as Jen is describing a delicious meal of oysters she and Peter had enjoyed on a rare night alone.

'How anyone can go on holiday without some kind of babysitting facility is beyond me – it's positively medieval,' she's saying, defending the fact that Juanita, their nanny, goes everywhere with them.

I discreetly grab Alfie by the blazer lapel and hold him to me despite his flailing around. I know if Jen spots this she'll call me a helicopter mother again, but I don't think I'm being overly protective given the size of the parents' four-wheel drives and the fact Oliver is a maniac. He is out of control and I'm feeling under a great deal of stress to keep an eye on the boys, but I don't want to offend Jen by appearing not to listen. However, when Oliver takes Charlie in a headlock and yanks him around by the neck,

I give a little yelp and say, 'NO, Oliver,' which finally brings Jen back from Brittany.

'Get here NOW, Oliver, you little SHIT!' she yells.

I cringe as a few looks pass between yummy mummies. I'm reminded of Simon's comment about the school mums' 'sows ears' status. Jen is no silk purse, he's right – but perhaps that's why I like her. Through Jen I can be more rebellious, if only in my head.

'Oh, Marianne, it's no use, we can't talk with these little sods distracting us, can we?' She's clamping Oliver down with one hand while with her other she's running her fingers through thick, blonde waves and pouting. 'Why do fucking nannies have to have a day off?' she hisses to me under her breath. 'I mean, it's not like Juanita has a life or anything – you've seen her, fat as a pig and twice as greedy.'

I laugh, even though I shouldn't, she's being so unkind, but I'm also laughing with relief because Oliver is finally being physically restrained and my kids will live to see another day.

Still manhandling her son, Jen starts on again about the French doctor and my relief suddenly spirals into agitation as I realise the time and glance at my watch. We're going to be late for the boys' music lessons. I virtually had to beg Mr Mendels to tutor Charlie in the violin. He's the best violin tutor in the area. Francesca's daughter Sadie has him, so he must be good, but when he told me he was fully booked, Simon suggested I go back and offer double what he was asking. 'Never take "no" for an answer; remember everyone has their price,' he'd said. As usual, Simon was right, and old Mendels agreed – he couldn't wait to get his hands on the cash. But he insisted on one thing: 'Promptness, Mrs Wilson – if the boy isn't here on time, I will cancel and charge in full.'

I'm thinking of his wrinkled, gnarly old face now but can't just run off because Jen's in full flow. I can feel the heat rising in my chest and I just want to shout at her that I have to go, but I dig my fingernails into my palm, smile politely and thank the God of

Mirtazapine that I'm under control. But after another six minutes and forty-five seconds of French doctor lust talk, I am forced to interrupt her. I feel bad but have no choice and placate her with vague plans for coffee later in the week.

'You won't let me down next time, will you?' she asks, as I open the car door and herd the boys into the back. 'Coffee and a catch-up – we're way overdue.'

'Definitely,' I say, pushing the kids into the car as they protest loudly.

'Don't you be getting one of your headaches,' she jokes, holding her head in both hands.

'No way, it's a date.' I smile and start the car, winding down the window to wave as I pull away, hoping she hasn't already translated this morning's headache into something else.

When we lived in the last place, I used to sometimes sneak off for coffee with Jayne, a mum I met at that school. But then I became ill and I don't think she ever really forgave me for what I said to her. Who can blame her? Anyway, that's in the past now, and I need to look forward.

Desperate not to be late for the boys' lessons, I drive too fast up the road from school, suddenly realising I've forgotten their damned after-school snacks of home-made hummus and carrot sticks. They'll never last through their music lessons without sustenance, so I stop at the first petrol station and, in the absence of hummus, buy two bags of crisps and two Mars bars. As I'm leaving, my hands full of contraband, I spot fucking Mrs Mallory stopping for petrol and make a run for it. Mallory's a neighbour and a member of Simon's tennis club and a snotty cow to boot – if she's seen me, she will no doubt report back with names, dates and serial numbers. So I open the car door, hurl the goods at the boys in the back seat and, like an action hero, throw myself into the car – much to the boys' delight. I start the engine and drive off quickly, causing the wheels to screech and the boys to squeal with joy. I'm now laughing loudly along with them – a crazy lady in charge of children, driving a big car with E-number-laden snacks. What could possibly go wrong? The boys don't know why I leapt back into the car doing a commando-style roll, but they do know never to tell Dad they've had crisps and Mars bars.

Once the laughter has died down and the boys have ripped open their crisps and are crunching happily, I chill a little. I must remember to vacuum the car and wind down the window to let the air in, so Simon won't detect the whiff of prawn crisps or chocolate. As a doctor he's very strict about their diets, and rightly so, but needs must and desperate times call for desperate measures.

With the boys' mouths full, the journey is pleasantly quiet. Some parents hate all the collecting, dropping off and general taxi-ing of kids, but I love it. For me it's a happy time. I'm on my own with my children, we are all safe and free and sometimes I wish I could just drive and drive and drive.

I head for Mrs Pickering's cello class at a relatively low speed to give Alfie time to finish his snacks before we arrive. I snatch his packaging before opening the car door and ushering him up the path. Once he's delivered, I take Charlie another 2.6 miles to his violin lesson, before picking Sophie up from dance class. I then enjoy another hour of splendid freedom in Sainsbury's with Sophie before doubling back for the boys. After this morning it's nice to have some one-to-one time with her, to give her the attention that I can't afford her as often since the boys came along. We wander the clothes section, where she admires a pale-pink bra. I put it in the basket and we smile conspiratorially, then I suggest we have a coffee, which she's keen to do. Sophie chooses a small cookie to have with her drink and eats it hungrily, which amazes me. She's unusually chatty too, and I wonder momentarily why she's not this happy at home.

We won't be back at the house before six, but that's okay because Simon said he'd be late tonight and I have plenty of time to finish the special dinner I'm planning for him. As he pointed out, now the kids are back in school I have to be organised, on top of things – it's good for me, for my mental health. Tonight I'm making my husband baked sea bass with a lemon and caper dressing, fondant potatoes and a green side salad. I'll light candles and we'll look into each other's eyes like we used to. I hope.

Pulling up outside the house with two tired boys and a now-back-to-stroppy teenager, I see Simon's car in the drive and my heart drops. He's home and I wasn't here waiting, dinner ready, kids bathed – it isn't my fault he's early, but still I feel guilty. The lovely dinner I have planned will take time, and that's after I've bathed the boys and put them to bed. The mental image I had of me standing in my beautiful kitchen by candlelight, the night ahead of us, is quickly melting. Panic flutters in my chest, and I grip the steering wheel with both hands to steady myself, but the boys are being particularly argumentative and within seconds a fight has broken out. I pull on the handbrake as they shout and wrestle with baby growls, the beginnings of testosterone urging them to destroy each other. The panic is now rising into my throat, I know it's irrational, but I want to scream. I'm on the verge of tears, and I know I've lost it.

I'm screeching loudly for them to STOP, STOP... forgetting the window is down and the nosy old sod Michael from next door is taking out his bin. He's looking at me like I'm mad, but I'm not. *I'm not.* The kids haven't even heard me. No one seems to hear me these days, except Michael, who's still staring, I want to roar at him like a wild animal, but my voice is screeching, 'STOP.' Charlie's now using his violin as a weapon and Alfie's using his fists (fortunately, his huge cello is in the boot and unable to be accessed as weaponry). Sophie's shouting at them both and trying to grab the violin as the front door opens. My mouth goes dry.

'What's all the racket?' Simon's voice cuts through the noise. It's calm, neutral – is he genuinely calm or just aware of the neighbours? What on earth will he think being greeted with no dinner and all this chaos? If he's had a stressful day, a difficult operation, God forbid a death, he won't be in the mood for this circus on the doorstep.

I take a breath, slowly look up and, to my great relief, he's smiling. I want to hug him.

I quickly gather myself together and climb from the car, attempting to look like I haven't just screeched at the top of my voice for several seconds and everything is under control.

'Come on boys,' I say, walking towards him, clicking the remote lock. 'I'm sorry, darling, it's all been a little bit mad this evening. I haven't even started dinner…' The words come tumbling out.

'Why not?' His face is suddenly unreadable.

I swallow. 'Because, because… I've only just got back, darling… and this morning I think you said that Theatre… 33 was booked for eight hours…'

'Did I?' He's now looking at me with a doubting smile on his face. I'm not sure what this means and am unsure how to respond.

'Sorry… I must have misunderstood,' I offer, knowing I didn't.

'Theatre 33? Well, you seem to know more about it than me,' he answers brightly, and I see his jaw flinch ever so slightly.

The kids are now running past us up the drive and we follow them. Simon steps back for me to enter the house. I thank him, taking the opportunity to glance at his face. I still can't gauge him. But as we walk together in the aftermath of children, he stops in the hallway and turns to me. He suddenly reaches out his hand and I stand waiting for whatever is going to happen next.

'Whoa, you're a little jumpy this evening, Marianne,' he says gently.

I don't say anything, don't give anything away. I don't even feel. I just do what I always do, and stand and wait. He slowly brings his hand to my face and I stop breathing, aware the children are suddenly quiet in the kitchen.

'Dad,' Sophie says, walking into the hallway. 'I did a French test today. Ninety-eight per cent.' I know what she's doing. She didn't have a French test today. I love her for this, but I don't want her involved. I just wish all the children would disappear. I don't want them to see anything.

Simon smiles at Sophie. 'Well done, darling.' And as he turns back to me, his hand makes contact with my face. He strokes my cheek with the back of his hand, as light as a cobweb – and for a moment I don't know which way this will go. I don't think he knows either.

Sophie's standing completely still just watching.

'So, you haven't even started dinner yet?' he says slowly, almost whispering.

'No… I'm sorry… I…'

Searching his face for a clue, I'm at a loss and, aware of this, he holds the unreadable expression for several agonising seconds. I slowly meet his eyes and see a flicker of uncertainty, until his lips finally break into an indulgent smile. I turn quickly to Sophie, who's still stopped dead in her tracks. It's like she's not even breathing.

'No dinner, Marianne?' he murmurs.

Fight or flight.

He's turning his head slowly from me to Sophie and back again. 'In that case…' He is looking straight at me and at times like this I believe he sees into my head. 'Shall we all go to that new pizza restaurant in town?'

Breathe again.

I want to cry with joy. My heart spills over with relief, gratitude and love.

I nod energetically, like a child, throwing my arms around his waist and hugging him. He laughs, like a tolerant father. Tonight will be a good night after all.

CHAPTER THREE

I know I'm not completely well yet, but I'm taking the medication. I'm supposed to take it at night before I go to sleep, but I have to confess I do experiment with timings. Consequently, I'm sometimes unfocused. I can misinterpret things and so I may be imagining this, but whenever Simon and I are together, there's an atmosphere.

Am I imagining this? Am I *creating* it?

Yesterday I stood in the kitchen watching Simon and the twins play football in the garden. He was in goal and every time one of the boys kicked the ball he'd hurl himself across the lawn, pulling silly faces and pretending to land in a heap. They roared with laughter and just watching them from the window I felt love blossoming in my chest. I never had a father, but my children do, and he's wonderful with them, and Sophie too – even though she's a teenager and a little bit trickier. Simon and Sophie had such a lovely relationship when she was younger – he was besotted by her, still is – and that's bound to stand them in good stead as we steer the rocky teenage waters. He's a good father, and he and the kids seem to have such happy times, like I do when alone with the kids, but when we're all together, I've recently felt like the odd one out. I feel like I don't belong, and I wonder if that's down to me, my illness, the medication or something else... Is it Caroline?

I feel like a detective trying to work out the crime from a million hidden clues. So, here's the evidence: Simon's been working late a lot recently. He's also been to two weekend conferences, with apparently more on the cards. He says as he's going for Senior Consultant he's expected to work longer hours, and attend more events, but is he also expected to speak to me like he's angry all the time?

It seems there's always edginess in his voice when he speaks to me. I see resentment in his eyes. Is it because I'm me and not her? I'm not, nor will I ever be, Caroline Harker, Junior Surgeon and enfant terrible of the operating theatre. Yesterday I bit the bullet and did something I shouldn't do: I opened up a vent of hell and looked her up on social media. She is stunning. Where I'm dark and short with a tendency to weight, she's tall and slender with blonde hair and icy blue eyes. She looks like a woman from a L'Oreal ad... 'because she's worth it'. Since then I have been spending far too much time googling her name too, which revealed a world of pain. She was one of the youngest surgeons to qualify in her field, comes from a family of brilliant doctors and her favourite drink is – champagne. Oh, the fun she has, this Caroline, with all her smiley, privileged young friends. Endless sunsets soaked in alcohol, shiny golden smooth faces crammed against the camera; a gondola in Venice, Caroline in St Mark's square, her arms outstretched embracing her wonderful life; a long weekend in Paris, Caroline standing alone under the Eiffel Tower looking like a young Uma Thurman. I have to tear myself away from her looking over her sunglasses in Rome, half-naked on a Greek island, driven insane by selfies of her grinning face, close-ups of long brown legs on fucking beaches everywhere. She's all over social media.

And I'm all over her.

Sophie tells me the phrase 'supermodel' is outdated now, but it's the only way to describe Caroline, with her long, coltish limbs and perfect bone structure. Our Caroline plays fresh-faced ingénue and vampish thirty-something with equal sex appeal, and the more of her I see, the more consumed I am.

I can almost hear her panting as she leers at me from her Instagram page – tiny bikinis on faraway beaches, filtered selfies in low-cut tops. The Facebook page is less soft porn and more PG, family-oriented, as she downs fun cocktails with friends, attends family weddings and holds friends' babies like Mother bloody Teresa. I don't know her status regarding my husband, but according to Facebook she's still single... but is she?

It's the PG version of the fragrant *Facebook* Caroline I encounter in the flesh when we bump into her in Waitrose. It's Saturday, two days after our pizza 'en famille' and the family togetherness over marinara pizza and ice cream sundaes has convinced me everything is going to be okay after all. We'd all chatted happily at Pizza Express, Simon was in a good mood, the boys were tired but not *nasty* tired, and Sophie chatted and even ate some of her pizza. It was a magical evening, one I'll always remember, and anyone watching through the window of the restaurant that night would have seen a picture perfect, happy family. #Blessed.

On returning home, the warmth of the house and the two glasses of wine I'd consumed with my pizza gave everything a lovely glow and once the kids were in bed, Simon and I shared a bottle of wine by the fire. I was amazed when he started to undress me on the sofa, something we've barely done since the kids because there's a chance at least one of them might walk in. But he seemed consumed with passion and I wasn't arguing. I was happy to be swept into his big strong arms and to be loved. He was so gentle, not the usual wham-bam let's do this quickly because I've got an early start, and none of that *Fifty Shades* stuff he quite likes either. No, this was special, like in the beginning, as his soft but urgent caresses brushed away my prickly paranoia, and when I woke the next morning, all traces of Caroline were gone.

She soon came back though, in the flesh.

Meanwhile, things are slipping again at my end and I've forgotten to buy the lemons for the sea bass and capers, now postponed to this evening's dinner. My forgetfulness meant an unscheduled trip to Waitrose with the whole family. Because, to the boys' irritation and Sophie's abject horror, Simon insisted we all go shopping together to buy bloody lemons.

'It's the weekend,' he says. 'I don't get many free weekends, and we need to spend quality family time with each other.'

I'm not convinced a supermarket is the best place for quality family time, but it's the thought that counts and it's nice he wants us all to be together.

'But why can't we stay at home and play Fifa?' Charlie groans.

'Because it's destroying your brain cells. If you're good, I'll buy you a footie magazine and Alfie can have...'

'A dinosaur magazine! Please, please, pleeeeeeese!'

The prospect of this is sending Alfie into a tyrannosaurus frenzy and he's leaping about. Now both kids are ridiculously excited about having a magazine each and chanting loudly. Meanwhile, Sophie heads back upstairs and I put my coat on and wander into the front garden to wait for Simon. I'm leaving the boys unchaperoned in the kitchen with their iPads, which is probably a bit risky, but I just need a few moments of peace. Having deadheaded the last of the season's late roses round the door, I wander back, always aware that two six-year-old boys can be wonderful, funny and loving – but potentially terrifying if left alone. I'm greeted by Alfie standing on the kitchen oasis, the island in the middle of the room used for food prep, which for the boys is now the stage of *Britain's Got Talent*. This in itself contravenes all my health and safety rules, but as Charlie is throwing apples at his face, causing him to lose his balance, it's clear we are one apple away from a major child injury incident. Had I not walked in at that moment, an apple would have hit him straight in the head and he'd have fallen from a fair height onto the solid stone floor.

'Charlie, don't be so stupid!' I yell loudly.

'I'm NOT STUPID!' he roars, which brings Simon downstairs, unaware of what's gone on before he jumps straight in.

'Marianne, please don't call Charlie stupid,' he says with unconcealed horror, making me feel terrible.

'Yeah, you hurt my feelings,' Charlie mutters sulkily. I want to cry because he looks genuinely hurt, but I could kill Simon for undermining me like this, and it isn't the first time. Yes I can sometimes be cross with them, but it's only ever out of love and concern. When Simon reprimands me in front of them, the boys naturally feel like I've done them a great injustice, when all I'm doing is what any good mother would do. Keeping them from harm.

'I'm sorry I said that, Charlie,' I say, knowing I have to do this, but at the same time knowing it's weakening me in the eyes of my little boys and any respect I have garnered will be lost. 'It's just that Alfie could have really been hurt...' I start.

'Please stop talking, I'm getting a headache,' is Simon's sharp response. I feel humiliated, like the fourth child in the family, but I don't argue. I don't want to start a row that could go on all weekend. Once in the car it's a free for all. The boys, having got off lightly, are given licence to yell and thump each other throughout the journey and I don't feel like I can step in again. My head hurts and I'm feeling on edge with all the noise, not to mention the potential for injury. I flinch at each smack they land on each other, every squeal of pain a trigger, but Simon drives along, apparently oblivious. I dig my fingers into my palms and look out at the passing shops and cars, trying to blot the noise from my head.

Arriving at the supermarket, all three kids stagger across the car park like zombies, unsure why they're here and what's expected of them. Buying bloody lemons is something I could so easily have done alone; in fact I'd have quite enjoyed a little drive into town and a wander down the aisles by myself. I'd also have done this more efficiently and far more quickly without any arguments, but once Simon gets an idea in his head there's no stopping him. I sometimes wonder if he just does things to upset me. But I shouldn't complain. It's lovely that he wants us all to be together – I should be grateful. I remind myself of this only a few minutes later as I physically and forcibly separate the boys who are in full ninja mode around the citrus fruit.

'Kill me now,' yawns Sophie as we walk through the greengrocery. She's on her phone whilst the boys have commandeered the oranges, turning everything citrus into a war zone. I'm attempting to extricate the 'hand grenades' (grapefruits) from their sticky fingers, when I hear Simon say 'Hey.' He says this softly, and for a moment I think he's talking to one of the children or even me, and I soften and turn towards him, warmed by the gentleness in his voice.

But he isn't talking to the children, or me, he's talking to a blonde stranger. Except she isn't a stranger. I've seen her before, in different countries with different friends. *Caroline.*

He seems genuinely surprised (and pleased?) to see her. 'What are you doing here?' he asks, suppressing a smile. It's obvious, isn't it? She's buying bloody groceries… either that or she's stalking us – or rather stalking Simon. It wouldn't be the first time a woman has taken it upon herself to be with him every waking hour. Margaret from the café where we used to live was always bumping into us 'by coincidence', pawing him while completely ignoring me. I soon put a stop to her little game. That's the price you pay when you're married to a man like Simon: women are ready to drop their knickers and climb into bed with him at the first hello. It puts me on edge, and that's how I feel now as I watch intently from behind a wall of satsumas as they chat. I ask Sophie to take the boys to the magazine aisle to choose their reading matter and grab a sack of unwaxed lemons, almost knocking a child over in my haste to join Simon so I can come between them, be present and stop anything being said that can't be unsaid.

I stand next to him wordlessly, an expectant smile on my face. It's my open, welcoming smile that says I'm secure in my marriage. A smile that lies.

On the surface they are conducting polite small talk; there are work references, then vague introductions. Simon eventually notices me and steps back, his arm vaguely gesturing towards me, but not touching.

'I don't think you've met Marianne… my wife.'

I stand there holding tightly on to my sack of lemons and my composure.

She smiles back somewhat grudgingly, or perhaps she's just shy? Then she reaches out her hand to shake mine. Her hand's cold, but not as cold as her eyes.

'This is Caroline… my colleague. Caroline Harker,' Simon says.

I'm stung all over again at the way her name sounds on his lips. Tonight she's having dinner with a friend, she says.

'I'm providing the wine.' Caroline smiles, all perfect white teeth, holding up her basket for his inspection, like a child seeking approval. I can't see the contents of the basket but glimpse a bottle of good white and an expensive fizz. Here's a young woman who's never known the meaning of poverty, tragedy… death, real life. *Ponies and private schools*, I think as she negotiates her way through the conversation, sure of who she is, laughing openly when Charlie runs into Simon's legs, causing them to buckle. I flash a look at my husband – he doesn't like being laughed at, but here he is now laughing along with her as they both look down at Alfie like he's their own. I have a sudden urge to grab my son and smash her bottle of bloody Sauvignon over her head. Then I think better of it. There's a good old Chateauneuf du Pape on the top shelf; it's red and so would be far more dramatic, and would stain more.

As they continue to chat, I smile and nod at their stupid small talk, while enjoying the thought of the bottle hitting her skull, cracking bone and glass, wine splashing scarlet on that baby-pink Armani coat she's wearing.

Watch out, Caroline, with your perfect teeth.

Sophie suddenly appears with Alfie and the promised dinosaur magazine, which he's holding like it's the most precious thing he ever owned. I smile at them, and quietly ask about the tyrannosaurus on the cover, relieved to have a distraction and back-up; I was beginning to feel like a gooseberry. I'm pointing at dinosaurs and feigning fascination while listening and watching the two of them from the corner of my eye. It's primal: my senses are heightened, my heart in overdrive at this latest threat to my survival, *our* survival as a family. I waited all my life for a family and I'm damned if I'm giving it all up to some simpering thirty-something who clicks her manicured fingers. I'm the only one who can keep this fractured family together. Even if I am mistaken and she's just a colleague, I can't afford to be complacent – I have to always be on my guard. I've been wrong before, but I can't relax, ever. Would you be comfortable with intelligent, beautiful blonde Caroline working closely with *your* husband? Unfortunately, this kind of woman is a prime target for what Simon and my therapist refer to as 'Marianne's paranoia'. She's ten years younger, with a tinkling laugh and a vivaciousness that belies her status as an esteemed Fellow of the Royal College of Surgeons. *And I hate her.*

All the signs are there: his perma-smile, the look in his eyes as he talks to her, the way she caresses her neck when she responds. To anyone witnessing this typical Saturday afternoon supermarket scene – the small talk, the polite laughter, the kids playing hide-and-seek behind the tins of beans – there's nothing here to see. *But I can see it.*

He teases her about some bloody comment she made in a surgical meeting and she nudges him playfully. Not only does this exclude me, but I can't remember the last time he teased me, not in a kind, flirtatious way like this. I turn away, can almost taste the sex in the air, not something I've experienced in Waitrose before. They continue a supposed conversation about the new surgical department, but I suspect it's some kind of secret sexual code. I move closer and take the opportunity to study the contents of her basket, because a shopping basket can tell you a lot about a person. And I want to know everything there is to know about this woman. A single bag of organic leaves, a punnet of late strawberries and the expensive wine and champagne. No carbs, no sugar and no dairy. Judging by the contents of her basket, this one isn't getting her kicks from food. *So where are you getting your kicks, Caroline?*

During our marriage, I've developed an instinct when it comes to Simon's female friends. She may, on the surface, be a colleague or acquaintance, somebody else's wife – but sometimes I see a potential lover, a mistress even. Friend or foe? I'm not completely sure yet what Caroline is, but she concerns me deeply. *This one will be trouble.*

Eventually, she politely makes a move. It's an uncomfortable dynamic of three when two people know each other well and the third is merely a bystander. But who is the bystander, her or me?

'I didn't know she lived around here,' I blurt, during the slightly uncomfortable aftermath as we head for the checkout, followed by our reluctant entourage. I touch Simon's arm as we walk, in what seems a futile attempt to claim ownership and sweeten the accusatory tone I can hear in my own voice.

'Sorry you didn't know she lives around here, but I didn't realise you had to be informed of all my colleagues' home addresses,' he answers petulantly without looking at me.

My heart jolts. The lightness of the past couple of days has gone. All the happiness that had continued after the pizza night just snapped like taut elastic. Why am I never satisfied? Why do I have to ruin things with my stupid, jealous questioning? I'm so bloody stupid, and small-minded – why can't I free myself from all this? But then again, how can I ever be free after what happened?

The queue isn't moving, the boys are whiney – they're hungry now – and Sophie's brow is furrowed in the light of her phone. I can't even begin to guess what's troubling her. Once upon a time I could plaster her knee, kiss it better, take her out for cake and everything would be okay, but as she's grown older I've felt a chasm open up between us, and there are times now when she feels almost out of reach. I have enough on my hands with the other two (now brawling by the checkout) but at times she seems lost and I have to help find her again.

I call the boys, wanting to regroup the family into our little hub, to gather us together.

Safety in numbers.

I may be the cuckolded wife, but I'm a mum first and my awareness is heightened to everyone's moods. I look at my kids as we stand in the queue; they are everything to me and I will fight tooth and nail for their happiness and safety. Like most mums, I absorb all their hates and hurts, disappointments and loves (Charlie hates losing, loves football and chicken crisps; Alfie hates sport, loves Maltesers and dinosaurs; and Sophie… What does Sophie love? I think she hates eating but loves Lana Del Rey, and… I'm guessing Josh in her French class, from the way his name keeps popping up). Every joy, every reward, every stinging slight I probably feel even more keenly than they do. I soak up my family like a sponge. I wouldn't have it any other way.

I look at Simon, oblivious to the kids, and wonder if he's thinking about *her* and want to intrude on those thoughts.

'What a coincidence, seeing Caroline.' I can't leave it. I have to do a biopsy, poke around in it and work out how dangerous she is.

'Why?' He's looking at me; he wants an answer. The intensity in his voice makes me uncomfortable. I immediately regret saying anything and grapple with my response.

'Because you only mentioned her for the first time the other day and… we live here too.'

'Coincidence? A coincidence that two people who work together also live in the same area? If you say so, Marianne.'

His sharpness catches me and I'm annoyed with myself for causing this change in his mood. The only reason we're here is because I forgot the fucking lemons for the sodding sea bass. If I'd remembered them in the first place, we'd never have had to come to Waitrose. And if we'd never come here we'd never have bumped into her, and I wouldn't have potentially ruined the weekend by quizzing Simon on where *she* lives. I glance up at him for a clue; he's looking back at me, his eyes boring into mine like he can read my thoughts.

'You okay?' I mutter, knowing he's not.

'I'm fine. But you clearly aren't. You need to calm down and stop being paranoid just because a woman I work with happens to shop in the same supermarket,' he hisses under his breath.

'Sorry, I didn't mean… anything.' But we both know I did, and now I've really upset him, which is the last thing I wanted to do.

Until recently we thought we'd come through our problems and with support it seemed I'd finally been able to control my obsessive, irrational behaviour. But no, I'm still imagining all kinds of ridiculous shit and I hate myself for spoiling every lovely moment with my unfounded suspicions. God, when will I learn?

'Sorry, I'm an idiot,' I say again, hoping I can pass for normal. *I'm not mad. Please don't think I am. I promise I won't mention her again.*

Gazing down into my metal basket, I concentrate on the meagre contents – four lemons, a dinosaur magazine and a copy of *Match!* What would my therapist make of this basket? She'd probably up my dosage and lock me away. *All he did was bump into a friend from work and Marianne assumes they're having sex.*

I'm shaken from my rather self-indulgent reverie by a kerfuffle in front of us in the queue. I spot two kids on their tummies snaking their way through shoppers' legs and for a brief moment feel smug that I'm not the parent – then I realise I am.

Simon leans forward, taps Charlie on the back and gently tells them both to 'stand up and stop being silly!' He does this with a twinkle in his eye that isn't lost on the cashier, who giggles as he rolls his eyes good-naturedly. 'Apparently they are in the jungle,' he explains. Soft, well-spoken voice, handsome face, charm oozing over the till. He is irresistible. I positively sparkle as he turns to me, still smiling, and in front of the queue says, 'Darling, we really must get a rope bridge for the garden.' My face beams, as I see other women in the queue look enviously on at this gorgeous husband and father I'm married to. *Simon could be with anyone but chose to be with me.*

'They watch too much inappropriate TV,' he mutters to me once we are outside, the charm dissipating at the exit. The boys are now 'firing' at each other from behind parked cars.

'I only let them watch what's on our agreed list,' I say defensively. 'I can't keep an eye on them all the time. I don't know what they see at school… the other boys…'

He flashes me a look and I shut up. We walk on and I decide if I don't speak for a while it might help – this is his day off and Simon doesn't need me antagonising him. I stare ahead and my stomach lurches as I spot her at the far end of the car park, climbing into a shiny, sporty car that looks like the roof comes off. I imagine her driving along a lonely coastal road, hair flying, sun on her back – the tight, perilous turns. The car swerving… it could so easily go right off the cliff, plunging hundreds, no, thousands of feet below, smashing on rocks… I must stop thinking like this. I have no evidence at all that she's more than a colleague, except for the fact that just seeing her causes every pore, every hair follicle, to open.

I watch her drive off, breathing a sigh of relief, trying not to imagine her upturned car at the bottom of windswept cliffs. Simon doesn't seem to see her, and if he does he isn't letting on; besides he's too busy commanding the boys to 'walk not run'. His jaw twitches with tension and I glimpse the real man behind the smiling charmer witnessed by the checkout audience.

'Simon, they're okay. Let them work off some energy,' I say quietly.

He turns sharply. 'What?'

'They want to run; they're just being... boys.'

'Oh, well, that's okay then, isn't it? I suppose that's what the mothers of thieves and murderers say – "*they're just being boys*",' he says in a whiney voice, presumably to emulate mine. I don't answer him; there's no point. 'Perhaps if you paid more attention to our children's behaviour and less to mine...' he hisses under his breath.

But I can't, I have to watch him. I am compelled to listen to his phone calls, check his texts, because if I don't, everything will fall apart, and our family will be over.

CHAPTER FOUR

The first time I suspected Simon was cheating on me was before we were even married – two weeks before, in fact. He went out for drinks after work and turned up quite drunk at 4 a.m. I was frantic and tearful, but he said it was nothing, just a night with colleagues that had gone on later than expected. But I didn't believe him and the following day I sobbed and pleaded with him to tell me the truth. I just *knew.* Exhausted from my near hysteria and unwillingness to drop this, he finally admitted to a mild panic setting in about the future. He described a drunken evening with work colleagues and guiltily confessed that he'd ended up talking to a young nurse from surgical until the early hours of the morning. He said he liked her – nothing more than that – and swore to me that nothing had happened, but at the time I was so devastated I threatened to cancel the wedding. Thank goodness he talked to me, showed he really cared and convinced me I'd be throwing everything away. 'I will make it up to you every single day of our lives,' he'd said earnestly. 'I adore you, there could never be anyone else – ever. You're the moon to all of my stars.'

I melted at this. It was just what I wanted to hear, what I needed to know. And, as he said later, I completely overreacted. Though sometimes I wonder if I'd merely heard what I wanted to hear – and buried those suspicions so deep they still live inside me. That he could leave me at any time. That he could have any woman he wanted. I feel it inside the marriage even now, eroding the very heart of who we are, changing who we could be if I could only let it go.

It's an uphill struggle keeping him to myself, keeping our family safe. It's not his fault he's faced with temptation every day; women have always fallen at Simon's feet. He has the looks, the wit, the intellect and charm to make a woman feel like a goddess. I know how that feels, because he used to make me feel like that. Even now, despite everything that's gone before, I would give anything to have that back. All that we've been through, all the terrible stuff that's been said, and all it takes is one caress, one night, to put me right back there in my veil on my wedding day, before all our lies.

If only I could feel like that again, but I've spent our marriage in a state of paranoia – I've imagined I'm competing with shop girls, barmaids and even my best friends. I've misjudged, overreacted, and there have been times I care not to think about when I've behaved like a wild animal, and in Simon's words, 'like a fishwife' and 'a savage'. We've had to move house more than once, Simon's changed hospitals, and it's all my fault. I even have a criminal record – whoever heard of a surgeon's wife with a criminal record? I'm a total liability, that's what he says, and he's right. I'm not the wife he deserves, or the mother his children deserve – what kind of mother does what I did? Why does he even stay with me? I love my home and my family. But I can't enjoy them because I spend my days worrying that I'm not good enough and Simon will find someone better and leave me, which is why I'm always on guard. I thought I'd shaken it off, but my demon's back with me. And this time her name is Caroline.

After years of therapy, I really thought I'd finally learned to live with my grief, my guilt and Simon's imagined betrayals. Moving here to this well-heeled road of elegant, double-fronted Georgian houses has been good for me, but I'm beginning to wonder if we will ever shake off who we are and the pain we carry with us. Being here also reminds me of who I used to be. It isn't far from where my mother used to live and I spent some of my childhood in the area – albeit on a different side of the tracks. I lived with a foster family just a few streets from here and used to walk past houses like the one I live in now on my way to and from school. I'd catch a glimpse of another world and daydream about what life might be like in these lovely homes. Lit by lamplight on cold winter evenings, a perfect family with good parents, a fire flickering in the grate, hot crumpets for tea. And now at Number 5 Garden Close, in our beautiful home with an elegant, manicured lawn and symmetrical bay trees at the door, I was beginning to feel like I'd almost made it, like I belonged. No one was going to send me away from here, no one was going to leave – it was all mine and I was safe. Until now. Until Caroline.

Our present is informed by our past, the fears, the insecurities – the loss. But why can't I just ignore these new fears and embrace what I have? When I've been ill in the past I planted roses, deep-cleaned the kitchen and baked enormous quantities of organic bread to take my mind off whoever I imagined was Simon's lover. But this is different; Caroline's different. She's not like the others. She's here all the time, in my head, in my kitchen, and the harder I wipe and polish the more I see her face in the shiny kitchen surfaces, and smell her perfume in the aroma of freshly baked bread. I feel like I'm about to lose everything. *But I thought I was better now?*

I wonder if I finished working with Saskia, my therapist, too soon? When we decided to move, I felt like this fresh start would be good for me and perhaps I could live my life again without the safety net – I had to start thinking for myself and making my own decisions without checking with someone else all the time. *But am I ready?* I've taken the lessons she's taught me and used the tools to get me through the day, but sometimes I feel like I need to talk to someone. 'Be positive, Marianne,' she'd say. 'Think about what you do have, not what you don't.' Okay, so I have a beautiful home, three perfect children and a gorgeous and loving husband who's also a great father and works hard to provide for his family – the family I always longed for. So what if my husband has women friends and female colleagues he's close to? There's nothing wrong with that. Is there?

Saskia would also tell me to 'feel the power of positive self-affirmation', or something equally unfathomable. But I get the gist, so tell myself I'm not unattractive, that I'm not stupid, and I'm worthy of a man like Simon. I am. Aren't I?

It's weird to think now that when we first met I was the one who was thriving and poor Simon was a mess. He'd just lost Nicole and was struggling with childcare, so his mother Joy was looking after Sophie – by that I mean taking her to and from school, making sure she was fed and putting her to bed at seven each evening, so she didn't have to actually engage with her. The woman, Joy by name, Joy-less by nature, was the coldest, least maternal person I have ever met and sometimes, when Simon's being mean, I try to remember this. We are the children our parents made us and though Simon can be warm and loving, especially with his kids, Joy's lack of maternal instinct must have had an effect.

Our love story would make a great film: struggling young widower meets party girl who's going places and against all the odds they make a go of it. I lived in London back then and my flatmate, who was in PR, asked me to go to a book launch with her, promising free champagne, so naturally I tagged along. It was a launch for a memoir about a pioneering surgeon, at Waterstones in Piccadilly, and as I knew no one and most of the guests were over seventy, including the 'distinguished' surgeon, I positioned myself near the refreshments. I was drinking cheap champagne like it was lemonade when I saw Simon in the 'medical books' section. Our eyes met – he was the most gorgeous man I'd ever seen – and when he walked over and introduced himself I was bowled over. I loved his confidence, the way his thick, shiny hair flopped over big blue eyes that twinkled like he knew how to have fun. I was working for a fashion company and he was a surgeon, and though we had little in common, we somehow just clicked. He invited me out the following evening and while eating oysters in a champagne bar we shared our stories.

Mine was very boring really. I lost my mum when I was ten and a foster mother spotted my potential for art and suggested I study it at A level. I then went to art school and became the head fashion buyer for a big Swedish company that was doing well. I loved my job and was good at it too, but after a few dates with Simon my career wasn't the most important thing in my life any more. My previous relationships had all been casual, without commitment, but here was the man of my dreams and not only was he kind, funny and charming, within weeks he had asked me to marry him. I was smitten, couldn't believe my luck, and despite my friends suggesting I was rushing into this, I also saw the looks of lust and envy on their faces when they met him.

Sophie clearly needed love and understanding (she was getting neither from Joyless Joy) and so as soon as we'd booked the wedding, Simon chose a new flat close to the hospital where he was working, and the three of us moved in. Unfortunately, the flat was perfect for Simon's work, but the commute was too far into London for mine, so I gave up my job. I was sad to say goodbye to a career I loved and had worked hard for but it was important that Simon was near to where he worked. I'd hoped to become freelance, but success in the world of fashion is about being in the capital, attending all the shows, and out in the suburbs I couldn't keep on top of things. Besides, I now had a ready-made family to look after. Simon worked long hours, Sophie had to be cared for, and within a few months I'd abandoned the idea of working from home and embraced a new life. And the first time Sophie called me 'Mum' made up for any glamorous fashion career I might have had. I cried with happiness. I was home.

I loved spending time with Sophie. It was good for both of us as she missed her mum so much, and to build our bond and fill the void left by Nicole's death I'd read to her, we'd go shopping and to the cinema, and we also shared a hobby. While she was at school I'd wanted something to do so started making small shoulder bags and hair scrunchies from scraps of fabric and bric-a-brac. And at weekends when Simon was working we'd scour second-hand shops for lovely fabric and old paste jewellery to decorate them with – and I taught her to sew. This was a happy time and most evenings, with Simon working late, we had great fun designing and sewing – and Sophie seemed to love it, with her wobbly stitches and scary but cute colour combinations. I planned to rent a market stall in the town at the weekends and sell what we'd made, but Simon was worried the whole 'project' was distracting for Sophie and she should be concentrating on her schoolwork.

'I'm sure the little bags and bits are lovely, darling, but I'd rather she did something more academic,' he'd said one evening when he came home unusually early.

This was a fair point, I had to admit. So I suggested I would perhaps continue alone – I'd had some interest from my old boss who'd asked me to bring my handbags in to show them to her. But, as Simon pointed out, they were 'eye-catching but not exactly Chanel'. 'And,' he added, 'it's not like you'd make any money. I mean, they'd bring in a few pounds, if you were lucky – but they wouldn't pay for our children's education.' I'd loved it when he'd mentioned 'our children', even though we hadn't yet had any of our own.

I know this sounds almost crazy in this day and age, but after struggling through my twenties to make ends meet, I welcomed being looked after by Simon. This was my chance to take a breath, to care for Sophie, to stop and smell the roses and look after our home, or 'play house', as Simon jokingly referred to it. 'You love playing house, don't you, Marianne,' he'd teased one evening after a particularly good dinner cooked lovingly by me. This was so true. Yes, I'd loved my party life but was now ready to grow up and move on. It had been a great job and I'd worked damned hard to get there, but I felt being with Simon and Sophie was the real meaning of my life. Simon, Sophie and our future children were now my career and I was ready to give them my all. When you spend your childhood in care and foster homes, you take nothing for granted and to be included in someone's future plans, and be cared for, was all I'd ever wanted.

I felt like I was damaged goods, but Simon took me on, whisking me away from the nightlife, the travel, the wine and the coke – the endless search for something to quell the raging sadness sitting heavy in my belly. He took me straight to his bed, made me feel like the most beautiful girl in the world, helped me forget the pointlessness and tragedy of the past and handed me a shiny new future. He was the beginning of everything and brought me to a new and perfect world, something I'd never thought possible – and for the first time I felt how I'd always longed to feel: just like everyone else.

Our first summer holiday together was spent in sunny Dorset where he'd grown up. His mother still had a holiday home there and our days were filled with picnics on the beach, acres of rolling lawn, open fires on cooler evenings and jam and scones for tea. It was magical, the kind of holiday I'd read about and dreamed of as a little girl and never had. Unfortunately, his mother joined us for a few days and took an instant dislike to me because I hadn't been to the right schools and, apparently, didn't know my cutlery. She was horrified and made it clear she thought I was beneath her son. But I was so happy, I didn't care. I was in love; so was he. And we had a secret – I was pregnant.

I think about that summer of hope, when everything lay before us, now as his phone lights up on the kitchen table. Recently, I've tried to stop snooping, but there's something in the air and I just know it's a message from Caroline. He's gone upstairs and I know I shouldn't, but I wander past, glancing over at the first few lines. It's from someone called Roger – which I don't for a minute believe. I just know it's from her.

CHAPTER FIVE

I stand over the phone and lean over to read it, totally wired to the fact Simon may walk in any minute but unable to stop myself.

What about tomorrow evening? Can you tell her you're...

I can't see the rest of the text. And I can't open the phone because it's fingertip recognition, nor do I know his pin code. It's so frustrating, so horribly tantalising. Even if I could unlock it, I daren't because then he'd know I'd read it.

I remind myself this isn't the first time I've been convinced he was having an affair from a half-read text on his phone. Last year I'd found myself in a similar situation when spotting the first few lines of a text message. 'You have my heart...' the message had said. I was desperate, convinced he was seeing someone else, but I didn't know who and was so crazed, so compelled to open it, I couldn't leave it alone. I tried the children's birthdays, and after a couple of misses, I guessed his pin code, which was the date he received his consultancy position – I knew it was one of the most important days in his life. I unlocked that phone with tears streaming down my face, hating myself and the new low to which I'd sunk. But in spite of the self-loathing and guilt, I clicked on the message, braced for the tidal wave of pain I was about to inflict on myself. 'You have my heart *patient...*' was the opening line. Just one word, *one* wonderful word, transformed the message from a lover's text to a request from one surgeon to another. Of course

I was completely wrong. I should have known, and *I should have trusted my husband.*

I remember laughing maniacally as I read the message, which went on to talk about some procedure that had to be adhered to when treating this particular patient. I was tearful, overjoyed, then worried about the fact that Simon would know I'd checked his phone and opened a private message. The information was sensitive and vital. I knew this, but I deleted it. I had to. It was pure madness, but I would rather delete the message and risk the possibility of someone coming to harm, than admit to Simon that I'd unlocked his phone. But afterwards I couldn't live with myself, and two tortured days later confessed to him. Understandably he was really upset and said as a result of this he hadn't been able to act on the information and the patient had died.

'It will be on your conscience forever,' he'd added, as I sobbed quietly, disgusted with myself and how, through my paranoia and wickedness, I'd as good as killed someone.

I'd cried for weeks. I couldn't cope with what I'd done and my self-hatred was at an all-time high, as was my medication dosage. Then, one day, out of the blue, Simon said the patient hadn't died, but my 'reckless and selfish actions' meant they *might* have died.

'But you lied,' I remember crying.

'Only a little lie, for your own good – to teach you a lesson,' he'd said. 'You must never interfere in my work again. I'm still shocked at what you did, Marianne. I don't think I can ever trust you again… my own wife,' he'd said, and left me standing there, chastised like a child.

So I hadn't been responsible for a death after all, but his disappointment in me cut like a knife.

After that Simon changed his pin code and all his passwords on his PC so I couldn't access anything. I don't blame him, and I'm glad, because I'm not sure I'd be able to resist looking now.

I can't trust myself.

I know I should walk away from the phone still sitting tantalisingly before me. I should have faith in my husband because he loves me – but I can't, because what it is I'm imagining threatens my very survival. All the pills in the world can't give me the peace I now long for. I can't rest until I know what's happening. Even though the rational part of me says it could be an innocent text between work colleagues, the mad part of my brain is screaming at me that it's something else.

My hand is reaching out for the phone just as Simon appears in the doorway. He's just read the boys a bedtime story and is smiling about something one of them said. I laugh nervously and he walks towards me, kisses me on the cheek and suddenly everything's okay again. I breathe deeply and sink into him. I am pathetic. I have to stop tormenting myself over nothing, because it's seriously affecting my mental health again, not to mention the damage to our relationship.

Now he's kissing the back of my neck, murmuring sweet nothings. Here, if I need it, is the evidence that my husband isn't having some wild affair with a woman he works with. Of course he's not, it's just a text message – I want to throw the bloody phone across the kitchen, smash it into smithereens on the new worktops, but I dig my nails into my palms and try to relax against him.

He eventually pulls away and as I go back to the oven and stir the sauce for pasta, I see him walk over to where his phone waits. I turn to reach for the bubbling pot of water, flashing a look over at him to see if he's responding to the text, but he puts the phone carefully down and starts shuffling through the day's post.

'I'm making your favourite pasta,' I say, hoping the domestic sing-song in my voice will keep everything sweet, like I'm spraying Caroline deterrent all over the room. 'You always say the sauce reminds you of that holiday in Sorrento. It'd be about ten years ago now.' Smiling at the memory, I turn to look at him. 'Do you remember how hot it was that summer? I was pregnant with…' I stop there.

'Yes, I love Italy.' He smiles absently as he looks through the credit card bill, my twittering voice swooping around him. He isn't listening, but he's frowning at something on the bill and I feel a little uneasy. 'You've been buying flowers, Marianne?'

'Yes... yes. I meant to say, I went to Mum's grave, put some roses there, for her anniversary.'

'You should have reminded me; I would have gone with you. The anniversary always makes you rather...'

'It's fine... I was okay,' I say, before he can add anything. My mother has always been a moot point between us – just the mention of her can bring up so much that I try to shut it down before it gains any momentum. Self-preservation, I suppose. Simon's own mother died two years ago and he's never mentioned her once, even on the anniversary of her death. I know there was very little warmth between them, but she was his mother. I suppose we all have different ways of dealing with loss.

I wish my own grief wasn't so all-consuming – so many layers, so many years. I stir the sauce and see scarlet water, white, blood-stained towels. The text on his phone has unsettled me, and I close my eyes tight so I don't see the blood.

Simon sits down at the oasis, and leans on the Calacatta Oro marble worktops, which the designer assured us would set off the clean lines of the sustainable European oak cabinetry.

I don't care about the origins of the fucking cabinetry, I want to know if you're sleeping with her.

I glance over again as his hand reaches for the phone, clicking open the text. The air is thick with steam and Italian herbs, but all I can taste is fear and hurt.

'Oh... looks like I'm working late tomorrow,' he says.

I plunge dry pasta into bubbling water, unable to speak. Silence hangs in the air between us, heavy and aromatic. Eventually, I'm able to respond.

'Oh. Why are you... working late?'

'What do you mean *why?*' he snaps, and I know I'm in danger of ruining a perfectly good evening.

'I meant what is it… an emergency?' I say, trying to sound interested, but not too interested.

'An emergency? Hardly. If it is, it'll be too late in twenty-four hours' time,' he mutters as he takes a bottle of red from the side and opens the drawer, looking for the corkscrew.

'I left it there for you, on the oasis,' I say. I always try and pre-empt anything Simon might need. A friend I had at the old house used to joke that I was a Stepford Wife, but it's not like that, I'm not that organised. It's just that Simon has a stressful job and the last thing he needs after a day of open-heart surgery is to lose it over a bloody corkscrew. But tonight it seems he has.

'Honestly, Marianne, you know I'm under pressure. I'm working so hard towards this senior consultancy. I had a really tough meeting with Prof. Cookson today. I'm not the only one in the frame for this and he's riding us all hard, and now I'm home and you're adding to my pressure, questioning, the *constant* mistrust… it's back and it's driving me mad!' He stabs his finger into the side of his head, suggesting madness. *My* madness. His face is red, angry, resentful, and I'm relieved when he finds the corkscrew where I'd left it and has something to do with his hands. Pushing hard metal into soft, pliant wood, he glares at me until the cork is released; there's a soft pop and he's pouring himself a large glass of red.

'I'll have one too,' I say fake brightly, pretending everything's fine. *Perhaps if I keep pretending everything's fine, then it will be?*

I look at his phone still sitting on the table – I can't help it. I don't want to go over and over the bloody text in my head like it's a crossword puzzle. But I know I will. I need to solve the conundrum, find out the answer to my question. I'm at the mercy of my own sick mind. *'What about tomorrow evening? Can you tell her you're...* 'What? Leaving her? Not in love with her any more? *What does the rest of the fucking text say?*

He hasn't poured me a glass of wine, so I go over to where he's now standing with his own glass and pour myself one.

'Are you sure you should be drinking wine?' he asks, like I'm a child.

I nod mid-gulp. 'I'm fine, not taken any pills yet today.' I let the warm red liquid fill my throat and soothe my soul, and when he turns away I take another bigger gulp.

'You haven't *taken* anything?' He's incredulous.

'No. I'd like to come off the medication for a while. I feel well enough, Simon.'

I'm all better – do you love me now?

But he rolls his eyes and looks worried. 'Marianne, you *should* be taking your meds. You can't mess about. You know what happens when you don't.'

'Yes, but when I don't take them, I feel better, more alert... more...'

'More what? Mad? Paranoid? Psychotic?'

I'm stung. I don't know why; this isn't new. I know what I am but still, hearing those words makes it all so real.

'I just hate feeling like I'm wading through cotton wool all day,' I mutter, going back to the safety of sauce-stirring and wishing I could down the bloody bottle in one go. I take a breath and turn around to speak to him. 'I want to be better, Simon. I used to take the prescribed 30 mg a day in the evenings and that knocked me out, but I could at least function the next day. But now Doctor Johnson's upped it to 45 mg... I think it's too much.'

'Oh, fair enough, you should know all about your dosage. After all, you spent years in medical school,' he mutters sarcastically.

'Don't be like that Simon, you know what I mean... I told you, I stagger through the day. Everything's cloudy on 45 mg.'

'But they calm you down?'

'Yes, I suppose you could say that. But along with the cloudiness I have unwelcome thoughts… and I find it all so distracting. Simon, I *want* to be present… I *want* to be a good wife, a good mother,' I add, hoping he'll at least try and see things from my perspective.

But he doesn't even look up from his phone. 'Good wife and mother? It's a little late for that, don't you think?'

I start to cry silently over the bubbling sauce.

Eventually Simon sees that I'm upset and wanders towards me. 'I'm sorry, I didn't mean *that*,' he says, and again I feel the sharpness of his blame for what happened all those years ago. 'I was talking about the way you become… agitated when you don't take your medication,' he's saying. 'It's not just about you, Marianne. You have a family to consider – what do you think your "episodes" do to them, to our surviving kids?'

'Don't… just don't… Simon…' I'm now back on the edge of tears and he can see I'm likely to become hysterical if he doesn't back off.

'You always think I'm saying one thing when in fact I'm saying something quite different,' he snaps. 'You really do have to stop jumping to conclusions, Marianne. I'm sorry if you're upset, but you need to sort yourself out, for everyone's sake.'

I turn to him, tears streaming down my face. This wasn't the way I'd hoped things would be for my pasta marinara. I was aiming for memories of Sorrento and loving smiles, not me hiccoughing and dripping tears into the sauce.

'Sorry, sorry.' He's holding his hands in a surrender gesture. 'It's just… I have such high expectations of you and… I shouldn't, because you aren't well, you're poorly, my darling,' he adds more softly.

I don't feel 'poorly', in fact until he mentioned the C word (Caroline) only a matter of days ago, I felt fine – never better. I'd put everything behind me, was moving forward and Simon and I were beginning to connect again. But the past has come raging into the present and is now swirling around like dark water at my feet. I know he doesn't mean to hurt me, I'm just oversensitive – but perhaps I'll always be 'poorly' and was never really better, just pretending to myself? I should take his advice and keep up with my medication.

Ten years ago, my GP prescribed antidepressants temporarily, but in a short time I became dependent on the pills and both Simon and I were concerned at the way I reacted when I stopped taking them. My anxiety levels went through the roof and so we went to my GP together and Simon suggested I needed something stronger that I could take long-term. That was years ago and though I've had my moments, on the whole I've stayed relatively calm, but the recent increase in dose has made me feel out of it. Perhaps it's the price I pay for not going mad and doing crazy things?

I should be sensible and take them again – we don't want a repeat of last year. I'm bloody lucky to have a husband who cares, who stuck around after everything that happened. Simon's picked up the pieces, including me, on more than one occasion. He was telling me only the other evening about one of his colleagues who just walked out on his wife for a woman ten years younger because she'd let herself go. It made me think – I've done a great deal more than letting myself go and he's still with me, for now. He's a bloody saint and the least I can do is take the pills and make life a little bearable for Simon. I need to stay on track, keep my thoughts to myself and not burden him with my trivia. I can't give him any excuse to leave me. I couldn't bear to lose him.

Suddenly the pan of pasta begins to boil over, throwing foaming bubbles over the cooker. I yell and run to it, reaching instinctively for the handle but managing to scald myself instead. I cry out in pain, but Simon doesn't flinch, just takes a long sip of wine.

'You go on and on about being a good mother, a good wife, and you can't even boil pasta,' he says bitterly and shakes his head like he can't believe it. Then he looks away, unable to countenance the flawed woman standing before him. In a kitchen she doesn't deserve, in a life she isn't worthy of.

'Mum, are you okay?' Sophie's suddenly at my side, pulling my hand under the cold tap, shooting her father a look that would kill.

'I'm fine, darling,' I say, grateful for her kindness, touched by her concern. She'll be leaving for university at the end of next summer and I wonder what life will be like without her.

She pats my scalded hand dry with a clean towel as Simon continues to play on his phone. He's probably sending Caroline a text, planning their cosy evening tomorrow night, telling her what he's going to do to her on her big brass bed (oh yes, I've seen it – she poses on it on Instagram. I try not to obsess, but I can't help but keep going back to the photo, as painful as it is to see).

When Sophie finally goes back upstairs to her virtual world, I discreetly open the handmade cabinet door and reach behind the tins of tomato soup. I see Simon watching as I open the bottle of Mirtazapine.

'And take the correct dosage, don't skimp,' he says, continuing to flick through his phone.

'I just don't want to feel so tired,' I sigh, more to myself than him. 'They sap all my energy. I haven't worked on anything for ages.'

'Worked?'

'My bags.'

'And what a great loss to the world of *handbags* that must be.' He says handbags like one might say *shit*.

I don't answer him. No point. Working with fabric and colour was my talent – I like to think it still is – but it isn't a talent Simon recognises, probably because his talent is science-based. He's never seen the point in fashion or design and though when we met, he said he admired my drive, I don't think he understood my world. It was so different from his. '*Vive la différence*,' he'd say. 'It makes us more exciting.' But within a year of being married I'd given birth to our child, and I didn't need to create any more – my new life filled me up and quenched any desire I had for design, even as a hobby.

I'd longed to be a mum, to hold that baby in my arms, but sometimes the things you wish for don't always work out. The whole experience of motherhood took me by surprise. I was so overwhelmed with love for my baby even Simon took a back seat. I was drained and had nothing left for him. In fact – and I find it very difficult to go back over this – due to my negligence, my husband sought comfort in someone else's company.

I found out from a friend when Emily was just a few months old. He'd been seen holding hands with a woman in a local restaurant; he hadn't even had the decency to be discreet. When I confronted him, he said he'd wanted me to find out, that it was just an emotional affair, nothing more, and that me knowing was a relief. But it wasn't a relief to me, it was pure agony. He'd promised me before we married that he wasn't that sort of person, that forever meant forever and he couldn't imagine being with anyone else. How could I ever trust him again?

Weakened by sleepless nights, baby weight and the endlessness of being a new mother, I eventually accepted what happened. I just wanted to keep my husband, and for our family to stay together, and if that meant forgiving and forgetting I had to do it. And it wasn't sex. According to Simon, he hadn't actually done anything – he may have thought about it, but he said he'd never do anything to hurt me. So I forgave him for even thinking about it. I don't honestly know what I'd have done if he had confessed to a full-blown relationship. I'd like to think I'd have been able to walk away, but back then I was unable to imagine anything worse than being without him. Then something worse happened.

My damaged mind still has problems going there, back to what happened, to those dark, lonely days of exhaustion and cow-like heaviness. I try to forget, but my therapist and Simon won't let me. Saskia said that facing up to what happened would help me to heal, move on, which is why Simon sometimes tries to make me talk about it. But I can barely say my baby's name, and I cover my ears when he says it, which is why I need the medication.

In order to get through the day when the children are at school, I sometimes try to avoid the extra dosage. It doesn't always work. Sometimes I just need it – if I didn't take the pills, who knows what I'd do? But on good days I can quiet my mind by making bags from scraps of fabric like I used to. I recently made a shoulder bag for Jen's birthday from scraps of silk and velvet in midnight blue sprinkled with tiny silver stars. I gave it to her at her birthday dinner – one of the few social occasions Simon and I have attended here. Jen was delighted. She loved the bag, clutching it to her chest and saying it was the most beautiful thing she'd ever seen. Everyone admired it and some of her friends asked if I'd make one for them and I remember looking over at Simon, who was looking back, his poppadom paused at his mouth, waiting for my response.

'No, I'm too busy at home,' I lied.

Choose your battles.

Though I had to admit that making the bag and giving it to Jen made me happier than I'd been for some time. Despite what I'd said in front of Simon about being too busy, I wanted to make more and considered starting a Facebook page to try and sell them. I mentioned this to Simon a few days later, but, as he pointed out, when on earth would I have the time with three kids, a huge house and a busy husband?

He's right of course; it was stupid of me to think it made sense to spend all that time sewing for a few pence when I could be spending my time more usefully. But I did enjoy making that bag for Jen and while I was working on it I was able to forget my medication, take a break from the dark, swirling water and land somewhere in the fabric stars. For a few hours anyway.

But now I realise this isn't the answer, it's a temporary stop gap and doesn't work long-term. I'll go back on the higher medication, to stop me overthinking everything. I've realised I can't control myself as well as chemicals can, but I can help myself. I promise myself I won't think about Caroline. I'll stop constantly checking her social media and imagining all kinds of ridiculous scenarios. I also make a vow not to put myself in any situation that might cause problems for me, or those around me. I'm being really positive. And trying hard not to crumble.

CHAPTER SIX

I spend the next few days attempting to achieve a calmer state of mind. But despite heavier medication, Caroline keeps rearing her ugly head. Even 45 mg of Mirtazapine can't keep her away. I see her in Waitrose, in Costa sipping a latte and I even think I see her in Simon's office when I drive past the hospital, which I sometimes find myself doing. But I know it isn't Caroline, it's the medication.

I feel like I'm standing on the edge of a cliff. Will I fall or be pushed? I have to stay safe, keep my mind healthy, not veer off and cause chaos again. So, apart from the school run, I stay home and do my grocery shop online, avoiding Waitrose and Costa and Caroline. I keep the house spotless, tend to the garden and cook for Simon and the children. Digging out recipes for some of his favourite suppers reminds me of how I cooked for him when we were first together, Sophie safely tucked up, wine flowing, sex on the menu most nights. I leaf through French-style family banquets, salivate over soufflés, recall the texture of steak tartare, the richness of creamy, garlicky dauphinoise potatoes. And it occurs to me that if I want the old Simon back, perhaps I need to be the old Marianne again?

So, for the next few days, I make a concerted effort to get my mind and marriage back on track and recapture some of those romantic moments. I scour Julia Child and Elizabeth David cookery books for the best, most difficult and most delicious recipes. I make their complex French and Mediterranean dishes that take hours, reducing stock, layering flavours, filling my mind and my time. I make home-made pasta just like I used to, filling the home with the warm aroma of robust, herby breads to dip in rich casseroles. Cooking is creative and it's one of the few things I do well – Simon's always appreciated my food, and I want to feed him, to please him, like I used to. I may not have a glittering surgical career or perfectly cut blonde hair, but I can beat her in the kitchen. *He will soon bore of your soft lips and tiny hips, Caroline, but my sourdough culture and bone broth will always excite him.*

I work to ensure supper is ready as soon as Simon walks through the door, the kids already bathed and in bed and that I've taken my pills. I feel exhausted all day and am mostly on autopilot, blindly driven to protect my marriage, my life – I can't let Caroline, or even the *idea* of her, invade our castle.

This isn't my first rodeo. Moving here was the third time we've had to move because of my illness. But Caroline is different. She bothers me even more than the others. This one is so much more – she's a colleague, a peer, someone on his level who he can share ideas and problems with. Caroline is worthy of him. He could go home to her and talk about his day, and she would understand because her days are the same. And Caroline would know how to behave at the Surgical Department's Christmas party. She wouldn't take pills with gin and accuse random women of having sex with her husband. She wouldn't burn the dinner, leave twin boys in a hot car, write profanities on another woman's Facebook page or scrub her skin so hard with disinfectant it bleeds. No, she's everything I'm not. This one is a *real* threat – and I suspect she isn't just a diversion, like I thought the nurse, the barmaid, the best friend or Sophie's friend's mother might have been.

Simon says his first wife, Nicole, was an amazing cook, and along with all the imagined women, I do feel the weight of her legacy. It's just another penny in the falls for me, more pressure to be perfect, to not slip and fall and crash into the rocks below. Simon often remarks on what a wonderful wife and mother she was too, and I know I don't come up to scratch – how could I, she was perfect. Nicole now has angel wings, whereas I'm still a mere mortal with all the faults that go along with it, as Simon is often keen to remind me. So, spurred on by the challenge to be 'the best' wife, along with my Herculean culinary achievements, I don't raise my voice, ask any difficult questions or make any crazy accusations. I scrub all surfaces constantly with antibacterial cleaner, dry shampoo every carpet and deep-clean each room in the house. I even get up after midnight sometimes to clean the kitchen floor so no one will walk on it. Sometimes I sit in the semi-darkness admiring the perfection in the early morning quiet, my surfaces unsullied by human feet or hands – everything's perfect. But nothing lasts forever and dirty footmarks soon appear, blighting the sheen, intruding on perfection, and I seem to be in a constant battle to keep on top of it all.

Today, the boys are at their French tutor after school and Sophie's revising upstairs. She's tense about her A levels, and the sudden change of school earlier this year hasn't helped. Simon says he'll buy her a car if she gets three A stars, but as I pointed out, she has to pass her test first. A driving test and A levels are both a big deal and I feel like she's under too much pressure. I suggested she might take some time out, have a gap year before university, but Simon won't hear of it. He says a year off is for 'spoiled brats' and she has to 'buckle down', which is the right advice I suppose, but sometimes, when I see her crumpled face and furrowed brow I wonder at the wisdom of forcing her to go to university at eighteen, just because it's the done thing.

As Jen's collecting the boys and Oliver, I have at least an hour to myself now and it's very precious. I've cleaned everything in sight and have a roast in the oven for dinner and I'm wondering how to make the best use of this uninterrupted time. I hate doing nothing – it makes me think, makes me remember. *I don't want to remember.* Should I start a new handbag? I'd love to make another bag, but that might irritate Simon if he comes home and I'm 'lolling around', in what I laughingly call 'my office', which is basically a corner of the utility room.

'Stitching bags isn't contributing to the household in any way,' Simon remarked the last time he found me working. 'It's just… self-indulgent sewing. Is it too much to ask that you bath the boys first and perhaps clear all this mess?'

There wasn't much mess, but I took his point. Besides, my medication kills any spark of creativity – but I can always find the energy to clean. Wiping away dirt is a compulsion and I can't rest until the house is spotless. And then I realise Simon's office is one room in the house I haven't cleaned in a while. It must be filthy – it's off limits to the kids and therefore I adhere to that rule too, but surely I can give it the once-over while the meat's cooking? I can even put some flowers in there, freshen it with room scent. He'd like that. So I gather all my cleaning equipment and head upstairs to the fifth bedroom, 'Dad's office'. I'm half expecting the door to be locked but am pleasantly surprised to turn the handle and walk straight in. The room is very minimal, with a white desk and chair, an open shelf containing various medical books and a small stone figurine of a young woman. Naked. It was given to him by a patient. 'She says it's her and it's anatomically correct,' he'd laughed, when he brought it home about five years ago. 'And is it?' I'd dared to ask.

He never answered me.

I push away unwelcome thoughts of my husband with naked women and take in the room. I have to smile; he travels light, my husband. If he was a celebrity and I was on one of those TV programmes where I had to guess 'Whose house?' I'd never guess, and I'm his wife.

Last Christmas, Sophie bought him a beautiful glass heart-shaped paperweight that she said would look good on his desk.

'Thanks Sophie,' he'd said, holding it in his outstretched palm like it might be contagious. Then he seemed to spot the flaw.

'It's scratched.' He'd winced, lifting it up to the light. I thought Sophie might cry.

'It's okay, darling. It's so beautiful, you can't see the scratch,' I offered.

'Of course. It's quite lovely,' he'd added, realising his mistake. But it was too late, Sophie was already disappointed in his reaction and had closed herself off again.

My heart broke for her. So I'm pleased to see the paperweight on the desk. It's a gift from a child to a parent, and it touches me still. I adore all my kids – all three of them. Simon says I'm a tiger mother, and I suppose I am. I'll protect my kids until the end. I've never said this to Simon, but they come first, even before him – always have, always will, even Sophie, who isn't my biological daughter, but feels as close.

I polish the shiny white desk, tickle the ceiling corners with a feather duster and vacuum the carpet vigorously. Twice. I give his landline a wipe with something smelling strongly of lemons, which tells me reassuringly on the packet it kills 99.9 per cent of germs. With that acidic smell of fresh lemons, I find Caroline wafting back to me. I wonder if Simon's ever seen her Instagram account, or peeked at her Facebook. I doubt it, because he doesn't dabble in social media – he says it wouldn't be professional, after all a patient might see him and, God forbid, try and 'friend' him. 'It's for sad teenagers with no lives,' he always says, which I think is a bit unfair, especially as I'm on Facebook and Instagram and put my recipes and household tips on Pinterest. I enjoy posting pictures of my new kitchen, the kids dressed up on World Book Day and Halloween and all the family stuff in between. It doesn't hurt to show the good bits. I haven't told Simon I have online accounts. He wouldn't approve and would probably ask me to close them. He says Sophie's 'online activities' leave us open to a cyber attack that could put his career in jeopardy. I feel he's a bit dramatic, but it's a testament to his love for Sophie that he indulges her, allowing his daughter to engage with what he perceives is a threat to his privacy. He's fanatical about privacy, says data companies are selling our secrets to Russia, but quite frankly if someone wants to hack my online accounts and steal my recipe for lemon meringue pie or my tips for getting mould off taps, they are welcome. Russian or not.

I suspect the real reason Simon wants me to stay away from social media is because he doesn't trust me; he thinks I'll go spying, put two and two together and make six. I once got it into my head that Simon was sleeping with a neighbour and wrote nasty stuff on her Facebook wall. She came round to the house, screaming at me and threatening legal action, which was all very embarrassing and Simon had to talk her down. That was a couple of years ago, and I have to remind myself of these incidents when I want to come off the medication. I really can't be trusted when I'm not on the tablets.

I go on to clean the table and the drawers, although of course, the drawers are locked because Simon sometimes brings home sensitive patient information. It wouldn't do for it to be open and accessible to anyone wandering in. Not that anyone does wander in. We all respect Simon's space, although he can be a little hypocritical and go into the utility room and move my bags of fabric when I'm not there. I know I don't sew much these days, but it's the principal, and I wouldn't mind, but he spilled a cup of hot black coffee over a piece of lovely material. I'd left it on the side, and I know it's stupid but I cried when I discovered it in a heap, ruined. He hadn't even tried to clean it or tell me about it, just left it there soaked in black, sugary coffee, treacle-stained. I mentioned it to him, and he said it must have been one of the kids. But I know it was him, because he's the only one in the house who drinks black coffee with sugar.

I waft the lovely fabric away like gossamer from my thoughts and stand back to survey my work on Simon's office. It smells fresh but doesn't look that much different as it was pretty spotless and empty to begin with. I wonder at these two words, *spotless* and *empty* – on bad days, I'd use them to describe my life, though of course it's not, it's just the way my addled mind works. As Simon often says, 'I've given you everything, but everything isn't good enough for you, is it Marianne?'

From the doorway, my eyes land on the laptop sitting untouched in the middle of the desk. I feel it looking back at me, or perhaps it's just the medication making me a bit weird again?

I've done so many terrible things when I'm off the pills and am 'unleashed', as Simon puts it. The last time was the reason we had to leave the house on Ellis Road. Such a shame because we were happy there, but I had to go and ruin everything by getting it into my head that Simon was having a raging affair with the twenty-three-year-old barmaid at the local pub. Stupid really, as Simon said she was young enough to be his daughter and keen to point out 'also not very bright'. But by then I'd already been in The Hare and Hounds, screamed in her face and thrown a glass of beer over her. Poor Simon, he was mortified – said he could never drink in there again and the next day he put the house up for sale. Within two months we were moving, much against Sophie's wishes, just when she'd finally settled at that school. We'd only lived on Ellis Road for about three years and the idea of leaving her hard-won friends and moving twenty miles away to a new town again really upset her.

Sophie's recently shown signs here of struggling with schoolwork and new friendships – life is hard enough as a teenager without being uprooted every couple of years. Her teacher has said she's finding it hard to cope with the new environment, and I know that's all my fault, but Sophie had got it into her head that we'd moved this time because Simon wanted to change his job. Anyway, it was soon cleared up when he explained it was because I'd been poorly again and we'd had to leave because I'd embarrassed them all. To my horror, Sophie seemed to know about my little visit to

The Hare and Hounds to launch a pint of beer over the young barmaid's head.

'Everyone was talking about it at school,' she'd said, defeated. *I know how that feels.*

'Darling, I'm so, so sorry,' I'd said.

'It's okay, Mum, I knew something was wrong, but didn't want to upset you.'

'What a pity your mother hadn't had the same respect for *your* feelings when she stormed into a public house and abused one of the staff,' Simon said, with fresh anger at my stupid actions.

I relive the shame all over again. *I am a stupid, selfish bitch who doesn't deserve to be loved.*

I'm still staring at the laptop, thinking. I'm trying to resist opening it, but I don't think I can. Something pushes through the mists of medication and I have no self-control. As Simon says, I can't blame my mental health because it's only part of who I am and even strong medication can't change someone's flawed personality. The trouble is, I am emotional, too emotional, and act on my feelings. *I have no control. I can't be trusted.*

I slide my fingers under the lid. It's cool to the touch as I gently lift it and the screen springs to life. Gazing at the now flickering screen, I wonder what secrets this sleek oblong holds? I imagine the tangle of explosive information twisting through the hard drive. The clandestine human knowledge living inside, inveigling its way through the circuit board, snaking along the keyboard membranes, waiting to pounce.

I press a key and suddenly turn around. *Is he watching from the doorway?*

Guilt and fear overwhelm me but are suffocated by my uncontrollable urge to access this Pandora's box. I bend down for a closer look and, with one hand on the table, dare to attempt a password. I go for the obvious and type in 'surgery'. The computer tells me I'm incorrect and suggests I try again. A part of me is relieved the password didn't work, because I don't want to go there – if I find something, it will near kill me. But if I find nothing, I'll have peace of mind. I long for peace of mind. I can live my life and be well again, safe in the knowledge that we're still a family and he won't leave me and take the children with him. This is my worst fear; it's what keeps me awake at night through the fog of Mirtazapine.

Then a thought occurs. What if there's a way Simon can find out that someone's been in his computer, poked around in the hard drive of his privacy? I don't know, but by now I'm beyond reason or consequence. I have to know if I'm *mad, paranoid, psychotic*, all the words he uses to describe me, where once he used words like *beautiful, bright, talented.* I want to be those lovely things to him again. I want to be the me he fell in love with and perhaps then he will finally forgive me for what happened to our baby and we can move forwards together.

I type in the long-shot password with hope. 'Marianne', I key in slowly, carefully. And my heart thuds to the floor as I'm faced with 'try again'. *Once I was his password.* I move around the desk like a hunter circling its prey and tell myself to give it one last go. I want to look away as I punch in her name. 'Caroline' – and there it is. Where once it was me, Caroline now unlocks his world. I don't need to know any more, but now I can't stop. I'm through the looking glass, and there's no turning back.

A generic sandy beach flickers onto the screen and I have the opportunity to take a dip into Simon's world, bathe in his secrets, splash my feet in the 'privacy' he so craves. I lean over the computer, unable to sit in his seat, knowing I'm trespassing on my husband's life, but intrigue and irrational anger spur me on. I need somewhere, someone, to channel this strange anger – or is it merely my madness again?

I check the clock on the screen. My vigorous and thorough vacuuming took longer than I thought and he's due home in less than half an hour.

I should just close the lid and walk away but of course I can't. Instead I open up his favourites. He hasn't thought to hide anything because it never occurs to him anyone will disobey him and go into his office, let alone on his laptop. So where do I want to go – emails, photos, documents? I click on email and it opens out before me, his life laid bare. Emails from the hospital, the tennis club, various colleagues and friends, and then I find her, nestling in a folder. She has her very own folder in his inbox. *Caroline.*

I click on Caroline more forcefully than I need to and even though I'm expecting a lot of emails I'm shocked at the sheer volume. Oh my God, I've hit the horrible jackpot -- and won the booby prize. I scroll down. He started working at this hospital in February but I can't see any emails to or from her before April, so I start there, at the very beginning… the beginning of what, I really don't know. But I sure as hell am going to find out.

CHAPTER SEVEN

I open the first email – it's from him to her. She's only just started at the hospital apparently; it's a sort of introduction, a 'hello, I'm here if you need any help or advice'. He points out he's only been there two months, but he knows what it's like to be 'the new girl or boy' and takes an interest in the careers of young surgeons in his department.

It's not just their fucking careers he takes an interest in.

Simon's email is friendly but not flirty, and as far as I can see there's no hidden agenda. Likewise, her response is equally professional. She thanks him and requests information about some surgical procedures blah blah blah.

This continues for another ten or so emails, a month or two just shooting the surgical breeze. He's her senior, her unofficial mentor, and as the emails continue to go back and forth I can see how they have developed a working relationship. So far so good. I'm strangely torn between relief and slight disappointment – so he isn't having an affair, it's my imagination and I'm crazy after all? I am a 'bunny-boiling bitch', to quote my husband, who referred to me this way after the fracas over the bloody barmaid. Or was it when I thought he was sleeping with Sophie's friend's mum? I can't remember – they all merge into one, and all of them in my head. Is this one the same, just a figment of my fractured mind?

I don't have much time, so I skip to July, where I find the first interesting communication, and my heart drops a fraction. It's from her. She's asking him if they can meet for a drink. She says she has a patient she wants to discuss, an op she's involved in with a different team the following day. She's worried and just wants to talk to someone senior.

I open his response: Yes sure, is The Dog and Duck 7 p.m. okay? I should be out of theatre by then, if not I'll call you. I bristle – is this the beginning? Am I mad to resent my husband going to the pub with a beautiful young woman?

He clearly has her number by now. Of course, there will be texts too, but I know he'll be more careful with those given my previous history. Presumably he thinks emails will be safer, more hidden and, unlike texts, they don't pop up on your phone and ping to alert nosy wives that something's going on.

I'm just about to delve further when there's a knock at the front door. Jen returning the boys no doubt. I wait a moment, unable to leave the unfolding story and, to my great relief, Sophie goes downstairs and answers it. I hear Jen asking where I am. Sophie's typically vague and monosyllabic saying she doesn't know, which usually irritates me, but on this occasion works in my favour. The boys will take advantage of the fact there are no adults around and go straight for the prohibited TV. This will buy me at least another twenty minutes before they feel hungry and roam the house searching for me to feed them.

I haven't got long, and scroll quickly through the next few days of emails: a polite thank you from her for talking her 'off the ledge', as she so wittily puts it. I imagine her literally on a ledge – the multistorey car park in town would be a good spot. I see her flying through the air with the greatest of ease. She's wearing that baby-pink coat. She lands horribly, making a real mess of the pavement, that lovely coat and her skull.

I continue to scroll through July. It proves uneventful – no sex talk or naked pics, but then again, I think people save those for their phones, don't they? Nevertheless, I think I'd know by the emails if there was a sexual subtext, an intimate undercurrent, and there's nothing here to see in July. Should I stop now? That was less than two months ago; what could possibly happen in such a short time? For God's sake, he was with me and the kids in Crete for the first two weeks in August, and apart from a few arguments, a little bust-up over the hire car and his rant about the boys' behaviour, we were okay. We had sex at least three times – it was perfunctory, a little soulless, if I'm honest, but better than the rough stuff he enjoys when we're at home and no one can hear us. I imagine sharing this with Jen in the way she shares her sex life with me. I'm sure she'd laugh loudly about the kinky slaps, the tight handcuffs. It would make me feel better to share things with a girlfriend, get them out in the open, but I'm not sure I can – besides, it would be disloyal to Simon.

I skip through a few early August missives and then notice the emails are becoming more regular, not one a day or every two days as they have been, but several times a day. I go back and open the first one in August. It was the 2nd, the day we actually flew out to Crete. I can't think why they would be emailing each other when he's on holiday. He's always strict about work colleagues not bothering him when he's off. 'It's the only time I get a break,' he says. 'I can't be discussing surgical procedures from a beach on my family holiday.' But looking at this little row of beauties lined up, it seems there was much to discuss with one work colleague on our family holiday.

'I can't believe you'll be gone for two whole weeks,' her email begins, and already I see the change in tone. If that isn't clear enough, the next comment spells it out: 'I'll miss you. I can't bear to think of you away for so long.' Bingo, I was right – and the pain I feel in my chest makes me wonder if I'm having a heart attack. Eventually I compose myself and find the strength from somewhere to read on. 'Will you miss me?' she asks and I recognise her insecurity. Those early days when you're not quite sure where you stand and need constant reassurance of your position in someone's life, someone's heart.

He answers that, yes, he will miss her and he doesn't know how he's going to 'get through' the next two weeks, like a holiday on a Greek island with his wife and children is something to be endured. But this is merely foreplay, and before long we are plunged into my worst nightmare. As I had feared, every little twitch of my muscles, the feeling that's been grinding deep in my bones is proven correct: my husband and Caroline are having a love affair. I am in no doubt at all – it's in every sentence, every utterance.

The first damning email that makes their relationship very clear is when she refers to him leaving her alone in bed 'on Sunday', and looking at the dates this would be the day before we left to go on holiday. He'd told me he was on call that weekend. We didn't see him for two days and when he came home on that Sunday evening 'exhausted' from two days of 'surgery', including a seven-hour heart transplant, I believed him. 'There was a moment when the heart stopped pumping, but I manipulated it with my fingers and gave someone their life back,' he'd said. I cringed slightly at his purple prose but forgave him because he was a hero and I loved him.

Manipulating a heart with his fingers? He was manipulating *something* with his fingers, and it wasn't a fucking donor heart. I feel my own heart now, beating in my throat, as though it might rise and rise, pushing up until I vomit it out onto the clean white desk.

I don't know if I can bear to look at the next email, but then again I can't stop myself. It's like watching a horror film – you know it's going to be distressing, but you can't tear your eyes from the sheer awfulness. I'm almost grateful for my drugged-up state. It's like feeling the pain through cotton wool; it's still unbearable, slightly dulled, less sharp. I want to cover my eyes as I read about my lovely holiday according to Simon; I am shocked to discover how lonely he was with us, how empty he felt, how nothing on the holiday gave him any joy. I learn that the delicious seafood we ate at a gorgeous little Greek restaurant in Chania was 'terrible'. Apparently the kids played up and I shouted at them, which caused a row, one of many apparently. I don't remember them. Did they happen – have I pushed them from my mind? *Did I only imagine the perfect family holiday?*

I find out so much from his emails to another woman. I find out, to my horror, that he doesn't trust me with the children, that he's scared to leave me because he doesn't know what I'll do. Apparently he wonders why he even married me, but suspects it was on the rebound from Nicole's death.

The pain on reading this is excruciating. I know people lie when they are having affairs; they have to. I doubt Simon means any of this, he thinks it's what she wants to hear. But for me it's such a blow, like a hammer to the head, followed by a slow, scary strangulation.

All these things I would like to do to you, Caroline.

I read on, unable to tear myself away. Horror and fascination are a toxic cocktail and someone with my issues shouldn't be doing this. I think of the saying 'that's where madness lies…' and this is it. These emails are my route to a breakdown, a world of pain and confusion that will cause me to lose control, and Simon's told me if that happens again he'll divorce me and take the children. But here's the proof of my madness right here – my eyes refuse to listen to the rest of me that's screaming to stop reading, so I continue.

It seems Simon can't bear to spend another minute with me and another without her. She's the best sex he's ever had and he can't wait to leave this Greek hellhole with his family and take her up to heaven when he lands at fucking Gatwick. I take a moment to digest this; I'm completely devastated, but I'm also right, and my instinct is spot on. I just never expected to be *quite* so right – it's so overwhelming, so brutal, so… intimate.

I click on more emails and, among the bitchy comments about work colleagues, the technical discussions about life in the operating theatre, I learn more interesting and agonising things about my marriage and myself.

'Darling, I can't bear to be apart from you this weekend,' he opens with, on an email sent only a couple of weeks ago. It seems she'd gone to stay at her parents' and the very thought of forty-eight hours without her made him 'incredibly sad'. He then goes on to tell her that 'Marianne is ill again, it isn't her fault but I find it so hard to deal with. Last night she screamed at Charlie, she told him he was being stupid, but he's only six. He was so upset at his own mother saying this to him. This happens when she's off the medication. I've asked her time and time again to take it, but she won't, she says it makes her tired but can't see what it's doing to all of us. She screamed at the boys, threatening to hurt them the other morning at breakfast – just because they wouldn't eat their eggs. Darling, I know I should be stronger, but when she's cruel to me and the children I just want to pack them all in the car and drive to you.'

I gasp, unable to take a breath. How could he say all this? Yes, these things happened, but not in the way he is telling her they did. It's all about interpretation, but whose version can I trust? He's threatened to take the children away before, but it's always been mid-row, in the heat of the moment – seeing it written in black and white makes the threat very real.

Finally I drag my eyes away from the screen. I can't bear to read on. I know we've had blips and there have been times in our marriage when understandably his love has been tested. But I thought we'd worked through all that, and despite me being a little paranoid, he's forgiven me and we are back on track now. I can't begin to comprehend the two of them having sex, but even more painful is the way he talks about me, revealing every little aspect of me, even the fact I take medication. I feel exposed, violated. They judge me, interpret my actions; my life, my past and my secrets are all plundered. I'm also hurt by the way he relates to her, and in this I glimpse the past, *our* past, and the Simon I fell in love with. I can feel and remember the warm, affectionate responses, the urgent need to make love. Tears roll down my cheeks as I watch his love fluttering across the screen like confetti. I see how we used to be and realise now how far away we are from that – and from being happy.

I'm on a tightrope with no safety net. Without Simon, what do I have?

As much as it pains me, I need to know the truth, and go back to the emails, swallowing hard, trying to focus through tear-blitzed eyes. These are more recent, a matter of weeks ago, and she asks if they can spend a weekend in Amsterdam; she's never been to Amsterdam. He sends her a link to a boutique hotel, suggests they hire bikes and trail along the canals. I am so envious. It should be me he's taking on romantic weekends. She says, 'I want to see the Van Gogh Museum.' He says they can see 'whatever you want to – I just want to spend all night in your arms and wake up next to you.'

Caroline's Simon is relaxed, happy, loving and kind... so kind. It's the Simon I met at the book launch, the one who took me out for oysters and champagne, who made me laugh. The man who, in that bookshop, bought a book about ballet for his daughter and talked about her with such love I knew I wanted him to be the father to my children. Back then nothing else mattered but his blue eyes and his arms around me and waking up next to him every morning. He told me he'd love me forever. But he lied. With Caroline, my husband is the man I fell in love with, and this is what really kills me – I thought he'd gone, but he's still here, he's just not with me any more.

I'm scared and feel sick. If I don't gather myself together and get a grip there's a very good chance I'll be clearing up vomit from the spotless white desk any minute now.

Suddenly I hear the front door and exit the emails with a vicious click. Everything disappears from the screen, like it never existed, but it did, I know it did because I saw it with my own eyes. Simon's home. I close the laptop down quickly, my heart still thudding, my breath short, as though I've been running.

I quickly scan the room to check I haven't left anything behind that will give me away and run downstairs to greet him with Elizabeth David's garlic and rosemary crusted lamb. *I will not give him up. She can't have him.*

I daren't mention the emails, because if I do he'll say I'm ill again. Three years ago when I'd had several 'episodes', he did what he felt was best for me and told me we were having a 'date night', and going to dinner at the new restaurant in a little village nearby. My best friend had the children and I bought a new dress specially – it was black and white with polka dots. I loved it, and Simon said he did too. I was so happy that evening as we drove along the country lanes. I remember telling him some story about something funny the boys had said – they were three then, and he laughed. He actually laughed with me at my story and I thought, yes, we're over the hump now, I'm well again.

But we didn't go to the new restaurant; we pulled up outside a clinic and I immediately panicked. I knew what this meant. I started to cry and when someone tried to force me out of the car I naturally hit out. The next thing I knew, I'd been sedated and was being interviewed by a psychiatrist, prescribed strong anti-anxiety pills and kept in for eight weeks of electroconvulsive therapy. This involved several sessions to send a strong electric current through my brain to trigger an epileptic seizure and attempt to relieve the symptoms of my mental health problem. It didn't work, merely left me with side effects: apathy, short-term memory loss and a loss of drive and creativity – not to mention weeks away from my children. All this because I'd suspected my husband was having an affair with one of the mums from the school. I know Simon had me sectioned for my own good, but it was the worst time in my life and I can't go there again, and that's why I can't confront him about the emails, because he'll think I'm ill again. And this time it might actually be convenient to send me away and move Caroline in.

Simon's in the kitchen by the time I get downstairs and already communing with his phone like it's a life support system. He's texting her, I know he is. She's with us now in our lovely home, in my kitchen. He doesn't even look up as I rush in and grab the vegetables from the fridge. I really shouldn't have spent all that time in his office. Apart from the obvious – that I shouldn't be snooping – I've now left everything until the last minute and the Chantenay carrots will take at least seven minutes to boil. Damn. I should have had the dinner ready, on the table when Simon got in. I have to show him I'm fine, in control and more capable of creating a home life than Caroline.

'Muuuum,' I suddenly hear coming from the sitting room. Fuck! I'd forgotten the boys. I was so engrossed in the bloody emails I hadn't even thought about them. I'm a terrible mother; how could I forget my own kids?

I quickly look over at Simon, fully expecting a cutting remark about the boys being 'plonked' in front of the TV, but he's still scrolling, apparently oblivious to my giant cock-up. I send up a little prayer of thanks that he hasn't noticed and dash out of the kitchen after putting the carrots and cauliflower on and checking the roast potatoes around the lamb aren't about to burn. I must keep everything on an even keel. I don't want him to know I know.

'Oh, my darlings, I'm sorry,' I say quietly, walking in to two sleepy little boys wide-eyed in front of the TV, biscuit crumbs everywhere, jam around their mouths. Sophie must have given them that packet of Jammie Dodgers I'd hidden away at the back of the cupboard. Simon doesn't approve of biscuits for children – too much sugar, he says, and he's right of course, but sometimes the odd biscuit or chocolate bar keeps us all sane. I'm grateful to

Sophie for giving them something, but keen to hide the evidence of her chosen child-taming tool.

'Boys, would you like some supper?' I ask, knowing it's a little late for them to eat but don't want to put them to bed hungry. They both shake their heads and snuggle further down into the sofa, weary and unable to move away from the giant screen mesmerising them. Selfishly, I don't really want to have to go back into the kitchen with them and explain to Simon that I haven't given them a meal. I decide to get them to bed with hot milk and text Sophie to come down and give me a hand. She knows the score. I don't need to explain to her that we need to keep Dad out of it or I could be in trouble. Within a few minutes she's at my side, walking Charlie, while I manhandle Alfie upstairs. We're both gently shushing them and giggling as we go. *Will I lose my children?*

'Thanks, darling,' I whisper, when we all reach their room. 'I don't want Dad to get annoyed about them watching TV, you know…'

'I know.' She rolls her eyes and helps me put them to bed. I wonder again what I'll do without her when she goes to uni next year.

The boys' heads hit their pillows and I don't even have chance to give them hot milk. They are instantly asleep and we both sigh at the relief and sheer madness of it all.

We close the boys' bedroom door quietly and are walking across the landing when she stops. 'Why do you do this, Mum?' she suddenly says, her face serious, her eyes searching for the answer.

'Because they need to sleep,' I say, brushing away the question.

'I don't mean that, I mean Dad. Why didn't you just tell him you were busy, so the boys are a bit late going to bed? Better still, why can't he put them to bed? He used to with me, didn't he?'

'Yes he did… he used to read to you every night too.'

She smiles at the memory, and I wonder if she misses the old Simon as much as I do. I know he adores Sophie, just doesn't always show it – I hope she knows.

'Darling, it's fine,' I say, faking a smile. 'Dad's just… he loves us all very much, but let's face it, I can't let him come home from a day in the operating theatre to those two crazies live and unleashed.' I roll my eyes. 'He works so hard and it just keeps the peace, you know.'

'I know.' She gives me a look I can't quite fathom and puts her arm on my shoulder.

I'm touched. Sophie isn't one for open affection but she's intuitive; it's like she knows I'm upset and in her own way is trying to comfort me.

'You know I love you, don't you, Mum?' This is so sincere, for a moment I wonder if she's about to tell me bad news. But when I look into her face, I see love. I don't see much love these days and my stepdaughter's kindness makes me want to cry.

We both stand on the landing, caught between sanctuary and what waits below. I have this sense of foreboding, like something terrible is going to happen, but I'm just getting carried away after reading the emails. Everything is going to be okay because I won't allow it to be otherwise.

'Come on,' I say, in a too bright voice, 'us grown-ups can eat even if I am a cruel mother and starve my youngest.' I wink at her and she gives me a vague smile.

'I'm not hungry, but thanks.'

'You don't have to eat the meat,' I say, 'but please eat something. There's Quorn?' I'm begging her to join us, and she knows it. 'Sweetie, you *are* eating aren't you, you're not dieting or anything stupid?' I take her hand in mine as we speak.

'God no. I had a *huge* pizza for lunch today – I'm still full.' She pats her flat-as-a-pancake stomach and blows out her cheeks like she's a big fat pig. I don't believe her. Then again, I'm not sure *who* I believe any more – I don't even know if I believe myself. I think again about the emails and wonder if I imagined them and it's just the pills clouding my mind. The words are so clear in my mind – I miss you, I can't bear to be apart, I just want to spend all night in your arms. Can I really have imagined them?

Sophie gives me a hug and I try to feel the weight of her in my arms but she's pulling away too soon and heading to her bedroom, so I'm left to face the music.

I go back downstairs to finish preparing Simon's dinner. To my deep joy, the kitchen's empty. I'm glad of the space. I need to work out what's real and what isn't. My head is full of him and *her*, our holiday in Crete, Caroline and Simon kissing, Sophie not eating, Simon loving Caroline, the boys having only Jammie Dodgers for tea, their faces sticky with jam, the sofa covered in crumbs…

Shit! The SOFA. I hurl myself into the sitting room to remove the damning crumbs that reveal at least two maternal sins – that they watched TV and ate biscuits. If Simon gets even a waft of my bad mothering he'll think I'm not capable of looking after the children. I throw myself face down onto the sofa, shovelling the crumbs from one hand to the other. I'm on my knees, desperate to remove every tiny sweet morsel of evidence. But I suddenly have the feeling I'm not alone. The hairs on the back of my neck prickle, and lifting my head slowly, I see him out of the corner of my eye. He's sitting in the big armchair, waiting and watching. Just waiting and watching me.

'Oh… Simon,' I start, 'I was just…'

'Go on… what were you *just*…?' He lifts his head slowly, questioningly.

His words hang in the air like a threat. He knows about the biscuits.

'I was just… cleaning the sofa.' I'm still on my knees, staring at him, wondering what will happen next.

'Marianne, tell me something,' he says, picking fluff from his trousers.

I wait. And wait. I'm still on my knees, looking up at him in the armchair. He takes his time. His face is unreadable; how much does he know? How much can I get away with?

He finally looks up and, putting his head to one side, asks, 'Do you think I'm stupid?'

CHAPTER EIGHT

'No, of course I don't think you're stupid.' I try an outraged laugh, but it comes out as more of a scared splutter. I hear Sophie on her phone – sounds like she's coming down the stairs. I hope she isn't; I don't want her around for this. A couple of seconds pass and I hear a door close upstairs. Sophie won't have to witness whatever happens next and for that I'm overwhelmingly grateful.

'So, am I right in thinking that you *don't* think I'm stupid?'

'No… absolutely… no, you're not…' I seem to be frozen in my prone position in front of the sofa, a handful of crumbs now warm in my clenched, sweating palm.

'In that case, why do you treat me like I'm an idiot?'

'I… I don't. You're not…' I can feel the ground shifting under me; the pills make me feel so dizzy.

'So what makes you think you can hide the fact that the boys were plonked in front of the TV tonight with no dinner while you flounced around the house?'

'I didn't try to hide anything… I just—'

'I'm sorry, you're not being very clear.' He's now glaring at me, his eyes boring into my face, my soul.

'I was busy cleaning… and when I came downstairs, they were almost asleep and…' I feel so guilty. If I hadn't been so obsessed with snooping around his emails, none of this would be happening.

At this he stands up, and still on my knees, I instinctively move across the floor away from him, practically crawling now. I feel like a trapped animal. I want to leave the room but my body won't let me; besides, I need to explain to him what happened, show him I'm not a bad mother, that I'm well, but Simon speaks first and I'm already lost.

'After… *everything*, I really would have thought you'd be on top of things where the kids are concerned.'

'I was… I am…'

'No, you clearly weren't and I'm seriously considering the situation, Marianne.'

'No… please… Simon…'

'I've told you before. The children have to be your priority. Those boys are six years old and they can't be left alone while you wander about doing as you please.'

'I was *here*, I didn't leave them, I just… I was busy.' Panic is rising in my chest. *He will put the children in his car and take them away from me… to her.*

'Busy? *Busy?* You don't know the meaning of the word. But here are two words you do know the meaning of, and I want you to think about them and the implications for the family's future – "unfit" and "mother".' He takes a casual step towards me and I look up at him, ready for him to give me what I deserve. He's right, I'm not fit to be a mother, and not good enough to be Simon's wife either. He stands over me and says through gritted teeth, 'Get up.'

I stand up slowly, moving in front of him, bracing myself for the slap that comes hard and swift across my face. The impact of his hand makes my heart jump, but I keep my eyes open so I can take in his hatred and loathing – it's what I deserve.

Give it to me.

'You are not fit, Marianne.'

I wait for the second slap, the punch. I welcome it and close my eyes. I'm ready for whatever physical or emotional pain he feels fit to inflict. I want it. Who can blame him after what I did? But it never comes.

'Go to our room, get undressed and wait for me.' He brushes past me roughly and I flinch, but there's no smack, no knock to the floor.

Not yet anyway, but later he will inflict pain, because I have to be punished.

And I know what comes after the pain. We haven't had sex for a while, but tonight he wants me... he doesn't want me in a loving, gentle way, but still he wants me.

He leaves the room, and after a few seconds I allow myself to breathe again when I hear the front door slam and the sound of his car starting up.

I go upstairs and do as he says. I sit up in bed waiting, but who knows where he's gone and how long he will be? I couldn't ask.

I am alone, and as insane as it sounds after everything that's happened this evening, I'm drawn back to her. *Caroline.* Grabbing the iPad like a drug addict, I log on, hungrily jacking up in my own bedroom. I always delete the history so it takes a few seconds to find her Instagram – but when I do Caroline's world opens up before me.

No locks on Caroline's life. No passwords, no secrets.

I go back over a few days of Caroline drinking and mugging to the camera, and a bunch of roses, apparently 'from my love #TrueLove'. I can barely bring myself to look, but it's a compulsion. My face is still stinging from the hard slap and I caress my cheek with one hand, feeling his touch as I gaze at her. A day at the seaside posted only last week, just her on the beach, but she isn't alone because the photographer's with her.

Is that you, Simon?

She's pensive, natural, like a beautiful girl on a poster for a trendy band. The photo is taken from behind, her short, blonde hair glinting in the autumn sunshine. The beach is pebbly and pale grey, and I'm upset to see how good this looks against her dusky-pink oversized cardigan. She looks like a model. Then I see something familiar on the sand. I look closer to see she's sitting on our fucking picnic rug, the one Simon keeps in the boot of his car.

I have to stop a moment and take this in: Simon's lover is sitting on our family picnic rug. We use it all the time: the boys sat on that rug as babies, Sophie sunbathed on it in Devon and Greece and now he's putting it under *her*. How fucking dare she sit on my family's picnic rug – my cheek throbs and my heart aches. I don't think I can stand this a moment longer, but I can't stop. I have to stay and walk through my private Instagram hell, each picture a fresh, searing pain.

I search for clues and find them easily: the back of his head, his car in the distance. Each picture is further evidence, if I needed any, that Caroline and Simon's lives are entwined on a personal level. They're twisted around each other in a complex network of veins and arteries thrumming through each other's days, each other's lives. And I can't keep her out – because she's already let herself in.

I'm still in bed on the iPad when Sophie knocks on the door – still scrolling, searching for my hit. I don't know how long I've been there. I wonder where Simon is, and hate myself for caring. Sophie asks if I'm okay, and I abandon the iPad and say I'm fine, just tired, and despite Simon's orders I say I'm going to make a cup of tea, and she follows me to the kitchen.

I suddenly smell the burning lamb and recall a vague memory of a planned dinner, but when I open the oven door, the meat's now black, inedible. I am a mess. I can't even make a meal without ruining it. What's happened to me?

I put the kettle on and ask if Sophie's hungry, knowing what the answer will be. I go into 'Mum' mode, where I feel safe and can pretend nothing has happened, that I haven't been waiting in bed for my husband, who hasn't returned home, and that he didn't spend the day with Caroline on a beach when he told me he was working.

'Sweetie, I wish you'd eat.'

'And I wish *you'd* stand up to him sometimes.' She's glaring at me across the kitchen. The air is acrid with burnt meat and I'm devastated that Sophie must have heard our conversation. She knows I went to bed to wait for him too. What must she think of us?

'Oh, Sophie, it isn't how it seems,' I try. 'Dad's stressed. He's tired and a bit grumpy and... I just don't want to wind him up and exacerbate the situation.'

'So, it's okay for him to hit you?'

I'm shocked by this. I don't know why. Sophie's probably seen enough over the years but I have to pretend. I have to tell her the little lies I tell myself... the lies I tell Simon and the one's he tells me. Our little lies.

'It... he's... he didn't. People do stuff... it isn't always as it seems.' I'd almost forgotten about the slap. I'm sure he'll be apologetic when he gets home. I assume he's gone for a drive to calm down – or to see her.

Sophie looks at me with his eyes, Simon's genes overpowering Nicole's brown-eyed genes, as they later overpowered mine, giving the boys their big blue eyes. The difference now is I don't see his hate in Sophie's baby blues, but I do see the same doubts about my sanity. Sophie's caught us fighting before now. She knows things can get a bit rough; she also knows I've suffered from depression, and she knows about baby Emily too. And then there's other stuff – like me falling out with women friends, mothers of her friends, and the small matter of me 'attacking' a woman in a bar earlier this year. I've never doubted Sophie's love for me – she's my child, even if it isn't by blood– but I wonder if, after everything, she trusts me and knows I'm there for her. I hope she feels safe around me and doesn't worry I may do something erratic, out of control. I wish I could reassure her that I'm safe – but I can't.

I want my relationship with Sophie to be different from the one with my own mother. It was difficult – with her frayed mind stitching together a tenuous reality. She suffered from depression and was unable to care for me, which meant most of my childhood was spent in foster care. I was finally allowed to see her when I was ten years old, and after supervised visits we were able to spend whole weekends together without any social workers. My mum was loving and kind, if a little sad, but I remember toasting mallows with her over the open fire in her little terraced house. She had a new baby, my half-sister Megan, and a nice new partner David, who I wished was my dad too. After the first visit, I dared to hope I might become part of a family – it was my dearest wish, even more than a Barbie doll. Then, one weekend, I went to stay and Mum seemed quieter than usual, almost listless. On the Saturday morning, David put Megan in her pushchair and took her to the shops to buy some groceries. He did everything when Mum wasn't well, cooking and cleaning, looking after Megan – and it didn't seem like there was much food in the house so he had to go to the shops. As Megan always seemed to be crying, I guess he also hoped some quiet time alone with me might help make Mum feel better. 'I'll leave you girls to chat,' he'd said kindly as he left. 'Keep an eye on your mum.'

Mum went upstairs soon after they'd gone, leaving me to watch *The Wide Awake Club* on TV. After a while, I realised she hadn't come back down and so I called her and wandered upstairs to see what she was doing. I found her in the bath; the water was scarlet and I was so confused at first I thought it was a strange new bubble bath. I kept telling her to wake up and when she didn't I pulled out the plug and let the scarlet water glug away, but the blood was still pouring – it was coming from her wrists. Apparently, David found me holding her with a towel, insisting she was sleeping. I must have been in extreme shock. Even now I can't think about it without shaking. And when I'm not well, I close my eyes and still see the white towels stained in my mother's blood. This had been my first experience of untimely death, but it wasn't my last.

It was over thirty years ago, and I didn't know her well, but she was my mum. For a brief and beautiful moment in my childhood, I was able to glimpse a family, but when I tried to grasp it, it disintegrated in my hand. I cried for the mother I lost, the mother I'd never had for many years, and still sometimes find myself in the midst of grief for a woman I hardly knew. It was only when I became a mother myself that I wondered how she could leave me in such a brutal way, knowing I would probably be the one to find her. Years ago, I spoke to David, who's since remarried, and he had no answers. 'Just try to forgive her, Marianne. She was very poorly, but she loved you.'

After years of therapy and having a family of my own I've been able to understand it and forgive my mother for leaving me. That's why my relationship with Sophie is so important, and I know how much she needs me, so tonight, with Simon gone and the boys in bed, I make us both camomile tea and we sit in the semi-darkness of the kitchen together. Eventually she kisses me good night and leaves to go to bed, but as she reaches the door she turns to me.

'Promise you won't let Dad hurt you again.'

I shake my head. 'I won't,' I lie, and hope she's reassured by my confident smile. Later that night when he returns, I bite the pillow and try not to cry so she won't know that I didn't keep my promise.

The following morning he arrives in the steamy kitchen, filled with toast crumbs and children's chatter, and stands behind me as I make coffee. His hands slip round my waist and move down to my thighs, giving them a gentle squeeze and reawakening the sex and bruises from last night. I want to cry out in pain, but I just turn and smile and make like I'm busy as my eyes fill with tears.

Later when I've taken the children to school and Simon's gone for the day I bathe my aching body in a warm bath and try to be kind to myself. I feel so desperately lonely and at times like this, I wish I had a mother to talk to, to share my pain and tell me what to do. *I don't know what to do.* Is this how marriage should be? I know I shouldn't discuss our personal lives – I mustn't open up our relationship for others to delve around in – but I would like a friend. I need a friend. I've never had much luck with my attempted friendships, until recently with Jen, but I know Simon doesn't approve of her, and I can see why, but I wish he'd be a bit more chilled about it – he can be a bit of a pain where my friends are concerned, if I'm honest. Early on in our marriage, when it was just me, Sophie and Simon, I was keen to invite Sophie's friends round and make things nice for her. So one day I told her she could invite her best friend Kate for tea after dance class. Sophie was about nine and excitedly took hold of her friend's hand and they ran up the stairs to her room squealing. Later, when Sonia, Kate's mum, came to collect her, I invited her in for coffee and we sat at the kitchen table chatting. I remember thinking, *this is nice, I should do this more often*, as we shared stories and experiences of being mums to nine-year-old girls.

Intoxicated by the whole experience of having a new friend round, I made a little joke to Sonia about wanting her to stay and chat all evening.

'I'd love to open a bottle of wine and tell Simon to get himself a pizza – I don't feel like cooking,' I laughed.

'Sod that. Let him get a pizza; better still get him to cook your dinner,' she was saying loudly as he walked in. I hadn't heard him arrive and was shocked to see him standing there. Sonia giggled, waiting for me to join her, but I felt awful. It was so disloyal of me to be saying stuff like that to a virtual stranger. I saw him stiffen, and the tell-tale flexing of the jaw muscle only I could see, and my heart sank.

'Oh, so to what do we owe the pleasure?' he asked, putting on his most charming smile.

Sonia immediately went all girlish and flushed and told him her name.

'Well, Sonia, it's lovely to have you here.'

'It's lovely to be here – you have a beautiful home,' she said.

I didn't say anything, just watched and listened with a rictus grin. It was like a game of tennis and I knew at any minute he was going to either hand her the winning trophy or hit the ball so hard it smacked her in the face.

'Yes, it's not a bad old place, is it?' he said, taking in the kitchen like he'd never seen it before. 'It takes a lot of blood, sweat and tears to own a house like this, Sonia… Mine,' he added with a grin and she looked a little confused, but smiled along with him.

'Coffee, Simon?' I heard my tiny voice ask into the silence.

'No, darling, I never have coffee after 6 p.m., you know that.' He turned to Sonia. 'It makes me jittery, Sonia.'

'Oh, yes of course, the caffeine.'

'That and not having a decent meal waiting when I've been working hard all day, and this one,' he gestured towards me, 'is just chatting away in the kitchen to you.' He added a flashing smile like he was joking. He wasn't.

'*Simon*…' I attempted what I hoped sounded like a flirtatious reprimand.

'Oh, I'm sorry, I didn't realise I was keeping Marianne from her chores,' Sonia said.

'Well it seems you are,' he replied, staring at her, unsmiling.

The smile fell from her face as she turned to look at me, then back at Simon as she stood up. 'I'm sorry – I didn't realise it was the 1950s,' she said, recovering well with a victorious smile to match his. They both now glared at each other as she picked up her handbag, called her daughter downstairs and left the house, banging the door as she went.

Simon was furious, I could see it in his eyes, but he pretended to find it funny and laughed. Squeezing my cheek, he asked me why I wasn't laughing.

'Because it wasn't funny,' I said, wanting to cry. I'd thought I'd made a friend. 'I'm embarrassed. She'll tell all the other mothers that we have a weird relationship… like I'm some kind of Stepford Wife.'

'Which is exactly why you shouldn't be mixing with these lowlifes,' he'd said, pouring himself a large glass of red. 'Just because a woman loves her husband and wants to welcome him home after a hard day's work doesn't make her a Stepford Wife,' he added. 'I *wish*.'

I gave him a half-smile, grateful he was still in the mood to joke slightly – and knowing it wasn't worth fighting over. I was smarting from the encounter though and wondering how I would handle it when I saw her again, but I pushed down my resentment, held back the tears and began peeling the vegetables.

I never spoke to Sonia again. I saw her in the playground and she smiled, but it felt like pity, and I didn't need pity, I needed a friend. I have a friend now in Jen. I feel comfortable with her, and what's even better is that she's met Simon several times and she knows how to handle him. He criticises her to me but responds well to flattery and flirting – and Jen's good at that. I'd love to bare my soul, tell my friend everything. I've hinted that he can be difficult to live with, but Jen didn't pick up on anything and just laughed, adding flippantly, 'Aren't they all?'

CHAPTER NINE

It's been several days since I discovered the emails and I've been on tenterhooks, not sure what or who I believe any more, including myself. All I know is that I don't have the strength to go through another drawn-out argument that escalates into physical and mental pain. So I've stayed away from Caroline. I've tried not to think about her and I've avoided going into Simon's office and checking on his emails. But I don't know how long I can live like this, knowing he is living another life, and that it is easily accessible to me with just a couple of clicks.

I can deal with Simon. I can just about cope with his moods and the way he sometimes treats me because I want us to stay together as a family. It's a small price to pay for the kids to feel secure and happy, but if, as I suspect, he's genuinely in love with someone else, I can't take it. 'When I promised to stay together til death do us part, I meant it, Marianne. I just hope you did too,' he said recently. But now I wonder if he just wants me here to punish me for not being the woman he wants me to be – and for what happened all those years ago. When will I have paid my dues? Isn't it enough that I think about my baby daughter every day, and cry for her most nights before I fall asleep?

Simon's a surgeon – he needs precision in his day-to-day life – but I'm concerned he's getting worse and it's tipping over into something else. He's always been a perfectionist and often tried to impose that on me, and now and then he'll be physical, nasty, but then he just carries on like nothing's happened. I'm guilty too: I lie to myself and say he's stressed, it's the last time he'll hurt me and the last time I'll let him, but then it happens again. Recently, his anger hasn't stayed in the bedroom, it has bloomed red and raw into our daily lives and he's started to pick even more at what I feel are the few things I *can* do. My beurre blanc sauce is too thin, the new duvet cover in the spare room is 'cheap looking', his books aren't in alphabetical order on the shelf, the kids aren't doing their homework correctly. These are all in *my* domain, elements of our life that I have some control over and some skill for, and I feel like I'm being erased. I'm slowly becoming invisible the more he criticises, bullies and humiliates me – especially in front of the boys. I've always prided myself on how I look after our family; it's important that the kids are happy and doing well at school. I attend most parents' evenings on my own, I know who the children play with, I'm aware of the boys' upcoming SATs tests and totally on top of Sophie's AS levels and the three A levels she'll take next May. And yet I still feel I'm not good enough. 'You need to make sure the boys are doing their maths,' Simon'll say, 'because Alfie couldn't add up three plus seven the other day. What's going on?'

These days, when Simon's around, I feel like I'm standing on the outside looking in. I had no family, but as a child I watched families on TV, watched my friend's parents, and this isn't how it should be. I remember the Oxo ad like everyone else, and the dad would come home for dinner and everyone would be included. But sometimes I feel like Simon alienates me from the kids – he pulls funny faces when I say things, and if he and the boys are telling jokes and I try to join in, he rolls his eyes and says 'girls aren't funny'. The boys enjoy this banter, but I think it's disrespectful. It's not good for them to see girls as less than boys and it hurts.

This evening, he directed this towards Sophie, making an unkind remark about the jeans she was wearing and how they 'do nothing for you', which caused her to burst into tears and run upstairs. I wanted to run after her, but I knew it would cause even more upset if I did.

'What the hell's wrong with her... what do they call it nowadays? She's a complete snowflake!' he'd snapped.

'Simon, she's a teenager. She hates herself and she's under pressure. You commented on her physical appearance – can't you see how upsetting that was?'

I know I'm treading on eggshells, but this is important; it's about an already struggling teenage girl who doesn't need her father's insensitive remarks. It worries me a lot, that like the boys, she may have been getting the wrong impression of relationships from the snippets of our life together that she sees. I try to hide the difficult moments – our little lies, the tension, the bickering, the fights – but we all live together and kids see a lot. I want our children to remember the happy times, and not have their childhood and their own relationships blighted by how they perceive their parents to be. Simon can be difficult, and currently I'm not making things easy with my concerns about him playing away, but we can also be loving and caring and I have every hope that we'll soon be okay again.

I know he is upset, but he's too proud to chase after her, apologise or at least give her a hug. I doubt he's too proud to give Caroline a hug. All of the issues in our family started when she came on the scene and the sooner she's out of his life the better for all of us.

Simon later made it up to Sophie by saying he'd give her a driving lesson, and she seemed happier, but something must have happened during the lesson because they came home late and she went straight up to her room in tears. He clearly felt guilty about whatever had happened – he wouldn't tell me, but I know someone's going to pay for that. And I know it's me. So now I'm waiting for the fallout and, just as predicted, he starts by calling through to me from the sitting room that the throws on the sofa are apparently 'messy'.

I'm with the boys in the kitchen, but as soon as he calls I leave them and wander in with an already defeated sigh. It's late, the boys have been a handful, I'm worried about Sophie – and I think the throws look fine. In fact, I spent the good part of an hour today folding them so each corner lined up with the other (as he'd *suggested* a couple of weeks back). I'd embraced this too much and it had become a monkey on my back: each time I passed the sitting room, I went in, and only after I'd done this about twenty times could I drag myself from the room.

I am on the edge.

'I buy you cashmere throws and you treat them like cheap acrylics,' he says, impatiently guiding me across the living room for a masterclass on fucking throw folding.

'Simon, they're fine…' I say, trying to keep the irritation out of my voice.

'To you everything's fine, you leave mess everywhere, the place is covered in dust and you—'

'Simon, I dust every single day. I polish until I can see my bloody face in everything.' I can't hold back, I'm so tightly wound today I feel like I'm going to burst.

'Don't swear, you're better than that,' he spits.

'I'm not though, am I? I'm not better than that. This is me, and I'm not good enough.' I'm almost shouting. I know this won't end well but I'm on the edge of hysteria. The tension of the past few days is overwhelming me. I can't stop myself. 'I've never been good enough, have I Simon? Your mother made that clear from the moment she saw me, and I've been proving her right ever since.'

He's now marching between the sofas, dropping the throws that I painstakingly folded on the floor.

'Don't speak about my mother like that, God rest her soul.'

I'm incredulous at his piety. 'God rest… Simon, you've never even been to her grave…'

'How dare you.' He stops what he's doing. I wonder if I've gone too far; why did I have to push his buttons? I could have just folded the fucking throws and left it at that.

'It's… it's true, but I'm not blaming you, your relationship with your mother was cold…'

'Oh, and you'd know all about families, wouldn't you? Your own mother dumped you practically when you were born.' He's glaring at me and I have this urge to hide from him.

'Simon, please, let's not… I was just saying…' I start, now wanting only peace. But the genie is out of the bottle. And I opened it.

He comes towards me, grabbing me by the collar of my jumper, almost lifting my feet off the ground. His face is in mine, and his eyes are so filled with hate, it's burning my skin. I should have kept my mouth shut. I could kick myself for saying something so mean about his mother. What kind of wife am I that I can be so cruel?

'Only *saying* are you…?'

I feel the heat from his face in mine, his eyes boring into me and I stand still, holding my breath, waiting for the blow. I think he might bang his head into mine, because both his hands are now round my throat, so he doesn't have one free to hit me. I can't take this again; recently his flashes of anger have become more frequent, more prolonged, more scary. And for the first time in my marriage I'm genuinely worried that he might strangle me and I'll become a number on a list of victims of domestic violence.

When I was single in my twenties, living the party life in London, I was strong and independent. I wouldn't even let a man pay for a meal. Never did I ever imagine myself in this situation, standing here in my own home with my husband's hands at my throat, genuinely fearing for my life but unable to stop it. When did I become this way?

I wait for my punishment, holding my breath, hoping it's quick and silent. But suddenly, Charlie's voice cuts into the thick toxic air – he's yelling for me and I make an attempt to pull myself away from Simon's grip.

'Stay here,' he commands, but I shake myself free – my child needs me. 'Marianne, if you go, you'll be sorry,' he warns, as I falter in the doorway. His anger is tangible, but I can't ignore my child.

'Mummyyy!' Now Alfie's shouting and Charlie's joining in; just the sound of their wails is enough to cause a physical reaction in me. I'm rushing through the hall to the kitchen where Alfie has banged his head on the island, and I immediately wrap him in my arms and kiss his little face.

'Darling, let Mummy see,' I say, gently parting his hair to see if he's cut his scalp or if there's a lump. I can't see anything but call Simon, who runs in, and in the wake of his child's injury, all anger towards me is momentarily forgotten.

He pushes me aside roughly and does a perfunctory check of Alfie's head. 'You okay, mate?' he asks, and I can see he's looking into his eyes, checking them with his own, gently touching the wound.

'He banged his head – shouldn't we take him to A & E?' I ask.

'No, he'll be okay, but I do think we have an emergency on our hands,' he says, alarmingly.

'Oh… what? What?' I can barely contain my fear and panic but he seems to be enjoying it.

He looks around at Alfie and back at Charlie. 'I think what we need is emergency chocolate ice cream.'

There are yelps of joy as Charlie mounts Alfie, almost knocking him over, demanding he also be included in this 'emergency'.

I laugh with relief and reach out for Alfie, hugging him and kissing Charlie on the head. I wonder where the chocolate ice cream is coming from. There's none in the freezer; Simon doesn't approve.

'Okay – so Nurse Mum… take out the emergency ice cream,' Simon says.

The boys look at me and I'm a little lost. 'I… don't… we don't have any… Doctor.'

Simon puts on an expression of genuine surprise. 'Have you eaten all the ice cream, Mummy?' he says, rolling his eyes, and the boys protest at 'greedy Mummy', who apparently spends her days emptying the fridge of treats.

'Okay then, if Mummy ate it, she can replace it,' Simon says.

I look from him to the boys – is he teasing?

'What... do you...?'

'Go and get us some emergency chocolate ice cream.' He says this with lightness in his voice, but only I see the darkness that's returned to his eyes.

'Yeah... go on Mummy,' Charlie joins in, delighting in this game.

'Now?' I ask.

Simon nods and looks at the boys who now nod along with him.

'But it's late... it's after eight o'clock. I'll have to drive to the supermarket on the other side of town.'

'Yes, you will,' Simon says. 'Won't she, boys?'

'Oh yes,' they say in unison.

'What do you *want* from me, Simon?' I say. He's in the kitchen holding a corkscrew, an unopened bottle of wine on the oasis in front of him. The boys have now finished the chocolate ice cream I drove twenty-five minutes across town to purchase. It's almost 9 p.m. and they've gone to bed, Alfie complaining of tummy ache and Charlie threatening to be sick.

'What I *want*...' Simon is flushed with anger and taking a bottle of red and twisting the cork. I feel like he's pushing the sharp metal into me, twisting it into my flesh as he grinds it into the bottle. I rarely if ever challenge him, but merely asking what it is he wants is seen as a challenge – it's all relative. 'What I *want* is for *you* to come to bed and continue the discussion we were having before you ran off hysterically screaming about calling an ambulance for a bump on the head.'

'I didn't say… an ambulance… I just thought we should have him checked over.' I'm trying to stay calm. I must keep calm.

'I'm a doctor. I've checked him over – or perhaps you would like a second opinion? Perhaps my "doctoring" isn't good enough for you?' he says, staccato, uttering each syllable like he's drumming it into me. He's standing in the doorway, holding his glass of wine, Alfie's injury forgotten. 'Time for bed,' he announces and my heart sinks.

To the uninitiated, one might assume he's asking me to join him in the bedroom to snuggle up in love and kisses, a little gentle foreplay before rolling together in marital bliss. But I know different. And in the middle of my fear and dread of what tonight will bring, I see Caroline. She comes to me at the most difficult times, slipping between the sheets next to us, showing me how he loves her, and how different it is from the way he loves me.

Does he roll in bliss with you, Caroline?

He gestures for me to walk ahead of him and knowing there's no alternative, but a loud fight that will wake and traumatise the kids, I get up on unsteady legs and he follows me up the stairs one at a time. In spite of everything, I'm usually filled with respect and love for my husband – but tonight I'm broken. Of all the things he's said and done to me, of all the affairs that are real or suspected, I've always known he loved me. But now it seems he might be in love someone else and the more he loves her, the more he's making me suffer. If she wasn't here we'd be fine, and he'd love me like he used to and we'd be happy again, but as it is I'm in danger of losing not just him, but my family.

I've always been a little scared of him, but the thing I've been most scared of is him leaving. I'm sad that he's prepared to ruin everything we have – our family, the gorgeous home, a future – for someone else. But my real fear is the children. I know losing them is a very real threat, especially if he has someone in his life who can look after them.

They say we go for the same type and though I was never the blonde supermodel, we have our similarities, me and Caroline. Just like her, I was once the single girl making her way through a promising career. *My supermarket basket was once filled with champagne and strawberries too, Caroline.* Simon always said he was attracted to the way I lived my life, the way I'd dance easily, laugh loudly, fill a room with colour; but instead of sitting back and enjoying the butterfly, he caught it. He framed me like a butterfly, pinning me into his frame, but the pins that hold the butterfly in place are not easily visible, and no one can see I'm being held down. Over the years the butterfly has faded – he's stripped me of everything that made me what I was, and now he's left with this dull, colourless woman who's scared to say what she really thinks. *And I can't dance any more.*

It's hard to reconcile the person I once was with the woman I am now, standing helplessly in my beautiful bedroom with handmade oak wardrobes and gold silk eiderdown. The only reason I get out of bed in the morning is my children; they are my reason to live, and without them I don't think I would survive.

Things have never been perfect between Simon and I, but until Caroline, my life was bearable, but now I see her curling up on our king-sized bed. She's lounging seductively on our sofa, arms around the boys, *my* boys, and she's in my kitchen serving breakfast. This woman wants to take over my husband, but she'll also take over my life, my kids, if I let her. Sophie's appetite will be restored by Caroline's perfect pancakes, the boys will eat noisily before demanding seconds, and using my pans in my kitchen she'll make them some more. Now she's sitting at my dressing table, covering her perfect skin with my favourite perfume.

She can't have it, it's mine, and so is my husband.

'Marianne, we need to talk,' Simon says as he takes off his tie and hangs it up, and I wonder if he's going to tell me about her, put me out of my misery. I hope not. I can't bear to hear it.

For years I've felt like I owed him something because he stood by me after what happened with Emily. He could easily have divorced me on so many occasions, but he didn't – and for that I've always been grateful. But now, with thoughts of Caroline stealing my children infesting my mind, I suddenly feel a boiling anger inside, like a volcano smoking, ready to erupt. I hate this woman I don't know and I'm scared of Simon leaving me for her, and what they might do next. But I'm also scared of what I might do next.

'You know you need help, don't you?' he's saying as he sits on the bed, still drinking his wine, sloshing it slowly around the glass like a wine taster.

'I'm fine.'

'But, Marianne, darling, you're a mess – you can't even take the slightest criticism...'

'If you mean the throws—'

'Yes, but far worse was the... the hysteria you displayed over a minor bump.' He turns to look at me, concern on his face. I'm not sure if it's real. 'Darling, you must understand, I'm worried about them... with you.'

I feel a rising panic. This threat is never far away. I know he's concerned about my behaviour around the kids, but he knows the thought of losing them petrifies me.

'They are fine with me,' I insist.

'Darling, you're not well... tonight's craziness goes to prove...'

'Alfie was hurt – it's not a sign of mental illness for a mother to run to a screaming child...'

'You completely overreacted, as always, and you're passing your anxieties on to the children.'

'And you're passing your misogyny on to the boys,' I hear myself say. I don't know where this bravery (or stupidity?) came from. I just feel angry.

'Oh dear, you really are losing it, aren't you? I'm not the one who's ill, Marianne – and I certainly don't hate women. It's clear that your paranoia is back.'

'Simon, when I last saw the psychiatrist, she said I was doing well. You can't make a mental illness diagnosis on what happened tonight.'

'There you go again, putting me down.'

I can't believe this; he's twisting everything around. 'No, I'm not, you just manipulate me, make me say things I don't mean...' I start, like I'm reading from a script.

'No, it's your illness that makes you say things you don't mean.'

I realise as I backtrack that my default position has always been to appease him – that way we'll get to bed at a reasonable time without a scene. But tonight, he clearly has a bone to pick and he's going to damn well pick it.

'Why do you take every opportunity to attack me?' he's now saying. 'All I ask is that you respect me. Is it too much to ask, Marianne?' he asks, playing the victim, the poor husband whose crazy wife treats him badly. Everything always comes back to him.

'I do... I... I have a great deal of respect, and being concerned about my child when he's hurt doesn't equate to a lack of respect for you.'

'You disrespected me.' His voice is now raised and I can see he wants to take this all the way; he isn't going to drop it. 'Earlier tonight you walked out on me while I was talking to you...'

'You were talking to me about folding throws... and something more urgent was happening in the kitchen.' I am careful with my words, but he's surprised at my retaliation. I know in the great scheme of things I'm not exactly a warrior, but I think he senses the subtle change in me. His affair with Caroline has strengthened me because I know it's real – I've seen it written down – so I'm not mad after all, surely?

He looks at me for a long time and I know he's waiting for me to offer myself up as the lesser mortal, the broken woman for him to heal. He's just waiting for me to break, and when I don't, he stands up and does something I would expect of the boys. He slowly empties his wine glass over the golden eiderdown, then onto the pale gold carpet and leaves the room.

The throws started all this. He sees them as some kind of status symbol. He insisted we bought them for when we invited our neighbour Renee and her husband over for dinner in the summer. She's an attractive woman with a talent for interior design, and Simon was very keen to show her our new cashmere purchases before taking her into the garden to look at his roses. At midnight. *And I didn't imagine that.* I can't think about this now – so many women, so many lies, but whose? Are they Simon's lies or mine? I don't know who to believe as I sit alone surrounded by the mussed-up covers clouded by maroon wine stains. I'm too exhausted to cry. I just want to sleep. But first I must clean the mess he's made of our beautiful, expensive bedroom carpet, the one he chose. Simon loves luxurious things in the same way he loves beautiful women, sees it all as proof of his success. I suppose Caroline began as just another *objet d'art* for his collection, like I was once. But now he has another newer, shinier trinket, I'm not worth showing off any more. I'm flawed like the ruined sofa throws and this once beautiful carpet. I watch the red stain spread slowly into the pale wool and know I'm in the way. Simon never lets anything or anyone get in the way of what he wants – and that scares me.

I clean as much of the bedroom carpet as I can and put the stained bed linen in the washing machine. Eventually I hear him come back – looks like he's been for 'a drive' again, and I can guess what that means. I give it half an hour and when I eventually go upstairs and climb into bed, he's already asleep. I think about poor Nicole, his first wife, Sophie's mother, and for the first time I wonder if the marriage was as perfect as he says. If so, why did she take an overdose? How could she leave Sophie motherless? Simon says she had her demons, an unhappy childhood that led to depression, and I can't help but think she sounds a bit like me.

I'm itching now to watch the next episode in my husband's illicit love affair and his loud snoring tells me he's had a lot of wine and is sleeping like a log. So I attempt to get into his emails from my phone, and after only a couple of clicks, I'm delighted and a little scared to see them open up before me. There's something equally thrilling and frightening about doing this as he lies next to me in the dark, blissfully unaware that I'm rummaging around in his secret places.

I find emails from the past couple of days and delve into his other life, searching hungrily for things I don't want to see. Caroline telling Simon he's the best lover she's ever had, that she loves his passion, the way he can go on all night and still wake early and bring her blueberry pancakes in bed. *Blueberry fucking pancakes!* This isn't the Simon I know; he's never been in the kitchen to do anything other than eat or tell me I'm doing something wrong.

I hurt as I open another email and see this parallel life going on alongside this one, where everything is different but the same, and nothing makes sense – a whole world uncovered at the touch of a screen. Their most intimate moments and feelings are laid bare before me in the darkness and I flagellate myself with the details. I am devastated to discover that she makes my husband go hard when she passes him in the corridor at the hospital, that he can barely concentrate on what he's doing in theatre because she fills his mind. Meanwhile, she can't wait for him to be inside her and thinks about him *on* her, *in* her, *all over* her, and he responds by reminding her how good she is on top, how he loves her breasts in his face and her long legs wrapped tight around him.

I am breathless with hurt as I open up each shared intimacy, each secret, each betrayal. Through their emails I can sit on the end of the bed when they have sex. I'm in the wardrobe, peering from behind the curtains, standing behind them. Watching. I'm the third wheel, the idiot in the room – the other woman. But I'm the innocent party whose life they are destroying with every thrust; every orgasm is shutting down my marriage. #GooseberryWife

I eventually turn off the phone, feeling like I've been sliced open. Despite his cruelty, his slaps, his contempt – I am still jealous of her, of the Simon she has and I don't. I am the wife, I wore white lace, I had hopes and dreams and he's killed them all, but *she's* provided the fatal blow. Most of the time, he can barely say a word to me, but he can write so much to Caroline; each sexually charged word passing between them through cyberspace is more painful than any of his slaps. But the real tragedy is that I still care, I still want him, he's mine and I'm not ready to give him up, and not sure if I'll ever be. We roll around in our mutual pain, hurting ourselves and each other, but it's all I've ever known. And I can't imagine loving anyone else but Simon.

I lie in the dark, going over every line in my head, torturing myself with their words, amazed at the way I want him now. I'm not sure whether it's reading the depths of his passion or the thought of needing to be touched in the way he touches her, but the ache is intense or similar. I want to make him mine again, repossess him. I touch him on the chest as he sleeps, then move my hand down under his pyjamas. I feel like I'm not in control, like someone else has taken over my body as I grasp him, holding him firmly in my hand. He stirs, and I kiss his neck. I am so conflicted, so drowsy from my pills, but aroused, and when he wakes I climb onto him, pushing him inside me and undulating my body around him. I lean forward, pushing my breasts into his face. *Just like Caroline.*

He starts to respond, thrusting, grasping my nipples and squeezing tightly. In between bites he's telling me quietly that I'm a bitch and I have to be punished. And he's right. I push down hard, thrusting as fast as I can until he groans his release. But I'm not finished, and despite his protestations I keep driving him into me, hissing my own filth back at him. And when I'm done, I roll off, my sweat and his saliva trickling between my breasts. My heart aches and my thighs burn, but I made him mine again, for a brief few moments. And I fall asleep, filled with love and loathing.

I thought I'd won him back with that one act, shown him that I could be what he needed me to be, that I could be like Caroline if that's what he wants. Anything to keep us all together, to keep my children safe. Keep me safe.

But the next time I venture into his office and open the laptop, I stand in the clinical space staring at the screen as he tells *her* how much he 'adores' her, how she is 'the moon in all his stars' and I'm amazed to feel cool tears sliding down my cheeks. It's like stepping back in time. I remember him using this exact phrase on me early in our marriage (when he was trying to convince me he hadn't cheated) and I'm filled with fresh hurt; it oozes from my organs, stings my flesh like salt on an open wound.

I'm not like Caroline. I don't love pain, but Simon says I need to try harder, that if I loved him I would do as he asks without making a fuss. But she doesn't *have* to try – she's tied up, abandoned in her pain and pleasure, smacked hard, taken quickly everywhere and anywhere. She's exciting and beautiful. How can I compete with this perfect woman? I long to tear myself away from the emails detailing the night before and how they fucked each other's brains out. But I can't leave. I am the voyeur in my husband's relationship and unable to let go.

'When can I see you?' he asks her. 'I can't spend longer than a few minutes away, I'm addicted to you, my darling.' Her response is equally yearning and rather more poetic. 'I watched you drink coffee this morning, your long, slender fingers circling the paper cup,' she writes, and I think about his long, skilled hands that open up hearts and bruise them. Those hands have held my own heart in their grip for far too long. 'I wanted those fingers on me,' she goes on to say. 'Right there and then, in the hospital canteen, I wanted your fingers caressing me, inside me, touching every secret part.' *Calm down, Caroline, you home-wrecking slut.* 'I keep thinking about last night. Oh God, I've never come like that before.'

I want to throw up. I can almost hear her staccato breaths, reaching a screaming crescendo on that big brass bed, and once more I'm strangely aroused and horrified. These few graphic lines make everything so real for me. As much as I try to tear myself away, I'm drawn back into her bedroom as they lie in each other's arms, watching like a stalker as she climbs on top. Now I'm caressing her, as she thrusts up and down, screaming with her as he bites her nipples, and riding him until he explodes, their cries loud in the darkness of my head.

I stop abruptly, click out of the emails, unable to read any more. Anger is the only thing that will make me strong enough to get through this, but my cheeks are still wet with tears. I think again of how we used to be, before the tragedy, before I lost my mind and he gradually gained control until we destroyed each other in our own special way.

Like all marriages there is light and shade and it hasn't all been bad. Simon and I were close in the early days, decorating our new flat, planning our wedding together. He even came with me to choose my wedding dress. The saleswoman said it was 'unusual' for the groom to be involved and potentially bad luck, but we laughed this off. Who else would come with me? My mother was dead, my friends from work and college had moved on. I had no other family; he was all I had. Besides, I wanted him there. I thought it was sweet and I wasn't superstitious – he was my good luck charm, not bad luck. But the saleswoman spoke to me like he wasn't there and created an atmosphere. I remember being aware of Simon's jaw twitching as she asked if I *really* wanted him to see the dresses I was trying on. I could feel the tension in the air as my hand brushed through various shades of white and cream clouds on hangers. She was ruining my day.

'I'm paying for it,' he'd said, 'so yes, I will see the dresses my fiancée tries on. That's what marriage is about isn't it, doing things together,' he added and winked at me. I glowed back at my knight in shining armour who'd come along to dress me in white lace and whisk me away to a better life. Finally 'love' had arrived, and Simon wouldn't leave me like my mother had, or send me back into care as the foster families had done.

I loved the fitted cream dress with the low-cut top and ruffle, and the saleswoman agreed. 'You look absolutely stunning,' she'd said and I turned expectantly to Simon for his approval. But I could tell by his face he wasn't enamoured and he suggested instead a white one he'd seen in the window, which the shop assistant went off to find in my size.

'I like this one,' I said, when she'd gone.

'Darling, you are so much better than that trashy dress,' he sighed, standing back and shaking his head.

'Oh, but it's lovely…'

'Marianne, you look like a hooker with a weight problem,' he snapped. I hadn't imagined him ever saying something like this to me, and I could feel my chin trembling as I stood there *like a hooker with a weight problem.* He spotted the way my eyes were filling with tears and sighed. 'I can't say anything to you these days, you're so touchy. I never expected you to be like this.'

It's a phrase I've heard often in the intervening years: 'I never expected this, because I always thought you'd be a better wife/ mother/lover.'

I'm a disappointing woman.

Anyway, in the end, my wedding dress was cool white, which the saleswoman warned me 'drains colour out of you'. It had long sleeves and a high neck, which Simon remarked was, 'Perfect. You look just how I've always imagined Mrs Wilson – my wife'.

I was young and in love. I didn't question anything, just couldn't believe my luck, landing a husband like Simon. Jill, one of the few friends I'd kept in touch with, was amazed at my good fortune. 'Well done, you jammy cow, you got yourself a doctor.' But other friends weren't so complimentary: they said he seemed a bit moody, that I didn't really know him and I shouldn't rush into it and rather wait until I was sure. I thought they were jealous. I didn't want to listen. I'd never been so sure of anything in my life and I wasn't prepared to risk the chance of losing him by hanging around. Despite being told I was pretty, I didn't have much confidence, and I couldn't imagine anyone wanting to marry me, let alone Simon Wilson, confident, charming, middle-class surgeon-in-waiting. What did he see in me? Let's face it, from a financial, familial and genetic perspective, I wasn't exactly a catch. Joyless Joy saw this inequality and offered to finance a research trip in Europe for Simon, and suggested he take Sophie with him. But he refused, said he loved me and, against all the odds, he stood by me and married me. I was stunned and delighted by his loyalty – no one had ever chosen me before.

It was now us against the world, and I was comforted to know he was even prepared to forego what was probably a great career opportunity and go against Joy's wishes to be with me. I was a very lucky girl. Simon was offering himself to me along with the chance to make a life, a family together – it was all I'd ever wanted.

He'd held me in his arms in our new house, with seven-year-old Sophie sleeping contentedly in her lilac bedroom next door, her soft, long hair on the pillow, her fluffy cat toy Muffin in her arms. We didn't have much back then, but we had each other, Sophie and a baby on the way, which was everything to me. In those early days, I never had any doubts about me or Simon, and when our beautiful daughter Emily was born I felt like we were complete and we'd found our happy ending. But I was wrong.

CHAPTER TEN

I'd had a difficult birth so stayed in hospital for a week with Emily. Sophie was staying with Joy for a while, but Simon collected her every day and brought her to see me. They'd always bring lovely things – little dresses for the baby, flowers and little cakes – and he'd sprinkle us all with kisses. 'My girls,' he'd say, and I felt so loved.

Emily and I came home from the hospital in a taxi to an empty house. Simon was back at work and, against my wishes, Sophie was still with Joy. As she wasn't actually my daughter, I had no jurisdiction, even though she told me she didn't want to go. I promised her I'd get her back as soon as I could – Sophie had already lost one mum, and was scared of losing another. I understood more than most how that felt.

Arriving back at the house alone with my baby, I felt bereft. There'd been no heating on for days and it was the middle of winter. 'Have you been saving money on the gas?' I joked to Simon when he finally got home late that evening. It's not something he'd even consider; when you come from a wealthy background like Simon's, lavish heating is a God-given right. I turned to him and smiled, waiting for him to giggle at this, but he looked angry.

'What are you trying to say, Marianne?'

The colour of my first evening home with our baby went straight from pink to grey.

'Are you accusing me of not staying here while you were in hospital?' he pressed. 'Are you insinuating I was somewhere else, Marianne?' he said this slowly, deliberately.

My blood chilled. It hadn't even occurred to me that he was anywhere but our home while I was away. I was too exhausted from the shock of a new baby and lack of sleep, to even think about what Simon had been doing. Despite my protestations and attempts at placation, he created a huge emotional scene and told me I was mad just like my mother. He stormed out of the flat, slamming the door like I'd done something terrible to him, and I was devastated, sitting for several hours clutching Emily and crying. This wasn't the homecoming I'd envisaged and I blamed myself for not trusting him.

Later, he returned in tears, said he hated himself for upsetting me and asked if I could forgive him. 'I was just so worried about you and the baby,' he said. 'I've missed you so much while you were in the hospital. I don't know what I'd do without you, you're everything,' he'd cried, and I stroked his hair and comforted him, happy to have him back. Although I was hurt and confused by his reaction to an innocent remark – who knows what happened while I was in hospital – all that mattered then was that he'd come home to me and I was everything to him, because he was everything to me.

I think my return home marked the beginning of postnatal depression. I'd been fine in hospital, with the support and kindness of nurses, the short visits from Simon and the adoration of Sophie for her baby sister. But now I was unsure about my role, my future and what was expected of me as a wife and mother. Worse still, I wasn't sure how I felt about Emily. I was her mother, I had to love her, it came with the territory – how could I not? And yet, I just didn't *feel* it. I tried so hard to conjure up love for my baby daughter; I'd gaze at her for hours as she slept in my arms and wait... and wait. I desperately tried to breastfeed her despite having little milk and feeling more and more stressed at each abortive attempt. And sometimes, on those long, dark, lonely nights as I longed for her to sleep, and cried as I paced the bedroom with her in my arms,

I wondered: was I like my mother after all? Was I destined to be the kind of mother she was, unable to cope, unable to love, forced to give up my child to someone who could?

Simon must have observed me and despaired. All he wanted was a mother for his children, something that came naturally for most women – an instinct, a need. But not for me, not then, and when I think about what he's doing now, I feel like we're even. I let him down back then and now he's letting me down, and when it's over we'll be straight and we can start with a clean slate. I wouldn't be the first woman to forgive her partner for cheating because they want everything to stay as it is. And I'm not ready to give up this life, so *she* will have to go.

I constantly wipe down kitchen surfaces with pure bleach to wipe the thoughts of them away. But as hard as I wipe, I can't get away from them. I'm tormented by their closeness and what it will mean for me. I'm also fascinated by their intimacy, and as I clean the bath, I imagine them sitting there naked in steam, his hand slipping between her tanned, firm thighs. I bleach the sink and imagine her sitting on my kitchen counter, his long fingers gently pushing her legs apart and taking her there. I scrub the floor thinking of the emails she sends asking him to be rough, to tie her up, hurt her because she's a bad girl.

CHAPTER ELEVEN

Tonight, the boys are both playing rugby for the school's junior team – the baby team really, as they are the youngest. On Simon's insistence, I enrolled them both in the extra-curricular training two nights a week. Apart from the fact Alfie didn't want to join the team, I felt that along with all their other after-school activities this was a heavy schedule for them. I shared my concerns with Simon, who was adamant and refused to listen to my plea for Alfie, who's less competitive than Charlie. Simon's in denial that Alfie hates sports and would rather do drama after school instead. His performance as Joseph at last year's nativity brought the house down. I cried, and so did Sophie, he was so good, but Simon was working late so couldn't attend. Some evenings, after a particularly vigorous game of what the sports teacher refers to as 'The Rugger', poor Alfie has emerged in tears. 'Please don't make me go again, Mum,' he says, and sometimes, unbeknown to Simon, I've created a fictitious illness and spared him the pain of being under the weight of fourteen other overexcited boys.

I can't count how many late winter afternoons I've stood on the sidelines watching, feeling every triumph for Charlie, and every moment of pain for Alfie. Tonight is the fruit of all the hard work, a game against another private school a few miles away, and the atmosphere is tense with competitive dads lining the edges of the pitch, mums posing with flasks and full make-up.

Simon has arranged to finish early at the hospital and is meeting us here; even Sophie offered to come along, for which I am grateful. The boys know Dad's on his way and I'm aware Alfie is trying extra hard not to cry because his leg has just been stood on deliberately by a bigger boy before the game has even begun. My heart goes out to him as the whistle is blown and the game starts. I watch them, while every now and then looking anxiously towards the car park, for Simon's car.

Simon should have been here almost an hour ago. But he isn't. The game kicked off at 5 p.m. and it's now 5.45 – the teams have stopped for a break and are drinking hot Bovril or something equally disgusting. Alfie's face tells me all I need to know: he hates every moment and longs to be safely home in the warm. I feel just the same.

Anxiety fluttering in my stomach, I check my phone – nothing from Simon – and I wonder if perhaps he's been called in to an emergency? And if so, what kind of emergency… and does it involve Caroline?

I push unwelcome thoughts away and watch the rest of the match in a blur, upset for the boys who wanted to show Dad their game. Even Alfie's putting everything into it, thinking Simon's here.

'Dad not coming then?' Sophie asks, as she bangs her hands together and moves her feet to keep warm.

'Probably an emergency,' I suggest, slightly resenting the way I have to explain his absence.

'Or a better offer,' she mutters and I pretend not to hear, but what she says cuts deep.

Half an hour later, after showering and changing, the boys finally join Sophie and I. They are both looking behind me, around me, for their dad.

'Dad's sooo sorry but someone has been really badly hurt and they almost died, but Dad saved them,' I add, my heart breaking slightly at the disappointment on their faces. The boys are too young to be impressed, but at least this feels like a justifiable excuse and I hope it will mean their father's absence is less painful. I avoid looking at Sophie, who lets out a big sigh as I tell lies to my boys. But as we walk together to the car park I convince myself that sometimes a lie is the kindest way of explaining something.

'So… I was thinking…' I start, as I put the car into reverse and turn it around quickly in the car park, causing it to veer across the frosty ground and create much excitement and whooping in the back. I laugh along with the kids – it's fun to be naughty now and then, take a few risks.

'So… you were thinking…?' Charlie says.

'Was I?' I joke and the boys laugh and shout 'Mum? Tell us,' in various degrees of loud.

'Okay, okay, I was thinking we might go… to… McDonald's!'

If I'd suggested Disneyland, I doubt the joy would have been any more rapturous. Nothing says 'sorry' like a Happy Meal, and in my own, small way, I just want them to have a good time and be happy. I want to erase for them the fact that their dad never turned up. I want them to laugh and let go, because in spite of my constant smoothing over, I know they are affected by the tension at home.

So we head for McDonald's on strict instructions that we don't mention it to Dad, 'because he will be really sad that we went without him,' I lie, as we pull into the car park of The Golden Arches, the boys singing songs about burgers all the way.

Ten minutes later, my children's faith in parenting and the world is restored as they tuck into what is regarded by Simon as the most toxic food on the planet. The boys have a Happy Meal and even Sophie deigns to pick at a vegetarian wrap. I've also ordered myself a quarter-pounder with cheese and, as we sit in the fluorescent light of the place whose name we dare not speak (in front of Simon), I watch them. The kids are all absorbed – the boys with their meals and toys, Sophie with her own phone. My babies, all safe. All happy. And with me. I log on to Instagram.

Don't ask me why; perhaps it's the headiness of being alone with my kids and eating the devil's own Happy Meal together, but I suddenly feel brave. As long as the four of us are together, nothing else matters and their father's absence can be compensated for with a burger, a free toy and a Coke. So, with this new-found courage, I decide to go deeper into the tunnel, not knowing how dark it will be, but knowing my kids are here in this brightly lit fast-food restaurant to pull me out should I need it.

I punch 'Caroline Harker' into the search box for about the millionth time, and there she is again, looking right at me, daring me to reopen the window into her life… the life that's intruding into mine.

'Mum, look how high it goes,' Charlie's saying about his *Star Wars* spacecraft, as he swoops it into Alfie's face, knocking his drink everywhere.

I wipe the table with bits of napkin and say 'Eat your burger,' and 'Don't hurt Alfie,' while clicking on Caroline Harker's photos. She's looking right back at me in close-up, a glass of wine in hand, perfect smile on her face – shiny lips, very white teeth. I expect she has them whitened, and that tan has to be fake. It's not like she's been away all summer; too busy hanging around my husband. And then I see it, posted ten minutes ago: rumpled bed sheets, a stocking on the floor, two glasses, a bottle of Merlot, his favourite. #LoveInTheAfternoon.

My heart is thudding in my head. How could he? I know he's hurting me, but now he's hurting my children. He's put her before his kids and that's unforgivable. My hurt and anger explodes like meteors all through my body and for a moment I don't know where I am. I feel a mist coming over me. Everything's dark and I'm fighting my way out of a nightmare. And then it's bright again; the kids are laughing at something.

'Mum's so old she can't see,' Sophie giggles, and I realise I have my phone right up to my face, trying to get inside the picture, to see who's there, behind the camera. I'm looking for clues, anything that will confirm for me that he's there now, with her. I try very hard not to imagine strangling her with that silk stocking. But the kids are still laughing and the sheets, the glasses and the stocking wipe from my mind. My children bring me back and I cross my eyes, which is always a favourite with the boys who can't yet do this. They roar with laughter while making their own eyes do everything except cross, and Sophie and I laugh along too. These snatched moments are precious and looking across the table at my beautiful children makes me even more determined not to let Caroline have them.

Later, when we arrive home, Simon's car's in the drive. I see him at the window, standing there, guiltily clutching a million excuses, ready to throw like confetti. I feel so sad as I open the door and the boys charge ahead, Dad's absence at the match either forgiven or forgotten. He's in the hallway now, catching them as they run, hugging them and offering placatory pizza tomorrow to make up for not being there tonight.

I say nothing, just walk into the kitchen where he follows and opens a bottle of Merlot. His second today. I listen to some long-winded lie about a patient walking the line between life and death and how he saved yet another life. I don't respond, just go to my default and blindly wipe down kitchen surfaces as he speaks.

'The boys were disappointed you weren't there,' I say simply, after he's finished his 'story'.

'Disappointed? Not as disappointed as the family would have been if my patient had died tonight.'

'That's hardly a comparison.' Even if it were I doubt he was even at the fucking hospital judging by his lover's Instagram.

'No, of course it isn't a comparison,' he sneers, 'because apparently me being at some school rugby match is far more important than saving someone's life.'

'I'm not saying...' Why is it he can always twist my words, make me feel like I'm in the wrong? 'It wasn't "some" rugby match, it was your boys' first rugby match, with the team you were so eager for them to join.'

'I've apologised to the boys, and after the day I've had I don't need you sulking...' he says, turning my anger into something petty and trivial.

'It's one thing hurting me, Simon,' I say, speaking over him, 'but it's another hurting the kids.' It hangs in the air like a thick cloud, and I hold my breath and keep wiping with the antibacterial cloth, wishing I could clean his slut away like dirt.

'How dare you of all people have the audacity to say I would hurt our kids?' he says.

Bullseye!

And back I go, down, down, down, plummeting to the ground. *He will always win.*

I want to tell him I know where he was; it's on the tip of my tongue, but what proof do I have? A photo of two empty glasses of Merlot? I can hardly accuse him of choosing her over our children with that flimsy evidence. She could have taken that photo any time, and he may not have been the fellow drinker, the one she'd just rolled around on those rumpled sheets with.

'The boys were upset you weren't there – you should have called me and at least I could have told them,' I say, trying to speak calmly, gently, so as not to ignite this.

'Oh, that's right, I should have called you while my patient hung on between life and death. I should have downed tools and said "I'm sorry theatre staff – I know the patient is bleeding profusely from his left aorta and may die any moment, but I really have to call my wife".' He looks at me with barely concealed disgust and takes another glug. 'I wish you lived in the real world, Marianne,' he is saying now. 'I wish I had someone to talk to, someone who understands.'

'You do have someone though, don't you?' I hear myself say.

He whips round to face me and I know this is what he wants – my wild accusations, my tears, my begging, because that way he can deny everything, say I'm mad, send me back to the hospital and set up home with Little Miss Caroline and her nasty rumpled sheets. 'What are you saying?'

'I'm saying, you can talk to *me*. I'm your wife, I understand.' I need to play for time. I need to erase this thing that's living in our marriage. If I argue or start accusing now, I know who'll be leaving our home tonight, leaving the kids – and it won't be him. I have the written evidence in the emails, proof that this affair is real and I'm not mad. I look at his handsome face, knowing his lips have kissed her, his hands have been all over her body, and I want to ask him why. I want for him to break down and tell me everything, what a mistake he's made, how he only loves me and can I forgive him? I don't know if I can, but it's immaterial, because he doesn't ask.

'I'm going to do some work,' he says, and heads for the door, then just before he leaves, he turns to me, landing one more fatal blow. 'Marianne, I've been thinking… are you finding everything too much… again?' A loaded question that doesn't wait for an answer. 'It's just that… well, you shouted at Charlie, called him stupid… and the boys abandoned on the sofa surrounded by biscuit crumbs for their supper the other evening, and now this… this *aggressiveness* in your tone… I have to say I'm rather concerned.'

'I'm fine, I told you…'

'Yes, but you told me you were *fine* with Emily, and look what happened there.' With a warning look, he walks out of the kitchen, closing the door behind him. Closing the door on me.

'Come on, boys, bath time. Mum's not feeling too good, she's a bit confused again,' I hear him call.

I run to the door and open it. 'I've told the boys no bath tonight. They showered after rugby, and they're already in their pyjamas,' I call, knowing it will confuse them to be given conflicting instructions.

'Come on boys, bath time,' he says calmly, repeating his command like I'm invisible. I hear the protestations from their bedroom as he heads upstairs. 'Yes, you *are* having a bath. I told you, Mum's not very well again.' He's now reclaiming the children. He'll be the perfect father: reliable, hilarious and loving. Meanwhile, I will fade into the background until I'm of no consequence, until they don't trust me any more, until I don't trust myself. They will live happily in Simon's world, a world where I don't belong, but where a shiny new mother waits.

I see the tableau in my mind's eye, Caroline in weekend casuals, blonde hair in a messy updo, make-up free with flour on her nose. The sun's coming through the window in that pleasing way and bathing her and my lovely Farrow and Ball wall in buttery morning sunshine. She's making pancakes in my kitchen again, just two feet away, using my pans, my ingredients, even my fucking handwritten recipe I keep in the drawer. The boys are excited. They love Caroline's pancakes – and Simon loves Caroline. He kisses the flour from her nose and she gives him a lingering 'later' look and, putting the children first, like all good mothers, she throws pancakes in the air and the boys whoop with delight. I've never been able to toss pancakes – they land on the floor or never leave the pan – but I bet Caroline can toss. Even Sophie is seduced by Caroline's youth and beauty; this mum is so much prettier and happier than the old one, and she doesn't disappear to hospitals for weeks on end or throw pints over barmaids in local pubs.

That was last year, when I got myself all wound up over... nothing, or something or... I'm not even sure what it was any more. Caroline will be a breath of fresh air for poor tormented Sophie. She'll help her with her homework, and they'll 'like' each other's Instagram posts – Sophie loves social media, she's always on it. Caroline will probably know someone in a cool band and get free tickets because that's the kind of woman she is. All things to all men and children. *My* children. #PerfectWife #CoolMum

I sit on one of my beautiful leather kitchen bar stools, put my head on the Calacatta Oro marble worktop and cry.

Yes, there were the warning signs, but I hoped after our troubles that they would become less and the love become more. But because of what happened with Emily, it was the other way round. And it was all my fault.

I was a new mum, my emotions were all over the place and so I retreated into numbness. I soon found I was balancing Simon's feelings with my own plus my baby's needs and just went through the motions of feeding, nappy changing and praying she'd sleep. She cried so much, and so did I. Simon said Nicole had never had these problems with Sophie; she'd been able to soothe her instantly and they bonded straight away, which made me feel even worse. I tried desperately to feel something more than a robotic, perfunctory caring for Emily, but my emotions were so frayed. I'd built a wall around me and no one came in or out. I had no friends, no mother to turn to, and then Simon's mother came and took Sophie again at Simon's behest. This made things worse for me. I missed her, and being without Sophie made me even more lonely, more lost. Meanwhile, I was struggling to care for Emily, who refused to eat and rarely slept – just screamed most of the time. Simon was working long hours and being alone all day I wondered vaguely if I should try and make friends by joining a 'new mums' club', which I mentioned to Simon, but he said it was beneath me. 'Sitting in a circle on a cold floor of a draughty town hall – is that really what you want to do with our child?' he'd said, shaking his head in despair at my suggestion.

I agreed, but not because I believed it was beneath me but because a gaggle of cooing mothers who knew exactly what to do when I didn't was the last thing I needed. I was sleep-deprived, covered in the aftermath of baby weight and deeply unhappy. It was difficult enough to comb my hair and appear 'normal'. I longed for peace. All I wanted was what I'd previously taken for granted: to go to bed and sleep. But Emily was colicky and fretful and the days rolled into each other in an endless loop, both of us helpless, in tears and alone. I'd wake each morning with new resolve that today I would get it right, but trying to calm my baby seemed to have the opposite effect and exacerbated her. I was also dealing with my own feelings, irrationally hurt when she wouldn't take my breast and feeling a personal slight when she slept happily in Simon's arms but yelled constantly in mine.

'You're too anxious, and you're passing it on to her,' Simon would say as he took her from me. 'This is what Nicole used to do.' He'd smile, rocking Emily gently, or holding her up and talking to her, making her little hands unfurl, big blue eyes on his. He was wonderful with her, but I never had these beautiful moments and, if I'm honest, I was jealous. I was jealous of Simon, of Nicole and of every other parent who walked down the road with a contented, sleeping baby in a pushchair, because they could do it and I couldn't. I couldn't even leave the house with her in case I had a panic attack and something happened, so I'd sit with her on my knee all day and turn the TV up to cover her screams. I'd sit there watching smug bitches on TV ads mock me with their perfect post-baby bodies while enthusing about their chosen brand of disposable nappy. It was a world of mystery to me, as inaccessible as the moon, and I wondered again if it was postnatal depression or because I didn't have a relationship with my own mother. Is being a bad mother inherited? Simon thought it was.

'Your mother's suicide worries me,' he'd said one evening when he'd come home from work and I was still in my dressing gown, crying.

'Does it?' I sighed lethargically over Emily's usual screaming as he took her gently from me.

'Yes. I was talking to a colleague, – she says you may have a genetic propensity to mental health problems. Plus, your mother's absence will naturally have an impact on how you respond to Emily… nature *and* nurture.'

'It's how she responds to *me*,' I said, through big, blobbing tears. Emotions and hormones whirled around my head. I was concerned about my mother's genetic input but I was more worried about the fact he'd discussed me with someone at work. Another woman too. It's the little things that eat away at you when you're vulnerable. I felt ashamed, and alone, so alone.

'I'm disappointed, Marianne,' he said, now cradling Emily who was sleeping peacefully in his arms. 'I thought you'd be a strong mother, that you'd cope.'

'I can… I will, I just—'

'And you know I'm not shallow – I didn't choose you just for your looks, but I have to say, I'd be embarrassed to walk down the street with you right now. Quite frankly, you're a mess. You spend all day lolling around filled with self-pity and completely letting yourself go. I could understand it if this was because you were busy being a mother, but it seems you have no mothering skills. I imagine your mother was just the same…'

'My mother was ill.' I'd been taken from her as a baby because there was a risk she might harm me. I wasn't like my mother, was I?

'You said yourself, you don't love Emily – what kind of mother says that?' Simon was right, and I was as scared as he was that my illness meant I would never be a mother to our child. This wasn't what he'd signed up for; he'd done his part, providing a loving home for me and the baby. I was here in this brand new house with my lovely husband and perfect baby, but for some inexplicable reason I couldn't be happy. Simon was right, I'd let myself go, sitting around all day in my faded blue dressing gown, hair unbrushed, face permanently wet with tears. I had to do something about it, because if I didn't I might lose him.

'I'm going to get dressed,' I'd said, quietly walking out of the room.

'About time,' he answered without looking at me, but he added a parting shot. 'Though I'm surprised you can find anything to wear, you've got so fat.'

This was like dunking me back underwater when I was already drowning. It was just one more blow to the heart.

I thought you were meant to mend damaged hearts, Simon.

I think about this now, sitting in my designer kitchen, the boys laughing with their father upstairs. We'd both known I wasn't worthy of Simon, so he tried to mould me, shape me into the wife he wanted. But unfortunately the real Marianne kept emerging and spoiling everything, but now he's found Caroline, a woman he doesn't need to shape, because she's perfect just as she is. And there's not enough room for both of us.

CHAPTER TWELVE

At the moment, I am permanently on edge and can't wait until the evening when I am calmed by a veil of medication. I've started to take my pills late in the day because I have to be alert to drive the kids around, but at weekends I sometimes dose myself up in the mornings. I don't want to take drugs, but I need them to calm the thoughts that have taken over since Caroline's arrival in our lives. Simon says the medication will help me get better, but I've been taking various pills for nearly ten years now, and I'm beginning to think they make no difference – this is who I am. My mother.

After finding my mother's body I was deeply traumatised for a long time. I had therapy, and professional support from social workers, and between the ages of ten and fifteen was placed with a lovely foster family. The mum, Mrs Fellowes, had been an art teacher, with two kids of her own and me, plus the odd little one who stayed on a temporary basis. Mrs Fellowes – or Jean as she liked me to call her – was the only kindness and consistency I had in my childhood. Jean was wise and caring, and when we came home from school to find her at the oven waiting for us kids with warm tray bakes and glasses of milk, I felt I was living a fairy tale. Jean was the one who gave me a sewing kit and saw the potential in my drawing and designs. She read women's magazines with glossy pictures of models and I'd pore over these, copying the pictures with my own handmade clothes made from old fabric and hand-me-downs. It was through Jean my love of colour and fashion was born, and without her I reckon I'd have probably ended up on the streets. Jean and Bob were thinking of adopting me when she became ill, but she was in and out of hospital for months and they seemed to have forgotten. Jean was going for regular chemo and Bob was beside himself with grief, so when, one day, I asked him about the adoption he was a little short. 'I'm sorry, Marianne, when Jean goes I won't be taking in any kids.'

I was terribly crushed. It hadn't occurred to me that Jean might 'go', I wasn't sure where to but it was unexpected because she was the one person I'd thought I could count on. When she died, I realised that's what happened to people I loved: they left me on my own. Marrying Simon and becoming stepmum to Sophie erased all that – at last I had my own family, and no one could ever take that away from me. *Until you came along, Caroline, with your perfect white teeth and rumpled sheets.*

I lift my head from the kitchen worktops; everything's quiet and for a moment I wonder if I blacked out and Simon's taken the kids, but then I hear a giggle and Simon's deep voice. He's obviously bathed them and is reading a story – everyone's home, everyone's safe. I have to be grateful. All is right with the world. For now.

Thinking about Jean and the calming qualities of art therapy, I wander into the utility room and open the cupboards where I keep my bag-making stuff. Everything's neatly tucked away in biscuit tins and old chocolate boxes and I open them up, touching the crispness of lace and the softness of velvet. Then I remember Jen's bag, how she'd loved it so much and how, a few weeks later, she had asked me to make one for her friend.

I was so flattered that she liked it, I suppose I got a bit carried away. I saw it as a first commission, a little chink of light in the navy-blue darkness. Business empires were built on these little things, a friend telling a friend, and before you know it you're in a *Vogue* spread. Jen said her friend liked green, and the ocean, so I bought some beautiful sea-green fabric and made tiny pearl starfish. I knew Simon wouldn't approve – he'd already said that my sewing was a waste of time – but I wanted to prove to him that I could make a success of this. I felt I might be able to persuade him to get behind me once he'd seen this latest creation so spent days sewing, creating, forgetting. When I'd finally finished it, I lay it on the kitchen table and admired it. I was so proud. It really was beautiful, and for the first time in forever I felt good about myself, like I had something to give to the world. Sophie said it was gorgeous, and even the boys noticed it on the table and said it was 'awesome' and 'wicked' and, later that evening, Simon spotted it.

'What do you think?' I asked proudly. Surely even Simon had to admit it was good?

'It's a bag,' he sighed.

'Oh, Simon, I think you're being mean,' I said playfully, covering my hurt.

'Oh, you do? Well, *I* think you have more important stuff to do in the day than play with your sewing kit,' he'd said slowly, almost with a growl as he walked away from the table.

'I'm not just playing, Simon,' I said with a fake brightness that bordered on brittle. 'This is my first commission, I've just finished it.' I lifted it from the table, holding it in front of me, admiringly, desperate for his approval. If I had his approval I could pursue this without him throwing landmines in my way.

He sighed. 'We talked about this, Marianne. You can barely cope with the kids without taking anything else on. And who exactly "commissioned" it?' This was said with fingers signalling quotation marks.

'Jen... she said her friend Suzie loved the one I made for her and Jen wants me to make it for Suzie's birthday.'

'Oh dear,' he sighed again, his head to one side, a look of faux sympathy on his face.

'What?'

'I'm sorry, darling, but I think Jen's probably making fun of you.'

'Why would she do that? I don't understand.'

'She didn't like the one you gave her; she's hardly likely to be asking for more.'

'But she said… you were there, at her party, you saw how pleased she was. She wore it on her shoulder all night. She said she loved it.'

'Of course she did, she'd hardly tell you she hated it, but I'm afraid I heard her saying something quite nasty about it to one of her friends later. I didn't tell you. I didn't want to hurt you, but I can't watch you make a fool of yourself all over again… darling. Think about it. She owns Prada and Gucci handbags. She doesn't want your handmade stuff… She was just being nice.'

So I abandoned the bag on the table and did the only thing I could still do well: I finished cooking dinner. I'd made lamb boulangère from Elizabeth David's *French Provincial Cooking* – a book David's mother swore by when she was alive. It had taken me all day to prepare, and if she'd still been with us I'm sure even Joyless Joy would have approved. But I stood over the lamb, my eyes brimming with tears, feeling so upset that Jen would say something 'nasty' about my handbag, my gift. I'd really believed she loved it, especially when she asked for one for her friend Suzie. I wondered if Simon had perhaps misheard, or was exaggerating – lying even? But why would Simon say it if it wasn't true? And I have to admit it had sounded like her – it's the kind of thing Jen would say in one of her more humorously bitchy moods.

Within a few minutes, I'd reduced the sauce, carved the lamb and steamed the vegetables (Simon liked his al dente). I laid the plate of food before him and stood back waiting for his reaction. Surely this would wow him, and he'd forgive me for 'playing' with my sewing kit all day? But I could see by his flexing jaw that the very sight of me sewing a handbag when I should have been tending to the house had angered him. He chewed on meltingly tender lamb, a bright, luscious jus, fragrant with garlic and thyme, soaked up by the crispy golden roasts now dancing on his tongue.

I waited… and I waited, standing near him like I was on bloody *MasterChef* and holding my breath for the judges' verdict.

Eventually, he put down his knife and fork, the plate almost empty and, reaching for his phone, looked up at me. I felt like a waitress as I collected his plate.

'Did you enjoy that?' I almost wanted to add 'sir'.

'It was okay.' He pushed his seat back. 'The lamb was over-cooked.' He didn't even look at me, just stood up and walked away. 'And sort the boys out, they're running round the front garden like savages,' were his parting words as he left the room.

I've been so good at creating this idea of our 'perfect family' with him that no one would believe me if I said my marriage was less than perfect. I happily gave up my career to be a mother and sometimes I wonder what my life might have been had I pursued both a career and a family, but Simon said there was no such thing as 'having it all' and this was right for us. But who is 'us'? Am I even part of us – recently I've felt like nothing, just an extension of Simon's needs and wishes, while he waits for the opportunity to get rid of me and put a ring on Caroline's finger. I've been waiting, knowing I was never good enough, knowing he will leave me one day like my mother, like Emily.

Emily would be nearly ten years old now, and I think about her almost all the time. She had Simon's blue eyes like the other children, who have all inherited his left-handedness too. It was too soon to know if Emily would have been left-handed, but I often wonder what she'd be like. But I'll never know because she died… and it was all my fault.

CHAPTER THIRTEEN

It should have been the best time of my life, but it was the worst. I had a perfect, longed-for new baby but was deeply depressed, unable to cope with anything. Simon was working long hours and he'd come home and reluctantly take over. Some nights he was tired and resentful and he'd get frustrated and angry with me. On these nights, I was glad Sophie was with Joy. It may not have been fun for her, but at least she wasn't lying in bed listening to her father and I rowing, while Emily screamed in the background. Then one night he just didn't come home.

It was after eleven when I really started to worry; if Simon went out for a drink he was usually home by then because he had to be up in the morning for work. I'd heard him talking quietly on his phone late at night and I'd smelled perfume on him, so on top of sleepless nights and depression I was feeling paranoid that he might be seeing someone else. I'd called his mobile and left several tearful messages, but now I was worried he'd had an accident. He didn't drive drunk, but he might take a chance in his fancy new car after a few pints and I just kept looking at my baby's face and wondering if she still had a father.

Over the next few hours I became more distraught. I called his friends, the various pubs he might have been to and then the police station. When there was no luck, I put Emily in her pushchair, wrapped myself in Simon's overcoat and set off into the night to look for him. It was stormy, the wind was freezing and the rain spattered like ice on my face, running down my chin into the opening of the coat, soaking me through. I was walking and crying and it was way after midnight when a young couple stopped me to ask if I was okay. I told them I was fine and to leave me alone. I was quite rude. I didn't care what anyone thought – nor did I want anyone's 'help'. I just wanted Simon.

But after walking for hours, while calling him constantly, I headed home in the vain hope he might be there. I imagined him sitting on the sofa, exhausted from a day's work, wondering where I was. He was all I had apart from Sophie and Emily – he was everything to me – and I trudged back to the flat like a homing pigeon. When I opened the door of our little flat and it was as dark and empty as when I'd left, I just broke down. I was desperate, crawling the walls with anxiety and fear. Was he with someone? Had he crashed the car? I didn't know which was worse, for him to be lying in a ditch or in another woman's bed.

Throughout most of this time, Emily screamed, her cries filling my head. I tried to soothe her, but found it so hard because I couldn't think straight. By 4 a.m. Simon still wasn't home and I could barely move for exhaustion and worry. I put my baby in her cot in our bedroom and lay on the bed, just willing him to walk through the door. I didn't care where he'd been and I daren't ask him, I just wanted him with me. He was the only one who loved me and the only one who could calm Emily.

Eventually I started to drift off into sleep, but it seemed the more I drifted, the louder Emily's screams were. As I fell into an uneasy sleep, her cries provided the soundtrack to my nightmares of her drowning and me watching, unable to save her. So I got out of bed and picked her up, holding her against me, rocking her and, miraculously, she stopped crying, and I held her longer, comforted by her downy baby head against my cheek, her snuffly little breaths.

Once asleep I put her back in her cot, but of course the minute I climbed back onto my bed she would start again. This happened several times until we were both crying again, and I gathered her up from her cot for the final time, my face next to her little hot head, our tears ebbing as we consoled ourselves in each other. I think that night was when I finally loved her. I'd bonded at last in the middle of a storm, and carried her back to our big double bed and gently lay her down next to me. I was happy; this was unconditional love. I'd searched for it all my life and, here in my arms, this little one needed me and I her. It was probably seconds before I fell asleep, and I dreamed of soft pillows and babies with angel wings.

I awoke in the morning remembering that Simon wasn't there but also remembering that my feelings for Emily had finally arrived. I glanced over to her cot, but she wasn't there and she wasn't crying, then I turned to see her lifeless body next to me. Her eyes were wide open. But she wasn't awake.

Simon turned up about the same time as the ambulance. All he could say was 'what have you done, Marianne?'

We both cried an awful lot. I never really stopped. It isn't just the loss though that is incalculable – it's the terrible, terrible guilt. And it's also why I don't blame Simon for the way he treats me and for never trusting me with our children. Why should he, when I can't even trust myself?

Simon's home late again tonight – he smells of expensive perfume and guilt. He also seems distracted; I'm not surprised, he's probably just left her bed. While I'm supposed to believe he's been working, she's probably been riding him into sexual oblivion most of the evening. No doubt she looks great on top and dismounts with grace, like the pony club tart that she is.

His slap from the other night has developed into a purple bruise down the side of my face. I usually cover my bruises in concealer to protect him from his own crime and pretend it didn't happen. But now I want him to see it, I want him to face what he is, what he's become. I walk towards him, turning my face slightly so he doesn't miss it. He looks up from his phone and doesn't flinch. I'm so conflicted; my feelings are all over the place. I hate him but I still love him, still want him.

'Have you been working late? I ask.

He nods absently, scrolling through his phone; I'm not even important enough to warrant a verbal response.

'I wish you'd called. The dinner might be spoiled. I've been cooking all day.'

I know I'm pushing it, risking a tsunami of rage – but then again it could be a passionate kiss as he tries to reclaim me, to convince me everything's fine.

He throws his phone down on the kitchen table with an exasperated sigh, like I'm a buzzing fly and need to be swatted. 'I've just stepped through the door and already the whingeing, Marianne.' He's holding out his hands in despair, like I'm the one who's at fault because *he's* late home.

'I'm not whingeing, all I *said* is I've been cooking. I've made something special.'

'Oh, I'm so sorry you've been here all day in our million-pound house *cooking*. How terrible your life is. I wonder, is there a support group you can join?'

I ignore his sarcasm and continue buttering bread for the children's school lunches tomorrow. But my anger at the thought of him being with her makes me brave and I can't help but say, 'It's just good if I know what you're doing… if you were working late I mean.' Our eyes meet. He's surprised at my bravery.

'As a matter of fact, I wasn't working late. I went for a drink,' he says, holding my stare.

'Oh, you had a drink with people from work?' I ask after a decent interval that implies polite small talk rather than interrogation. When he doesn't answer, I look up, waiting for his answer. I hold my breath. I don't want to know. And yet I do. I *do* want to know. Will it be elaborate lies involving people and places that don't exist, or something closer to the truth? If it's a good lie that means he wants to keep her a secret, but if he's open, then he's not scared of me finding out and he wants me to know.

I can tell by the way his eyes glitter that he's about to hurt me.

'Not people, a *person*,' he says, defiantly. And without taking his cold eyes from mine, he adds, 'Someone whose company I enjoy. Do you have a problem with me enjoying a drink with someone I admire after a long, hard day?'

My heart flinches, but I don't outwardly react. I let it go and open a jar of peanut butter for the children's sandwiches, glancing at him as he picks up a breadstick from the kitchen table and breaks it in two. I feel the break in my bones, aware he's looking at me still, saying nothing yet challenging me to ask more questions. But I won't. His confession would mean I have to take action and I can't. I'm not ready for that. Not yet.

I stand with my back to him, both of us far apart but covered by the same thick blanket of silence.

'Have you ever considered your mother might have been psychotic?' He says this calmly, picking up a bottle of wine, his head to one side like he's contemplating a philosophical question to be debated. He plucked this from his kit of emotional weaponry – now sharpening the knife to jam into my back as I make sweet little triangle sandwiches for the boys.

'I don't like to think too much about my mother,' I answer, spreading organic peanut butter briskly. I'm trying not to engage my emotions. I have to respond in a rational manner; I don't want to light any fires. Thing is, I don't feel rational. I feel crazy – his comment punched me hard in the stomach and I'm still reeling, but he mustn't see this, so I continue with the conversation, trying to sound objective. 'I think my mother was a manic depressive, but perhaps this was compounded by postnatal depression which presented in a way that was hard to diagnose.'

'*Presented? Hard to diagnose?* Have we been on the internet again?' He gives a mirthless laugh and pours himself a glass of red. 'Marianne, she was a zombie for years, then she slashed her wrists in the bath. It was hardly the baby blues,' he says, insulting my mother's memory and trivialising postnatal depression in one sweeping sentence.

'She wasn't a *zombie*… she was ill. I just remember someone saying she seemed worse after she had me, and then she had the baby and that's when she…' I stop, unable to go on and too weak to argue.

'Yes, and all I'm saying is she was probably psychotic… and you may be the same.'

Yes, okay I'm a psycho, if that's what you want me to be, Simon.

I don't answer him, and after a while he realises he won't get any fight out of me tonight.

'I'm going to bed,' he says, picking up his wine glass, and without turning back he leaves the room.

I keep going like I'm programmed to do, and despite knowing everything is crumbling around me, I put hummus in a little pot for Sophie's lunch. Then I take a large, sharp kitchen knife and slice carrots, imagining they are Caroline's long fingers. Even when there are more than enough carrot sticks, I keep chopping, chopping, chopping.

Look at me, Simon, chopping your girlfriend's fingers off like a psycho.

The conversation we just had was telling – it's the first time ever that Simon hasn't tried to hide where he's been or who he was with. She must be very special. This isn't an imagined one-night stand with a waitress, or a female figment of my fractured mind. No, Caroline is real. I know the pills can make me confused, but their dirty little secret is written in black and white, smeared across months of emails.

I hate her.

Apart from the fact I still love my husband, I don't really have any choice. I must stay and fight to keep my family together. I'm not financially independent and having not worked since we married don't even have an up-to-date CV, so couldn't support me and the kids without him. Besides, he'd never allow me to leave and take the kids, even if I had the means – so I'm stuck, because I'll never leave my children.

I can live with a man who doesn't love me. I'm used to being unloved; I spent my childhood with people who didn't want me. Yet I can't help but wonder after almost ten years and four children, three of our own, if he really has nothing left for me. He loved me once and I can't help but be reminded of that when I read what he says to her, but I worry that all I am now is what comes between him and Caroline's happy ending. Will his next move be to have me locked up again, making the coast clear for her? She could step in and take over my role – which is why I have to appear to be calm and stable and not do or say anything rash. I don't feel calm and stable.

Caroline is waiting in the wings and I have to do something. Because of her I am suddenly surplus to requirements. Simon has found my replacement.

I was here first. I want my life back. I want her gone.

CHAPTER FOURTEEN

The following day, Simon's gone by the time I head downstairs. I'd slept in the spare room; I felt uneasy about lying next to him, like lying with a stranger. I couldn't sleep and heard him leaving before 6 a.m. I lay alone in the double sofa bed meant for guests, knowing he was going to her, no doubt giving her an early morning wake-up call before their working day of performing miracles on mere mortals. I try not to think of them naked, wrapped in her sheets as I cover my bruise in Touche Éclat and yell at the boys to 'hurry or you'll be late.'

Toast pops up briskly from the toaster, making me jump, and I laugh a little too loudly. The air is filled with the fragrance of morning, burnt toast and strong, sweet coffee, but instead of providing comfort, it makes me want to puke. Perhaps I should take a pill now and not wait until later today? I'm on edge – my skin feels tingly, as though the nerves are on the outside, exposed to the elements.

I take a pill and before the tiredness kicks in I get the boys to school, enjoying the freedom of driving along, listening to the radio, and therefore unable to log on to a device and watch my husband's affair. I tell myself if you look hard enough, you can always find a silver lining. And while Simon's doing his mistress, I can do what I want to do too. So when I encounter Jen in the playground, I'm delighted to catch up and take our chat to a nearby coffee shop. I feel raw and I need to talk to someone.

'Peter's being a twat,' is Jen's opening gambit over low-fat muffins and skinny flat whites. She then goes on to regale me with a story about how tight he is with money and how he baulked at buying her a Chanel handbag for her birthday. I dream of having such a simple problem but nod and shake my head in all the right places, something I'm used to with Simon. But Jen seems to pick up on my mood and stops talking about herself – eventually. 'I know, I know, first-world problems,' she sighs, taking a sip of her coffee. 'You okay, sweetie? There's me going on and on and I haven't even asked you about your weekend.'

'Oh, it was fine, nothing special…' I want to tell her everything. I want to tell her about the emails, about Caroline's sparkly teeth, her crumpled sheets, her fucking basket of champagne and strawberries. Stupidly I want to ask her if she thinks there's a chance my husband might still love me. I need a friend. It used to be him, but not any more. He has Caroline now – and she has him.

'You seem a bit down, sweetie. What's that… oh, is it a bruise?' Jen looks concerned.

I nod slowly, unsure of what to say, but tell her I banged my head opening a cabinet door.

'Oh… I thought for a minute you and Simon had been having fisticuffs.' She giggles, but she's probing.

I smile and shake my head.

'But something's bothering you isn't it, darling? I understand if you'd rather not… talk about it, but, hey, we're friends, that's what friends are for, to share worries… and…' She leans forward and touches my hand. She's looking at me with such concern I want to throw my arms around her and cry.

'I think Simon's having an affair,' I hear myself say over the babble and crockery.

Jen looks at me, her mouth wide open, her spoon held mid-air over her cup, like she physically can't move with shock. I almost want to laugh but realise this would be inappropriate given what I've just said.

'Jen, are you okay?' I say, as she sits, stopped dead in her chattering tracks.

'Sorry, sweetie,' she says, coming round. 'But I can't believe he'd... What makes you think he's...?'

I shrug.

She abandons her spoon and touches my arm again. The diamonds sparkle on her fingers as she clutches at my jacket sleeve. 'Do you know who it is... this... woman?' She crosses her long legs and leans in even closer for the details.

I explain a little about Caroline, a vague sketchy outline about 'a colleague', with a few choice words thrown in. She seems incredulous, doubtful even, and I'm tempted to tell her about the emails. I know what I saw, but I don't want to say it out loud. It makes it too real, and I'm not sure I can trust Jen not to tell the whole playground.

She raises her eyebrows, calls the waitress over and orders two more skinny flat whites. 'I shouldn't have a second one. Too much dairy. I'm trying to lose weight but I'm just so... surprised and upset for you. We need the caffeine, my love.'

I'm soothed by how the inclusive 'we' makes me feel like there's finally someone batting for my team. I excuse myself and go to the toilet, where I start to cry, I'm so overwhelmed by Jen's kindness. Then I throw up. So much for the extra tablet I took this morning, that's now sailing down the pipes. I just hope I can keep everything together. Telling Jen has made it real; until now it was just inside my head.

'So have you said anything to Simon?' she asks on my return. Our fresh coffees have arrived and she puts her spoon in her cup, stirring too slowly for too long, her eyes on me all the time.

It crosses my mind that he may have already got to her: 'Marianne's ill – she imagines things. She might tell you I'm having an affair, several in fact. She always does this when she's ill.' I can hear him saying it now. 'Of course it isn't true, she's not herself, poor love – we call it a headache, but it's so much more.' I know the script because he's used it before on other friends I've dared to have over the years.

I shouldn't have said anything, I want to swallow my words back down with the second skinny flat white.

'No,' I say, taking a sip of the hot, milky drink. 'I haven't confronted him.' I say this quietly.

Jen now has her head in her hands, shaking it slowly, eventually emerging to announce loudly, 'But Simon's the perfect husband. You two seem so happy… I can't believe he'd *do* this to you. Like on the first day of term when I saw him in the playground, he'd left you in bed, he was so worried about you being ill, having a headache…'

At the word 'headache', I bristle.

'I didn't have a…' Her interest is so piqued, I feel like she's interrogating me and I want to run away. 'I… I don't know, Jen, I can't be sure, perhaps I'm putting two and two together and making an affair,' I say, backtracking now.

I feel claustrophobic. I've said more to her in half an hour than I have to anyone in weeks and as much as I like Jen, Simon's right. She's a gossip, and I can't trust her to be discreet. I shouldn't be discussing this with her; apart from anything else, what if I've got this all wrong – again? I was sure last time, and the time before that, and then after having a total meltdown resulting in all kinds of shit for everyone, I realised I'd imagined it all.

I need to take another pill, but I don't have any with me, so check my watch deliberately. 'Oh damn, almost forgot, I have a doctor's appointment,' I lie. I get up to leave and, shocked at my sudden departure, Jen grabs my hand as I stand up.

'Doctors? Nothing serious I hope, sweetie?'

'No, it's nothing.' I'm on the verge of tears, which Jen sees and becomes even more cloying.

Still clutching my arm, she tries to make me stay, but I have to get out of here and pull my arm away. 'Marianne, you can't leave like this, you're upset… what are you going to do?'

I say I don't know but I'm fine and run out of the coffee shop, leaving her standing by our table, filled with half-drunk coffees and uneaten muffins, pleading with me not to go.

I feel bad. Jen's such a caring person, and that's what I need at the moment, but I panicked; I find it hard to judge people these days. In spite of my sudden doubts about telling her, Jen made me feel like I have a friend. And even for a little while it's just what I needed. I hope I haven't offended her by leaving so abruptly, but, as Simon says, if a friend's worth having she'll accept you whatever.

Arriving back home, I feel like I left something behind at the coffee shop and it's made me uneasy. I question myself again about telling Jen. If she's the gossip Simon makes her out to be, she could be repeating what I'd told her to one of the other school mums right now. Then again, Jen's my friend and is concerned about me. Surely she knows that I told her my fears in confidence and wouldn't discuss them at the school gate?

I am drawn upstairs to Simon's office; now I've shared my suspicions with Jen, albeit briefly and vaguely, I feel the need to double-check I'm right. I can't help but doubt myself after everything that's gone before. It's easier to access the emails from his laptop and as he sometimes checks the history on my phone he's more likely to find out I've been snooping if I use that. I have to smile. Jen would be horrified at the prospect of Peter checking *her* phone's history. Recently I've asked myself how Jen would react to the way Simon treats me. She wouldn't sit by and watch him have an affair, she wouldn't allow him to usurp her in the family, talk disrespectfully in front of the kids. Then again, Jen has a family who love her and isn't grateful for any crumb her husband throws her because she's scared she might lose him, and everything else she has.

I open Simon's office door and once again step in, like Alice in Wonderland – the nightmare version. I open up the laptop, and go through the looking glass again, uncertain of what I might find. I type 'Caroline' and, like magic, his secret life emerges before me, and I wonder what fresh hell there is for me today.

I go straight to the emails and, yes, there's no doubt – I didn't imagine this. But today, among the heart emojis and kisses, there seems to have been a hint of trouble in paradise. Apparently she's still upset that he was a little 'grumpy' when he arrived late at hers the other evening.

Ah, so she's disappointing him already? Isn't it the wife who's not supposed to understand?

But even a sign of trouble in paradise can't stop the sting when I read the next few lines.

> Babe, I just can't help but feel upset that you didn't tell her last night. I know these things can't be rushed, but it's been six months now and I can't bear for you to stay there in that hellish atmosphere. You adored Nicole, and if you ask me, you were grieving when you met Marianne and clearly don't love her the same way, the right way. I hate to say this, but do you think you may have married Marianne on the rebound? She's not your forever person, is she? And clearly not the mother you'd choose for your children.

I feel like I've been whacked in the face and ask myself again why I keep flagellating myself with this. I am filled with hatred for this woman, this stranger who, having met me once in the fucking wine aisle at Waitrose, thinks she's qualified to asses my faults, my personality, my capability, my marriage. How dare she condemn me with her tin-pot psychology and thirty-something naivety. It isn't all marriage by numbers, and it isn't all black and white. *There are grey areas, Caroline, but don't dig too deep into your lover's marriage – you might not like what you see.*

I scroll down for his response.

Oh darling, it's so like you to think of the children, if only Marianne had your thoughtfulness – but she doesn't and that's just one of the problems. I know I've been dragging my feet, but trust me I'm working on it, we'll be together soon. I hate that you feel insecure, darling, and you might be right, I think I probably did marry her in a state of grief.

He's working on it, they'll be together soon. Over my dead body.

Our marriage has been a sham. As you know, we haven't had sex since the boys were conceived and we barely speak, except for her whingeing about how bored she is and how she hates spending time cooking meals for me. Last night she was so angry she hadn't made me anything to eat and, of course, I'd have made myself a snack, but after a long day in surgery, I was too tired so just went to bed.

I am furious. The injustice, the lies. Yes they might be little lies about the minutiae of domesticity, but these little lies define me. He's making me look like I'm cruel, incapable, unwilling to even try to be a wife and mother. None of this is true. He'd come home late after drinking with a colleague he 'admired', opened a bottle of wine, tried to start a row about my mother's mental state, thus implying mine was inevitable, and stormed off to bed.

And we haven't had sex since the boys were conceived?

He's lying to you too, Caroline.

I scroll to her response. Surely she's not buying the well-worn cliché that this married man doesn't have sex with his wife?

Babe, that's outrageous, she's supposed to be your wife, your teammate. I know your sex life has been non-existent, and I think you're a bloody saint, but there's no excuse for her laziness. She's at home all day, the least she could do is make you a sandwich.

I laugh to myself at this – I'd love to see his face if I handed him a sandwich one evening. She really has no idea. And my *laziness*?

I read on, barely able to contain my anger at his lies, at the homewrecker's sanctimonious reaction to his far-fetched stories...

It's clear that your wife doesn't appreciate what she has and, as you've always said, it's not like she cares about you. Simon, babe, please just take her to the doctor's and get her some appropriate care. I know how it is. After we talked last night, it helped me to understand what you've been through. I know there are times you wish you could turn back the clock, but you can't, you married her and you now have to extricate yourself from this damaging situation. You've tried your best for her, God knows you've given her everything, including your love and support, but illness aside, she seems to get off on complaining, on being permanently unhappy and all she does is moan about her privileged life. I understand the dynamic so much more now. She is one of those people who just take and don't give, and however much you try to love and help her, she can't love you back. From what you tell me, she clearly set her sights on you, a surgeon, and got pregnant quickly so you had no choice but to marry her. I know you only got married for your lovely mum, but Marianne tricked you, she knew you'd do the right thing by her because that's the kind of wonderful man you are.

Oh, my God, he's even lied about when I got pregnant and why we married. He wasn't forced to marry me. He loved me, he wanted marriage and a family – with me. But he can't even admit that now. And 'your lovely mum'. I don't think so – I have to smile at this.

I continue to read, drinking it in, all the lies, all the posturing, all the 'babes' and the fucking 'darlings'.

You've given Marianne so much, please don't give her the rest of your life, because I don't know how long I can wait. I don't mean to sound horrid, but you'll be doing the kindest thing by saying goodbye to her and she can then find her own life and hopefully some happiness, because she isn't happy with you.

Oh Caroline. I expected more of you.

I bet she calls herself a fucking feminist. Well, what about her sister over here who's bleeding while she sticks the knife in even further?

And his response to her diatribe of crap is... even more crap.

Darling, I will finish things, but before I do I have to check with David and make sure everything's watertight. He's been my solicitor for years and he knows the score. I've arranged to have drinks with him next Wednesday evening and I'll lay it on the line. He'll know exactly what I need to do so we can keep the house and the children. This is all new to me, darling, as you know I've never strayed before, never even thought about another woman until you. I'm afraid you've changed everything, in a good way, but I just need you to hang on in there. I need you and can't imagine the rest of my life without you. I love you so much. X

So, he's seeing our solicitor next Wednesday? This is even more serious than I'd feared. This isn't a fling that he'll get over and leave behind, but the end of our marriage – sooner rather than later if Simon has his way.

My mouth is dry, my chest tight as I scroll down to see one final message from her.

Oh babe, sorry to go on. She needs to be somewhere safe where she can't hurt herself or anyone else for that matter. I'm going to say this now because I can't say it to your face, it's too

painful – but, Simon, you already lost one child because of her.
Aren't you worried you might lose another?

I am so hurt; each tiny shard of information pierces my heart
and lodges in my brain. Yes, I figured he'd tell her that I was mad
and a liability as a mother, but I was thinking biscuit crumbs and
McDonald's. This is on a different scale – I honestly didn't think
he'd tell her about Emily.

Finally something's going to happen for them. And to me.

CHAPTER FIFTEEN

'Hello, darling.' He's back from work and I'm strutting down the stairs, greeting him with a confident hug. I feel different, empowered. Reading today's emails made the fog clear from my head. I'm not mad. I'm not delusional. He wants an end to us, to our marriage, our family and our lies. And now I'm reading his thoughts – his perception of me and our life together – I'm beginning to feel the same. So my marriage might be over, but if Simon and his homewrecking mistress think they're going to take my children they have another thing coming.

There is a chink of light in the darkness. I don't have to sit helplessly waiting to be destroyed – I may not win, but I can at least fight this.

I kiss him on the cheek while wanting to punch him in the face. 'Had a hard day?'

You lying, cheating bastard.

'A very good day actually.'

I wander into the kitchen and he follows me.

'Oh really?' I say, almost flirtatiously.

'Yes… you can now address me as Mr Wilson *Senior* Consultant Surgeon!'

'Wow! Well done, darling,' I say, hugging him, wondering if he told her before me, while gazing longingly at the row of kitchen knives.

'Yes, it's been a tough few weeks. I heard Cookson wanted to give it to someone else, but I convinced him with my amazing skills and talents,' he only half-jokes.

'Well, congratulations. No one can say you don't deserve it.' I mean, he's been sliming up to the revolting Professor Cookson for some time, and that can't have been easy.

'Well, the prof says he has faith in me, says he's impressed by my credentials, my work ethic… the other guy is a bit of an unknown quantity, single, rented flat, no roots.'

'Oh yes, well having a wife and family in the background always helps in these things – settled family life.' I smile through gritted teeth.

'I hardly think you can take credit for my new position, Marianne,' he spits.

I'm so raw with emotion I want to lash out, want to hurt him like he's hurt me. But instead I smile and go into Stepford mode while harbouring wicked thoughts about getting rid of Caroline. I have this urge to ask about her, how she is, just to see his face, but if I do, he's likely to call Saskia my therapist again, 'concerned' about 'Marianne's erratic behaviour', my apparently 'obsessive and irrational jealousy'. He isn't the only one. The mums at previous school gates, the neighbours from the places we've lived – they've all turned against me, assumed I'm some deranged madwoman who's likely to kill them all in their beds.

Yes, there have been times when, driven crazy by grief, pills and life, I've overreacted, when I must have imagined those things that never happened. But not this time. This time is different, because I *know*. I *know*. This time I will be smarter. There will be no pints and insults hurled across a bar at some woman. I won't scream and shout and behave like 'a fishwife'. I won't accuse anyone of anything – yet. I will bide my time and tear them apart from within, as they are doing to me.

I think of Caroline, lying in *our* bed, and newly promoted Senior Consultant Surgeon Mr fucking Simon Wilson next to her, reading Thackeray or something equally pompous and impenetrable. She'd be in a strappy little nightgown and would lean over and take the book from him, remove his glasses and…

I need to take a couple of pills, but I want to be aware, focussed. I know I'm in danger of being removed from my life and being doped up would only assist this.

'I hope you've taken your meds,' he says absently, sitting down at the table, waiting for the food I've slaved over all day. I sometimes think he reads my mind… or watches me.

'Yes,' I lie. 'Just now, in fact. I need to get you served up before I go all groggy.'

'Good. I don't know which is worse, you falling about all over the place and blacking out or attacking perfect strangers… On second thoughts, I prefer the former, the medicated version,' he says without a smile.

I don't react – it's what he wants – but I'm not biting. I swirl salted butter into green beans and place them with the beef on his plate. 'I've made your favourite, boeuf bourguignon, a perfect celebration meal for a Senior Consultant,' I say, smiling brightly.

I hope it chokes you, Simon.

I present the plate to him with a pretend flourish, wishing I'd crushed the pills up into his beef so he could feel what it's like to see the world through a mist before blacking out, not sure who you are or where you've been, what's real and what isn't.

He bites into the meat and I wait for his comment. 'Not bad… not bad,' he says.

Oh, so nothing to complain about tonight?

'Oh…'

I spoke too soon.

'What's wrong?' I ask.

'What on earth have you done to the green beans? They're like old rope. I can't eat these; they're overcooked.'

Ah, I thought it was too good to be true.

'Oh, I'm sorry, darling. I can cook you some more?' I suggest brightly, suddenly wanting to ram his head into the plate with all my weight.

'No, don't put yourself out.'

I won't, but I'd like to put you out.

I wander into the living room before I do or say something I'll regret. I'm suddenly filed with such rage, my feelings fighting each other constantly. I hate that he loves someone else. I don't think I want him any more, but I want to keep our life. I feel like she's stealing my life from under me and he's handing it to her – it makes me mad as hell. The kids are in bed and I tidy around a little, then read my book, a romantic comedy – I need some of that in my life.

Eventually Simon comes in looking for something to criticise.

'What's that trash you're reading?' he says, right on cue.

'It's good actually, it's funny – a love story about this couple who meet on holiday. They don't speak the same language but they get married anyway. Jen lent it to me.'

'Sounds like her kind of nonsense,' he huffs as he picks up his *Telegraph* newspaper from the coffee table and turns to leave. I asked if the *Guardian* could also be delivered, but he said it was 'for leftie luvvies', so that was that.

'Darling,' I call brightly after him. He turns around, anger waiting in his face. 'Congratulations... on the promotion. You make me so proud.'

You will not get to me. I won't give you an excuse to remove me. I'm here to stay.

He shrugs and leaves the room – his celebrating will be done elsewhere, with another woman.

Now I'm alone, I pick up one of the boys' iPads lying on the coffee table and log in, thinking how nice it would be to have my own tablet or laptop. I was delighted when I got my iPhone, an old one of Simon's, but he told me I had to share my password and he has some kind of tracking device so he knows where I am. I recently suggested I have my own iPad, but Simon says anything I want to do I can do on my phone. This is true, but he checks my history, the things I don't delete, and I can't see pictures of his mistress so well on the little phone screen. I want to scrutinise every detail and when I have to use my phone – sometimes I have to get my fix any way I can – I feel like I need a magnifying glass, which would be taking the Sherlock Holmes analogy a little too far. I remember the pin codes for the boys' iPads because I set them up for them on their birthdays when they received one each and thank God they haven't changed them. I can only do this when they are asleep because they spend their waking hours glued to the things, despite us putting restrictions on screen time. They are always smuggling them upstairs and protesting the usual defence when caught: 'It's for school!'

Anyway, I now have peace, quiet, no interruptions from husband or children, and can lurk wantonly all over Caroline's social media. I go to Facebook first, and the bigger screen shows even clearer skin, a face that's never had sleepless nights over children, no worries, a shiny happy girl with a supermarket basket full of alcohol and a penchant for rough sex with my husband. This new photo isn't a selfie. She's glowing for the camera. The man she loves probably took it – clicking away, telling her how gorgeous she is. She's clutching a glass of what might be G&T, and her face has that 'just had sex' flush. Her lipstick's been reapplied though and her white teeth compete with dazzling lips. I feel an unwelcome lurch in my belly, a moment of recognition, recalling a time he made me feel like this. Glowing. Flushed. Dazzling.

I pore over every detail of the picture – even the backdrop is beautiful. Expensive wallpaper, huge green fronds on navy blue. Stunning really. It gives her an exotic air, and I imagine, by the pile of terracotta pots and the forearm of bangles, that she's travelled.

She probably had a great gap year, no doubt funded by Mummy and Daddy.

Even if my husband doesn't love me any more, I refuse to allow some surgical slut to plan my destiny, thank you very much. I lurch between hating him and hating her; I don't know who I hate the most. I know it should be him – he's married, she's single – but still I hate her more.

Looking at her photos makes me anxious, so I pop into the kitchen and take a pill after all, as Simon suggested – just to get me through the night. I can't trust myself without them. If I slip up once, then Simon will be straight on to my therapist, who'll be straight on to my psychiatrist and before I know it I'll be back in hospital – and I don't want to give him or his bloody solicitor any more ammunition. People listen to a surgeon when he says his wife is sick, that she needs more medication, that she *has* to be in hospital. Doctors listen because he's one of them; he speaks their language. He can come up with all kinds of jargon, translate the simplest most sane act into madness, and because of the medication I don't always remember what I did or said so find it impossible to challenge him. Not knowing reality from fantasy is a scary place to be and you need to be able to trust the one who holds your hand as you walk together. I used to trust Simon, but not any more.

I go to bed, but I can't sleep and find myself sitting on the toilet at 3 a.m., my phone providing all the light I need as I move on from Facebook to investigate her pretty Instagram account. I can only imagine how I look, my phone up in my face, eyes screwed up so I can see every detail, capture every moment, every visual nuance. I'm like a crazed drug addict – exhausted, scared, but unable to tear myself away from her curated online life, only satisfied when I'm looking at her photos, checking where she is. I have become obsessed, from her smiling face, to the jangly bangles and shiny lipstick. I look at her again, framed by the tropical wallpaper and clutching the same glass of G&T. She must like this photo a lot to put it on all her social media accounts. I don't. I hate it. I think she looks smug, like she stole something precious and got away with it.

The cat that got the cream.

I'm tired. The medication has knocked me out, but not enough, and I'm overwrought. I'm my own worst enemy. This addiction, like all addictions, is never sated. It's always 'just one more click', and it leaves me empty, more desperate for a hit than before. I should never have gone on her Facebook page before bedtime. I do one more click, see another photo and remember how Simon went out last Saturday night to play tennis. He's never gone out on a Saturday before. Always said we should spend time together as a family. In spite of everything, we've stuck to that and most Saturdays we'll take the kids to the park and after their tea the boys go to bed, Sophie disappears into her room and we binge on box sets. I usually make a light supper, bake warm bread to dunk in a piping hot shared bowl of home-made broccoli and stilton soup. But thinking about it, the last time we did that was weeks ago, and he said my soup was 'too rich'.

I see the photo now on her Instagram: white, tight shorts, a little T shirt, a racquet in one hand a bottle of Peroni in the other after a sweaty, vigorous session with my husband. #Tennis #TennisDrinks #TennisAlmostAsGoodAsSex.

I wish I could add my own hashtag – #WithSomeoneElsesHusband.

I'm trying to click off. I have to stop this agony of a front-row seat on my husband's other, better relationship. But unable to leave, I take one last glance at her page, and then I see in the last few seconds she's added a new photo…

And there it is, the tiny phone screen framing the room in an eerie cold light. Grey amorphous limbs, an almost face, blurry lines made blurrier by the tears springing to my eyes. A baby scan photo.

'Look who we met today!' #BabyScan #Pregnant #NewMum #LoveIs #MyBaby.

CHAPTER SIXTEEN

I don't know how I've got through the past few days. I've wanted to say something so many times, but resisted, and it's making me so anxious and tearful, I have to keep disappearing to the loo to cry when anyone's home. I wonder how Simon feels? Is he happy, worried, angry? He's so keen on his privacy. I know he would hate that she's put it on Instagram, but he wouldn't know because he doesn't have Instagram. Maybe that's why she puts these pictures on there – a secret life she's desperate to share but can't because he's married. Or maybe she wants me to know?

You could have anyone, so why take my husband?

I can't sleep at night, and my fists are permanently clenched. I imagine a staged suicide pact, pushing them both under a moving train and feigning distress and surprise when the police arrive to tell me.

What have they done to me? What have I become?

I must try and think of nice things, so I think of kittens and bunnies, then wonder if she has any. No, I'm not a cliché – her bunny is safe. But her cosy future with Simon and their new baby isn't – it's about to hit a few roadblocks.

This morning, I woke up and felt okay for the first time in days. I'm coming to terms with the situation, but that doesn't mean I will accept it and lie in the road waiting for their truck to go over me. She's pregnant with my husband's child, my children's half-sibling, and they think I'll be the last to know.

I busy myself by cleaning rooms that don't need cleaning, scrubbing and spritzing and wiping away the unborn baby. But I see them all in my shiny, scrubbed surfaces, my glistening windows, and when I look at my beautifully painted walls in my favourite shade, there they are.

She's even taken away my Borrowed Light.

Like an old-fashioned projector, they are on my walls, a moving video of her and Simon cooing over their baby. The tableau widens in my head and I start to cry as I see Sophie and the boys are there too, all simpering over their newborn sibling.

Daddy's little bastard.

I look closely at the image on the wall… or is it in my head? I look into her baby's face and my heart misses a beat. She looks just like Emily.

But Caroline won't let her baby die like I did. She will give birth quietly, her milk will flow and she will calm and soothe. She will be the perfect mother that I could never be.

I am so hurt, so bruised, so empty; my breasts ache and the emptiness in my belly is fresh and raw. I turn away from the tableau, the perfect family – and remind myself this is *my* family, and she can't have it. She can keep her bastard, but she's not having my children.

I have to do something to stop this. Her email suggestions to get me the 'help' I apparently need (no doubt in a long-term psychiatric ward) will now be fast-tracked. Who knows what she'll be prepared to do to get what she wants and have one big happy family now? Yes, I need to do something. Quick.

I tried the nice way, tried to win him over with my delicious cooking. I made his home life more perfect than ever. But clearly my lemon roast poussin wasn't enough to pull him away from her firm young thighs. Extreme times call for extreme measures, so plan B will now take shape. I'm quite breathless with excitement as I make a call to the hospital. I dial the number I know so well, and when a woman's voice answers I say, 'Could I possibly speak to Caroline Harker – she's a surgeon in Cardiology?'

CHAPTER SEVENTEEN

I'm now on hold after speaking briefly to a bouncy-sounding receptionist who is, apparently, 'Katie speaking.'

A moment later, Katie is back on the line, and I'm devastated to be told that Caroline is not currently available. I express my disappointment and Katie's now on script, telling me some rubbish about how I need to email the department and someone, one day, might get back to me, if there's a fucking 'r' in the month or something like that. I don't hear Katie's stupid words; I'm formulating my own.

'Oh, I'm so sorry, I should have explained. I'm Simon Wilson's wife… Dr Simon Wilson, Cardio… Senior Consultant?' I add in a you-may-have-heard-of-him voice.

'Oh… Mrs Wilson…' That changes Katie Jobsworth's tone – suddenly she's all melted chocolate.

'Obviously, I have Caroline's mobile number already. We're good friends,' I cut in before she can continue the fake fawn. 'But, silly me, I changed phones and now I don't seem to have it on my new one. Between us, Katie, I'm trying to organise Simon… my husband's… promotion party. He's just been made Senior Consultant and I'm throwing a surprise party to celebrate… Thing is I'm trying to get hold of all his colleagues. Top-secret stuff!' I add in my surgeon's wife voice.

'Oh… oh… well, I'm not supposed to give out staff mobile numbers, Mrs Wilson.' I hear the wavering in her voice – she doesn't want to break the rules, nor does she want to disrespect a senior surgeon's wife.

'Oh dear... of course, I understand. The last thing I would want is to get you into trouble, but it's just that I'm at a loss because Caz – I mean Caroline – promised to help me out. I have to admit, I do need her help...' I giggle girlishly, while wanting to puke. 'It would be such a shame to let Simon down...' I add.

'Oh, I'm sure it will be fine on this occasion...' she says. I wonder if not wanting to upset Simon is what persuades Katie; is she yet another one under his spell? I will never know, but suddenly it's 'open sesame' and Katie gives me Caroline's mobile number.

I thank her profusely and am really over the top, grateful the rumours about me haven't yet started, because at the last hospital the sodding 'Katies' used to cut me off.

No sooner am I profligate at Katie's feet, I'm straight back on my mobile and this time I'm licking my lips. It only takes two rings for our worlds to collide.

'Hello... hello, is that Caroline?' I ask, confident, breezy.

'Yes, this is Caroline, who's this?'

I savour the moment. I've caught her off guard. I'm in control. And that's how it's going to stay.

'It's Marianne...' I say after a pause, then give it another couple of seconds for my name to sink in, for her to fear the reason for my call.

'Marianne...' I can hear the shock in her voice. She wasn't expecting this. I love it.

Then before she can say anything else I'm straight in: 'We met a while ago, in Waitrose of all places – you work with my husband. Simon?' This is said in the voice of a woman who's happily married to the Senior Consultant Surgeon.

'I know this is completely out of the blue...' I continue. 'I got your number from Katie... you know, at the hospital,' I say, like the receptionist is a mutual friend.

'Oh, I don't know a Katie… '

No, but you know a Marianne, don't you? You're shagging her husband, you shameless cow.

'She kindly passed your number on because I didn't want Simon to know but I need to speak to you about something quite urgently,' I say, talking over her. Then I stop, and hold this for a beat. I want her to think, if only for a few seconds, that she is about to be questioned regarding the contents of her rumpled sheets.

'Oh… okay.'

Worried are we?

'You may be aware that Simon now has a more senior surgical role.' My voice is all excited. 'And I want to do something special for him, so I'm going to throw him a surprise party.' This is not something at this stage that I intend on doing. I'm hoping my plan to get rid of Caroline will mean she's running away with her tail between her legs long before I need to throw any promotion parties. No, the party is a backup if Caroline is still around after I've fed her all my info over lunch.

She doesn't answer, so I channel Jen and just keep talking. 'Thing is, to celebrate anything big, we usually like to do our own "private" thing, if you get my meaning,' I say in my sexiest drawl, which probably sounds like I'm having a stroke, but I keep going. I need to drop in a few little intimate hints to entice her. If I can give Caroline the impression that we're a blissfully happy couple, she'll be horrified and intrigued and want to know more. I'm hoping this will entice her to agree to meet me – so she can find out if Simon's telling the truth about the state of his marriage. I don't care how secure a mistress is, she always suspects there's something he's not telling, because if he's lying to his wife, the mother of his kids with whom he's shared a whole life, then why wouldn't he lie to the woman with whom he's only shared a bottle of Merlot and a pile of creased bed linen? I'm counting on her not to tell him I've been in touch, because if she's as bright as

I think she is, she'll want to know about the marriage from my perspective, without him shutting it down. That's why the party has to be 'a surprise'.

'Anyway, thing is, I want to make sure all his friends are there, but I also want to invite some new blood. Especially women – as you know, it can get a little "old boys club" down in Cardio.' I introduce some tinkling laughter now to hint at female cama-raderie. I have to be careful because my 'tinkling' laughter can sometimes sound manic. I press on: 'It was the same at his last hospital – crusty old things they are –… and I don't want a party full of old men. Simon's talked about a few female colleagues,' I say, sticking in a little sharp point of the knife, 'but I can only remember *your* name.'

'Oh?' she asks. A little twinkle of hope laces her voice; she's hoping I'll say it's because he talks about her all the time.

'Yes… from when we met before in Waitrose?'

'Oh, yes, of course.' I can taste the disappointment in her voice. It tastes good.

'Anyway, Caroline, I was keen to touch base with one of the women he works with because I'd like to get the lay of the land.'

'In what way?' she asks coldly, but I skate across her ice.

'I just think women are better at people – we know who's friendly with whom and who'll be good in the mix. I don't want to invite someone if it's going to be awkward for anyone else, if you get my drift.' I giggle, knowing the irony will be lost on her.

Oh, Caroline, with your brilliant mind and flexible pelvis – you don't have a clue. While you were riding your pony at your private school, I was learning to survive. How dare you fill your womb with something that doesn't belong to you and expect no consequences. I will shut you down.

'Simon is a waste of space when it comes to anything social. I think men are, don't you? Oh God, I'm being sexist; my seventeen-year-old daughter will kill me.' I hear myself laugh again.

Note the possessive pronoun, Caroline? MY seventeen-year old – not yours. Never yours.

She doesn't respond. I have her like a fish with a hook in its cheek, and I ponder the image as she sits there, trapped on my phone.

'So, I was thinking it would be just lovely to get together with one of the girls who works with Simon, conjure up a guest list and find out who's who.'

'I'm sorry, I don't really socialise with work colleagues so I don't know who...' she says, feigning vagueness.

'Oh, that's a shame. Do you find it difficult to socialise with your colleagues?' I ask, like it's a problem.

After all, you aren't finding it hard to socialise with my husband.

'No, I don't find it difficult. I choose not to.' I hear the affront in her voice. She'd hate to be thought of as anything less than perfect.

'Oh no, I'm sorry. I shouldn't have said anything – it's nothing to do with me how people get on at work.'

'What do you mean?'

She's clearly worried. I can hear it in her voice. Caroline's not as strong as she thought she was and now she thinks Simon's said something about her not coming up to par. Good.

'Well, even if you don't have any friends at work, I'm sure you know...'

'I have friends,' she snaps.

'Oh. Good,' I say, like I don't believe her. 'It's difficult though sometimes. God, the things I hear from Simon, and he's a senior.'

I put my head to one side like my therapist Saskia does when I tell her something sad. I know Caroline can't see me, but it helps my performance.

'Oh Caroline, I've upset you... I'm sorry. I shouldn't have said anything. It's not like Simon would discuss any... of your... difficulties with colleagues – he only talks to me. Look, you clearly don't want to be involved and I can't say I blame you. I only asked you because we bumped into you at Waitrose that time and I thought you might be able to help. There's that nurse... Alison? Oh, I don't know, Simon's always talking about her. They're quite good friends I think... I'll try her. I'm sure she can give me an accurate perspective on who should be at Simon's party, and don't worry, I won't add you to the guest list if it's going to make you uncomfortable.' I smile down the line at her.

She says very little during our exchange, thanks to my Jen impression, and I wonder if it's going to work. Will she simply tell me to fuck off, put down her phone and go running to Simon?

I just hope I've dropped in enough doubts, enough tempting titbits about our marriage, to make her want to get involved without telling him. Then she and I will have a secret like they do. The rather delicious thing is that I'll be in on everyone's secret, without them knowing. Knowledge is power, and I'm finally taking back some power, not sitting around waiting for shit to happen to me.

'I'm sure... I could give you an accurate perspective ... I think there's a theatre nurse called Alison, but I wasn't aware she was friends with your husband.'

Oh, she's so jealous I can hear it sizzling down the line. I'm rather chuffed because I only made a wild guess because Simon mentioned an Alison as being 'too young and totally incompetent'.

'Okay great... In that case I was wondering, are you free to meet up for lunch next Monday or Tuesday?'

Ideally before my husband tries to seal my fate with the solicitor on Wednesday.

'Lunch?'

'Oh, I know, we're not even friends yet – and it all sounds a bit formal – but perhaps you could pop out in your lunch hour? My treat. There's this lovely little Italian, Gianni's, in the town. Do you know it?'

Of course you do. It's where you enjoy foreplay and fagioli with my husband.

'Yes… I…'

'Fabulous, shall we meet there, say at twelve-thirty on Monday?' I pounce before she has a chance to backtrack. I have her; now all I have to do is reel her in. 'Oh please, say yes, I don't get chance to go out with girlfriends. Simon isn't one to babysit – always ends in tears and chaos.' I laugh, hoping to cast doubt on his self-made image as the perfect father.

'Okay. Yes,' she says. 'About twelve-thirty.'

I can't wait.

CHAPTER EIGHTEEN

Today is the day. I'm lunching with the lovely Caroline, who, according to last night's Instagram, was having drinks with friends. In a low-cut top in a trendy wine bar. I doubt Simon would approve of either.

I dig out some nice faded jeans, a soft grey sweater and a blush scarf. Non-threatening clothes in soft shades. *I want you to think I'm harmless and want only to be your friend.*

Arriving at the restaurant, I feel strangely calm, possibly because I've got this, or because I took a tablet at 9.15 after I'd dropped the kids off at school. I'm cutting down, but today I needed a safety net to prevent me from raging at my husband's lover over the main course or pouring red wine over her lovely blonde hair. So I took only the minimum dose so that I'll be calm (I hope!) for lunch and should be able to remember everything, or at least most of it. I won't be me mixing it with alcohol either – I'll stick to soda water. You never know.

I take my seat at a discreet table; I don't want anyone to see us. I check out the menu; she'll probably have a salad. I saw one on her Instagram. No humans in the photo, just an inanimate salad with walnuts and copious leaves, but the two plates and two glasses of red gave me all the information I needed. #Healthy #MeatFreeMondays #EatYourGreens. God, she makes me want to puke. *How about #HusbandFreeWednesdays, Caroline, let's make that a thing eh?*

Eventually, she arrives and I surprise myself at how warm and welcoming I am. None of the vitriol I feel inside has come to the surface – let's just hope it stays that way. She looks good. She obviously made an effort, but whether that was for lunch with me or work with my husband I don't know. She's wearing a light-blue chunky cardigan over black – a short skirt, high shiny boots.

Not exactly mother material.

I try to glimpse her stomach before she sits down, but she's not showing yet. I look at her and see Simon next to her in bed, the baby between them, and immediately push the image from my mind.

'Drink?' I ask, sipping my own clean soda, picking up the menu as the teenage waitress wanders over.

'Water please... still,' she says to the girl without a smile.

'Let's order before we chat. I'm aware you're on your lunch hour,' I say, like I'm the most considerate woman in the world, when in fact it's my greatest desire to stab her right in the hand with the fork that's resting on the napkin.

I glance at her over my menu as she looks at hers and I wonder not for the first time at the injustice of all this. She could have anyone, with her gorgeous body and perfect face. She was free, she had no ties – she could have travelled the world, become head of something medical at MIT or UCLA and lived the life of a beautiful academic in Boston or California. She could... She could have done all these things, but instead she chose *my* husband, *my* kids, my *life*. She must have known what she was getting into, must have liked the look of my life and decided to take it for herself. Caroline must have lurked on my social media as much as I have hers. What self-respecting mistress worth her salt wouldn't seek out the competition? And while checking out the wife, she saw the nest and thinks she's going to bring her baby cuckoo into it. But it's *my* nest, I've worked hard to make it perfect, to make our family happy. I've learned to deal with the darkness and to concentrate on the light.

Borrowed Light. Stolen husband.

As soon as I found out the baby news, I went to town on my virtual life of course. I put my stamp on it. There were already family pictures, holidays, school events, but I went full-on PR and curated our lives online. I shaped it into something wonderful on Instagram and Facebook and with the help of Photoshop, some clever filters and some ingenious cropping, my online presence reads like something from a glossy celebrity magazine. Our summer holiday in Crete is like a photo shoot for a high-end travel company, our beautiful daughter lay in her hammock and our gorgeous sons playing in the sea with their perfect father. #FathersAndSons #Family. The reality of course was quite different. What the photos didn't show was that Dad couldn't wait to get out, get dry and get sexting his mistress. #SextingDad #CheatingHusband. Even I don't recognise my life. Then there's the picture of the kids in the park transformed into a *Vogue* layout, laughing, throwing leaves in the air, creating a beautiful bronze blur of happiness in the early autumn sunshine. #BrothersAndSister #SiblingLove. Of course, I had to edit out the litter, the dog poo and the condoms lying among the leaves, and didn't photograph Charlie and Alfie's meltdown, with Sophie calling them 'fucking little bastards' and storming off. #FilthyMouthedDaughter.

It's mine, mine, mine.

We are not perfect, no one is, but as a family we've had more than our share of stress and it's not been easy. Over the years I've put up with all the pain, all the blame, all this torment and managed it into something we can live in. And now *she* turns up with her just-washed hair and her ripe uterus and ruins everything.

Get your own life, bitch, because you can't have mine. #Thief.

'So,' I start, clasping my hands together on the tabletop to anchor myself and appear to have control at lunch with my husband's mistress. I need to establish the upper hand early on or I will fall apart. I must convey as much information to her as I can in this fake-news lunch. I want to introduce doubts and darkness as she has done with me – she may not have done this directly, but I don't care. I want her to suffer. I want her to question everything he's told her, everything she believes to be true – I want her to know how it feels to be paranoid. I want them both to feel the other has secrets, and I want her to know he's lying – because, trust me, there is nothing more painful than believing the person you love is lying to you. Just because she's special and he wants to make it official and move her in doesn't mean he'll be exclusive. He's married to me, but still can't seem to stop himself from straying.

Once a cheater always a cheater, Caroline.

The other day I found a few restaurant receipts in his wallet that I can't account for; naturally, he wasn't with me, and through my obsessive online stalking of Caroline, I can't place her in these romantic venues at these times either. It makes me wonder if he's already established Caroline as wife number three and is auditioning for a mistress to go with that marriage. I wonder if it's a pattern: will he do to Caroline what he's done to me? Will he fill her with doubts and fears until she's broken and he then has to find a newer model? Not that I give a damn about Caroline, but perhaps it's happened before with Nicole and her suicide was due to life with him? Nothing about Simon surprises me any more.

He once told me she was 'very fragile', but when they met she had a career in banking and, according to Joy, who never missed an opportunity to remind me of Nicole's qualities, was 'a strong woman'. Did he break her spirit like he tried to break mine?

I'm more determined than ever. I won't be another Nicole. I will not go to sleep and leave my three children. More than anyone, I know how that can destroy a child. Long after the discovery of my mother's body, I still see her – it's like her ghost lives with me. My mother's life is even more frightening to me than her death; it's made me compliant and scared. Every forgotten name, each unwelcome thought, is a sign I'm living her life and will one day lie with my mother in a cold, red bath.

I sometimes wonder if it was my fear that Simon was drawn to. A flawed vulnerable woman who wouldn't answer back or try to control him, as his mother always had. Joy was a wealthy woman and indulged him with new cars, homes, holidays – and continued this after his father died and even after he'd married me. But despite this, she never showed him any physical affection. As a result, Simon puts value on things rather than people. He sees women as disposable, just pretty trinkets to make him look good and tend to his needs. I'm beginning to wonder how disposable I am to him… especially as he now has a new, pretty play thing.

I'm sitting opposite the new play thing now, making inane small talk about guest lists and canapés. I try to be animated, exude fun and naughtiness, like Jen would. I don't want Caroline to think I'm meek or boring. I'm sure he's told her that, along with my 'illness' and my 'obsessive jealousy', I'm bland and uninteresting, so I'm going to turn her world upside down, make her question everything he's told her, everything she thinks she knows. After all, it's only what she's doing to me.

'I love it here,' I sigh, smiling. 'Simon often brings me here on date nights and, I don't know… however many times we come here, there's always something incredibly romantic about it. We just kick back and forget about the exhausting – but wonderful – hurly-burly at home and we… regroup.' I toy with my breadstick, slowly raise it to my mouth and bite off the end. 'It's like we're on our honeymoon again, you know?'

Haven't had sex since the twins were conceived? Really?

'Lovely,' she splutters. Early signs are my campaign is having the desired effect. And what's more, I'm enjoying myself. Her drink arrives and she almost grabs it from the waitress's hand.

'Yes, the Italian music reminds me of holidays,' I smile. 'Do you like Italy, Caroline?'

'Yes… I love Tuscany.' She tries to smile. She's so uncomfortable she's making me itch. And I love it.

'Ooh, Tuscany, me too! Has Simon mentioned we're thinking of buying a place out there?' We're not, but one more lie to add to all the others we're telling each other won't make any difference. In fact the more deceit the better, eh Caroline?

She shakes her head and almost chokes on the huge gulp of water she's taking. I want to laugh. I want to roar with laughter in her face at how easy this is, how delicious it is to inflict pain on someone who's caused me so much. God, why didn't I do this before instead of torturing myself stalking her on social media and trying to win Simon over with fancy dinners and his kind of sex. No, this is much more fun.

'Oh yes, we're thinking a small farmhouse. As Simon says, we have three kids and if *they* have kids, then we need somewhere we can all go and just...' I continue to press at the wound that I've made, opening it further and further. Even Simon the surgeon won't be able to stitch this back together.

THREE kids – count 'em. You and your blurry baby will not be welcome.

I lean forward with what I hope is a sincere look on my face. 'Simon has to destress, and he says he's only ever really able to do that when he's happy, with his family,' I lie. 'I've always said it's about family. We want to just *be,* you know?' Of course, he has his little hobbies on the side, but they mean nothing to him – the only thing that matters, that really counts for him, is us.

I'm nodding and she's nodding back, no doubt searching my eyes for signs of psychosis.

'When we're in Italy we're going to treat it like a second home, the usual stuff – we'll have friends over, cook on the barbecue, open a few bottles, just chill around the kitchen and garden with all the kids. I'm very, very lucky,' I add so smugly I almost hate myself. I look at her, relishing the uncertainty on her face.

'Sorry,' I say suddenly, pretending I've just realised I'm talking too much. 'Oh, will you listen to me going on about second homes and the family and… and you're being so lovely listening, but you must be starving – we haven't even ordered yet.'

I call the waitress over and I order a seafood linguine; she orders a salad.

I know you better than you know yourself, Caroline.

'Anyway,' I say, taking a sip of soda. 'Needless to say, you'd be welcome to come and stay with us in Tuscany any time. You could bring your husband… or…?' I wave my half-eaten breadstick in her face – because I can.

'I'm not married,' she says, moving her fingers agitatedly up and down the stem of her glass. #Anxious.

'Do you… live alone?' I fold my napkin, feigning slight indifference to her answer. I don't want her to think I'm interviewing her.

And where do you see yourself in five years, you conniving bitch? Making pancakes in my kitchen with my kids? Think again, slut.

'Yes… I have a little cottage, just outside town.'

'Lovely. Anyway, enough of my interrogation,' I joke. 'Caroline, I can't thank you enough for coming to meet me today, I know your help with the guest list will be invaluable,' I start, referring back to the party, I don't want her to cotton on to the fact I'm just playing with her like a cat with a mouse.

'I… can give you a *few* names, but as I said on the phone, I haven't been around for long.'

She's not keen on shooting the breeze with her lover's wife and maintains a business-like demeanour. I'm expecting her to grab her coat and leave at any moment – either she finds me terribly dull or perhaps she has a conscience?

'If you can text a list to me that would be wonderful,' I'm saying. 'Caroline, I'm so grateful. And I know Simon will be…' My phone rings. I'm expecting this because when a cold-caller bothered me with his fucking double glazing yesterday, I realised it could work for me. So I told him I'd love double glazing and asked if he could call me back at 1 p.m. today to discuss this. So in the absence of a trustworthy friend, I had to rely on some annoying salesperson to make my phone ring when lunching with Caroline.

'Hello, is that Mrs Wilson?' the cocky young man asks. 'This is Jordan from Wonderful Windows.'

'Oh, darling, thanks for calling me, but I'm having lunch…' I look at Caroline and roll my eyes with an affectionate smile directed at whoever's on the other end. Chippy salesman Jordan's probably very surprised to be addressed as 'darling' so soon in our double-glazing relationship. But he seems quite unperturbed.

'So sorry, Mrs Wilson, you said you'd be free at 1 p.m. so I was just calling back to talk to you about…'

'Oh, you are sweet… yes, and I know, darling, you'll have to save that until you get home and the kids are in bed.' I giggle girlishly and mouth 'my husband' to a shocked-looking Caroline. Admittedly she's only slightly more surprised than cocky Jordan must be, but like all these relentless telephone intruders, he's a true salesman and keeps going. I want to laugh. It's as if what I've just said is perfectly normal – he's probably just grateful I haven't cut him off.

'Wonderful Windows can provide draught-free windows at half the…'

'Sweetie, I'm with a friend and you can't say embarrassing things like that,' I purr. I'm now shaking my head and feigning my embarrassment with a shy smile. 'Yes, babe, I do too, and I always will… Oh and in other news, don't forget the boys' rugby like you did last week.' I wonder if she'll clock this; after all she was the reason he didn't turn up to see his sons play. 'I know. I know you were busy, but they cried so much when you didn't see them in their special game… Okay, I forgive you. Oh, you've already made it up to me. Love you too.'

I put down the phone, ignoring Jordan the salesman's promise of 'a very good estimate and a ten-year guarantee'. I don't believe in guarantees any more. I glance over at Caroline and know at this moment she is hurting even more than me. I wish I could say I am sorry, but I'm not – it gives me pleasure, makes me feel alive and like I actually have something to contribute instead of just letting it happen. I'm taking action. I've had time to accept the situation, to know what Simon is, but she has no idea at all. I know he's manipulated her by misrepresenting me, and for a while he's been controlling both of us. But not any more. I'm in the driving seat now.

'So sorry, that was Simon, he's hopeless.' I smile indulgently as I place my phone carefully on the table. 'Such an old romantic, but he'd forget his head if it wasn't screwed on. He should have been at the boys' first rugby match last week. They're only six… they're twins,' I say, like I'm assuming she knows nothing about our lives – why should she? 'Anyway, they were devastated. He said he was busy, said he wished he could have come, but a colleague was being really high-maintenance and demanding he stick around. He's too soft for his own good.'

I look at her face. My account of our life is so far away from Simon's, perhaps she's thinking that he may not be telling her the truth about everything? He probably isn't.

This is what it feels like to be betrayed, Caroline.

Our meals arrive. She's said very little – she's finding my words hard to digest – and it looks to me like she might vomit at any moment, but seems to gather herself together.

'So… how long have you been married?' she asks, evidently deciding to play along and get as much information as she can. Caroline is as thirsty for more marital revelations as I am for her online posts. #ThirstyGirls #LadiesWhoLunch.

'Almost ten years,' I sigh contentedly. 'And they've been happy… well, mostly,' I add as a little tease, while piercing a prawn on the end of my fork.

'Mostly?' she asks, instantly looking up, then feigning disinterest and picking absently at a lettuce leaf.

'Yes, I mean, it hasn't always been a bed of roses. We've had our ups and downs… like anyone, I guess,' I say, putting down my fork. I'll be up for a bloody Oscar for this – I'm surprising myself at my skill. Subtle nuances, averted eyes. I am believable and brilliant, if I say so myself.

'Oh... are you okay?' she asks, going through the motions – if she really cared if I was okay she wouldn't be shagging my husband. No, she can see from my acting that I'm upset and wants me to expand on this hint that there have been shadows. She's leaning forward, all ears to find out what happened inside my marriage. She thought she knew, she thought she had every single moment of a decade pinned down, the hopeless mental case married to the kind, brilliant man. But I'm giving her my version – and like his, it makes a very good story.

'I'm fine,' I say, clearly not.

She orders another water for her and a soda for me. I'd love a big glass of wine, but daren't mix alcohol with my medication. I have to be clear-headed, feed her enough information and take enough in. I mustn't alert her to the fact that I know.

'But you seem upset...?' she pushes.

I nod. 'Yes, I just find it hard... it doesn't matter when or how many times... I just... Oh, it's all in the past now.' I look away, hoping I've piqued her interest.

'The past?' she asks, eager to know more. #Bingo.

'Yes, well... I shouldn't really say, it's just... my husband's had a few little *indiscretions* during our marriage... It happens.'

She sits back. 'What do you mean?' She probably doesn't believe me. He's told her I imagine this stuff, so she's ready to consign it to the lunatic ramblings of a madwoman. I need to give her just enough to doubt him, but not so dramatic that she thinks I'm fabricating. Just a drip, drip, drip to keep her on her toes.

'You know, just the odd indiscretion with women who've meant nothing to him, but oh, it's very indiscreet of me – you're a colleague of Simon's. It isn't fair.'

'You're right, I don't think this is appropriate.' She looks relieved and disappointed at the same time.

'No, of course, and I apologise.'

'It's fine… really.' She takes another large glug of water, probably to stop herself demanding names and telephone numbers. I know I would, but then I'm supposed to be mad.

Sometimes I am.

'Anyway, I want to throw this lovely party for Simon because I think it's important to celebrate good news. We've been through so much stuff over the past year, but we had a long talk last weekend. He says he wants a fresh start and asked that we put everything behind us.' I'm amazed at how easy it is to tell my stories, my lies. I suppose it's wishful thinking really. I'd love to be in a secure marriage where a promotion is celebrated because it's good for our future. But because of Caroline my future's hanging in the balance.

'Yes, Simon's been under so much pressure with the consultancy,' I continue, 'but promised he's going to focus on our family now.'

'Oh…?' She's absolutely *dying* for more information. But I'm not giving it away. I want her to really want it; after all, that's how she likes it. #ForbiddenFruit.

'Oh… that's nice.' She's absolutely horrified at the prospect of Simon focussing on his family, but is desperately trying to cover it. I want to laugh out loud in her face, but manage to resist.

'Look, Marianne, this has been lovely, but I really have to get back…' Her salad is barely touched.

'Oh no, we haven't even talked through the canapés.' I look crestfallen. 'I'm sorry, I probably seem really sad to you, don't I?' I say, in an effort to get her back on board and surprise her with my self-insight. 'It's just that I'm fairly new to the area. I don't have any family, the school mums are all a bit cliquey and…'

'I'm sorry about that, Marianne. But really I…'

'Look, I'm not trying to play the sympathy card, it's just, as I said on the phone, I really want to do this for Simon. I haven't thrown a party for a while and you'll know everyone there because they'll mainly be his work colleagues I just would *so* appreciate your help.'

'Help?' She has no intention of giving me a moment's help with anything. She wants nothing to do with me or my sad party, but I see something around the edges of her eyes. I think it's pity.

I don't want your fucking pity, Caroline. I want your unease, I want your fear, I want you to taste it like I taste mine.

'Look, I'm setting the date for a week on Friday…' I say, then I offer her the bait I've been holding back, that I know she won't be able to refuse, a peek at what she imagines will one day be her home, a glimpse into her future.

Over my dead body.

'Why don't you come over to ours early evening? We can have a little drink, I can show you round before the other guests arrive…'

She looks vaguely interested now, and seems to sit back in her seat; her need to leave has suddenly become less urgent.

'Friday? I don't know. I'll have to check with…'

'Your boyfriend? Bring him too.'

'No I meant check with my schedule. I don't know what I'll be doing… I sometimes work late,' she says, but we both know she won't be able to resist.

'Of course, I understand if you can't make it, but I just know you'll have fun. Along with his colleagues, I'm inviting some of Simon's oldest friends…'

The idea of meeting Simon's friends in his beautiful home must be bringing her to the point of orgasm, which according to her emails she reaches easily when my husband's around. She thinks knowing his history will bring her closer, but I *shared* his history – it's one of the few things a wife has over a mistress. She can't wait to have a good poke around the nest too… *my* nest.

Cuckoo Caroline laying your eggs in other women's nests.

'No pressure,' I say, piling it on, 'but give me your address and I'll pop an invite in the post. I so hate those email invites – so impersonal.'

I find a pen and notebook in my bag, hand it to her and she writes her address. How can she refuse?

I take it from her and put the notebook safely back in my handbag.

I know where you live.

'You can be there from the beginning, so at least if Simon's early, it won't be just me surprising him. And you *have* to see my new kitchen, before it gets all messed up.' I giggle like a middle-class idiot.

'Marianne, that all sounds lovely and I'll try to make it,' she says and I swear I hear something like guilt in her voice.

'Great! I'll call you and we can talk through the canapé list…?'

'No, er, I'm not very good at…'

'Oh, I just thought… as Simon's out on Wednesday, I'd be able to go over the canapés with you on the phone without him listening in… Let me check my diary.' I open up my phone and gaze at a photo of the twins. 'Yes, he's out Wednesday seeing our solicitor.'

'Oh?' Her interest is so fucking piqued; he told her he's seeing David about a divorce. He probably is, but as he lies to me, I'm going to lie to her and use his solicitor's meeting to drop another little bomb into her life, which she will hopefully detonate into his.

'Yes. David our solicitor's an old friend; he's helping us with our plans for the place in Tuscany. If ever you need anything like that, he's your man. Simon wanted me to go with him as we're all old friends – the Merlot will be flowing and David's wife is hilarious,' I add in a cheeky aside, making like we're all besties yet unable to remember his wife's bloody name. 'But Sophie's out and I can't just leave the boys. My husband's terrible, sometimes forgets we even have kids.' I giggle. 'One of the boys said the other day that he wished he had a dad like his friend Josh's. I said

"Why darling?" and he said because Josh's dad actually talks to him.' I shake my head as she glares at me; she can't believe this. 'He's outrageous, honestly,' I continue. 'I have to do everything. He's hopeless – loveable but bloody hopeless.'

Her hand instinctively touches her stomach – protective, defensive.

What do you think of your baby daddy now, Caroline? #Perfect-Father.

'Do you have any children?' I ask, trying not to laugh.

She shakes her head.

'Would you like children of your own?'

Do you want mine too? You already have my husband, perhaps you'd like the complete set?

'I… yes, I'd love children. I have two younger sisters…'

'Lovely. We have Sophie who's the seventeen-year-old, then the twins, who, as I said, are six and a handful, often in trouble at school. The other day they found a toy gun and pretended to "kill" another boy,' I lie. 'His parents went mad and threatened the police, all sorts of trouble – I'm still untangling all that with the help of the rather stroppy headmistress and hundreds of pounds' worth of therapy. Simon's completely unaware of all the drama, of just how hard it is to manage two wilful boys with a death wish.'

'Shouldn't their father be aware of what's…' she says judgement-ally, and I see the strong second wife emerging. I doubt her line of questioning would go down well with Simon.

'Yes, absolutely he should, but if you ask me, he makes them worse with his pretend wars in the sitting room and gunfights in the garden,' I lie. This is quite delicious – not only am I scaring her, I'm describing Simon as some psychotic jingo dad who encourages gun play and war games. It couldn't be further from the truth, but I'm only doing what he does when he misrepresents me and my actions.

'Gun… fights?' she stutters.

'Yes. Simon loves guns, but when I try to tell him that it's not good for them and we need to talk about the boys' wild behaviour, he says "not now, Marianne, give me a massage," or sex or whatever he wants that evening. He finds the children far too demanding. I mean, he has three kids and has never changed a nappy in his life.' I laugh, like this is something to be admired and amused by.

I can see by her face that the father of her unborn child, the man she wants to spend the rest of her life with, may not be who she thinks he is. I also hope that I'm not the woman she thought I was, the woman he painted me to be. Hopefully now she now knows I'm invested in this family, in this life, and I will cling to it like a limpet on a rock. I will not be the easy part of their plan.

You can't have my life; it's not for sale.

I insist on paying the bill. When Simon queries it – and he will – I'll tell him I took Jen out to lunch to thank her for collecting the boys from the French tutor when I had to pick Sophie up from dance.

We get up from the table and when we part outside the restaurant, I give Caroline the warmest, most sincere hug I can fake. I think she buys it, and with a girlie wave I thank her *so* much for her time, threaten to call and talk canapés on Wednesday and *desperately* hope she'll be able to make the surprise party.

I will not be disposed of, Caroline, I'm here to stay. Whatever it takes.

Walking back to the car, I think about how I fed her the pretty little crumbs, and how hungry she was to take them. Caroline isn't going to tell Simon about meeting me because we both know he'd put a stop to it – and she wants more. She longs to find out what's really going on inside our marriage; she probably doesn't trust him quite as much now. And if she's trying to muscle her way into my new German kitchen, she needs to know exactly what to expect, and I can tell her what I want her to know.

My glee at the apparent success of my plan starts to wane when I get to the car. I climb in and pull down the mirror to check my

face and seeing myself brings me back to reality. My eyes are wild
and the grin on my face looks painted on and I see the Joker staring
back. I quickly put the mirror away. What the hell am I doing?
Who have I become? I just had lunch with my husband's mistress,
I probably tortured the woman and despite what she's done to
me suddenly I'm not sure I feel comfortable causing someone so
much hurt. She's pregnant after all. But then, I remind myself,
it's *my* husband's child and if I want to keep my own kids I might
just have to play hardball, even though it's against my nature. I'm
a mother who will do anything to protect her family – who knows
what I'm capable of?

I start the car, tell myself I need to toughen up and check my
make-up again in the mirror. I look better than I have for a long
time. I'm taking something back, and it's about time.

I'm not a mean person, but Caroline had to taste the pain of his
betrayal today over her salad. I think she was trying to come over
as cool, detached, just a work colleague, but it translated into cold
and snooty with a rather smug, superior topcoat. She doesn't know
that I know who she really is. She unwittingly shares with me her
deepest thoughts, her darkest desires, her most profound orgasms
every time she sends her lover an email. Despite her superior air I
know she is a homewrecker with the morals of an alley cat. Simon
is equally to blame of course and between them they've conjured
up this image of me that is ill-informed and judgemental, based
on his lies. How dare she take his word and condemn me as a wife
and mother. How fucking dare she get herself pregnant and push
me out of my own nest. She thought she could see our marriage
very clearly, but the truth is many-faceted and, today, I was able
to offer her a different perspective. I hope it's given her food for
thought, and I hope she will at least now question some of what
he tells her regarding me and our family life. I hope this lunch will
stop the 'Marianne needs help…' line and start Caroline thinking
about how much Simon's lied to her about his 'mad' wife. But

more than anything I hope this lunch will result in her fucking off and leaving us to get on with our lives.

As I pull away, I see her climbing into her sporty little Mini. Her shoulders are stooped, her face is filled with angst. Caroline looks ten years older – and I almost feel sorry for her. Almost.

CHAPTER NINETEEN

I don't go home. I want to enjoy my victory with a lap of honour round the supermarket. I throw random things in my trolley as I go over our conversation, again and again. Yes it must have been awful for her, but each time I feel a tiny twinge of guilt at her pain, I remind myself how much fucking pain she's caused me. She really thought she could just sail through lunch with her lover's wife, the woman she wants to put away and replace. But guess what Caroline, you're not as strong or secure in your relationship as you thought you were. #PuttyInMyHands #SurprisedSlut.

I'm so wicked and I love it. I think I may have discovered a latent talent for emotional torture – no surprise, I learned it from the master. And the lunch went so well, I'm thinking that instead of pretending I'm going to host a surprise party for Simon's promotion, why don't I actually do it? Until now I had a vague idea of stringing her along and cancelling at the last minute, or even accidentally on purpose forgetting to tell her it had been cancelled and allowing her to turn up. I rather liked this scenario, the three of us sitting awkwardly on the breakfast stools in the kitchen while I prattled on about our perfect life. But no, I might as well go for it, and throw him a surprise party. Simon's worst nightmare – his stuffy colleagues, his boss, his lover and a few of our friends for surprise drinks and nibbles in our lovely home. What could possibly go wrong?

Before I know it, it's time to pick up the boys and, arriving at school, I wave to Jen and call to her that I can't chat as I have to get home for 'the plumber'. There is no plumber. It's another little lie – I don't have time to hear all about the minutiae of Jen's life today. I finally have one of my own. I'm dying to see the email fallout from lunch, and I'm hopeful I managed to convince Caroline that I'm not mad – well, not as crazed and cruel and horrible as Simon has inferred to her on email. God only knows what he actually says about me when they're together.

As for the surprise party, Simon will loathe it; he's a very private person for obvious reasons and to arrive home in a foul mood and be confronted by work colleagues and yummy mummies is his worst nightmare. (Oh yes, in a delicious twist, I'm inviting all the women he flirts with at the school gate that I'm not 'allowed' to fraternise with because they are beneath me. I'm hoping they'll do their bit by getting very drunk, saying stupid things and embarrassing him in front of his stuffy old colleagues – and, of course, Caroline.)

This party will be where I finally come out from under his thumb, where I prove I'm okay, where I show the world I'm a sane wife and mother, and he's the dysfunctional one. After all this time doing his bidding, walking on eggshells, I'm going to reclaim my kids, my life and the Marianne I used to be. I am suffocated by him. He has to know where I am all the time and has opinions on anyone and everyone I so much as talk to, yet I've always been kept away from his world. He's always had his secrets – never involved me in his working life. I know few of his friends and, as much as he can, he avoids doing anything with me that involves other people. Perhaps he's worried I might bump into the skeletons in his closet or the women sharing his bed? Too late Simon.

I collect the boys, give them home-made vegetable soup and when they've finished let them play in the garden to run off some energy. Sophie's already home from her driving lesson and doing her homework. I've never known her to be so conscientious – I'm hopeful she's finally settling in at school. I make a cup of camomile tea, take two pills, dig out Alfie's iPad and sit in the kitchen, watching the boys through the window. I feel a little guilty using my six-year-old's tablet to spy on my husband and his lover, but needs must.

Delighted to see there's been a flurry of emails this afternoon, I settle down to read them.

Hi babe, sorry I missed you earlier, had lunch with an old friend.

So, Caroline, you kept our secret?
'Are you coming over tonight?' she asks.

Yes, but only if you promise to wear my favourite underwear.

Underwear? God, he's such a cliché. I almost regurgitate my seafood linguine. I bought new underwear last year, when I thought he was seeing the barmaid. I ordered it from the internet. It looked great on the model – black silk slip, stockings and suspenders, not brash but classy. So all dressed up by lamplight I waited on our bed for Simon to come home after drinks with 'colleagues', hours after the pub had closed. I was sure he'd been with the twenty-two-year-old who served his red wine at room temperature, but I'd also tried to convince myself I was mistaken and hoped that if I wore something nice he might just love me again. But when he walked into the bedroom, the look on his face wasn't one of passion, it was one of disgust. I'd felt so vulnerable and quickly reached for the sheets to cover myself before he could say what he was clearly thinking. I wanted to protect myself, but I couldn't, and he tore the sheet away and beat me with his words.

'For Christ's sake, Marianne, you're a mother not an ageing streetwalker.' Remembering it stings afresh, even now, like salt in an old wound that won't heal. But I'm not the old Marianne any more and my husband's longing for another woman in lingerie will not be the end of me.

I'm sure our lunchtime meeting has cast doubt on Caroline's relationship with my husband. I find it hard to believe that she will be 'normal' with him having just found out that Simon and his wife are buying a 'forever' holiday home. My references to our sex life and marital bliss including 'fresh starts' and 'past indiscretions' will all be in the mix in her head now. She'll be torturing herself and, hopefully, torturing him soon.

And just then a new email pops up from her that indicates everything is going to plan. Their emails are instantaneous, just like texts, but so much safer, more hidden. Think again.

Hey I didn't realise you were thinking of buying a place in Tuscany?

I'm not, why would you think that?

Oh, just something Roger was saying this afternoon about buying a place there, he seemed to think you were doing the same?

Telling him little white lies already, Caroline? Naughty girl.

No, but I'd love to buy a holiday home together with you one day.

I'd rather talk about how you're going to take all my clothes off and…

My heart sinks a little – she isn't exactly pushing him on this, is she? In fact she seems to be over our lunch already, and back to seducing my husband! God, Caroline, what the fuck is wrong with you? Are you that desperate?

I read on as the emails get heavier, more intense, the sexual dialogue hinting at different, more adventurous acts, involving sex toys and pain. Simon loves to hurt, be it in the kitchen or the bedroom, the mind or the body, and this comes through in his sexual proclivities too. The first time he wanted to slap me during sex I was horrified, but over the years I've endured more because I was scared he'd might leave me if I didn't. He knows how I feel but rolls his eyes at my tears and slaps me harder if I don't pretend to be enjoying it. It's become more frequent over the years, but I've learned how to escape in my head.

Once, I asked him to stop and he was so angry with me, I cowered on the bed, waiting for my punishment. But instead he slowly got up, got dressed and left the house, leaving me tied to the bed. I couldn't release my wrists from the manacles, and I just lay there naked in the dark crying silently, waiting for him to come home and release me. At 7 a.m. the next morning my alarm went off and when I couldn't reach it to turn it off Sophie came in to find me, shivering and crying, on the bed. She let out a little yelp when she saw me and I told her, through tears of humiliation and hurt, that Daddy and I were playing a game and he'd run away to tease me. I told her where the key was and she opened the locks on my wrists. She never mentioned it again, nor did I. She was ten.

CHAPTER TWENTY

I call Caroline on Wednesday evening. After the briefest of greetings, I waffle on to her about drizzled olive oil over bloody figs and Parma ham and then channel my inner Julia Child and talk long and hard about the pros and cons of unmoulded chicken liver custards. 'A Julia classic,' I guffaw down the phone like a lunatic chef on crack. I don't give a fuck about canapés for Simon's 'promotion' party. My primary aim (along with a desire to irritate her and ruin her evening) is to establish whether Simon's with her tonight – and after about forty-five minutes of my culinary nonsense, I think I can safely say she's alone. This means, he's with our solicitor – planning my future without my knowledge. Oh how I'd love to lace those pretentious liver custards with the finest arsenic and serve them to him on a dainty platter at his surprise party.

I'd honestly hoped that by now our lunch meeting would have taken seed and they might have split. But it looks like she's not budging – the explicit emails and constant smiley selfies confirm this – and it seems Simon is also continuing with his plans to divorce me. So before I find myself certified and locked up in a mental institution for the rest of my life, I will bring out the big guns, throw my party and ruin them both. Let's see how long their love lasts after that.

I put the phone down, angry and hurt that he's with his solicitor right now going through with his plan to get rid of me. But I am comforted by the thought that I have a plan too, and I log on to his emails for a rummage around in his tawdry love life. Simon said it was a waste of time making handbags and, compared to this latest hobby, he's right – there are far better ways I can spend my time. I love coming up with new ways to inflict a fresh sting of insecurity on Caroline, another layer of doubt into her smug life, then checking the fallout online. She won't forget what I've said. I just need to prepare for the party while building on my already good work of layering on the perfect marriage, the perfect kids, the perfect life – and all the time revealing the lies her lover tells her. Along with my perfect Instagram posts, I feel like I've finally discovered a way to erase his lies and have a voice.

As much as I'm enjoying all this, there are days when I just wonder if I should confront him about the affair and be done with it. But the emails won't be enough – he will deny it or, worse still, use it to justify the divorce and ensure I'm the one who comes out of it childless and homeless. No, I'm doing the right thing. I have to confront them both. I have to be clever and end this once and for all. I want his relationship in tatters, his career over and I want him on his knees. And if that sounds harsh, I have to remind myself that this is exactly what he's done to me – and he recruited help in the form of the fragrant Caroline, who will go down with him. I don't want to be too cruel, but she started it and whatever happens to the pregnancy would be collateral right?

I'm just about to log off when I see earlier he made an order for silk underwear; seemingly his favourite set needs an upgrade. He'll be with David now, so won't be accessing his emails and I open it and see the lovely scarlet set, frilly and silky and soft to the touch. I feel sick but realise that life is handing me these lemons to make lemonade, so I immediately go through the order and see there's a two-hour window to make changes to the order. So I change the delivery address to our home – how delighted I'll be when it arrives, and I'll thank my husband and tell him how wonderful he is, as he stands there dumbfounded, unable to work out exactly what happened.

Next, I go on to *her* Instagram and officially follow her. That will freak her out and make her feel exposed, but now we're friends, ladies who lunch, I think it's perfectly acceptable for me to 'like' all her posts. How frustrating for her. No more glamorous pictures with cryptic notes and secret hashtags bragging to her girlfriends about the married lover. So I've now 'liked' all those, and congratulated her on her 'wonderful baby news' under the photo of the bloody embryo – talk about too much information. She'll be posting her bloody smear test results next!

Finally, I take a photo of a half-drunk bottle of Merlot with two glasses by the bed. #DateNight #EarlyNight #MarriedLife #TwoCanPlay.

Read it and weep, Caroline!

My underwear parcel arrives a couple of days after I ordered it, and I open it, lay the red silk on the bed, photograph it and put it straight on Instagram. #AGiftFromMyHusband.

Hope you like it, Caroline – apparently red underwear is your favourite.

Then I text Simon one of the photos, thanking him profusely for the lovely gift. He doesn't respond; he probably thinks *he's* going mad.

Welcome to my world, Simon. #GaslightingForGirls.

Later in the week I suggest 'a great idea' to the kids: that we put up our Christmas tree early. The boys are on the ceiling with excitement and I ask them to text Dad and tell him their great idea. Simon has to go along with it when he comes home because the boys are so excited and Sophie thinks I've lost the plot but also finds it hard to say no to two excited six-year-olds waving tinsel.

I post our early family Christmas with gusto; it's early October but I reckon I can get away with it – #Only12WeeksToGo. I'm worried if I don't bring Christmas forward and really screw with her head I could be locked up by then. My three gorgeous children are sporting matching Christmas jumpers and drinking hot chocolate and the five of us are decorating the tree (which Simon did under duress). We are all smiling for the camera, and it hasn't even occurred to him in his stupid elf hat that these photos will be seen by his sophisticated lover. It's hilarious. I even dig out some plastic mistletoe and ask one of the boys to take a photo of Daddy and I 'under the mistletoe' and kiss him just as it clicks. I'm delighted with the results; you could mistake the grimace on his face for a smile as I pucker up. #EarlyChristmasKiss.

If I could make a wish, I'd love for Caroline to disappear into thin air and for us to continue as a family. I know he isn't perfect, but Simon has been less present of late and I've been able to keep up appearances and keep him happy by cooking and cleaning. He's been so busy with his new role at work he didn't even notice an errant throw over the back of the sofa, and the empty bag of Monster Munch Charlie left in the car. Even the sex has been quick, perfunctory and painless. I could carry on like this: no highs and lows, just life and lies in my handmade German kitchen along with my family of five. But while she's waiting in the wings, I'm in serious danger of finding myself back in the clinic and I can't let that happen, so I have to fight. My ultimate goal is to keep my children together – with me. I won't move my family again, nor do I have any intention of leaving – I've messed the kids around so much, I owe it to them to stay here. So the only answer is to scare her off, get her out of Simon's life and therefore mine – if I don't, I could spend the rest of my days sitting on a bench in an over-manicured garden doped up to the eyeballs.

I've spent the whole week preparing for the surprise party – planning canapés with the catering company, ordering several crates of champagne and flowers, so many flowers. I've also bought my dress – midi-length red velvet – which will set off my new highlights and be perfect for this evening's soiree. I'm sure Simon will hate me being blonde, after all he already has one blonde, but tonight he'll have other problems to deal with.

Tonight I'm going to show Caroline what I have, and what I hold. Till death us do part. I want her to be under no illusions: these are my kids, it's my home, it's where I live with my family, and I've worked hard and endured much to remain here. Despite everything, I still have feelings for Simon. He's the only man I've ever loved and the father of my children. He's the man who saved me – but he also destroyed me.

Now it's my turn to destroy him.

I've filled the house with white roses, huge hydrangeas and lilies, inspired by Simon's beautiful, fortnightly bouquet.

Expensive, out of season blooms, Caroline… because I'm worth it.

His bouquet arrived yesterday and I couldn't help but remember the time when we were first together and the first time he came home one evening with a dozen roses.

'Who are they for?' I'd asked. 'Is it someone's birthday?'

He'd laughed and said I was so sweet, so unaffected, and that's why he loved me. #Vulnerable #RipeForThePicking.

No one had ever given me flowers before, and he was incredibly touched by my delighted, tearful response. He'd held both my hands in his and said, 'I promise to fill your world with flowers, Marianne… flowers and happiness always.' I still get the flowers, every two weeks; the happiness is more sporadic and rare these days. But that will all change tonight when I take back my life.

Does he bring you flowers, Caroline?

Ironically and hilariously, given that I forced her to meet with me and hand over names of ideal guests, I've invited no one on Caroline's list. As it all began as a ruse and I never intended on having a party, it wasn't important whose name was on her sad little list. But now the party is really happening I can't bear to think of her friends in my home; it's bad enough that she'll be here. I've invited my friends though – Jen and Francesca, and some of the other mums too. I need tonight to go viral, and with the playground gossips that's guaranteed. I mentioned at the school gate that I was planning a surprise party for Simon and if anyone would like to pop in it would be an open house, but not a word to Simon. I want to take him by surprise. I've never done anything before that I haven't checked with him first – I'm feeling rather rebellious. What have I got to lose?

Everything.

CHAPTER TWENTY-ONE

Since I found out about the affair, I've focused all my resentment on Caroline – she only had to say no to save me and my children. But now I realise that she is merely the symptom, not the cause and, as much as I dislike her, she isn't the one who lies to me, puts me down, controls me and hurts me physically and emotionally – that's all my husband's work. It's taken a while for everything to sink in, and for a long time I believed I loved Simon, thought he was everything – and in a way he was, because, thanks to him, I had nothing and no one else. But just reading the emails has slowly brought me out of the hibernation of my marriage. The brainwashing that he inflicted on me turned my head to mush and I needed this wake-up call. Yes, Caroline is the catalyst, and she's been instrumental in breaking up my family, but he's my husband, the father of our children, and he is happy to tear us apart from within. So now I'm turning my focus to both of them, and however difficult my life might be as a result, I just need all my children with me. No more moving house, no more affairs imagined or otherwise – I will take control of my destiny, and tonight I'll cut the cancer out of my life.

It's 5 p.m. and the caterers have just arrived. I say caterers – they are a group of young women not long out of catering college, very confident for their age, full of ideas and creativity. I'm finding them quite inspiring with their plans for edible flowers and shaved beetroot. Simon loathes beetroot – it gives him the most terrible indigestion – so I've ordered a double quantity of that canapé and requested beetroot be included as much as possible in all the canapés, because it's my husband's favourite. I know it's petty, but these tiny acts of rebellion are as delicious as the canapés themselves. These catering girls aren't cheap. They probably saw the size of the house and thought they'd take the piss, but so what, it's his money and, quite frankly, he won't care about the canapés or the cost – there'll be far more for him to worry about after tonight.

I'm not wasting time and energy on a full dinner, especially as I despise all the invited guests, except Jen. But I need Caroline to see me as a hostess. I want her threatened and defeated – and gone. I need to make it clear that I will not lie down while they walk all over me, and they certainly won't separate me from my children… Simon can go where he pleases, but my kids stay with me.

I'd sincerely hoped she would take up my offer of arriving early and seeing the house before other guests arrive, but she texted to say she has to work late and will arrive the same time as everyone else. I wonder if that's true or if she just can't face being here alone with her lover's wife – either way, I want her to have a peep into my perfect life, see my fabulous home and want it, because Caroline's clearly never wanted something she can't have before.

I'm dotting Jo Malone candles everywhere when the door chimes, bringing the first arrivals – and it's Jen with a gaggle of mothers. She's brought them early which is nice because I want everyone to see how in control I am, how very solid my life is in this house. God only knows what Simon has told his colleagues about me, but I imagine he's already laid the poison to pave the way for moving her in. 'His wife was ill, you know, he was a saint.' I can hear them now and it makes me bristle, so I grab a couple of bottles of champagne and pop them, hoping the fizz will calm me down.

As the caterers unload trays of canapés and place glasses on trays, I welcome Jen and the girls. She's brought Suzie and Francesca and someone called Yvonne who is quiet but nice enough. I pour us all a flute of cold champagne and make small talk. I'm not taking any medication this evening, which is risky, especially as there's champagne around and I'm feeling celebratory, but I don't want to be drugged up. I've been asleep for the past ten years and tonight I don't want to miss a thing.

'You look lovely,' I say to Jen. She has great taste – tonight she's in an apricot long-sleeved dress with matching high heels. 'You've got such a fabulous figure. I couldn't wear anything so fitted.'

'Yeah, but I'm tall. I'm five foot ten in heels.'

'Lucky you.' I smile, feeling short and dumpy next to her.

'No, it's awful! I could never get a boyfriend when I was a teenager. I can't wear these shoes with Peter – makes him feel inadequate. Fucking little midget,' she mutters as an add-on, which makes me laugh.

'You are awful, Jen.' I smile. I'm looking forward to being friends with this feisty woman, and Hope to see more of her once tonight's over. I will be independent, live my life on my terms, see who I want and go wherever I please.

'No, I'm not, he's such a dickhead. I hate him. These are my sexy bedroom shoes,' she says, forgetting Peter for a moment and twisting her ankle around to show me the full shoe.

'They're gorgeous,' Francesca sighs.

'Yeah, they're the kind you keep on after you take everything off – they're wasted on Peter.'

I smile at Francesca and she rolls her eyes. We both look at Jen, blonde, beautiful, tall and willowy and – yes, it's not just her shoes that are wasted on Peter.

'We had a huge row before I came out tonight. He's so fucking jealous all the time. Says I only married him for his money. Wanker.'

'You did, didn't you?' laughs Suzie.

Jen looks like she's about to defend herself and come up with some false declaration of love, then thinks better of it and nods, giggling. 'You got me there.'

We all laugh, and I'm surprised and amused again by her rather brutal honestly. I sip my champagne, wondering what Jen and the others' reaction would be if I suddenly announced that Simon checks my phone and hits me for fun.

'When I was looking for a husband, I didn't go for love or looks. But now I realise that there's a compromise,' she says ruefully.

'Between you and Peter?' I ask.

'God, no. I mean a compromise to be had in relationships. There are some gorgeous guys out there who could keep me happy in the bedroom *and* all the way to the bank. Peter buys me things, but he doesn't make me happy – never has. He's a crap lover who made his money in market stalls. I want a man with intelligence, wisdom. Someone who can teach me, and not just in the bedroom.' She sighs.

'And he'd have money?' adds Francesca.

'That's a given.' Jen giggles.

I giggle too, enjoying this conspiratorial 'girly' chat. I haven't been able to get this close to anyone for a while, but Jen's different. I admire her independence and drive, the way she's able to steer her own ship in spite of being married, but then again, she's not married to Simon. Jen sometimes says the most awful things, especially about Peter – but I can't help but enjoy her company. I think she likes me too. Most of all, Jen's there for me and she cares, which I so need right now because I'm very much alone.

'Anyway, let's not talk about men,' Francesca says, clapping her hands together like an excited child. 'Oh, darling, I am *loving* the flowers – ooh it's positively bridal in here,' she gushes, alighting on my floral displays.

'You don't think it's too much?'

'NO, NO, NO – you can never be too rich, too thin or have too many flowers,' Jen agrees loudly.

I know the other mums probably only came tonight because they wanted to see our house. It's the biggest on the road, and with the new extended kitchen it's even larger. I've never had good vibes from 'the girls' at the school gate and I'm hoping no one has picked up on why we moved from our last place. That barmaid pressed charges and thanks to her I've now got a police record; they'd probably only have to Google 'Surgeon's Wife in Bar Fracas' and there you go. But Jen's already seen the house. She isn't interested in my expensive German kitchen and my fridge that's big enough to hold its own reception – she came to spend time with me and I appreciate that.

'Oh my God, the girls all hate you.' Jen's taken me aside and is now hissing in my ear. I whip round quickly, almost knocking over the child-caterer who's doing something clever with pickled walnuts.

'Hate me?' I ask, a little alarmed. My propensity for paranoia is wide, especially when I don't take my pills – and along with imagined affairs, I sometimes think people are talking about me when they probably aren't.

'Yes, hate you… you bitch,' she jokes, but it comes out like she means it and for a moment we're both a bit awkward. It's funny really, but we still don't know each other well enough to joke like that, and I'm really rusty on new friendships, so can't rescue it. 'Because you have such a fabulous house and such gorgeous stuff,' she says, holding up her champagne flute and clearly coveting it as the others chat and gaze around the kitchen, commenting on the size of the two-acre garden through the bifold doors.

'Oh, yes, Simon spotted these champagne flutes in a magazine, had them shipped from Paris. They cost a bloody fortune, but that's Simon for you. He takes after his mother when it comes to beautiful things – the woman never once, to my knowledge, hugged him, but I bet she hugged her bloody French antique furniture every night.' I giggle.

Jen guffaws and I'm flattered she thinks I'm funny; it gives me the confidence to take this further.

'Simon's terrible – has to have designer clothes, labelled sportswear, and don't get me started on his tennis. I reckon he'd rather spend the night with the new tennis racquet than with me,' I half joke. But she doesn't laugh at this, she gets all serious and looks at me like she's waiting for me to say more and when I don't she puts down her glass.

'Marianne, you know you can talk to me?'

I nod, warmed by this more serious, caring side of Jen. 'Thanks Jen, but I don't think...'

'Look, I'm your friend, and I know you're not happy. You were upset that time in the coffee shop and we haven't really had chance to talk since. It's not easy at the school gates with the little monsters tearing around. Tell me to mind my own business, but didn't you say something about Simon and...?'

'Oh, I... Things haven't been too good.' Because I haven't taken my pills, I'm feeling quite anxious and hear myself talking, unable to stop myself in time. 'Yes, it's Simon and... you know, the woman I told you about.'

'But I thought you imagined it?'

'Is that what Simon told you?' I feel a rising sense of panic – has he been laying his poison among all my potential friends?

'No... you said it yourself, when we talked in the coffee shop. You started to say something, then you said you could be imagining it.'

'Oh... well, I thought then I might be. Now I know I'm not.'

'Wow!'

'Yeah. She wants my kids... She's going to move in, Jen. She wants my children, my life and...' I realise at this point I sound mad, so shut up.

'The home-wrecking slut!' She's absolutely furious on my behalf and I love her for it.

'Oh, it's not just her… He's as much to blame. I feel so angry at both of them.'

'Damn right you do,' she says, cheerleading me on – not that I need my flames to be fanned.

'Yes, I can't eat or sleep and…'

'I'd be *more* than angry – I'd be stalking the bitch, then rooting her out on social media and posting pictures of her head Photoshopped onto a pig's body!' she says this loudly with such venom, I touch her arm gently. I don't need her to be in full force when Caroline turns up… if Caroline turns up.

'She's coming here – tonight,' I say as calmly as I can.

Jen is open-mouthed. 'What the fuck?'

'I know, I know, but I want to make a stand. She doesn't know I know, so don't start anything.'

'But why would you…?'

'I want her to see me on my territory, see me owning it and giving her the message that it's not up for rent or purchase… and after tonight I think she'll get the message. In fact I know she will.'

'Ooh you dark horse.'

'Jen, she'd take everything if she could. I've seen the emails,' I add, without mentioning her and Simon's plans to have me certified. If Simon's given Jen any doubts about me that might just confirm it, I need to keep Jen believing in me and on my side.

'The kids, the house, are mine – and they are staying that way,' I hiss, and take a large swig of champagne, the kind of swig that isn't meant for such elegant flutes and would horrify Simon. Good.

'Whoa, Marianne – you want the kids and the house, but you're not letting her get away with the husband, are you?'

'She can keep him, as far as I'm concerned, but I doubt she'll want him after I've finished.' I don't mention the pregnancy; even without my medication I know this isn't the time. Not yet.

'You are quite the dark horse, aren't you? Well, good luck to you – you know me, I'm here if you need muscle.' She laughs and sips her champagne and I love that she said that, because I finally feel like someone's on my side.

I'm strengthened by her cheerleading, and go on to say more. It's good to get it all off my chest. 'I don't want to lose my temper or my dignity, but it makes me so bloody angry. Caroline wants everything I've got – but she could have anything. Why doesn't she just fuck off back to her double-barrelled boyfriend?'

'She has a boyfriend?'

'She did, but it seems to be over now.'

'How do you know this?'

'Because she's with Simon – oh, and because I stalk her on social media,' I admit, taking a glug of champagne, the bubbles making me almost want to giggle.

'So what else have you managed to pick up from social media about this… this surgical… slut!' she hisses.

'Oh, that she's popular, has travelled the world, she's in love with my husband and she's into pain… Or did I see that in her emails? I can't remember now.' The champagne is making me a little giddy. I must stop drinking.

'Emails? You've read her emails?'

'The ones to my husband, yes.'

'What, so you accessed his emails without him knowing…?'

I nod vigorously, relieved to share this. 'I know it's not nice, but I had to know.' I half giggle out of embarrassment more than anything else. I'm ashamed of who and what I've become – sneaking around, poking into their relationship.

Jen looks shocked, perhaps even she thinks I've gone too far?

'I only did it because I knew something was going on,' I say defensively. 'I wouldn't normally read his emails… I just logged in and the email account came up as his favourites, and there was a whole folder with their messages. He hasn't exactly hidden it.'

'Wow! Do you think he *wants* to get caught?' she asks, sitting on the kitchen bar stool and slowly crossing her legs.

'No, he just isn't very good at online stuff. He doesn't even have a Facebook account.'

'Will you confront him about her?'

'I want to, but he'll say I'm mad. I've imagined things, in the past... I've thought he's having an affair when he hasn't. I can be a bit jealous. I even thought he was having an affair with a barmaid at the pub where we lived before... and my best friend before that... and others.'

'Bloody hell! I hope you've never thought *I* was up to anything with your hubby.' She swigs the final dregs of bubbles and heaves the dripping bottle from the ice bucket, pouring herself another.

'You? No.' I laugh, incredulous.

'Why are you laughing?'

'Because you're not his type,' I say, wishing I hadn't been so honest and gone down this route. I don't want to offend her.

'Oh, thanks a million.' Too late.

'Oh, I didn't mean it like that, I... Oh, who knows what his type is, and now you come to mention it, I do remember you dancing close up to him at the school barn dance.' I wink.

'Yeah, but that was just to keep warm – that bloody old school hall can get very cold, even on an August night.' She pouts at this and I feel a bit uncomfortable, like I've accused her of something and offended her. I can't ruin this friendship like I've ruined the rest with my stupid insinuations. We're new friends, and if I want us to be old friends I shouldn't even joke about things like this. Besides, she's the only ally I have.

We both sip our champagne and the doorbell rings; a couple of Simon's work colleagues arrive with their wives. Next is my personal favourite and master stroke, his boss – Professor and Mrs Robert Cookson, staunch right-wing religious types who will probably think this is the most decadent gathering since Caligula was on the party scene. I introduce everyone, open more champagne and remind them all that Simon is due home in about half an hour so we have to be ready to hide and leap out when he comes in. I'm feeling a bit twitchy as there's still no sign of Caroline – perhaps she won't come after all and this will be for nothing? I wonder if after our lunch she decided that Simon's telling the truth, his wife is mad and she wants to steer well clear until the divorce is finalised and the house is hers?

Each time the doorbell rings I hope it's going to be her and brace myself, and like the good friend that she is Jen seems to sense my agitation.

'You okay, babe?' she asks, pouring us both another drink. I should say no, but she's already pouring and I need to take the edge off.

'Yeah, thanks, Jen. I just feel vulnerable, you know? I'm angry too and I don't want that to show, but I could honestly kill her for what she's done to me.'

'I don't blame you, sweetie, how fucking dare she…'

'I know, I know. But just do me a favour, keep it all to yourself.' I nod, squeezing her arm affectionately.

'Hey,' she says gently. 'Don't you worry, Marianne, I've got your back.'

I smile and touch her arm; it's good to have her onside.

I move over to the sink with a couple of empty glasses and I'm just rinsing them when the doorbell rings. The contents of my stomach rise to meet my throat. Why am I putting myself through this? Then I remind myself it's my attempt to break Simon and Caroline from within, to hurt and ruin them and, at the very least, it's a shot across her bows to show her I mean business and won't roll over. I have to make her think I'm in charge of everything, including what's in my own head… and the way I'm feeling just now, that might be a little tricky.

I head for the door and open it, the smile already plastered across my face. She's standing on the doorstep, looking totally amazing – her hair is blonde, shiny and tousled in a 'just got out of bed' model kind of way.

'Heyyyy,' I hear myself say in that fake way people do when they see someone they hate.

CHAPTER TWENTY-TWO

She's in a loose navy dress and, at what I guess must be fourteen weeks pregnant, looks bloody amazing and I feel like crying. All the time he's been seeing her, sleeping with her, he must have been comparing me, and though I don't want him any more and I know our marriage isn't good for me, I still mourn what we had, what we might have been without her. It's hard to just switch off.

'Come in, so lovely of you to come along.' I smile, guiding her through the door.

Move quickly through my hallway, Caroline, or I might be tempted to smash your perfect face into the mirror on the wall.

We walk together into the kitchen and I can tell by the way Jen's lips are tightly pursed that she's with me. She looks angry on my behalf and it makes me feel so much better, so much stronger, to know I have my friend with me, urging me on.

'So, welcome to chez Wilson,' I announce, introducing Caroline to the other women, the doctors she probably knows from the hospital. But before she joins the gaggle of medics and disappears, I want some alone time with her, so I gesture for her to sit on a stool next to me, which she does easily, clearly happy to mount anything. She's clutching a flute of what looks like water and I hold up my glass. 'To new friends and big surprises,' I say, and use my glass like a battering ram on hers as she tentatively holds it up. 'So, glad you came after all, Caroline.' I smile. 'You couldn't resist a little taste of what was to come?' I'm wagging my finger at her, aware I may sound a little tipsy, so put down my glass. That's enough to drink.

'Did you get my suggested guest list?' she asks, looking round, puzzled, as most of her cronies aren't here.

'Yes, thanks for that,' I say, vaguely. 'It's just that, most of the names on that list weren't exactly... Oh, I'm being very indiscreet, but quite frankly Simon doesn't *like* them.' I think it only fair to disrupt his work relationships; he's ruined all my relationships ever.

'Congratulations,' I say, and clink her glass with mine again. 'What for?'

I nod my head towards her still-flat belly. 'The baby.'

'Oh it's... not ... I haven't told everyone yet. I'd prefer it if you didn't...'

'Absolutely. Completely understand – you mustn't tempt fate.' I smile as Jen catches my eye and immediately rallies.

'So, hello, and you are?' she asks, staggering over to us and giving me an exaggerated tipsy wink that I'm sure Caroline has seen.

'Caroline Harker. I'm a colleague of... Simon's.' She puts out her hand to shake and Jen half grabs it, peering into her face, scrutinising it for a moment too long, and things have become even more uncomfortable. 'Oh, you're a *colleague*. It must be very... exciting being a nurse,' Jen says, knowing this will be received with some distaste. Caroline's air of superiority is plain even for tipsy Jen to spot.

'I'm not a nurse... I'm a surgeon...'

'Yes, she works very closely with Simon,' I add, enjoying the show and loving Jen, who then makes it clear to Caroline that we're all very good friends.

Caroline, if you even try to replace me, there's a high wall to climb. Her name is Jen.

'Simon's always telling us his hospital stories. Oh. My. God. That guy... Marianne, what was it, a car accident?' She's waving her hand up and down in my direction like that will give me a clue. 'He was twenty years old and his heart stopped... for thirty minutes. Everyone thought, that's it, he's gone, but Simon just had this feeling, this intuition, and he kept working on him. And, hey presto, he brought him back to life.'

I have to commend Jen for her improvisation. I don't remember Simon ever telling that story, and as Jen's only met him a couple of times I have to assume she's just laying it on thick. Who knew that Jen would provide such fabulous additional PR? She's certainly earning her keep, despite guzzling vintage champagne like it's bloody Fanta, but she's backing me up as promised.

'Yes… I remember that one,' Caroline says. 'That was one of the first operations I assisted on at the hospital.'

So Jen's 'improvised' anecdote wasn't that imaginative after all, it was real – he must have shared this with her at the school gate. I can only imagine the other yummies joining them as he chatted, rubbing up against him like bitches on heat. I can see Caroline watching the dynamic between us as we laugh about something that happened with the kids. I want her to think Jen and I share this perfect life, with our families socialising, popping in and out of each other's homes, opening a bottle of wine and chatting, feeding the other's kids, collecting them when the other can't. This isn't how it is at all. Jen's invited us over to hers a few times and occasionally we've said yes, but as Simon doesn't really like her I've had to say no a lot too. In truth I barely see Jen other than at school pick-up – her nanny does most of the school runs – but Caroline doesn't know that. I want her to think we're all best friends, that there's shared history between us built on school sports and fun days out with the children.

So there's another knot you'd have to untangle, Caroline, if you wanted to be me, and take over my life. So fuck you, Caroline.

'Where are my manners?' I hear myself say. 'Caroline, let me give you the tour.'

She looks a bit surprised, but if she tries to get out of it, I'll physically force her up those bloody stairs to our bedroom, because that's what I *really* want her to see.

I lead her first to the boys' room. They are on a sleepover tonight, which I'm suddenly a bit disappointed about. Because there's every chance they might have committed some atrocity before bedtime and the very prospect of being their stepmother might have sent Caroline running for the hills. I've put their toys strategically around though, so the room looks lived in, but still very *Homes and Gardens*. On one of the walls I've hung a big picture painted by Alfie and I'm keen to point it out to her.

'Lovely,' she says absently.

'Hardly,' I sneer. 'It's his father being eaten by a dinosaur – it's clearly labelled,' I say, going up close and pointing this out like a teacher at the blackboard. 'The child psychologist had a field day.' I laugh.

This isn't strictly true, because Simon wouldn't allow any of his kids to see a child psychologist. 'Nothing wrong with him,' he said, when he saw the painting. He was also adamant when Charlie tried to strangle Alfie, calling him 'a jealous psycho', that he had no idea what he was saying, but Simon and I both know where he'd heard the words, and I made a mental note to close our bedroom door from then on. #PillowTalk.

Caroline isn't sure what to say. She stands hesitantly in the doorway and any minute I'm expecting her to ask 'why are you showing me your kids' bedrooms and their unhinged paintings, you crazy bitch?' But she doesn't because her curiosity is getting the better of her.

I then knock on Sophie's door. 'She's revising,' I say. 'Our Sophie takes after her dad – wants to be a doctor, a forensic doctor in fact. She's crazy for *CSI* and all that.'

'Oh…' Caroline says. 'Don't disturb her… it's fine, I don't need to see…'

'She won't mind,' I say and, as Sophie calls 'Hi', I open the door. She's sitting on her bed, books all around her. She looks lovely, just sitting there, long hair brought round in a knot on her shoulder, glasses on the end of her nose. She's pretty, with small features, and looks a bit like Nicole, but people who don't know we aren't biologically related say she looks like me. We both like it – gives us a sense of belonging to each other.

She looks up. 'Hi Mum.'

'Darling, this is Caroline. She's a friend of Dad's; she's here for the party.' I bring Caroline into the doorway. She really doesn't want to be presented to the daughter of the house and shuffles in the doorway.

'Oh…?' Sophie goes back to her books. Sophie can be monosyllabic like most teenagers, but she's never rude.

I want this inveigler to see how close my stepdaughter and I are. Through my gentle, loving Sophie, I want Caroline to see yet another wall that she can't penetrate. But Sophie's reticence might give her a false dawn, a chink of light in the darkness, imagining she is difficult and hates me and she's looking for a new mum.

'Sophie, darling, it's usual to say "hello" when you're introduced to someone,' I half roll my eyes at Caroline. *Teenagers.*

'We've met before,' Sophie mutters, and Caroline shuffles again in the doorway.

'Oh, of course, in Waitrose when we were all buying lemons.' I laugh.

'No, we met before that,' Sophie says disinterestedly, going back to her laptop. My stomach drops like an elevator and is now crashed on the ground floor.

Who, what, when, where, why?

'Oh, I didn't realise.' I keep smiling, even though it hurts my face.

'Yeah… we met at the tennis club. Hi again, Sophie,' Caroline tries, but my daughter doesn't raise her head, just mutters 'Hi' and pretends to work.

'Okay, we'll leave you to your studies, sweetie,' I say, feeling like the rug's been pulled from under me. 'But do pop downstairs if you're peckish and say hello to Jen.'

'Jen?' she asks. She's barely even met Jen, but that doesn't match with the 'all families together' image I'm trying to present, so I close the door quickly.

Tennis. Fucking tennis. Taking her to his club to play is bad enough, but to introduce our daughter to the woman he's shagging is unbelievable, and makes me feel violated. I don't care any more what he does, but I do care when he's bringing our kids into it.

Incandescent at the audacity of him introducing Sophie to her next stepmother, I am unable to speak as I guide her to the bathroom. I try to come up with an interesting story about the tiles to give me time to compose myself and also to justify this grand tour. I'd like to smash her head against my tarnished metallic tiles and then put her head under the waterfall bath filler. 'I mean, who still has taps?' I laugh, running my hands under the bathroom equivalent of a minimalist Niagara Falls.

'So, you're a member of the tennis club too?' I ask, feigning disinterest.

I can't probe too much because if I do, it's clear I haven't a clue about Simon, or what he does. To be honest that's true, but I don't want her to know that.

'Yes, I joined a few months ago. I haven't seen you there?'

'Oh, I go… sometimes. Simon's always nagging me to join him for a game,' I say, and even I think that sounds desperate. I ignore the bathroom and push open our bedroom door so we can move on. 'Anyway, this is mine and Simon's room, the master bedroom,' I add with a flourish. I long to tell her we had sex here last night, that it was wonderful – loving sex between two people who've been together a long time and know each other well. I want to tell her it didn't involve anyone being hurt, that it was warm and emotional. But I resist saying any of this; it wouldn't be appropriate. Or true.

She's looking around, taking everything in, almost sniffing the air. Fresh flowers, staged rugs and cushions, books placed strategically on bedside tables. I've planted a few contemporary classics on mine. I felt Jane Austen would be a cliché and suggest a buttoned-up life/wife. So I've piled Jack Kerouac, Tom Wolfe and *Fifty Shades*. I want her to think I'm wild, artsy and sexy too. The tragedy is – I think I was all these things once, before Simon. I've played my own little joke on him and put the *Kama Sutra* and *Harry Potter* by his bed, to which I gesture with my hand and remark, 'Says it all about men, doesn't it? Little boys who love sex.' I let it hang – the implication's clear that the two of us are at it like rabbits, but he's so insatiable he then goes off and gets it where he can.

Work that one out, Caroline.

'Nice… nice colour on the walls,' she says. I can see her faltering but still clocking every little thing, including the pants from my red silk underwear lying on the floor. Staged of course, which I think is a really nice touch. I'm even more creative than I'd realised.

Enjoy your inventory, Caroline – it's the last time you'll be allowed in my home.

I make an embarrassed face and bend down to pick the pants up and push them discreetly under the pillow.

'Yes, it's all right, isn't it? We like it. Farrow and Ball's Borrowed Light. It's in the kitchen too. They describe it on the website as "evoking the colour of summer skies". That's what drew us to it. Simon says it reminds him of our holidays in Greece. We went to Crete this year – it was spectacular,' I say, erasing in one swipe those complaining emails he sent to her. I want to develop the idea that he lied to her when he said he was having a horrible time on holiday with his family. So I tell her what a wonderful time we had and how we plan to go back there alone, 'just the two of us, for our next wedding anniversary'. 'My husband is such a romantic,' I sigh.

I pick up the silk nightgown then that I casually dropped on the bed earlier – a gift to myself recently when I saw another email order for lingerie on Simon's account. I bought one exactly the same and I'm pretending to fold it, running the silk sensuously through my fingers, making sure she sees the label. I mustn't miss a thing; this is a small window I have with her and it has to work.

Yes, Caroline, it is exactly the same as the one he bought you, 'for being a good girl'. Not that good, eh?

'Wedding anniversary... when is...?' She can barely get her words out, so amazed is she at the marital love-fest I'm laying before her.

'It's not til next summer.' I smile. 'We're going to renew our vows... Simon's already chosen the hotel, the meal we'll have and even told me he plans to work out the moment the sun will dip into the sea on that night – give or take a few minutes. He's all about the detail is Simon. He chose the villa we stayed in with the kids – he wanted the one where the master bedroom was on the other side of the building, for obvious reasons.' I roll my eyes in mock annoyance, but my voice is laced with affection and, I hope, sensuality. 'We love the Greek islands,' I sigh. I want her to believe that her textual and email presence in our lives didn't affect our family holiday, or our marriage, because he's been lying to her all this time. 'You too?' I ask, clutching the nightdress, being deliberately provocative.

'What?' she snaps, confused, unable to take her eyes off the nightgown. She must think she's going mad. Been there, done that, got the pills.

Caroline, welcome to my world.

'The Greek islands? Do you love them too?' I ask innocently.

'Oh... yes....'

'Oh, we love Greece... and the South of France. We had a fabulous time there.' I leave a pause, like I'm remembering a beautiful moment – a sun-drenched beach, my husband's hand in mine, tangled sheets and warm bodies. 'But it isn't just about the location, is it? For us a holiday's about the family being together.

There's nothing quite like it – no one else, just us in our bubble. The kids in bed with us each morning, Simon making pancakes for everyone. It's the happiest I've seen him for a while; he said he dreaded coming home,' I add, just in case she's in any doubt. Of course, it wasn't like this, but then neither are the stories he tells her about me. We're both perfect liars. 'I hope you don't mind me asking,' I suddenly say, like I've only just thought of this, 'but for him to dread coming back from holiday – well, it's not like him and I have this feeling something's troubling him… at work. I wondered if…?'

'Oh?' She's gone a bit rabbit in the headlights. I could just drive right over her.

'Do you know if there's anything…?' I leave it hanging, look into her face, waiting to see what she'll say to this. It's obviously upset her to think he wanted to stay on holiday with his family… away from her.

'No, I don't know anything… I really… I don't get involved in other people's business.'

No, just other people's husbands.

'Oh, I'm sure it's nothing, it's just he's seemed a bit down recently, says he doesn't enjoy being at work like he used to.' I sigh, laying the nightdress neatly back on the bed, running my hands along the silk gently. 'I expect someone on the team is pissing him off… It happens.' I suddenly put my hand to my mouth like I've said something I shouldn't. It's Oscar winning; my talents in this field have surprised even me. 'Oh… how tactless of me, Caroline,' I gasp. 'Obviously, when I said *someone on the team…* I didn't mean *you*. No, not at all… I should hate for you to think Simon has a problem with you… in all honesty he's never mentioned you, even in passing – so nothing to worry about there. Oh, except that time when we bumped into you in Waitrose, and he said you were new to the job and he was really father-like about the fact that you were struggling a bit? He does like to take people under his wing.'

'Does he?' She's visibly shocked at this. Perhaps the penny is finally dropping. If he can say all those awful things about the apparently sane wife and mother in the happy marriage standing before her, what lies might he tell about her?

The truth according to Simon number 59,983.

I'm standing on one side of the marital bed now, her on the other, both braced over the battleground.

'I'm sorry,' I say, putting my hand over my mouth like I've spoken out of turn. 'Here's me, standing in our bedroom with one of Simon's colleagues, being very indiscreet. Forgive me – we're very close and I just know when my husband's unhappy at work. You get a sort of sixth sense as a wife.'

'Beautiful nightie.' She changes the subject. 'Where is it from?'

'Not sure – it was a special gift for being a good girl.' I wink and see the blood drain from her face. I wait a moment for this to sink in, then give her a big, beaming smile. She doesn't respond; she's clearly processing everything she's seen and heard and with that baby brain she's probably all over the place. 'Oh, Caroline, you mustn't mind me. I've had a few drinks and I'm being very naughty – though I sometimes get gifts for that too.' I laugh loudly at this, and put my hand back over my mouth. I do think it's quite funny, but not as hilarious as the look of sheer horror on Caroline's face.

How does it feel, Caroline? Oh, wait… I know exactly how it feels.

I show her the spare bedroom, which I've styled beautifully and is clearly not the product of a disturbed mind. I stand there a moment like an art gallery attendant, allowing Caroline to take it all in before moving on.

Like anything you see, bitch? Enjoy it while you can – you won't be seeing it again.

'Oh… fresh lavender,' is all she can mumble as I open the door. Staying with the Farrow and Ball palette, Dayroom Yellow smothers the walls in sunshine, broken up only by the grey bed linen and scattered cushions in fifty shades of grey. This is accessorized by a jug of fresh lavender and a diffuser in the same fragrance to give it some oomph. 'I love a room that smells nice,' I say, with a bright innocent smile. 'Covers up any nasties lurking around,' I add.

She really has had enough. I can tell by her face – she looks like she might be sick at any moment.

Oh, Caroline, but we're having so much fun, aren't we?

'Simon loves this room,' I say. 'Sometimes we just snuggle in this little bed and spend the night in here together. He likes to ring the changes – gets bored easily.' I roll my eyes like he's a child to be indulged, and, closing the door, I walk with her down the stairs, and try not to think about pushing her all the way down.

CHAPTER TWENTY-THREE

Caroline's clutching the bannister and taking the stairs two at a time. She can't wait to get him alone and ask what the fuck is going on.

But of course he's not arrived yet and when we get back into the kitchen, Jen is there like the welcoming committee, canapés laid out, cold champagne waiting in the ice bucket.

I can see the look on Caroline's face as Jen embarks on yet another story about Simon's prowess in theatre. I love her but she doesn't quite get it.

She's there in the theatre with him, you daft cow – didn't you hear her, she's a surgeon too. She stands next to him when he operates. She hands him the bloody scalpel and later, when they're alone, she does other things and I'm trying really hard not to think about them because she's here, in my kitchen.

I fill our glasses and down mine quickly – it's cold and prickly on my throat, and I'm already quite tipsy. Caroline looks like she's seen the proverbial ghost and I'm announcing the 'utter' deliciousness of prawn, mango and cucumber on crispy pitta chips, with 'a soupçon' of beetroot when I hear the front door open and so does everyone else.

'Hide,' I yell, and guests rush to every corner of the room, but mostly behind the curtains of the large French windows. The women from school remind me of eager meerkats up on their hind legs, waiting for the man of the house as I stand too close to Caroline, longing to wrap her so tightly in my beautiful curtains that she can't breathe. In palest slate linen, they are certainly to die for – and I have to stop myself thinking about her perfect, lifeless body and concentrate on the task in hand. Eventually, he wanders into the dimly lit kitchen where I can see his face is the usual miserable, unhappy one. I want to laugh hysterically as we all scream 'Surprise', making him leap in the air with shock and completely blindsiding him. The uninitiated might think he's okay with all this because his recovery is swift, but I see the horror turning to fake brightness as work colleagues and drunken school mums appear from behind the curtains.

'Ah, what a... surprise?' he gasps, suddenly surrounded by the little gaggle of work colleagues congratulating him on his new position.

I smile to myself – this has been worth it just to see the discomfort on his face – and I rush over to him, gently push through everyone and kiss him full on the lips. I know she's watching me. I can feel her cold blue eyes piercing my flesh. I don't hang around to see his reaction to my kiss. I flounce around, digging out more champagne to refill everyone's glasses. I nod to the catering girls, who do another whip-round with their trays of fabulous canapés, then I sit and watch.

As I watch on though, I notice the ticks in Simon's behaviour, the little telltale signs that show inside he's fuming and part of me is scared. I suppose I will always be scared of him to some extent, of the way he manipulates me, the power he has over me. But finally I'm not scared of losing him, and because of that I'm less vulnerable and, for the first time, able to envisage life without him if he leaves me, which, after tonight, I'm sure he will.

Simon is soon fawning all over the professor and his lemon-lipped wife, who apparently also hates beetroot with a passion. #Bingo #TwoForOne.

I have another drink with Jen and Francesca, whose husband has now arrived – which I'm glad about because it seemed odd just having the yummies without any partners. They like a man to bounce off and Francesca's husband is easy on the eye, so they're all having a giggle and Jen's flirting like mad.

When I look over to Simon's colleagues, I'm pleased to see Caroline isn't being included in the work gaggle – and that's because I haven't invited any of her friends. I only asked the Prof. and other eminent but crusty old surgeons and their wives, because they have to be here for my speech. The old buggers aren't interested or even aware of Simon's surgical ingénue, so with nowhere to hide, she's now being talked at by Jen, who's abandoned the yummy mummies to play cat and mouse on my behalf. #GoJen.

Amusingly, she is hurling a torrent of information at Caroline, detailing the minutiae of her family life, including a detailed account of her husband's lack of talent in bed. Caroline's face is frozen, and if I wasn't so busy, I'd take a photo and post it online – #PartyPeople. But I can't enjoy this for long because I have to play the perfect hostess and I get caught up in some small talk about Christmas with one of Simon's colleagues.

I eventually extricate myself and glance over to see Jen now has Suzie in a conversational headlock. So where's Caroline?

I can't spot her anywhere – maybe she's in *my* downstairs bathroom, sniffing *my* towels and marking her territory. Or I wonder if perhaps they've wordlessly made arrangements for him to join her alone in *my* garden, where he can wow her with his winter-flowering Japanese quince. He seemed to enjoy showing our pretty neighbour Renee round his roses at midnight and judging by their emails Caroline's no stranger to dropping her thong in the long grass.

I will not have the two of them engaging in some sordid little fumble in my lovely home, tainting the interior with their illicit sex. Besides, I don't want them to miss the best bit that I have planned so I'm relieved when I spot Simon is still talking to old Cookson.

I wander over, pushing my arm through his. 'Happy Senior Consultancy, darling.'

He smiles, but it doesn't reach his eyes and, raising his glass, he looks around the room and murmurs in my ear, 'Why would you do this?'

I laugh lightly and put my hand to my mouth as though he's made an improper suggestion, just as Caroline comes back into the kitchen. I catch her eye and I try to smile warmly, but it comes out as more of a sneer.

I'm finding it hard to hide my feelings tonight. Of course it could be the fact that I didn't have any pills. Or the three, four, five glasses of wine I've had? No more, that's it, I just have to hold it together a while longer.

'Simon,' I suddenly say loudly. 'This is a party. I don't want you talking work all evening – come and chat with the ladies.' I virtually drag him away from a rather irritated Cookson across the room to where Caroline has returned to her perch next to Jen.

Any port in a storm eh, love?

Simon is furious; if there was one saving grace about tonight's horror show it would be his chance to creep all over Cookson. But now I've put a stop to that.

'Darling, you know *both* these ladies, don't you?' I say, gesturing to Caroline and Jen, sitting awkwardly together but apart.

He looks uneasy. 'Yes – lovely to see you again, Jen.' Ever the charmer, he steps towards her, planting kisses on both cheeks and hugging her with fake warmth, but I know he can't stand her. She's well gone by now and smiles girlishly. '… And Caroline,' he's saying awkwardly, hugging her with one arm as she softens into it. He gently pulls away and I catch the look that passes between them – it's so tangible I could grasp it and bang it hard against the kitchen worktops until it dies like a caught, wriggling fish. 'It seems like only hours ago we were standing over an open chest…' He laughs, and she shifts on her seat. I'm surprised at the residue of jealousy lodged in my throat; an immovable fatberg of hurt wedged in my thorax forever.

I loved you, Simon, and in spite of everything I think a little part of me always will.

'So, what do you think of your surprise party?' I say, reaching up and kissing him full on the lips.

A kiss goodbye?

He's irritated by my open show of affection and discreetly pulls away. No one seems to notice, thank God. Jen's pissed, Francesca's arguing with her husband and Caroline's pretending to look down into the bubbles of her drink. I don't care what his crusty colleagues think – well, I do, but not in a good way, as everyone is about to find out in the next few minutes.

Always concerned about image, Simon has to be seen as the charming host and in spite of himself takes a bottle from the ice bucket. There'll be trouble when they've gone, but until then he'll play the perfect husband. He refreshes all our glasses, except Caroline's – she hasn't drunk a drop. She's obviously thinking about the baby. She puts her hand firmly on top of her glass when he brings the bottle to her and I get the feeling it isn't just her glass she's covering up from him. She seems so stiff, uncomfortable, and I see hurt in her eyes. Thanks to my evening's work, I reckon she's going to take some convincing that this marriage is over. Good.

It wasn't that easy after all was it, Caroline?

'So, what do you think of your little surprise party?' I ask again, in front of the throng of mostly school mums.

'You know I hate surprises.' He grimaces.

'I know, but you *love* Caroline… oh and Jen.' I smile, as Jen almost chokes. I wonder for a moment if I've been too direct but then carry on; it's nothing to what I've got lined up for tonight. 'I know you're a bit of a hermit,' I say, then address 'the girls'. 'He's never liked parties… or anything social really.'

'I wouldn't say I don't *like* parties…' he starts, gritting his teeth, flexing that jaw, keen to sell Caroline the 'party guy' image that I assume he's been falsely peddling.

'But, sweetie, Caroline and I have been planning this for weeks,' I say, like she and I are conspirators.

He shoots a look at her; she doesn't meet his eyes.

Turns out Caroline has secrets from you too, Simon.

'I wasn't planning... I just gave... her... your wife a list,' she's muttering.

'What do you think of the canapés – we're *loving* them aren't we, girls?' I say brightly over Caroline's small voice, watching her shudder at the 'girls' inclusion. And for the first time tonight I realise that despite the tension, the threat hanging over me – I'm having fun... Yes, I'm actually having fun, because I'm in charge for once and I like how that feels. In addition to this rather heady autonomy, I feel like Simon's focus has shifted. He doesn't care what I do any more, but he cares what Caroline does. 'So, have we made you happy, darling?' I say, gesturing round the room. 'We had to keep this a secret... the guests, the catering... even the champagne had to be delivered after you'd left for work this morning, didn't it, Caroline?'

'I have no idea. I merely gave you a list of names.'

I see a look flash between them – he's clearly annoyed that she was involved, however minor her role, and she's in denial. And, despite myself, his cold glare chills me to the bone, because it's a look I know so well, and it's usually directed at me, but tonight it's her.

Be careful what you wish for, Caroline.

Could this be the real Simon after all, and not the one who writes the loving emails? The man who writes those is the one I thought I'd lost because of my irrational behaviour, but he isn't here for Caroline either. Who is the real Simon: the one who is tender and warm and sends flowers every fortnight, or the one who pins me up against the wall with his hands around my throat? Have I been fighting all this time for a man who doesn't actually exist?

'Ooh, smoked trout nibbles with beetroot,' I say, trying to keep it light, taking a canapé from a passing tray. 'They described it as "a whisper of dill, a crunch of radish and the *acidity* of pickled beetroot" – but I think it's just yummy.'

Jen is smiling at me, not sure what it is I'm saying, but enjoying the running commentary. Caroline is itchy. She so wants to leave.

Not yet Caroline. The night is still young; there's so much more to come.

Simon's asking if there are actually any canapés without beetroot, when the mini fig tarts arrive.

'Ah… blue cheese and fig… A nice little *tart!*' I say, too loudly.

I take a bite from the miniature slice and make an 'mmmm' noise. I don't know what's more delicious, the taste of the tart or Caroline and Simon's deep, deep discomfort.

I will be happy when he's ruined and she's leaving with her tail between her legs, the bloom from her bastard child dulled.

'This…' I announce, holding it aloft, 'is *very* good. You love tarts, don't you Simon?' Then I laugh, loudly, and glare at him. I know, I know, it's a cheap shot… and childish, and to quote him, I'm better than that. But turns out I'm not, and I don't even care. I take another bite. 'Mmm, these flavours are a marriage made in heaven,' I sigh, as Simon looks on, horrified. Caroline looks pale, defeated, but I can't forgive her for the things she's said, the way she encouraged his plans for me. 'Talking of marriage, do you think *you'll* ever get married, Caroline? By that I mean – will you get your *own* husband or will you marry someone else's?' I say this loudly enough to alert the other guests, who turn to look, half-smiles on their faces, imagining this is some joke I'm making to start a speech. But this is no joke. Caroline doesn't know where to put herself and Jen titters into the deafening silence.

Simon is looking at me over his glass, not sipping, just holding it to his mouth, ready for what might happen next.

I see Caroline flash a quick look at Simon – she's threatened and wants him to save her.

He won't save you, love, he'll only save himself.

'Caroline?' I turn to her, deciding that now is as good a time as any to light the fireworks and let the sparks fly. I've been building up to this for a long time, and I will relish every moment.

'Lovely, fragrant Caroline… Do you mind if I give you some smart advice…?'

She is looking at me with fear in her eyes, which turns to abject horror at my next sentence.

'… That when you're looking for a husband, you pick one who isn't *already* married. Do you get me?' I say, my head to one side like I care.

'I don't know what you mean,' she stutters, her face an embarrassed scarlet.

'Oh, I think you do. You see, Caroline, I have one hell of a life. It isn't the easiest, it isn't the best and it's far from perfect. But I've endured it for so long, put up with his moods, his selfishness, his womanising, his cruelty for so bloody long, I feel like I should have a *medal*, and I am damned if you think you can walk in here and take over…'

Simon walks towards me – he's also red, but it's more on the purple side, and the vein is standing out in his head.

'Don't hurt me, Simon,' I say, dramatically lifting my hands up to protect my face for effect. Simon's a bully but he'd never hurt me in a room full of people, his pain is private. At this he immediately pulls away lest anyone should even consider this perfect man to be in any way violent towards his wife. Free to continue, I start to bang my spoon on my glass. 'Speech, speech,' I shout. I want *everyone* to hear this.

Silence lands with a thud in the middle of my beautiful kitchen.

'Thank you all for coming here tonight – it hasn't been easy keeping this from Simon, and thank you all for conspiring with me.' A faint waft of uncertain giggles. 'So, tonight's all about Simon's wonderful promotion that he's worked for, fought for, and really, really lost all dignity to achieve.' I smile; no one else does. 'Tonight is a celebration of my husband's amazing skills and talent… and it isn't just a surgical talent he possesses. Oh no, Simon has many skills – he also has lots of secrets and this wouldn't be an adequate celebration if I didn't share some of these with you. It seems that while everyone's been busy in the operating theatre, Simon's been busy too. He's not only been campaigning for his new role as Medical Director, fawning round old Cookson, but all the while he's been screwing Junior Surgeon Caroline Harker in empty operating theatres, hospital toilets and over the desk in his office.' I gesture towards a red-faced Caroline, pointing her out so all the eminent surgical minds can clock her and consider her toxic if ever she should go for promotion. Cookson and his wife's faces are a picture and will be forever be captioned in my head… #HappyDays #PulledItOff.

'That's enough,' Simon hisses and rushes towards me. For a moment it looks like he might hit me, and I flinch dramatically for everyone to see. Francesca's husband steps forward, my potential bodyguard – I move towards him and continue in safety, knowing Simon won't tackle me while he's around.

'As I was saying, Caroline, the femme fatale of the operating theatre, darling of the triple bypass, and enfant terrible of the Cardiomyoplasty department, also has a little surprise for us all.' I'm nodding now, building up to the big one – everyone is shuffling, drinking, desperately embarrassed but unable to tear themselves away. 'Because she is *pregnant* – with what we can only assume is my husband's baby!'

I start clapping during a murmur of shock and disapproval. Jen almost collapses; she's playing it to the hilt and I love her for it. Meanwhile, Cookson's jaw is on the floor and I reckon he's realising what a big mistake he's made in promoting immoral, cheating, empty-theatre-abusing Simon.

'Regrets, Professor?' I ask, and he snaps at his wife, who is trying to placate him, before grabbing her and storming out. 'Just one more thing before you all go,' I say to his retreating back. 'I imagine Simon has informed you all about my "headaches"? But despite perhaps evidence to the contrary, I am not mentally ill. Not at all. Increasingly, I'm realising that my behaviour is and always has been a perfectly natural reaction to life with my violent, cruel, cheating husband. Thank you and good night.'

Caroline grabs her bag and makes for the door, quickly followed by Simon. There's then a muffled discussion in the hallway, which everyone is pretending not to listen to. It's followed by the slam of the front door and the guests from the hospital and their wives and husbands suddenly realise how late it is.

After a montage of 'Is it really that late? Lovely evening,' and 'The babysitter has to leave by 9 p.m.,' they head for the door. Everyone's embarrassed, but no one as much as Simon, because this is his worst nightmare: a public humiliation, a shaming and, hopefully, a career crash. He can't believe I know – he can't understand how I've found out about the baby, which he apparently knew nothing of judging by the look on his face. His new position at the hospital is no doubt now in jeopardy, and he's been made to look a fool in front of his work colleagues and all the yummy mummies he uses for a quick ego trip in the playground when he drops the kids off.

Nice job, Marianne.

'What is *wrong* with you, Marianne?' He's now hissing in my face, having swept back into an almost empty kitchen after chasing the professor down the drive. 'Why do you *always* have to do this?'

Jen is the only guest left and is staring at me, mouth agape. Simon's shaking his head slowly, like I'm the problem, the burden in his life.

I gaze around the room. The poor catering girls are just like Jen with their mouths open wide.

'Can you invoice me?' I say with a smile. They nod and wordlessly throw the rest of their plates into a box and hurry out, as Jen pours herself another drink. She's already very drunk.

'Do you want me to stay – if nothing else as a referee?' She flicks her head at Simon, addressing him too. Presumably, she's hoping he'll pick up her little joke and laugh, but Simon never laughs at little jokes. He strides towards the huge French windows and stares out onto our perfect lawn. 'I can stay if you'd like me to?' She's nodding to me, while sneaking a mean glance at Simon.

He turns round quickly. 'No, Jen, but thanks for being here for Marianne,' he says, like I'm not here, like I've already been sectioned.

'Oh… okay… I'll call a taxi… shall I?' Jen's saying, almost expectantly. I know she's looking out for me, and I am a little scared of being left alone with him, but surely now I've told everyone what Simon is he daren't touch me. 'I'll wait outside then… for the taxi?' she says, without stirring.

'Please,' he snaps back at her, and she jumps down from her stool. The air prickles around him; even his glass of champagne is fizzing like it's been shaken as he stands glaring through the window.

Jen picks up her bag. 'Erm, bye then, Simon…' she says as she reaches the kitchen door. She doesn't really know him, and yet she seems to need his approval, his permission to leave – he has this effect on everyone.

In response, he turns his head vaguely in her direction, but doesn't look at her. 'Bye Jen,' he says, like it's a command: *Go, Jen.*

'I'll call you… tomorrow,' I say, hoping he'll take the hint that I have someone on my side who's waiting for my call. If he does anything to hurt me, Jen will know and she will come running. She has my back.

But she's clearly upset and doesn't look at me, just teeters from the room on her bedroom shoes. They don't look sexy or funny any more – just silly and a bit sad. Without even a goodbye to me, her friend, I hear the door slam for a second time.

I look at my husband of over a decade and wonder what's going to happen. He isn't going to make this easy, despite the fact that he's the one in the wrong – he will make me suffer for this.

But I want to lay it out for him. 'If you want to leave, if you want to be with her and your baby then go, because there's nothing left for us.'

'And whose fault is that?'

I hesitate, but this is the time for truth. What's happened these past few weeks has given me the strength to finally be honest and stand up to him.

'We're both to blame. You've spent our married life hurting me in so many ways, and I let you. Because of my guilt over Emily and my weakness, I allowed you to brainwash me into believing that there was something wrong with me as a wife, a mother, as a person.'

He's silent, glaring at me now, and I'm scared, but I carry on.

'You don't take any responsibility for the pain you cause... and I always end up apologising,' I hear myself say.

'Responsibility?' He turns quickly and rushes towards me. I put my arms up to my face in an instinctive act of self-defence. He can't bear to be close to me, but now his face is in mine and his eyes are on fire. 'You have the audacity to talk to *me* about *responsibility*?' He enunciates each syllable, spittle on his lips, pure loathing in his eyes.

'Don't... just don't,' I cry. 'You can't keep bringing everything around to that. It *happened*. Don't you think I feel it, the guilt, the pain? I wake up every morning and she's the first thing I think of. She's with me until I go to sleep at night. I dream of rolling back the clock, if only I could. I see her little face in my sleep, I see eyes wide open just like my mother's were when I found her. I understand why you hate me – I hate myself – but you can't go on hurting me for the rest of my life. I've welcomed your punishment, made myself vulnerable just so you can hurt me, because it's what I deserve. But Simon, no one can torment me about this more than I torment myself. I've built my life around it, because I live with it and always will... just being alive is my penance.'

I am crying; my heart is bursting. The only conversations I've allowed myself are the blaming ones, where I apologise and Simon gets to torture me and use it like a cattle prod to keep me in line. I'm pleading with him now, to put down his weapons, to call a truce, but all he does is look at me, shake his head despairingly. And then he walks away. I'm amazed... it was that easy. I've done it – the war is finally over.

'Simon, are you going to leave?'

'No.' He looks at me with incredulity. 'I'm not leaving the house I've worked for and have no intention of leaving my children with you.'

My heart bounces to the floor. I should have known he'd want one last fight, one last chance to control me, but I'm not that weak, insipid shadow any more.

'Then we're at a stalemate,' I sigh.

'No, we're not – tonight you put me firmly in the driving seat, Marianne. That stunt you pulled proved to everyone that you're ill, unhinged, paranoid. I don't have to leave this house or my family. But you will.'

I'm angry now and fighting for everything. I'm not scared of him any more. I'm just furious. 'You can dress tonight up as my breakdown, but this time I've not been so stupid. This relationship isn't a figment of my imagination – I've seen the emails, and the woman is pregnant.'

'Marianne, there are no emails. There's nothing going on with Caroline. She's not pregnant – to my knowledge – and if she is it's certainly not mine. I'm not having an affair with anyone. You need to let it go; you're not well.' He's talking to me in his calm, clinical voice. I remember it from last time when he left me at the clinic; it chills me to the bone.

'No, no... I *saw* the emails, Simon.' I'm not mad, I'm not. This time I know it's for real.

'Will you *calm* down and take your medication?'

I storm into the living room and grab the iPad, type in the passcode, then try to log into his emails, but all I get is 'this account does not exist, try again'. No... no... I saw them. This can't be happening.

He pours two glasses of champagne and calmly hands me one. 'Look, Marianne, we've been here before, so many times. You get yourself into a state and accuse me of all kinds, but this time it is serious. Caroline is a colleague, a junior colleague who looks up to me, and yes we have a friendship, a mutual respect. She admires me for my experience, my skill, and I admire her for being so young and bright. But that's it... and what you did tonight...'

'BUT YOU'VE BEEN SEEING EACH OTHER!' I yell in his face. 'I know... I've been reading all about it...' I pick up the iPad and frantically try again, my hands shaking. I press the keypad with the combination I know so well, but... nothing. 'They were here... I've been reading them for months.' I fall into a chair with my head in my hands. Forget it. I don't need some emails to prove I'm *not* ill... I look up and see him standing over me – is that a smirk on his lips or am I imagining it? Then it dawns on me, 'Where are they, Simon?' I ask, now as cold and calm as he is.

'You've deleted the account, haven't you?' I say, looking into his face, but he doesn't answer. He's holding out his hand, and in his palm are two tablets, which I slowly take from his palm and wash down with champagne.

CHAPTER TWENTY-FOUR

I lean against the kitchen worktop and cry. Have I imagined the emails after all – is there anything else that I have to prove I'm not going mad?

'Look, you have to ask yourself why you make these things up, and it's Emily's birthday in a few weeks. I guess you've been building up to it.'

'No… I…' I sip the champagne for comfort. 'Simon, I saw them.'

'So why aren't they there now?'

'Because you've deleted the account…'

'If… and all I'm saying is "if" I suddenly decided to delete anything, why now? I didn't even know you thought you were looking at these fictitious emails, so ask yourself why, if this was my email account for arranging rendezvous with junior colleagues – why would I delete it now?'

I can't answer that.

'You check my phone…' I make a final, dying twitch, a vain hope that I'm not mad, but I'm worried that he might be right. 'Perhaps you saw my history?' But I know I deleted it.

The emails don't exist. They never existed.

I stare at him. I know how this looks – it was almost a year ago that I accused the barmaid, and a year before that my friend and neighbour. There have been other accusations and paranoia in between, but it seems to reach a head around this time of year. Is he right? Does Emily's birthday always cause me to become anxious and ill again?

He sits down. He's speaking more gently to me now. 'I am at my wits' end, Marianne. Tonight wasn't the first time you've embarrassed me in front of friends and colleagues. You get drunk, say inappropriate things – you've made my life a misery. But I've stayed... I've always stayed, because it's my duty... and I love you. But I wonder if the children and I would be better off alone?'

'No, no, you can't say that... I won't leave the children.'

'You might have no choice if you continue on like this; you made a spectacle of yourself tonight and I don't want you near my children.'

'No, please, no. I love my kids and even you can't change that. I might be mad, I might black out sometimes, make mistakes, drink sometimes, but I do everything for them. I'm capable of loving and caring for them. I'm here when you aren't and I know who their teachers are, their friends... I know them, Simon. I know Alfie hates rugby and cries when you force him to play, and then you don't even turn up to watch. I know your competitive nature is making Charlie more aggressive... like you. And I *know* you love them all, but you won't acknowledge their flaws. Sophie's developing a destructive relationship with food, and this will, if it continues, probably lead to destructive relationships with men. You want them to be perfect, but they aren't and that's okay, Simon. I'm not perfect either. I've made mistakes, but I *know* our kids. I may not have a career, I can't operate on anyone, shit I can't even pull pints,' I say, taking a mild dig at last year's model. 'I don't earn an amazing salary, but I love my kids and I'll do *anything* for them. They need me.'

'Knowing the minutiae of my children's lives is a luxury I can't afford because I'm too busy working to keep you in champagne and with a roof over all your heads. And now, after tonight's debacle, you've probably lost me the promotion.'

'You love your kids and you're a good dad, but you don't see enough of them. You blame it on work, but one day they'll see that you find plenty of time for extra-curricular activities.' I sigh. 'I've called sometimes when you say you're working late and you aren't even there.'

'You're really not well; you need some time away.' He's shaking his head and looking into my eyes with such pity, I'm beginning to doubt myself. Yes, it's *possible* that I imagined all this with Caroline, but I'm not convinced.

I take another sip of champagne while he guides me into the sitting room where we sit together on the sofa.

'I accept that perhaps I haven't been the most sensitive when it comes to Emily,' he says. 'But she was my child too – and I hurt every day, just like you.'

I was already tipsy, but this glass and the pills are going straight to my head.

'I love you, Marianne, in spite of everything you've put me through. I still love you.'

Does he mean it? Do I care?

I look at him, but he's swimming before my eyes and I can only just make out his face.

'All I want is for you to get better.'

Is he jumping ship on Caroline, or is this just a way of luring me back to the psychiatric ward so he can move his woman and her full womb into my house?

Or did I imagine everything after all?

'What if the kids had seen you tonight? Do you think they'd be proud, because I don't,' he snaps, slicing into my chest, opening up a fresh wound with his words.

I feel bad. Whatever the truth, it's a fact that I've become obsessed and turned it into some crazy campaign.

'You can't rely on me to force you to take your meds, Marianne. You need to go back on the higher dose – remember when we went to the GP a few months ago? She suggested you take 45 mg of the Mirtazapine a day.'

'She said that because you told her I was in the garden at night with no shoes on. You said I was putting books in the fridge, that I would lose it over nothing and scream at the kids.'

'And you *were*. That's why I went with you to the GP. You don't realise, and you can't face up to it. Marianne, your illness isn't just destroying you, it's destroying everyone you touch… including our children. You can blame me for Sophie's eating problems and Charlie's aggression, and Alfie not wanting to play sport, but you're the one who cooks for Sophie, who disciplines Charlie and takes Alfie to practice. It's you they're railing against. And if you can't see that, then I don't think there's any hope of you getting better.'

I don't know what to say.

What if he's right?

Am I to blame for the kids? Am I a bad mother after all? Would they be better off without me?

'I spoke to Caroline before she left – in tears I might add – and she told me about the Instagram stalking, the weird invite for a secret lunch at the Italian and the way you forced her to send you a guest list and didn't even use it. She says you've been making late-night phone calls too. Heavy breathing. You're sick, Marianne.'

'I didn't make any late-night phone calls,' I say, unable to deny the other crimes levied at me. I don't recall phoning her, but then again I do have her number. 'Did she say it was me? If there was no caller ID, it could have been an old boyfriend. She's had a lot, you know…'

'Marianne, please, let's not split hairs. Who else would it be? Caroline says the weirdo whispers vile stuff, but it's a female voice – who else would be sick enough to make obscene phone calls to one of my female colleagues late at night? You're the only person I know who has an unhealthy obsession with Caroline Harker… wow, I'm a lucky man to be married to you, aren't I?' His face is filled with loathing; he can't bear to look at me.

I look back over everything I've done, concluding with the 'spectacle' tonight. Could I really have imagined everything again?

But, oh God, the stuff on her Instagram made me crazy. Then again, a staged photo of two glasses of wine and rumpled sheets does not an affair make, and it may have been his favourite wine, but it didn't mean he was the man with her. Could it be possible I did just put two and two together and make six? It wouldn't be the first time.

He's now pacing the kitchen – he looks terrible and I watch him going back and forth like a caged animal. Behind him on the wall is the blown-up black and white photo of our wedding day. It's mocking us, because the difference now is scary. We're older, of course, but my once rounded face is hollow now. No smile, no hope like back then. Simon's still handsome, but looks so much older than forty-two; he's a shadow of the man I married, and it's partly my fault. Because of my behaviour we've had to move house, lose friends, the kids have had to change schools and tonight I finally stripped him of his privacy and dignity by inviting his boss and colleagues into our home and humiliating him. Looking at him now, pacing, his face unshaven, his eyes unslept, I can see what I've done. I know he's been cruel to me, but I've also been cruel to him.

'Whatever's happened between us, I'm sorry – I apologise,' I say, offering the olive branch. 'I don't want a reconciliation and I'm sure you don't either – but we need to be able to talk to each other in order to move on, even if it is in the opposite direction.' Even if I've imagined it all and there was a chance for us, I couldn't stay with him, not after what we've done to each other.

He leans on the wall, his back to me, both palms flat, his whole body limp.

'I'm used to being talked about, used to the whispers as I walk by,' he starts. 'But this… this… tonight was something else… I'll have to put in for another a transfer – I'm taking the children with me.'

I can't see his face – he's still standing with his back to me – but I go over to him, try to make some kind of contact, if only to see his face.

'No... no. Simon, please... let's talk about this, you can't take them...' Tears are streaming down my face, I am pleading with him, but he doesn't move, just stands against the wall, his head down. He's threatening to take them but can only do this if I'm locked away and she goes with him. Without Caroline, my replacement, he can't take the kids to another place, start a new job – he needs me.

'Simon, let's not do anything stupid... the kids can't be moved again, they've only just settled...' I try to sound rational, practical even. I need to work out what to do next, but in order to do that I need to know what *he's* going to do next.

He shakes his head. 'Marianne, you've driven me to it *again*. I can't face anyone at the hospital after tonight. I'm going to bed. I need to clear my head.' And with that he walks from the room, leaving me alone with his words ringing in my ears. My worst fear. The end of everything.

I'm taking the children with me.

I sit on the sofa alone, hugging a cushion for comfort, and rock back and forth. Despite the clouds of doubt, something is pushing through my brain. I know I saw those emails, our picnic rug on her Instagram, the fact she drinks his favourite wine with an anonymous friend and her timelines fit with times he was 'working'. I saw them together tonight. I know they are together but it wasn't snatched glances or smouldering looks that convinced me, it was the change in her. I couldn't quite put my finger on it, but she was different – not the bubbly, bright career girl with the basketful of alcohol in Waitrose. Not the strong, independent woman who took an hour from her vital work to lunch with me, smiling benignly as I wittered on. No, this was a different Caroline, who in Simon's presence became quieter, duller, less assertive, meek even – and I realise he's turning her into me. His criticism, his disapproval and his slaps are all for the one he loves – and now it's Caroline's turn. And that's how I know I'm not mad.

Tonight everything I said was real, and the emails, the social media, the clues all lead to one thing – that this is not my paranoia. But there's only one way for me to prove it. Only one person who can help me by telling the truth so he can't say I'm crazy, and take away my children. The one that can save me is the one person I never thought I'd turn to: Caroline.

The following morning I wake up, make breakfast and when Simon disappears, I ask Sophie to keep an eye on the boys, who were deposited at dawn from their sleepover by the birthday boy's mum. I notice Sophie's wearing her hair scraped back with the scrunchie I made her and it reminds me that I still have the bag meant for Suzie. I never gave it to Jen after what Simon had said, and it gives me an idea. After last night, Caroline will be defensive and understandably might think I've come to cause more trouble. But that's not what I need now. I need confirmation, assurance, clarity, and Caroline can give me that. If I arrive with a gift, it will feel more genuine and the sea-green bag will be perfect because I made it with my own hands – a true gesture of goodwill. So I grab the bag and a bunch of flowers from one of the vases and set off to see Caroline.

I feel ready. We need to talk directly to each other and not through his filter of lies. But pulling up outside Caroline's cottage, my mouth is dry. I feel so nervous. I really have to force myself to leave the car and knock on the big wooden door. It's cold, and the swirling, biting December wind chills me through. I pull my coat around me and knock again a little louder. I open up the letter box and peer in, calling her name, but nothing.

Standing up, I see the curtains next door twitch and an older woman's face peer through. I make a waving gesture. I'm going to ask her if she knows if Caroline's in, but just then the cottage door opens. I feel the warmth from within, but Caroline is cold and unsmiling and I have to stop myself from running back to the car. Why am I putting myself through this?

'I'm so sorry about last night,' I blurt out, standing on the doorstep, shivering. 'It was inappropriate and, given your condition, I hope I didn't cause you too much distress.'

She stands there, no make-up, in leggings and an oversized grey cardigan. The designer gear, perfect lipstick and dazzling smile is gone – she looks pale and lethargic.

'I think we need to talk,' I say.

She doesn't budge, just stares at me, glassy-eyed.

'I've not come here to upset you, Caroline, I just want the truth from someone, because Simon won't give it to me. And I don't think he's been truthful with you either.' We both stare at each other across oceans, and I know this isn't going to be easy.

'Please?' I ask gently.

There's a moment's silence and then, defeated, she says, 'Come in.'

She stands back to let me in and, still unsmiling, leads me through a tiny hall into a small kitchen with beams, an Aga, oak worktops and a little mug tree holding Emma Bridgewater mugs with little hearts on. I think I may have misjudged Caroline; her home isn't the cold, minimalist setting I'd imagined. It's warm and cosy, romantic even. Caroline isn't the wild and worldly woman I imagined her to be, she's just another girl who's been seduced by Simon's devastating charm.

'Tea?' Caroline murmurs and I nod as she flicks the kettle on.

I put the flowers down on the worktop with the bag.

She turns to pick out some mugs and sees my 'gifts'. 'For me?'

'Yes… I… come as a friend,' I hear myself say. It's something I never imagined – yet here I am in my husband's lover's kitchen, she's making me tea and I'm asking for her help.

'It's beautiful,' she sighs with sadness, putting the mugs down momentarily and running her fingers along the velvet bag.

'I made it...' I think about how Simon said Jen hated the bag and I wonder for a moment if she'll do the same and say something nasty about the bag to Simon later.

'Thank you, but you didn't have to,' she says and pours boiling water into the two mugs.

'I saw your neighbour.' I smile, desperate to try and keep the conversation going but not sure what to say.

'Oh?' She puts a steaming mug down in front of me on the counter.

'Yes, the old lady next door, a real curtain-twitcher. I bet you can't do anything without her snooping?' I realise what I've said. Do I sound like I'm referring to nocturnal activities with my husband?

But before I can add anything, she shrugs. 'I don't know her. I work long hours.'

We stand opposite each other; it's similar to the previous evening when we stood over the marital bed, but this is different. She is different. She isn't the girl on Instagram who seems to spend her time holidaying and rumpling sheets – and when I look more closely at her face, it looks like she's been crying.

'Have I upset you? I mean, apart from... the obvious, last night?'

'Oh. No... though last night was horrific.' She looks at me and I feel awkward.

'I'm sorry... it's just...'

'Oh God I know, I know. Please don't apologise.' She reaches for her mug and on the inside of her wrist I see a deep-purple bruise. I suspect it's the result of their bedroom action. She's a grown-up, she can do what she likes I suppose, but it makes me wonder if he came here last night. He went to bed before me but he could have come here after I'd gone to sleep in the spare room. I wouldn't know. I'd had pills, drunk a lot of champagne and slept heavily.

'Are you okay?' I ask, and she nods her head and runs her long fingers against the velvet of the bag again, like she's seeking comfort.

'You're very talented,' she says.

'Oh, not really, making bags is a bit of an indulgence...'

'But you are. I could see it in your home, the way you've made it so beautiful. The kitchen, stylish but homely, the children's bedrooms all fitted out to their tastes, the way you talk about them...'

'I'm a mum first, Caroline. You'll know soon enough how that feels. You'll do anything for them, even stay with a man who destroys you... bit by bit.'

For the children.

She lifts her face and I see something like recognition in the other woman's eyes.

'Marianne...' She looks down again now, into her mug. I get the feeling she wants to tell me something, like when Alfie's done something wrong and he feels bad.

'It is Simon's baby, isn't it?' I ask.

She takes a ragged breath, the kind of breath you take after a long crying jag, and she lifts her head and looks away from me. Then after what seems like a very long time she nods, and turns back to me, tears in her eyes.

Here is my proof and in this moment we seem to come together, two mothers both protecting their children, protecting themselves. She could have lied, she could have said what he did, that I'm mad, and people would have believed her... and him. But for some reason she chose not to. She decided to tell the truth – it's about time one of us did. 'It's okay. You're not telling me anything I didn't already know, and as you probably gathered after last night – I've known about the two of you for some time.'

'I hate myself,' she suddenly says, and the tears flow. 'Just meeting you and realising how nice you are, how...'

'Sane?'

'I suppose... I'd fooled myself that this was a harmless fling.'

'No such thing.'

'I know that now. But the more I fell for him, the more I convinced myself that you didn't deserve him, that you were somehow… in the way.'

'Simon convinced you of that, I'm sure.'

'No, I take responsibility for my actions, Marianne. I… I became a villain in someone's life story. I wanted what you had because I thought you didn't care, that you were unhappy, a bit crazy, permanently bitter. I got pregnant deliberately. I wanted Simon to make me his wife and I didn't care what happened to you.'

'I understand… He told you lies about me, and you believed him.'

'He did, and maybe I'm stupid for believing him. As much as I can move on, take responsibility, apologise to you and step back from him – that kind of experience lives with you, Marianne. It takes up residence in your soul.'

How deeply she's been hurt and manipulated by him too. Perhaps she isn't the surgical slut, the man-chasing harlot I'd believed her to be.

She looks at me through blurred tears. 'It was fine at first. I didn't know you, I had no idea about your life, your home, your children… your holidays, then I find out I'm pregnant and I was delighted.'

'Does Simon know about the baby?'

'Yes… he was shocked… He wasn't okay about it, but said we'd work it out that you'd be… leaving soon and I could move in with him.'

'I know what that means. He had big plans to have me sectioned… again,' I sigh.

'I'm sorry. I know you've had your… issues, and I'll be honest Marianne, I believed what he told me, that you were ill, unable to cope and that you needed help. But as soon as I met you at lunch, everything changed for me. I didn't see the woman Simon had painted. I saw your happiness and your pride in your kids, your love of life. I saw your posts on Instagram, the kids' innocent little smiles everywhere, family days in the park, last year's summer holidays, and I felt so guilty. I realised I wasn't helping Simon by being with him. I might be responsible for ruining those children's lives… and yours too. I hated myself, but then I started to hate him, because he was doing this too, but he was worse than me… because he was hurting his *own* family. Then, last night… after the party, he came here, but I plucked up the courage and told him it was over.'

'Did he hurt you?'

She instinctively pulls down her jumper sleeve to hide the purple finger marks. 'He was upset… understandably. He said I led him on. I knew what I was getting into… and then, when he's about to leave you, I just dump him. He said he could have lost everything: the house, his kids… you.'

'He already has lost everything.'

'This mess… it's all my fault. You were probably happy before me.'

I smile at this and she's surprised, asks me why and I explain that this is Simon's talent. 'He has this way of making you feel guilty, like he's the innocent party,' I say. 'But know that he isn't. I don't want you to go through this pregnancy hating yourself, because trust me, it will end in tears. I know from experience that an unhappy mother means an unhappy baby and the pain of…'

She touches my arm. 'I know.'

'I'm sure you do, and one day perhaps, when this is all over, you'll allow me to tell you what happened from *my* perspective.'

She smiles, and I tell her that my marriage was over long ago; she must stop beating herself up and leave Simon to me.

'It wasn't you, but this has taken its final chunk out of a dying marriage. I just need to do it the right way and make sure the children are with me.'

Marianne, I know how hard it's been for you. Simon told me you'd been reading the emails. That's why he deleted the account – he didn't want to hurt you.'

'Thank you for telling me. You've no idea how grateful I am. You've just given me my sanity back.' I sigh with relief. 'I just wonder how he knew about the emails; he deleted them before I'd told him I read them.'

She shrugs.

'Oh well, I guess we'll never know. I should have confronted him straight away. It wasn't fair of me to play that game. The same with your online accounts. I used them to try and work out who you were, where you were and when you were seeing him… that's how I saw the baby scan.'

'I wanted my friends to see it. I never thought for a minute you would see it and know it was Simon's…'

'I know, I know. And I won't be looking again.' I feel rather stupid. We both stand together in the hallway, and for a while we don't say anything. The only sound is the rain lashing down outside. I realise in these silent moments that this woman was never a threat – she was a fellow sufferer, and now, hopefully, a fellow survivor.

'To be honest, Marianne, I understand the online stalking. We all do it. I checked out your Instagram more than once. But… it was the late-night calls you made that bothered me more… They really freaked me out… That was really nasty stuff, and all the heavy breathing.'

'Simon told me about that, but I didn't make any late-night calls… At least I honestly don't remember,' I add. 'God, if I did…' I don't know what to say; sorry wouldn't be enough because they sound like really scary calls.

She shrugs. She doesn't believe me and who could blame her? I don't even know what I did. All the online stalking, the obsessive jealousy, inviting her for lunch, ordering the same underwear – perhaps I was a little crazy for a while back there? Now I'm just confused and conflicted and all I'm left with is me and Caroline drinking tea from Emma Bridgewater mugs and trying to make sense of what has happened to us.

I don't remember how I got home from Caroline's. I took my pills earlier this morning because I was so anxious and by the time I got home they'd kicked in. Sophie was around, but Simon was nowhere to be seen when I got back, and I remember thinking so much for 'family Saturday' and laughing so loudly the boys came running into the sitting room to see what was so funny. I spend the day on autopilot and simply make sure the boys are fed and safe and later wake up in the spare room and wonder what happened to Saturday. It's pitch black but I'm woken by the sound of Simon leaving the house. It's 2 a.m. I guess he's going to Caroline's. I just hope she was telling the truth and it's over – and I hope she stays strong when he turns up at her door, because if she lets him in now – he won't let her go.

CHAPTER TWENTY-FIVE

The following day is Sunday and I wake in the spare room, feeling completely disorientated. I remember my meeting with Caroline and I'm uneasy, but I don't know why. She'd seemed a little happier for getting it all off her chest, and I was grateful to her for her honesty. I didn't imagine this affair. I was right all along, and knowing what happened I can now justify pursuing a new future with my kids, but without Simon.

Within minutes, the boys come thundering down the stairs and I go into the downstairs loo, wash my face and discreetly take my tablets.

'Can we have pancakes, Mum?' Alfie is asking. This request is added to by a roar from Charlie, so I quickly turn into Mary Berry and start the process as they attempt upside-down gymnastics on their stools. There's no sign of Sophie, so when the boys are eating, I pop upstairs and tell her there are pancakes waiting – she isn't very impressed. She looks tired, and I know it's because she isn't eating, so I try and tempt her by offering all kinds of things, but she refuses. I dread to think how Sophie will react when Simon and I break up, but for now I just want her to eat something.

After breakfast, I steel myself to go upstairs into our room, but there's no sign of Simon, and no sign that the bed's been slept in either. Did he spend the night with her? I feel like fucking Goldilocks.

Did you lie to me, Caroline? Did you simply tell me what you thought I wanted to hear?

I know this may sound mad – let's face it, I have a history – but I resent the fact he's probably with her again instead of his kids. It's Sunday, and earlier in the week he'd promised to take the boys to play football in the park today. This would have left me free to take Sophie shopping. She needs some TLC and just because Simon and I are in a state of flux it doesn't mean the kids have to suffer. I'm sure all the parenting rules have already been broken and I wonder at the state of our family after all the hurt and the hate they've probably seen. But we need to think about healing now. So where is he?

I try not to think too much – it hurts my head – so I go back into Mum mode, head back down into the kitchen and try to make things nice for the boys by offering second helpings and sprinkles for the pancakes. No one asks where Dad is and I don't want to pass my worry onto them, so we eat and tell jokes and the boys regale me with stories of Alex in their class who does the loudest and most 'awesome' belches – I imagine his mother is very proud. The belching stories are enlightening, and disgusting, but not distracting enough to stop my mind wandering back to Simon's whereabouts.

By mid-morning the pancakes are a memory, Sophie's appeared and the four of us are playing Monopoly. I join in with gusto, but have to feign excitement when I buy Park Lane and Mayfair and put hotels on them. I just keep wondering where Simon is and what he's up to and if he's got Caroline back in his clutches or he's with David working out the divorce. The doctor and the lawyer – two heads together, plotting some drugged-up, straitjacket life for the woman who won't leave.

I *will* leave, but on *my* terms with *my* children, and that includes Sophie because I'm sure if she was given the choice she'd want to be with me and her half-brothers.

I roll the dice and end up in jail, which is good because I have to miss a turn and that gives me the opportunity to think.

Sometimes we shape our partners into what we think we want them to be – and for me the revelation was seeing how Caroline had clearly changed so much in a matter of months. Just like I had. Simon married a free-spirited, vulnerable girl who was bright and fun, and he was fascinated. Like a child watching an exotic fish in a garden pond, he wanted to catch her and keep her. But in doing so he turned me into someone else. I always thought the person I'd become was my fault: my flaws, my mistakes, my madness – the terrible death of our baby. But seeing Caroline, the once strong, independent career girl, standing in her kitchen shivering, shadows and tears in her eyes, a dark bruise on her wrist, made me realise – it was never my fault. I didn't have to spend all that time being punished, because I hadn't done anything wrong – I was the perfect specimen to be seduced into Simon's warped idea of love.

Whatever I may have imagined in the past, I know Simon doesn't want me around any more. He and I both want an end to this marriage now, but he doesn't want to lose the house or his kids any more than I do. He also knows that the worst thing he could do is stop me having the children – and being an emotional sadist, that will be top of his list.

He could be at the clinic now, explaining how erratic my behaviour is, that he's worried for the children's safety, and signing papers for me to be taken in, like last time, when he said we were going on a date, but he took me to a clinic.

After everything that's happened in the past forty-eight hours, I'm so worried at the prospect of being committed again that I barely register when Charlie lands on my property, owing apparently 'millions'.

'Mum, Mum… I landed – and I'm *not* paying,' he's shouting.

I tune back in to my beautiful family, demanding this money in full, threatening to tickle him until he pays up and instructing Alfie and Sophie to hold him down. It makes a nice change for Alfie to be the one winning over Charlie and I go in for the tickle. It makes me think about the power struggle between me and Simon;

I always win, Marianne. Not this time, Simon, I won't give my children up under any circumstances.

Charlie's now screeching with laughter which makes us all laugh and as he tries to escape we grab him in a rugby tackle, all rolling around the floor, hysterical... Then we hear the front door open. The kids go quiet and Simon walks into the kitchen.

He looks dreadful, like he's had no sleep, and for a moment I almost feel sorry for him. He seems to have the worries of the world on his shoulders.

Sophie looks horrified, and Charlie asks shyly if he's going to join us in a game of Monopoly, but he just shakes his head. No one needs to say anything, but we all know Monopoly is over and Sophie immediately disappears to her room. The boys aren't so sensitive and Charlie sees this as the perfect opportunity to take Alfie in a brutal headlock and slam him onto the floor. I don't think this is unconnected to Simon's arrival. Charlie always seems to become aggressive and shows off around his father. I can't help but feel that without Simon in his life he would be a calmer child.

'Boys, boys... Charlie, that's enough! Just calm down,' I say and suggest they watch TV for a while in the sitting room. They look at Simon, waiting for permission; he's the only member of the household that can sign this off. *Pompous, controlling prick.* For a second I think he's going to object just to wind me up, but he eventually finds the strength to nod and, roaring their approval, they leave.

'Where have you been?' I ask him after a few minutes' silence. He isn't going to volunteer his whereabouts.

'Nowhere.'

'All night?'

'Marianne, when is this going to stop – this constant questioning?'

'I'm sorry,' I say, then hate myself for my default position of apologising. 'I don't care where you've been, but I just want to know what's happening.'

'I just drove around. I went to see a friend, we drank too much and I stayed over at their place.'

'Caroline?' I ask, remembering the sadness, the defeat in her eyes and feeling weirdly protective of her.

'No, not Caroline.'

'Who then?'

'I really don't believe after everything that it's any business of yours. I can spend the night with whom I choose.'

Why do you keep lying Simon, even when it doesn't matter?

I don't care where he stayed, and I don't have the energy to fight. 'I went to see her yesterday,' I say, looking at his face for a reaction. 'We had a talk. She told me you deleted your email account and she confirmed it's your baby.'

'Okay, well, you win.' He says this like he's given up – his heart isn't even in the lie any more.

'Christ, Simon, it's not about winning, it's about you lying, trying to destroy me.'

'It isn't unusual to lie to your wife about an affair,' he says pompously.

'No, but to deny it and imply your wife is insane is *unusual*, to say the least.'

'Do you blame me? Your obsessions, irrational behaviour, the ups and downs – if I'd told you about Caroline, you'd have slashed your wrists.'

'How could you…' He always knows where to hurt me. I once told him that I'm haunted by the vision of my mother's body, the red-stained towel, the slits lengthways up her arms from her wrists. White towels, pale flesh, red blood. He always conjured it for me.

'I've had enough of this, enough of you. It's impossible to have a conversation with you,' he hisses, already walking through the kitchen away from me. 'I'm going to get some sleep.'

Unfortunately, what he does next will impact on all of us, but I have no idea what his move will be. My instinct is to take the kids and leave but where could I go with no money? And if I did try and run away with the children I'd be playing straight into Simon's hands. He's hoping I will react (because I always have) and this will justify him keeping the kids, having me locked up. So for now I just have to be patient and wait, but for what I don't know.

While Simon takes himself off to bed to sleep off last night, there's no such luxury for me. Being the mum of two six-year-old boys, I don't have time to ponder my own life, and when I hear the latest argument becoming physical between them, I decide to take them to the swimming baths. I need to get out of the house and so do they.

I sit in the humidity, watching the boys like a hawk as they flail around in the pool, splashing each other and everyone else around them. I almost fall asleep – the warmth and the residue of medication still in my system makes me drowsy – but I manage to stay awake and get us back home.

By mid-afternoon, I can barely keep my eyes open. After a snack, I allow the boys an hour on their iPads, while I take a much-needed nap on the sofa, grateful there's no sign of Simon and the toxic atmosphere he brings with him.

I wake with a start, and discover it's 6 p.m. and I've been asleep for more than three hours. I'm so out of it, I find it hard to come round and immediately call the boys, who aren't in the sitting room where I left them. I open the French windows, calling them over and over, and it's only when I run back in to grab my phone to call the police I see a note on the worktop. It's from Simon and says he's taken the kids to the cinema. He's never taken them to the cinema in their lives. It's not something he'd do – I hope this isn't his revenge, and he's decided to leave and take them with him?

With my mind going into overdrive, I text him, and immediately get a message back, which is unusual for Simon, and he says they will be home in half an hour. I am calmer but still a mess and only manage to anchor myself when I put the kettle on and turn on the TV. I'm sipping my tea and feeling edgy, hoping his considerately quick response wasn't just a ruse to appease me while he takes them out of the country. I think I'm being irrational and overanxious, so take a tablet and sit down and try to concentrate on the news. Sometimes it helps just to be distracted by something outside my own little world.

I stare at the screen – stories of *real* turmoil, wars, terrorism, murder – but still my personal turmoil intrudes, pushing its way through. Even if I managed to get custody of the children (which would be touch-and-go given Emily and my mental health record, not to mention my police one), Simon would make things very difficult for me. He'd probably sell the house, the kids would be taken out of yet another school, there'd be no money for extra-curricular activities, no more lovely holidays. In truth, I haven't always found holidays to be pleasurable. Simon usually manages to find something wrong with the way I've packed the kids' clothes, the type of sun cream I've bought, the way I look in a bikini. But the kids have a great time, I make sure of that – and despite the ups and downs, there have been golden moments as a family.

There was the time when we hired a boat in Greece. Simon said he was the captain – the boys were only three and beside themselves with joy and Sophie screamed with terror and delight when Simon put his foot down. 'Faster, Daddy, faster,' she'd yelled. Later we found a little restaurant on the beach and ate freshly caught fish with chunks of lemon as we watched the sun go down over the sea. Alfie was asleep on my knee and Charlie on Simon's and I remember looking over at my husband and baby and feeling nothing but love.

Life wasn't always this perfect at home, behind closed doors, but the difference between then and now is that I had hope. I honestly thought if I was well Simon would love me and treat me better – but it was naïve of me. I believed that if we could string together these good times like fairy lights through our life, then I could endure the rest – the cruelty, the way he likes to torment and control me. I thought that was love, but he simply brainwashed me, like he has Caroline, transforming us into spectres of our real selves.

I think of the photo on her Instagram – smiling with those shiny lips, short, choppy blonde hair, clutching a wine glass – but the picture isn't in my head, it's on my TV screen in in my kitchen. I know it's the pills, but I can't keep going under like this. I thought I was over my obsession with Caroline. But it *is* her... or at least it's the same photo I've seen a thousand times online. The wallpaper, huge green fronds on navy blue, and the forearm of bangles, the glass of wine...

I turn up the volume and walk towards the screen, never taking my eyes off it as she comes closer. It seems so real. Perhaps I'm not seeing things; perhaps she's suddenly become famous overnight? Has she carried out a pioneering operation and saved a child's life? Then my head clears and I hear it.

'... Police are treating her death as suspicious and asking for any witnesses to contact them.'

CHAPTER TWENTY-SIX

I am hallucinating, aren't I? The bright blonde star of her own Instagram. The woman I've fixated on for weeks. The woman I feel like I know so well we could be friends. Except we're not. In the photo, she's beautiful, happy, vibrant and alive.

But now she's dead.

I hold my breath, and try to swallow, but my mouth's too dry. A reporter is standing outside the cottage.

I was there only yesterday.

I can't take it in – there's an interview now with the neighbour, the one I saw peeping from behind the twitching lace curtain, she's saying what a lovely girl Caroline was, but she didn't even know her.

Vultures.

The news is over, but I'm still staring at the screen, where two people are doing the Argentine tango and apparently 'the results are in'. No wonder I'm going mad. I'm surprised more people aren't mad, the way they switch so quickly from real-life murder to ballroom dancing. As the woman kicks and swirls and the man plays matador, I am seriously questioning myself. Time slips away and suddenly Simon's back with the kids.

Was I the last person to see Caroline alive?

I can't articulate what I know. It would make it too real and I need to think about it, come to terms with it in my own head before I say it out loud. *Caroline has been murdered.* I immediately go into my default mum mode where I feel safe and prepare food, ask the boys about their film, which apparently was 'sick' and involved 'awesome' Smurfs, who, according to Alfie, discover 'the biggest secret in Smurf history!'

'Wow,' I keep saying, sometimes followed by 'and then what happened?' But I'm not listening. Simon wandered off into the sitting room as soon as they came home – he clearly didn't engage with the film in quite the same way. Does he know?

After I've fed and bathed the boys and read several stories on autopilot, I go back downstairs and into the kitchen. Sophie's in there and I pick up one of the boys' iPads, for once genuinely hoping this was all in my mind. I'm frightened of finding this piece of news, but equally of not finding it. If it's there, Caroline's dead, if it isn't I'm mad.

I log on and ask Google, and within seconds she appears in the news stream, sparkly, smiley Caroline, the one before Simon, clutching her wine glass and smiling at me.

'Sophie.' I have to think how to ask this – I don't want to freak her out. 'Can you tell me: is this the woman who was here the other evening?'

Sophie looks up and comes over to me, looks down at the article, and when her hand goes over her mouth, I know I'm not imagining this.

'Caroline Harker,' she says, her eyes filled with horror. 'Shit Mum, what happened?'

I press play and we watch the news coverage, horrified yet mesmerised. As if the body they're putting in the ambulance now isn't someone we know. But it is… it's someone we know very well. 'I think she was stabbed,' I say, reading the copy and feeling a chill run through me. How many times had I wished that woman dead? I'd imagined her twisted body in car wrecks, at the bottom of car parks, smashed, her beautiful face unrecognisable. But that was just my state of mind back then. I was upset, a little overwrought, it was all a dark and horrible fantasy. I'd never do anything like that. Would I?

Sophie's phone tinkles and she's soon back in her own world of texts and teenage angst, Caroline almost forgotten as she wanders off upstairs, her face glued to her phone.

Knowing there is no doubt, that I haven't imagined or misunderstood what happened, I rush in to Simon, who doesn't even look up.

'There's something you must see.' I thrust the iPad at him, but before he can refuse, he looks up at me, the expression on my face compelling him to look at the screen.

'Christ,' he says as he takes it from me, slowly sitting up, his face ashen. Then he turns on the TV news channel, and is now scrolling his phone at the same time. 'Oh God, what happened? This is terrible... terrible.' I think he might cry. I think I might.

'We need to call the police. We have to tell them,' I say.

'Tell them what?' He's surprised at this.

'That we *know* her – they are asking for witnesses. This wasn't suicide Simon, someone killed her, she's been stabbed... She was at our house two nights ago. I was at hers yesterday.'

He seems to straighten up, compose himself, and says very calmly, 'Which is exactly why we *shouldn't* be calling the police.'

'What?'

'You had a confrontation with her in front of witnesses in your own kitchen. And then you were over there yesterday... and now she's... Well, this happens. You can see how it looks. You were probably the last one to see her?'

'Yes, which means I should tell the police...'

'You're not listening. You accused her of being pregnant with your husband's baby.'

'I know, but that doesn't make me a murderer. I went round there yesterday and we talked, that was all... I even took her a gift. We made up. Simon, whoever killed her must have gone there after me.'

'But who...'

I wait a moment, and then I say exactly what's on my mind. What's the point in holding back now?

'You?'

'Don't be ridiculous – why would I do her any harm? She's...'

'Carrying your baby? We don't have to pretend I'm imagining it any more. That's where you were last night. You were with her, weren't you?'

'No, no I wasn't... Oh my God...' He drops the iPad onto the floor. I'm standing over him as he looks up at me from the chair. His eyes are strange and dark; I've never seen him like this before. 'Marianne. When she told you... about the baby, that it was mine... did you... hurt her?'

'NO. NO. Simon, what the fuck?' I can see how this looks, but he can't turn this on me. He's just as likely to have done something.

'But you've been obsessed. Do you actually remember leaving her cottage?'

'Yes of course,' I snap. But I don't. I don't.

I grab my phone. 'I have to call the police.'

He stands up now; his hand is round my arm and he's squeezing. 'You were there yesterday... Did you stay long, did anyone see you, did you touch anything?'

'I don't... yes I suppose... but...'

'Right, so your fingerprints are all over the place... and you had a confrontation with her the night before... You were obsessed with her and when you went over to the cottage she told you about the baby... *my* baby...'

I stand in front of him, frowning, just frowning. I'm trying to show my displeasure at where this is going, but I'm also trying to remember what happened at the cottage yesterday. I went round, I gave her the bag and the flowers, she had a bruise on her wrist she tried to hide, we drank tea from mugs with little hearts on, she told me the truth and I left. Didn't I?

'Then there's the small matter of your mental state, your history – a previous assault on someone who you mistakenly thought I was involved with.'

'That wasn't assault and you know it. I poured beer over her...'

'You were charged with assault; you have a criminal record. You also stalked Caroline online, liking all her Instagram posts, just letting her know you were watching. What about the late-night calls, the weird lunch, the even weirder surprise party at which everyone witnessed your breakdown, and then the next day you just went off to Caroline's cottage to visit her without telling anyone? Have I missed anything out?'

I don't respond – what can I say? For once what Simon is saying is all true. He reminds me of a prosecuting lawyer giving his closing, damning speech, and he's not quite finished.

'Oh yes... and finally, the death of a baby, *your* baby – in *your* care.'

I doubt myself now, but I know this is what Simon does. He always lays the blame on me and I always accept it – gratefully – but not any more. I just wish I could remember what happened. I thought we'd made friends, that we understood each other. And yet... yet I remember doubting her, wondering if she was strong enough to say no to Simon, worrying that he could convince her to be with him and send me away. How far would I go to keep my kids? Would I really do something *that* terrible? Would I? Could I? I don't think so, but I don't know, because the pills make me wobbly and I've been under so much stress. I once threw a pint of beer over a woman behind a bar. I once wrote profanities on a woman's Facebook page because I thought she was with Simon. Who knows what the fuck I would do under duress? I don't know myself.

Am I insane... Am I unsafe? Am I a murderer?

I try and focus. I can't let him brainwash me into thinking I did it, though I really don't know and the more I think about it...

'Anyway, where were *you* last night, Simon?' I suddenly hear myself say.

'I was with David.'

'I hope David vouches for you if this gets messy.'

'For God's sake, Marianne, why on earth would I do something like that to a woman I'm… involved with?'

'Caroline told me she'd finished with you, that she was upset. She hated herself for what she was doing to me and the children. I can't think you'd just accept her dumping you and walk away.'

'I *did* accept it. I agreed we should part. I told her I would finance the child until he or she was eighteen as long as she could provide proof it was mine.'

'You old romantic.'

'I'm not stupid.'

'No, and neither was she, because she realised how evil you are and if you could hurt your wife and kids, you weren't what she was looking for.'

'Rubbish. As usual you're fantasising.'

'Like I was fantasising about the affair and the baby? I know exactly what was going on, and it wasn't in my head – it was real, I saw it in writing. You wanted me out of the picture so she'd move in, take over the house, the children, and you could carry on with your career and eventually when you got bored of her, whoever else you fancied. Caroline was the brand new model. The old defunct one had to be locked away and with no chance of her causing any more problems, throwing drinks over barmaids, accusing every woman within a five-mile radius of sleeping with you. But Caroline had moral backbone somewhere in that supple spine. When she met me, she could see I wasn't the hapless madwoman in the attic that you'd lied to her about, so she couldn't bear to help destroy me so said goodbye to you. You don't like goodbyes, do you, Simon?'

'Oh, Marianne, you're rambling again…'

'The police will see your emails. I know they were there.'

He laughs – he really laughs. 'Yes, they can probably still find them, but I'm not denying I had an affair. The emails put you firmly back in the frame. Caroline was killed by a jealous wife. It was the act of a woman scorned; the police will soon work that one out.'

Oh God, is he right? I don't know what to believe. I don't know *who* to believe and that includes myself. But I'm clearly not the only one who's faltering, because Simon is white as a sheet and has just gone to the downstairs toilet. I can hear retching and I don't know if his reaction is because he's upset, or he did it... or he thinks I did?

I shouldn't have taken those bloody tablets, I feel so out of it. I just wish I could remember things more clearly, but there's one thing that I remember loud and clear: I hated Caroline and had wished she was dead.

CHAPTER TWENTY-SEVEN

I'm scared. I remember the police arriving when Emily died. I was still screaming and trying to wake her. I didn't believe she'd died; she was everything to me. But the police were circumspect, not sympathetic – I suppose until the coroner decided it was 'accidental death', everyone involved had to be aware it could be more than what it seemed. And now, this has brought it all back and I feel guilty for doing something I don't think I did.

I keep checking the iPad for news. *Where was Simon last night?* Scrolling through all the information. Reading and re-reading the same facts, but all I see is that there were multiple stab wounds. *Where was Simon last night?* There's her smiling face once more, everything to live for. But something to die for? There's the cottage, the fucking cottage with its big wooden door and the nosy neighbour. She soon came from behind the lace curtains to grab her fifteen minutes of fame, didn't she? Perhaps she was the last to see her? *BUT WHERE THE FUCK WAS SIMON LAST NIGHT?*

If he was with David, why hadn't he just said that before instead of saying he was with a friend? Maybe he had gone to David's after he'd stabbed his mistress and his unborn child.

And now he's in the bathroom purging himself.

I want to scream. My insides are on fire. I am turned inside out by the shock and the not knowing.

A new line on the news feed. An older woman, standing with a man. Oh no, it's Caroline's parents. Her mother's name is Alice. My heart is bursting for her.

I know what it's like to lose your little girl, Alice.

She's asking 'If anyone knows anything…'

Alice's husband is holding her up. I want to put my arm around her and tell her one day it will all be okay. But I can't. Because it won't.

Your child's death will define you, Alice, and you will wake every morning and for that first miniscule, golden moment you will have forgotten that you don't have her any more. And then the darkness will come rolling back in like fog and you'll want to die to be with her. And that's how you will start and end every day of the rest of your life.

If I have anything to do with Caroline's death, then I don't deserve to be standing here in this beautiful house with my three perfect children sleeping. If I have caused Alice one second, one modicum, of the anguish that I suffered, then I need to pay for it.

I pick up the phone just as Simon walks in. I've never seen him look so terrible. I can't begin to fathom what he's thinking or feeling. I'm not sure I want to.

'Marianne, no,' he says firmly when he sees I'm holding the phone. 'You can't call the police. How many times do I have to tell you… Don't bring them here… You will be arrested.'

'Then so be it. The police can work it out, but I won't live a lie, Simon, I've been doing that for too long.'

'What are you talking about?' He sounds exasperated.

'I've buried myself so deep in this marriage, I don't know who I am any more. Over the years you've made me so bloody paranoid, so needy, so guilty, with your games and your blame. I don't know what happened last night, but either way we both have to take some responsibility, because I believe this young woman died because of one of us.'

But which one of us was it?

'One of us? Marianne, there's only one of us who could have done this, who's capable of doing it. The minute someone comes along and threatens your existence you try to get rid of them. And it looks like this time you have.'

'I'm not listening to you any more. I can't, because I've listened to you for years and look at me. LOOK AT ME, SIMON!'

We both stand there in our beautiful tomb, buried alive under the rubble of deceit and blame, and he can't look at me. He can't actually bring himself to meet my eyes.

I pick up the phone again and this time Simon doesn't stop me. He knows I'm right but whether that's because he did it or he knows I did, I'm not sure. There's only one way to find out. I punch out the number on the news feed for 'anyone who has any information'. I don't believe there is anything worse than losing a child. I have battled with this myself for so long, and I feel I owe it to Alice to help find who killed her daughter. Even if it's me.

CHAPTER TWENTY-EIGHT

Within an hour of my call to the police, there's a knock on the door. Simon and I haven't uttered a word, just sat in the kitchen waiting.

Dead men walking.

He's on a stool at the island. I'm leaning against the kitchen cabinets, arms folded, staring into space. Behind me is my shiny white backdrop, the beautiful pale walls, the fucking Calacatta Oro marble worktops. I almost laugh to myself. This is the kitchen I believed could change my life, bring us together. A new house, a fresh start – a state-of-the-art kitchen with the clean lines of sustainable European oak cabinetry. What a joke. How superficial I'd become. Now I know it takes more than a high-end kitchen to heal a mess like ours, and all the antibacterial spray in the world won't clean away the detritus we've created between us.

We wait in the heavy silence, the children sleeping upstairs, blissfully unaware of the juggernaut that's about to crash into their lives and change everything. When they wake up in the morning, nothing will be the same again; I feel a cool tear run down my face and look over at Simon, his head in his hands.

This is all we are now.

One of us knows who did this, but neither of us is prepared to either admit it or, in my case, dig deeper and find it. I've never been really good at digging, at pushing beneath the surface to see what's underneath, because in my experience, it usually isn't something I want to see.

'If you think I'm lying for you again, you can forget it,' Simon suddenly says into the thick silence. It hangs there like a stagnant smell – his loathing for me permeates the atmosphere around us like swirling fog.

I've taken another 30 mg of Mirtazapine, a slightly smaller dose, but it still packs a punch. I had no choice. The anxiety was swelling in my chest, my face was hot and my heart was thudding too fast. But through the medicated mist, something is pulling me to the surface – like a drowning woman, I am fighting for survival, for truth. I know if I believe in myself and my own truth, then I will get through this, and as painful as it may be, I can survive. I know this, because I've been in a similar place before, ten years ago with my baby's face like porcelain, her body cold and my mind racing through the screams and the tears. And when we arrived in casualty I was treated with caution, unsure if they were dealing with a bereaved mother or a baby killer. I was beyond caring where I fit into their story, what my footnote would be. I just knew my baby was dead and I wanted to follow her. I'd have happily died for Emily, and if they believed I did it, then prison was almost as good as dying to me.

'Inmates mete out their own retribution to cellmates who hurt children,' Simon had murmured at the time, and I was glad. I welcomed my atonement; the bloodier and more painful the better. The weeks dragged on, and through the cocktail clouds of medication all I remember is his hate. The only time he touched me was to have sex; it was rough, and painful, but it was what I deserved and when he'd filled me up with his loathing, I was grateful. Everyone else was sympathetic, from my GP to my health visitor, all mewling around me, telling me how awful it was for me, but I didn't deserve their sympathy. I'd let my own baby die next to me and Simon ripped out my already ragged heart, smashed it against rocks, pushed it through a blender and then handed it back to me. And along with my own self-flagellation, he lashed me daily with the fact that all I'd had to do was keep her alive, and I couldn't even do that. Simon didn't stuff me with clichés, touch my arm and tell me 'in time' it would feel better – he forced me back down the black hole until I couldn't see the light again. And I was okay with that. Because I didn't want to see the light; it was safer in the dark.

'Just like your mother after all,' he'd say. 'It's in the genes, tainted blood,' and therefore Emily's death in my care was inevitable. But even all this wasn't enough for me. I craved more punishment, because that's what I deserved. And even Simon couldn't hurt me enough.

Harder, harder, don't stop until I'm dead.

I remember standing in the bathroom of our new house, a modern new build with bay windows and a little pocket-sized garden, all ready for a young family. Emily had been dead for almost two years and I looked out onto that neat little square of green, thinking of summers that would never be. I imagined Emily's paddling pool, her bike with stabilisers, her birthday party in the garden, bright balloons dancing against a blue sky. In one hand, I clutched several packets of Paracetamol and in the other a pregnancy test. I waited then, like I'm waiting now, the clock ticking, my destiny on hold – and only when the line appeared did I know what happened next. Another baby needed me, and in spite of everything, including my own fear of the same thing happening again, I stayed – for the next one... two as it happened... and flushed the pills down the toilet.

Giving evidence at the inquest, I was so racked with guilt, convinced by Simon and myself that her death was all my fault and if only I'd done things differently she'd still be with us. Had I fed her too much too late, too little too early? Was it because I was lying next to her that she died? Had I smothered her by rolling over? Should I have sat by her cot all night instead of bringing her to my bed? Is that what other, 'successful' mothers do? I didn't hear any of the legal jargon, the paramedic's evidence, Simon's and my health visitor's assurance that all was well at home (which Simon has since referred to as 'lying' for me). After the verdict I remember standing in front of the coroner, hiccoughing with tears and asking, 'Did I kill my baby?' His face immediately softened and he reassured me that Emily had died of Sudden Infant Death Syndrome and I was in no way to blame.

But that didn't stop me blaming myself. It didn't stop Simon from blaming me either, and as we wait for the knock I feel like we're back there and it's all my fault again.

Even though we're both expecting it, and we know exactly what it means, we both start at the abrupt rap on the wood. My finger ends tingle and I reluctantly pull myself in the direction of the hallway. But Simon's off the kitchen stool and already passing me, putting out his hand to prevent me going first.

'I'll deal with this,' he hisses. 'This could be curtains for you… do you realise? You won't see the children again, Marianne. *My* children will not be going anywhere near a prison.'

He's right – they will throw the book at me, and I can't even say I'm not guilty, because maybe I am. Can I stand up in court and say I didn't do this? I don't know. And what about when they question me? Will I be able to convince them to look at other people who also have a motive before they condemn me? Like my husband?

I'm now in the hall standing a few feet away from Simon; the shadowy figures are on the doorstep as he puts on the porch light and turns to give me a final warning look. I don't trust him. He's also fighting for his life and I know if it came to it he'd throw me under the bus. For me this is not a battle to blame Simon, it's about discovering the truth, and if it *was* me who killed Caroline, then I'll take my punishment – but for Simon this is a battle between the two of us. And he's used to winning.

As he opens the door, I stand braced. I have an awful lot to fight for.

'My wife is in a state of extreme distress,' is his opening gambit, which doesn't put me in the best light with the two hard-faced women standing in the doorway.

The slightly older one introduces herself as Detective Inspector Cornell and the other one is apparently Detective Sergeant Faith.

'Your wife called us...' DI Cornell starts.

'Yes,' Simon says, 'but you need to know my wife hasn't been well.' He's standing there, and I'm behind him, like he's shielding me from the police. But I know his game – he's trying to stop me from telling my side of the story. 'But of course you can speak with her. She was very upset last night after seeing Caroline, but I'm sure my wife has nothing to hide,' he says.

I want to protest – he's making me look guilty before they've even met me with his faux concern. They may as well just handcuff me now.

I can't see his face but I know just how it looks: apologetic. He wants them to believe he's trying to cover for me, for something I might have done. I'm angry, so angry I want to punch and kick him. But I need to be calm. I need to be true to them and true to me – no fake happiness, no faking perfection. Not any more. It's time for the truth.

CHAPTER TWENTY-NINE

Simon ushers DI Cornell and her sidekick into the hall where I introduce myself. We shake hands and Simon suggests we go into the sitting room.

'Can we offer you a drink... tea, coffee?' he asks.

I'm relieved when Cornell shakes her head and Faith presumably can't say yes now her boss has refused. I know who'd have been sent off to provide the officers' refreshments and I'm determined not to leave him alone with them. God only knows what he'd say about me.

I've now taken a seat opposite them and Simon's standing in the middle of the room, rather rudely blocking our view of one another.

'You called us, Mrs Wilson – you think you might have been the last person to see her?' Cornell has to lean round to address me.

'Simon, do you mind?' I say and gesture for him to move.

He whips round and, for a split second, he looks like he could kill me. He's so wound up, I think he's almost forgot we have 'guests'. Then he realises we're not alone and he will have to do as I say – for once.

'Yes... I may have been the last person to see her.' I wait for Simon to interject, to add that it might be him, that he was there after me. And when he doesn't, I point this out. 'Though I think my husband may also have called round... later, I think. Am I right, Simon?' All three of us turn to look at him and Cornell turns her body round to face him. This has piqued their interest.

He's wandering the room, rubbing his hands together like he's waiting for something. I've never seen him like this before – he's a mess, and I wonder if he killed her, and if he did, would he try and blame me? I don't doubt it for a minute.

What are you hiding, Simon?

'So, can we establish your… relationship with the victim, Mr Wilson?' Cornell's saying, tapping her pen with those stubby fingers. She's distracted by Simon's pacing and looks relieved when he eventually sits down, still rubbing his hands, clearly anxious.

'A colleague…' is all he says and I just know he's going to deny he was anything more.

So, to his horror and increasing embarrassment, I explain everything. I start from the beginning and when I say, 'I assumed my husband was having an affair – we've had problems of this nature before,' he interjects, keen to establish that I was mistaken on previous occasions.

'My wife is prone to flights of fancy… not her fault, she is mentally ill…' he starts, but Cornell is too engrossed in my story, which she and Faith are both writing down.

Cornell's clearly an old-school 'copper', the type you see on TV, hair scraped back, no make-up, no wedding ring. I doubt those bitten nails have ever scratched a man's back in ecstasy. Funny what goes through your mind when you might be arrested for murder.

'Mr Wilson, I'm taking a statement from your wife – if you would just allow me to continue, I'll take your statement after this.'

He isn't pleased, Simon hates being told what to do, especially by a woman, and he sits with his arms folded, like a sulking child, while I carry on talking, punctuated by the detective's questions. When it comes to the point where I went to see Caroline, she visibly perks up and leans forward.

When I finish, I feel purged. I've told them everything in a calm and ordered way, no half-truths, no lies. I've laid everything before them, and I'm trusting them to find out what happened – and who did it.

When Simon tells the detectives about his own 'friendship' with Caroline, he says that they were 'close' and he's 'worried my wife may have given you a rather dramatised version of events'. He clearly thinks these women are stupid, which is the problem when you're a brilliant, but arrogant man – you think no one else can think for themselves. I believe the fact they are women makes him feel he can manipulate them, like he manipulated Caroline and God knows who else. But no-one believes me. I want to scream at them that he's lying, that I did nothing, but I don't know. And Simon's talking and talking, so smooth, so confident, so sure – and I'm not.

Eventually my worst fears are realised as DI Cornell informs me that I'm being arrested for the murder of Dr Caroline Harker. And, as she cautions me, I am filled with blind panic – how can I convince the police I didn't do it, when I can't even convince myself?

CHAPTER THIRTY

It's all so distressing. I've had a consultation with a solicitor and I'm now in a police cell with a little serving hatch so I can be looked at and checked on every now and then. I feel like an animal in a zoo. I left home in the clothes I was stood up in, surrendered my phone and keys and I'm now staring at a paper cup of coffee sitting in front of me. It's lukewarm and going colder by the minute, but I daren't even sip it because I might vomit. I'm trembling with fear and feel like my skin has been peeled off and I'm exposed, just like the roughly painted brickwork all around me.

I thought I was better, thought all the trouble was behind me, but do I carry it with me? What did I do?

I'm surrounded by nothingness, I have no newspaper, nothing to read, and there's nothing in here I can hurt myself with, which explains the tepid coffee in the paper cup. I don't know what time it is, how long I'll be here or what the outcome will be. But all I'm worrying about are my kids. They'll wake up in a few hours with no mum and though Sophie will be able to comprehend what's happened, the boys won't.

Is their mother a murderer?

After what feels like hours, there's a rustling outside the room, a rattle of the door and I'm taken out of the room, along a corridor to another room, where DI Cornell and DS Faith await.

They are sitting next to each other at a desk facing the door and when I walk in Cornell doesn't smile, just nods and gestures

for me to sit down opposite them. Faith rustles papers on the desk
and my solicitor sits down next to me.

'Mrs Wilson.'

'Marianne... please call me Marianne,' I almost beg. I know how
these things can escalate. I was 'interviewed' for several hours after
Emily's death and it was one of the worst experiences of my life as
they tried to break me down and make me confess to something
I hadn't done. It was only much later after the postmortem that
the police started to treat me differently, with more sympathy and
respect. But this is not the same; this is a vicious stabbing with
a motive. The 'good' news, if you can call it that, is that sitting
alone in a cell for a few hours enabled me to really search my
brain and relive my visit with Caroline, but I can't recall actually
leaving. I remember rain lashing down, mugs of tea, she talked
about late-night phone calls, which she and Simon seemed to
think I did. But I didn't... did I? If I'd gone there intending to
hurt her or kill her surely I'd have had the presence of mind to
cover my tracks or hide the fact that I was there. Christ, I virtually
announced myself to the neighbourhood, waving to Mrs Nosy
and banging on Caroline's door. I even called through the letter
box like some obsessive, but this doesn't help, it makes me look
guilty, makes me *feel* guilty. I have to force myself to concentrate
on DI Cornell, who's now telling me that some of the guests from
the surprise party have been interviewed and confirmed that there
was an accusation made by me about Caroline Harker.

'So... you had an altercation with the victim, Mrs Wilson?'

'Yes, but I didn't do anything. I just got a bit... too much at
the party. I thought she was having an affair with my husband.
Well, she was.'

'So, you had a good reason to want Dr Harker out of the
picture?'

'Yes, but I didn't want her *dead*... I mean, I may
have... felt... Look, I was upset. I thought Simon and her might

try to take the kids...' I stop. I'm not doing myself any favours and Cornell is positively glowing at the prospect of charging and arresting within the hour. 'I may have been worried, desperate even – but I would never hurt anyone... And anyway, the last time I saw her we kind of made friends.'

'Really? Well, while you've been filing your nails enjoying the room service at Her Majesty's pleasure here, DS Faith has managed to do a bit of digging.' Obviously some police humour, which I don't appreciate. 'And, according to our records,' the other detective hands her the notes which she reads from, 'eighteen months ago you assaulted a barmaid.' At this she looks up and stares at me. 'Yet you say you'd never hurt anyone?'

'I didn't *assault* her, I poured a glass of beer over her. I didn't *hurt* her.'

'Define hurt. She wasn't too happy about it – had to have six months off work with the trauma.'

'Yes, well I'm sorry about that, but I heard she'd had six months off *before* that too – probably because she'd been taking time off "sick" to be with my husband,' I spit, then immediately regret this – sounding like a bunny-boiling wife will not help me here.

Cornell just carries on, like I'm an irritating noise in the background.

'On Friday night you publicly accused a woman of sleeping with your husband – you say yourself you were worried about her plans to get custody of your kids. Forensics have been all over Dr Harker's cottage. Now we're just waiting on the DNA results. Do you think we'll find yours?'

'Yes... of course. I mean, I was there. I was in the kitchen, I drank tea, I touched a mug, knocked on the door... I don't know.' I'm starting to panic, and that never ends well.

Cornell doesn't react. 'There's a bag belonging to you at the scene... green velvet with sea stuff all over it. Your husband has identified it as one you made...'

'Yes, I took it as a gift for her. I wanted to make peace.'

'Nothing says I'm sorry like a green bag with sea urchins all over it.'

DS Faith smirks, but I look down, rolling the now empty paper cup between my fingers.

DI Cornell stares at the papers in front of her, presumably forensic results and titbits from DS Faith's research haul. 'So, to summarise the story so far, you had a hissy fit because you thought your hubby was having a hot blonde from the office...'

'Theatre. A colleague in theatre. He's a surgeon.'

'Whatever, a hot blonde in the office is the same the world over – and I can vouch for that from experience. Anyway... in a nutshell, you have this party, invite her over, accuse her of being pregnant with your husband's child, she storms off and the following day you go round to see her.' She stops abruptly and looks up from her notes, glasses on the end of her nose. 'You can probably see where I'm going with this?'

I don't answer, just glare at the table and try not to cry.

'And...' She goes back to the notes. 'There are witnesses from your... what did you call it, a *surprise* party?'

I nod, feeling very silly. I must look so pathetic – the scorned wife. The housewife's ultimate revenge, a fucking surprise party. What was I thinking?

'And a day later,' Cornell continues, 'Dr Harker is found stabbed to death in her own home, the home you admit you visited only hours before. You can see my dilemma here, Mrs Wilson?' She leans forward, tapping her pen on the desk. 'I'm not saying it *was* you, but it's not looking good...'

I am in a TV drama, aren't I? This isn't real. I want to be home drinking camomile tea and making the children's packed lunches for tomorrow. I don't want to be here being accused and patronised.

'Oh dear,' Cornell is looking down at a piece of paper, about to spring something on me no doubt.

'What is it?' I ask anxiously.

'And just when I thought things were getting boring. We now have a Mrs Jennifer Moreton saying you threatened to *kill* Dr Harker…'

Jen? What the fuck has any of this got to do with her?

'No… oh, you've got this wrong. She knew I didn't mean it. I… it was an expression I used. I said I could *kill* Dr Harker for what she'd done… I didn't mean I *could* kill her.'

'Oh, so you don't mean what you say?'

I didn't. Did I?

'No, I mean yes… you've taken this literally, that it isn't how I meant it… Jen knew I didn't mean it. You'd know if you'd been there…'

'Well I wasn't, was I?'

'Look, what I'm saying is Jen can be a bit of a drama queen. She may have exaggerated, taken it out of context….' I'm now deeply regretted discussing it with Jen – I just hope to God I didn't say anything else without thinking. I know she wouldn't say this with malice; she probably doesn't realise the implications and is just running her mouth. It's what Jen does. Too swept up in the drama of the moment to realise what harm she's causing. 'She obviously got the wrong end of the stick. Anyone who knows me knows I'm not capable of… anything like that, but I suppose she doesn't really know me that well…'

'Really? At the moment, she's looking after your kids so I hope we're not adding stranger danger to the list of potential problems with this case.'

I'm part of a 'case'. I'm involved in murder whether I like it or not.

Did I do it?

'Why is she looking after my kids?'

'She was the person your husband called.'

'I hope they're okay.'

'Why do you say that?'

'Because she'll probably get her nanny to take them to school while she goes off on a bloody spa day!'

'So,' DI Cornell continues, bored with my middle-class childcare concerns, 'to get back to the situation in hand… you've got form, a motive, there's probable forensic evidence, a nosy neighbour who witnessed you arriving at Dr Harker's cottage and another witness, a good friend no less, who's telling us you said you wanted to kill the victim. So what am I to think?'

I don't know what to say, but I know I'm not the only one who should be a suspect here.

'What about the emails between Caroline and my husband? He deleted them, but surely you can find them?'

DI Cornell doesn't look up, just continues to study the papers in front of her. 'All his and your devices will be checked,' she says absently.

That isn't going to play well for my defence – I must have googled Caroline Harker at least a thousand times on my phone, not to mention my constant lurking on all her social media.

'Simon once told me how you could kill someone swiftly. Because he's a surgeon he'd know exactly where the jugular was…' I press.

At this, the junior detective pipes up, 'Mmm, the perpetrator didn't seem to have a clue where it was.'

'Well, perhaps it was a double bluff?' I offer.

'The victim bled out for a while before she died. It didn't present like a premeditated attack. Whoever killed Dr Harker did it instinctively – it wasn't clean, it was done in a frenzy.' DS Faith takes a moment and looks at me before repeating, 'A *jealous* frenzy.'

I look away. This is too much, I can't handle it, but before I have chance to regroup Cornell hits me with something else.

'Do you recognise this, Mrs Wilson?' She's now proffering a photograph of the velvet bag I gave to Caroline. I don't understand why they're so interested in the bag; it was a gift – why don't they just get it and move on?

'Yes… that's the bag I made, the one I took to give to her as a gift.' I look closely. The strap from the shoulder bag has been broken. It's thick twisted silk, very strong – I use it for my handbags so you can carry quite heavy stuff, like a tablet, phone, bag of make-up… and I'm surprised it's snapped. 'What's happened to it?'

'You tell me?'

'I don't know.'

'Fibres from the bag have been found on Dr Harker's neck, and we're waiting on forensics but it looks like she was probably wearing it when her assailant attacked her. The strap was probably pulled across her neck. They got into a struggle, the strap was broken – before the victim was stabbed with the bread knife.'

'Amateur,' Faith's saying, and shaking her head in despair at the calibre of murderers these days.

What can I say? I have no idea what happened. I don't think I had anything to do with this, but innocent people have been convicted of murder before. I wouldn't be the first.

My solicitor asks if he can 'have a word with his client'.

The detectives leave and I reassure him I know nothing about the strap of the bag being used to try and strangle Caroline Harker.

'When will I be able to go?' I ask. I'm worried about the children.

According to my solicitor, they can keep me here for twenty-four hours. After that if they haven't charged me but still think I'm 'of interest', they can apply for extensions to keep me longer.

'The maximum time they can detain you is ninety-six hours, by which time they have to either charge you or let you go,' he adds.

During this conversation, I keep bursting into tears – my main concern is the children, and I try and comfort myself that at least Jen's there. She may not be mother of the year but at least she's familiar to them. The boys are used to her collecting them from the French tutor when we take it in turns and they've stayed over at hers once for Oliver's birthday sleepover. As for poor Sophie, she'll be so worried. Simon won't try and reassure her; he'll probably convince her I'm ill and that I did it. But this is only the beginning. What if I'm guilty? What if I end up spending the rest of my life in prison? I'll never see my kids again; Simon wouldn't allow them to visit. No birthday parties, no wonderful watershed moments. I won't be at their graduations, their weddings… I'll never meet my grandchildren… I start to cry again.

Richard attempts to reassure me, but I'm tired, confused and wondering if I've had my last few hours as a free woman, but I don't have long to think about this because Cornell and Faith are back, I'm cautioned again and the interview is resumed.

'Now, we've been talking to your husband,' Cornell says. 'Do you have anything else you'd like to tell me?'

'No.'

'Can you categorically say that you didn't do this?' I'm surprised at this sudden question.

You've told them you think I did it, haven't you, Simon?

I pause. It's time to be totally honest. 'Not one hundred per cent, no.'

'Really?' she says, sitting up like she's about to get a confession.

'Look, I'm just telling you the truth,' I say, and go on to explain my medication, how it makes me woozy, which is why I can't remember leaving.

'What's the last thing you remember?' she asks, monotone, like I'm using my lack of memory as an excuse, a defence even if I end up in court.

'I was confused… it might be the illness, or the medication… but I just can't remember sometimes. I don't trust myself.' I hear these final words and know I'm only compounding the problem. Richard Black shifts in his seat, and we both know that 'no comment' would have been so much wiser.

I'm ninety-nine per cent sure I didn't kill Caroline, it's just the bloody medication that provides that one per cent of doubt in my head, and after a lifetime with someone like my husband I think I'm more suggestible than I should be. If Cornell tells me she has evidence I did it and I'm being 'banged up' for life – or whatever catchphrase they use at times like this – I would probably go along with it.

Cornell's now asking me to go over everything again, and I explain about the emails and my suspicions and how Simon tried to convinced me it was all in my head.

'I just think… if I didn't do it, then who did? I wonder if my husband knows?'

'Really? Why?' She sounds intrigued.

'Well… when I saw Caroline she told me she'd ended it with him. I doubt he'd have been too pleased about that. I think he loved her in his own twisted way and he'd be hurt to think she'd leave him, especially as she was pregnant. And I told you, she had a bruise on her wrist. Simon can be violent… in the bedroom, but also if he doesn't get what he wants.'

'Did she actually tell you Simon hurt her, that he gave her the bruise?'

'Not exactly, but I feel that she was *trying* to tell me…'

'What you *feel* won't stand up in court.'

'I'm just explaining to you honestly what I think. I'm hoping you or your forensics people… can come up with something more tangible. I know one of us did it and I think it was him,' I blurt.

'Forensics are currently going through stuff but that could be days away,' she says, ignoring my last comment. 'We also have to look at other elements. Yes Dr Wilson had a motive if she was dumping him – he may have been angry about that.'

I nod vigorously in agreement.

'Tell me, Marianne, what's your height?' she suddenly asks, which seems a bit odd. I'd hoped she'd ask me more about Simon's motive.

'I'm five foot three.'

She writes this down, then looks up from her paper. 'Right-handed or left?'

'I'm right-handed...' What?

She nods. I have no idea of the relevance of these questions, but feel if I answer honestly the truth will out.

'Can you tell me anything at all?' I ask. 'It's the not knowing... and I'm worried about the children.'

Cornell is shaking her head and my heart drops. 'It's early days yet – and the CPS won't authorise a charge without enough evidence. I've worked on cases over the years where we've been so sure we knew who the perpetrator of a crime was, and we didn't even want to go through the tortuous interview process... but sometimes, just sometimes, we're wrong.' She looks up from her papers and her eyes drill into me.

You think I did it.

'Now, you said your husband left your home on the night Dr Harker was killed?'

'Yes, he left about three in the morning and he's never really said where he went, just that he drove around and ended up staying at his friend's place.'

'Mmm, yes, and his friend has confirmed this to us, so he does have an alibi for the night,' she concedes.

'Well, he would. His friend's his solicitor. He knows the score – they'll be in it together.'

'Solicitor?' She looks at Faith, puzzled. 'I wasn't aware Mrs Moreton was a solicitor.'

'No, not *Jen*, I mean David. That's who Simon stayed with.'

'Not according to your husband – it seems Mrs Moreton was kind enough to offer him a bed for the night.' She's looking at me now, waiting for my reaction to this.

'Jen?'

'Apparently. And she's backing him up on this.'

'Why would he go round there?'

'Who knows? Does that seem odd to you?'

'Yes. He hardly knows her…' And then I think about her girlish giggles, the way she waited to see if he'd drive her home at the end of the party. The way she was always interested in anything to do with my marriage problems.

Jen… what the fuck?

'Do you believe your husband and Mrs Moreton are…'

'I don't know what to believe any more, but let's put it this way, I *can* believe he spent the night with Jennifer Moreton. Her husband works away… and women find it hard to say no to Simon.' I'd imagined all kinds of things with other women, but never seen that one – Simon and Jen.

It didn't take him long to find someone else to use. Jen's bored of her husband, desperate for adventure, and it would explain the receipts for dinners and nights in hotels when I know from her online presence that Caroline wasn't with him. It seems, then, that he'd had more than one mistress. Caroline and I had both been played.

'She's confirmed he was there and provided his alibi,' Cornell continues. 'His fingerprints are probably all over the deceased's home, of course, but that isn't damning, he's not denying he spent time there.'

Cornell's looking straight at me, and I know exactly what she's saying. Tears are filling my eyes. My heart is thudding. I'm about to be charged with something I'm increasingly sure I didn't do.

CHAPTER THIRTY-ONE

'Can't you see he is guilty? Jen is lying as much as he is… Yes he may have been there, but I bet she can't account for all night.' My frustration is boiling over.

'Yes… she can.'

God, I can't believe it when I think about our girly conversations, the way I confided in her. She must have been running straight back to Simon; she played me as much as he did. And this also explains how he knew to delete his email account before I confronted him – Jen must have told him.

Cornell's looking at me, like I can provide a clue, a confession even, but I can't. As much as I can't say I didn't do it, I certainly can't say I did and until then I will try and stand my ground.

'Jennifer Moreton has provided your husband with an alibi right up until the next day, when he took your sons to the cinema.'

'I have an alibi too. I was home…'

'But you told us you don't remember saying goodbye, and being asleep with no witnesses is not an alibi.'

'He must have drugged me.'

'According to your husband, you drugged yourself… on a regular basis, and that was some strong stuff you were on – 45 mg of Mirtazapine… the usual dose is about thirty, according to our doc.'

'My GP said to take the higher dose when I needed it, but Simon kept on at me and said to keep up the forty-five dosage. He told me it would help… he's a doctor. I believed him.'

She shrugs, allows me to continue ranting, but I'm not sure this is doing me any good at all.

'I've had issues… I've done stupid things, I've even lost control sometimes – but wouldn't you if your husband was constantly bloody cheating?'

'Absolutely. Murder is usually madness in the moment, a loss of control, of reason – as I think you well know, Mrs Wilson.'

Faith is nodding, in agreement with her boss. 'Yep, one person pisses another one off and that's it… and, like I say, this was frenzied… nothing premeditated about *that* scene.'

Tears are now falling as my solicitor insists the interview is stopped because 'my client is distressed'.

I'm escorted back to the little cell, where I lie on the bare mattress, bring my knees up to my chest and curl into a ball and eventually fall into a restless and confused sleep. I wake every now and then, and an officer checks every so often presumably to make sure I've not come to any harm. After the fifth or sixth visit, I manage to drift into a deeper sleep and I dream.

I dream about my children walking through a huge field. They're alone, Sophie's holding the boys' hands and I can see a sinister figure dressed in black waiting for them, I'm shouting at them to come back, but they can't hear me.

I wake up screaming my children's names; someone is shaking me gently.

'Marianne, Mrs Wilson… wake up.'

I jerk and sit up suddenly to see a police officer standing over me. I'm in shock, caught between sleeping and waking, permanently alert waiting for news. 'What? What? Am I going to prison… Are you here to take me away? I have to see my children.'

'No, you're not going to prison, and you can see your kids when they get out of school.'

'Today?'

'Today.' He smiles.

'Really?' I'm crying. I don't know what this means.

'The Custody Sergeant will release you shortly, but DI Cornell is on her way – just wants a few words before you go.'

I almost leap up. This is wonderful, amazing. Am I dreaming? Why?

'Mrs Wilson, I see the sergeant has given you the good news. We have our perpetrator.' Cornell is walking into the cell, rubbing her hands together. 'Yep, while you've been languishing in your five-star hotel room here we've been busy. Good job too, because you've been here almost thirty-six hours and it means loads of paperwork for DS Faith to keep you a minute longer.'

'Great, but trust me, it's no five-star hotel.'

'No… it's more… *boutique?*'

I shrug. I've had enough of her banter, I just want to get home to my children, but I need to know.

'Was it Simon? Have you got him?'

'Your husband has been charged with the murder of Dr Harker,' she says to my great relief. 'I have to say though, there was a point when it was a toss-up between you and him. Both of you had a motive, both of your fingerprints were lighting up that scene and we're still waiting on DNA, but I suppose that's academic now. At one point we even thought you'd *both* killed her in some ménage à trois murder. The papers would have loved that,' she says half to herself. 'But you don't strike me as the threesome type – given your issues with jealousy.'

I shift slightly in the tiny cell. I'm feeling claustrophobic after all this time.

'Yeah, and you'll be pleased to know we recovered the emails – torrid to say the least.'

'Good… is that what finally caught him out?' I ask.

'As a matter of fact, he came in, asked to see us… and confessed.'

I'm shocked. I knew if I hadn't done it then he must be guilty, but I never expected him to actually confess – after all truth isn't his forte.

'You look surprised, Mrs Wilson?'

'I am… not surprised that he did it, but just surprised that he volunteered himself.'

'Yeah, that's what we thought, but the emails and the evidence tie in… He had a motive, and as you suggested, he was angry with Dr Harker because she wanted to finish things. He went over there the night she died; we've got his car on CCTV heading in the direction of Dr Harker's cottage. On initial investigation the entrance wound and trajectory of the knife was at a downward angle which would suggest whoever stabbed her was at least three or four inches taller than the victim, and left-handed.'

Simon's left-handed, and I'd imagine he's around four inches taller, so it all adds up.

'So why did you think it might be me?'

'Stranger things have happened. After all, Mrs Wilson, even *you* thought it might be you.'

I shrug. I'm saying nothing – if he's confessed then I'm okay with that. No point in adding any more of my confused thoughts to all this.

'So he just went round there and they argued and he ended up stabbing her?' I say, pulling the blue blanket over me, chilled at the thought that it could so easily have been me. It's difficult to imagine Simon doing something so rash, so unpremeditated, but there you go. I never really knew my husband.

I'm so sorry, Caroline. After everything I wish I could have saved you and your baby.

'He said it was her fault he'd lost you and the kids and wishes the whole thing had never happened. Funny, I never expected a man like him to be so…'

'What?'

'Frenzied… he seems so cool, and controlled. I was also convinced it was a woman. I don't know… copper's instinct?'

The way Cornell's studying my face for a reaction, I reckon she still thinks I know more than I'm letting on and this is some kind of code between husband and wife. Perhaps she thinks he's confessing to save me, but I know he'd never do that – after all he was the one who wanted me out of the way. Prison would have been even better than some clinic.

'Anyway, onwards and upwards,' Cornell says, shuffling papers, keen to send me on my way. 'Oh, I almost forgot, he asked me to pass on a message to you actually…'

'Oh?'

'Yes, he said he'd like you to be Sophie's legal guardian while he's away… I reckon he'll be going down for a very long time.'

'Of course. I wouldn't have it any other way. I'd like to officially adopt her. It was something Simon never wanted. I think he liked to hold it over me.'

I can barely comprehend everything that's happening; it's as if Simon has suddenly been overcome by his guilt. Perhaps he wants to make amends.

'He seems to have a lot to answer for. Anyway, social services will have to get involved in all that, but for now we're more than happy to let you go. Oh, and he wanted me to give you this.' She passes me a piece of paper which he's scrawled something on, and I eventually decipher it.

Marianne, you are right, I may not have been father of the year, nor have I been husband of the year. But I'll do anything for my kids. Tell them I love them. I know you'll look after them well, and Sophie will be safe with you. Simon x

It seems this horrific act has finally focused his mind.
Too little too late, Simon.

'Does that help?' she asks.

'A bit of paper with a few words doesn't help me or the kids recover from what he's put us through. I don't doubt he loves them, but words are easy, aren't they, and he isn't exactly going to be tested over the next few years as a father.'

She shrugs. 'Those kids have you and that's enough… they'll be fine. And you'll be fine. Just take it easy. These things have a way of hitting you where it hurts further down the line.'

'Thanks, DI Cornell,' I say and go to shake her hand.

'Call me Janet… I'll keep in touch,' she says.

'Okay, speak soon.' I smile as the police officer escorts me from the room to reception, where I'm given back my phone and keys and life. Then they call me a taxi.

I walk out into the winter sunshine – the air is freezing. I'm still numb from everything that's happened, but DI Cornell… Janet… is right, we'll be fine. The kids are better off without a dad than with one like Simon Wilson. I climb into the waiting taxi ask the driver to take me to the boys' school, then dial Sophie and tell her to meet me there. When I arrive I'll sweep them all up into my arms, and we'll go for burgers, plan our future, make silly jokes and sing rude songs that Simon doesn't approve of. Just because we can.

TWELVE MONTHS LATER

This Christmas will be a very different one to last year, when Simon was charged. We still had the house and his salary was paid for a few more months, but soon after, we had to move to a small flat where there's no European oak or Farrow and Ball walls. There's no extra French tuition, no music or tennis lessons any more for the kids either. But there's also no tension, no walking on eggshells, no violence – and I've weaned myself off the medication. Now I know that our relationship was a mess from the beginning. The flawed man and the vulnerable woman. That I was only ever allowed to feel what he wanted me to feel. That I was only ever happy when he chose for me to be. I believe my 'obsessive behaviour' was prompted by the fact that Simon was having the affairs he said I imagined. Sophie told me she'd seen him in a clinch with the barmaid. She's also since told me that she felt his friendship with one of her friend's mothers was 'weird' too. And then there was my so-called friend Jen, who I now know had been enjoying secret liaisons with him for a while, while constantly telling me she had my back. Perhaps some of Simon's women were in my mind, but that wasn't my madness, it was his manipulation. I don't care any more. I'm just angry that not only did he lie about what he was up to, he turned it into *my* problem, *my* 'illness'. I blame Simon for his first wife Nicole's death – not directly perhaps, but in my view, Simon could turn a woman to suicide… and who knows what he was capable of? I'm just glad I got out alive.

So with Simon out of our lives, I'm not anxious or obsessive, Sophie's eating again, Alfie's joined the school drama club and the only time Charlie gets wound up is on the football pitch, where he's scoring goals for the junior school team.

I moved the boys from the fee-paying school Simon had insisted on but I have a part-time job in a local shop and, with Joy's inheritance, I'll be able to send all my kids to university if they wish. Meanwhile, Sophie stayed on for the last few months of Year 13, as it's what she wanted and in the middle of the madness I was keen to keep everything stable for her. At her age Sophie knew what was happening. It hit her the hardest, and she struggled emotionally for a long time. Many nights I would hold her as she cried herself to sleep and I think, even after all this time, in Simon's absence, she allowed herself to finally grieve for her mother. She knew more about me and Simon than I'd realised and told me that her dad used to hurt her mum too, and she's been holding on to all this hurt, both for her mother and for me. She says she feels guilty that she didn't save her mum or stop him from hurting us, and I tell her she couldn't possibly have made any difference, but I know she needs to work through that.

Despite resenting Simon for his treatment of her mum and me, she seems to have accepted the fact he killed and in her own way forgiven him. She even insists on going to see him in prison, which surprises me. She says he's still her dad and she loves him, which makes me so proud of her – she's a bigger person than I am, but perhaps it's her way of coming to terms with everything.

Sophie took her A levels over the summer and, against all the odds, she achieved the required grades to study Forensic Science at university. She's passionate about it – but has taken a year out, says she wants to be home with the family. We all feel the same. The boys are more clingy too; our therapist, appointed by social services, says it's perfectly natural. We all need to heal, and the best way is to talk openly to each other about how we feel and spend time together as a family. The therapist says children as young as the boys can pick up on abusive behaviour, without actually seeing it and without parents even realising, and this can have a lasting effect on their lives and their own choices. But together we're working on that, I can't change the past, but I can help shape their future.

I still think about Caroline. I feel guilty that I couldn't save her, and after our last meeting, I even wonder if we might have been friends. We were both destroyed by the same man – but I got out just in time and though I'm glad I did, I do suffer from survivor's guilt. I know we only met a couple of times, but Caroline's social media was shut down after she died and weirdly, I felt the loss. Her Instagram and Facebook was all I'd known of her, and now it's like she never existed, which is why I can't bring myself to delete her phone number from my phone. It would feel like I was deleting her memory too, it's all I have left. But I try not to dwell too much on Caroline or Simon – they chose their path, I just got caught up along the way and finally I'm beginning to think that one day I'll be free of the past and not feel a painful twisting deep in my stomach when I have to pass her cottage, or see a woman with short blonde hair in Waitrose.

Until today it felt like we were all emerging into the sunlight and finally putting the past behind us. But this morning I have a visitor.

DI Janet Cornell's on the doorstep, says she's passing by and could she have a cuppa. It's not the first time. Janet sometimes calls in when she's in the neighbourhood, keeps me up to date with everything.

I put the kettle on while she chats away, sitting at the kitchen table, and when I turn around, I almost drop the two mugs I'm holding. There on the table is the sea-green velvet scrunchie that I'd made for Sophie from scraps left over from the bag. At first, I'm puzzled – what's that doing here?

'Do you recognise this, Marianne?' Janet's saying between mouthfuls of chocolate digestive. 'It was found at Caroline's cottage… not far from the body. Looks like someone dropped it.'

How on earth did Sophie's scrunchie turned up at the murder scene?

'We found it hours after the murder and wondered if it might be relevant and asked Simon. He said Caroline was wearing it the day she died – it must have come off in the struggle... he told us it was part of a set, and you gave it to Caroline when you gave her the bag. But then it was mislaid in evidence and when he confessed it didn't seem relevant anyway. But it has bugged me Marianne because... I don't recall you mentioning that you gave Caroline this hair scrunchie too?'

It wasn't part of a set. I didn't give it to Caroline. It was Sophie's.

I don't know why, but something stops me from telling Janet the truth.

'Yes... it's the one I made...' I say, looking more closely. 'Part of a set, yes... I made it to match the bag, gave them both to her.' I'm hoping my words make sense while my mind is elsewhere, somewhere it doesn't want to go.

We finish our tea while she tells me all about a burglary up the road, but I'm not listening and minutes later she's heading for the door.

I walk back into the silence and sit at the rickety little kitchen table – inside my head feels like a box of jumbled thoughts that I don't want to look at. But I have to force myself. Sophie knew Caroline from the tennis club; she was rude to her when I opened her bedroom door on the night of the party and introduced them. Perhaps she knew all about Caroline and her father? She was old enough to see what was going on. But then I come to my senses, all this is just me putting two and two together and making six again... isn't it?

The killer was left-handed. That's why we know it was Simon.

But Sophie is also left-handed.

The killer was three or four inches taller than Caroline.

Sophie's three or four inches taller than Caroline.

I go into Sophie's room, search her desk, cupboards, drawers and find nothing. I'm relieved but unsettled. I want to walk away from the very idea, the horrible images filling my mind – but I have to know. So I pace up and down, thinking, thinking; if there's anything it will be here.

But I don't want to find anything.

I go through her suitcase, handbags, and then, just as I'm about to give up and tell myself it's fine, I'm being stupid, I discover her old iPhone tucked at the back of a bookcase. The battery is dead and I know it's nothing, just an old phone, but I'll do one last check and then put this crazy idea to rest. Without Simon's mind games I've been so well and managed without medication for twelve months now – surely my paranoia isn't starting up again? I bring the iPhone downstairs and charge it, waiting for the bars to light up, my heart beating, my mind raging on and on. I doubt the phone will give me any clues, but something tells me I have to make sure, and there might just be something. All the time my mind is whirring, desperately trying to come up with an answer, a reason why these terrible, terrible thoughts in my head must be wrong. In his note after he confessed, Simon said 'I know Sophie will be safe with you.' What exactly did he mean by that? I'd always assumed it was because he was finally giving me custody, the chance to adopt her even. But now I remember what else he'd said in the note, that he'd 'do *anything* for his kids'. Did he do *anything* for Sophie?

Did Simon take the blame for murder?

Eventually the phone lights up and I click on it, not sure if I should even be doing this and not even sure what I'm trying to find. I'm now an expert at guessing pass numbers. I try Sophie's birthday, the boys' and then finally mine, and I'm in and I'm instantly touched by the fact that I'm so special to her that my birthday is her pass number. But I can't dwell on anything, my emotions mustn't overwhelm me. I have to know… though what

I'm not even sure. I'm trembling as I open up the contacts, looking for Caroline, stopping at every C but after much searching there is no Caroline, and I'm temporarily relieved. But I can't relax yet because I know that if Sophie's guilty of something she'd know not to put Caroline's number under Caroline's name in her phone. So I check the call log, and when I see the word 'whore' my heart almost beats out of my chest. I compare the number against Caroline's number in my phone. And the breath is sucked from my lungs as I begin to realise. I'm standing in the middle of the room holding two phones and looking at my worst nightmare. I check the log for this number on Sophie's phone and my suspicions are confirmed. So many calls were made – they were all just a few seconds long, the most about one minute – all at around three in the morning.

Sophie was making the anonymous calls to Caroline.

She probably knew about Caroline, and was calling to freak her out, even scare her off, or just hurt her like she was hurting us. This is evidence of phone calls made, a cry for help, a child protecting what's precious to her – family. It is not evidence of murder.

My mind is hot, whirling, and when I open up the photos on the phone I'm grateful to see nothing incriminating, but then I see a folder: 'The C Word'. I open it up and there are screenshots of Caroline's Instagram, the day on the beach on our picnic rug, the photo of rumpled sheets and wine posted on the night her dad didn't turn up to see her brothers play rugby and so much more. So Sophie had been watching Caroline too.

While I was obsessing and scrolling the internet in my corner of the house, our daughter was doing the same. Both hurting, both threatened, both scared.

Both of us keeping the same secret.

That night, I wait until the boys are in bed and Sophie and I are alone, before I mention DI Cornell's visit. I have to talk to her, I can't go over and over this in my head any more, because I can't come up with a rational reason for this all on my own. Surely Sophie will have one though… won't she?

'Janet… the detective, told me the police found your velvet scrunchie, the green one I made like the bag… it was at Caroline's cottage,' I say, unable to think of a subtle way of revealing this.

Sophie's face pales – she stops looking at her phone and looks directly at me.

'Did you tell her it's mine…?'

'No.'

I sit for a while. I want to know so much, and yet I don't.

'Did you… did you go to the cottage… Was it you?'

She doesn't answer.

'Mum, it's in the past – I don't want to talk about it.'

'We *have* to talk about it, Sophie.'

'Dad said I can't tell anyone, not even you.'

She starts to cry and I go over to her, putting my arm around her and kissing her head – it smells of apple shampoo. I'm reminded of the little seven-year-old who awkwardly shook my hand and asked if I was going to be her mummy now.

Yes darling, I'm your mummy now.

'Was it the baby?' I ask. 'Caroline's baby. Is that why you…?'

She doesn't respond directly. It's like she's in a world of her own, remembering life before Caroline. Eventually she nods, very slowly. 'I was frightened of losing you… of Dad bringing her and her baby into our house, his perfect new family… He wouldn't want us any more…'

'Oh darling, you should have talked to me.'

She'd been as scared as I was that Caroline was going to change our lives. Sophie was worried about me being sent away, she saw the baby scan and knew something had to be done.

'How could I? You weren't well. Some days you were like a zombie and I didn't want to tell you about her and make you even more sad. I hated the way he'd text her all the time, sending her heart emojis and treating you like shit. He'd take me to the tennis club, but it was only so he could see her – they'd disappear for ages when he was supposed to be spending time with me. I once asked him if you could come along. You were always asking me about what it was like there and he said no, that you were too ill, and might cause a scene. He was with her all the time, even gave me a driving lesson and made me drive to her fucking cottage. That's how I knew where she lived.'

'Darling, I'm so sorry, you shouldn't have had to be part of that,' She was just a young girl dealing with adult emotions, just as angry as me at the abandonment and betrayal.

'Tell me Sophie… about that night. Was it you… who … hurt Caroline?'

She nods, slowly.

'Did you mean to… for her to die?'

I don't want to ask, but I need to know.

'No.' She shakes her head and more tears. 'Not in the beginning – it's not like it was premeditated or anything. I found out about the baby. I saw a picture of a baby scan on Instagram… and I just knew… I just fucking knew it was his. Then there was trouble after your party. I didn't know what happened, but I knew you were upset, Dad was angry and I was worried. The next night, when you were asleep and he'd gone out, I picked up the spare keys I used when he gave me a driving lesson and took his car from outside Jen's.' She looks guilty. 'I knew where he was.'

'You knew about Jen?'

'I kind of guessed. I saw the way she looked at him, the way they were dancing together at the school barn dance last summer and… she dropped the boys off here once. You were in the kitchen. I think they kissed in the hallway.'

I don't hurt any more because he numbed me, but I'm hurting for Sophie.

'So you drove over to Caroline's in Dad's car?'

'Yeah, I went over there to tell her to back off.'

That would explain why his car was caught on CCTV driving in the direction of Caroline's cottage the night she was killed.

'I went there, knocked on the door and when she opened it I was upset and it was raining so she let me in. I told her to leave my dad alone, I didn't want another stepmother, you're my mum and... I'd heard Dad saying something to her at the tennis club about coming to live in our house and I was fucking mad. I didn't want her thinking she could do that. I just wanted to scare her off.' She breaks down again, huge, childlike sobs that I don't think will ever stop. I put my arm around her. I want to take her pain and guilt away, but I know I won't ever be able to do that.

'What happened?' She has to share it with me and unburden her guilt.

'She tried to make out it was all over with Dad...'

Caroline must have felt so guilty. I'd been round earlier, and then Sophie was back on her doorstep fighting for her dad, defending me, just trying to keep her family safe.

'She was being mean, telling me I didn't understand, that I was "just a child", but I *did* understand. I'd understood since I was really little, when my dad came home smelling of perfume that wasn't my mum's. I started shouting at Caroline about the baby and said she was a slag and a whore, and I think she realised then that I'd been the one calling her... I used those words.' She looks down, ashamed.

'The late night phone calls?'

She nods, unable to meet my eyes.

'So what happened then... just talk to me, Sophie.'

'She looked sort of scared, said I was upsetting her, told me to go and when I said no, she said she was going to call the police. Then I saw that she was wearing that bag and... I... I thought Dad must have given her one of your beautiful bags that we used to make together and I thought about you and how sad you were… and just lost it.' Sophie's sobbing in my arms. I can barely hear what she's saying. 'I wasn't trying to hurt her. I wanted the bag back and I tried to pull it off her, but it was round her neck and she started fighting. She thought I was trying to hurt her and screaming and… then she fell.'

'It's okay, darling,' I say, stroking her hair to soothe her like I've always done. 'So what happened then?'

'She got up off the floor, yelling that she was really going to call the police. She was shouting in my face, really freaking out and I panicked, I just grabbed the knife and…' She cries again, but I need to know everything.

'I know this is hard… but what happened then?'

'She was coming at me, telling me to get out, pushing me, and I was holding the knife out to stop her… I never meant to… The knife went in… We both screamed and then she started screaming for help and shouting about her baby and I was scared… I just … the knife went in, again and again, until she stopped screaming. I wanted to just run away, but I stayed and tried to clean it up. I knew what to do and tried to take everything that might have my DNA on. Then when I got home, I realised I couldn't find my scrunchie, it had been on my wrist.'

'So what did you do?'

'I was frantic, I couldn't go back to Caroline's to look for it even if I'd wanted to because I'd already taken the car back to Jen's. I stayed awake all night crying and worrying, then Dad came home the next day to take the boys out. You were still asleep. He shouted at me, knew I'd used his car. He checks the mileage – he was angry, thought I'd been out joyriding with my friends. I *wish* I had. I ended up telling him everything, it just poured out and then I told him I'd lost my scrunchie. We both just sat there looking at each other. We were both crying and after a bit he told me to just do as he said and not question anything, so he put the boys in the car – we all went to the cinema. He bought four tickets and came in with us but sneaked out through an exit when the film had started. He said he'd find the scrunchie, and I wasn't to tell anyone, just stay there with the boys. I was so upset I just sat staring at the film until he came back.'

'But he didn't find it?'

She shakes her head. 'He looked everywhere, but just couldn't find it and had to come back. Later on, when the police had taken you to the station I sat at the top of the stairs and watched you go. Dad came to me and said the police thought you'd done it. He said there was always a strong chance the murder would be traced back to you or him – both of you had been at the cottage. Your DNA would be everywhere. He said it would be best for everyone if they found you guilty, that you had a motive and it would be good for you because they'd put you in a clinic and make you better. He said Jen would come and live with us, bring her kids and look after the boys so I wouldn't have to miss out on going away to university. He said I had to live my life… he just kept saying it. But I knew he was just trying to pin it on you and I said no, I'd go to the police and confess… tell them it was me. But he said no because it would devastate both of you if I went to prison. Then he asked me who I wanted to stay and look after us all and I was so upset because he's my dad and I love him… but I said "I want Mum".'

'So that's when he decided to confess and came to the station after I'd been arrested?' I said, stroking her hair, maternal love surging through me.

'I didn't want either of you to take the blame for something I'd done,' she's saying. 'But Dad was adamant, said I was young and had my life in front of me, and if I tried to confess he would do something stupid.'

So he fell on his sword. He finally did something meaningful for his family.

'I'll do anything for my kids,' he'd said – and he had.

I've often wondered how I ever got involved with a man like Simon, but perhaps we aren't so different after all. We're both parents, and despite everything else that was wrong with us, with him, he was prepared to do anything for his kids. I lost my first little girl; I couldn't keep Emily safe. But Sophie *chose* me to keep her safe. And I will. A grieving child and a grieving mother, who found each other when they needed it most, and the father paid the price so his daughter didn't have to.

'How do you feel now… after what happened, Sophie?' I ask.

'I feel like shit. I cry. Every fucking day. I hate myself for what I did… Are you going to call the police, Mum?'

She's looking up at me, her nose running, her face wet with tears, and I think of the little girl sleeping peacefully in her lilac bedroom. I remember her soft, sweet-smelling hair on the pillow, a fluffy cat toy in her arms. Who could possibly imagine the horror that lay ahead?

'No darling, I'm not going to call the police,' I say, and I put my arms around her, trying to absorb all her pain and hurt, because I'm a mum and that's what we do.

Later, in bed I'm alone with my thoughts, I wonder if Janet Cornell ever suspected that Simon's confession was false? I've always had a feeling that she didn't quite believe he'd killed Caroline. 'I was sure it was a woman,' she'd said at the time, putting it down to 'copper's instinct'. Perhaps she still thinks it *was* me… or she might even know it was Sophie? Perhaps Janet *chose* to lose the scrunchie, *chose* to believe Simon's confession and let him pay for all he's done? After all she said herself, 'he seems to have a lot to answer for.'

Sophie was wrong, but ultimately I don't believe it was her fault; it was the fault of her parents. She shouldn't have to pay for something she was forced to do because of the irresponsible, selfish behaviour of the adults around her.

Our children are shaped by us, by our behaviour towards them, other people and ourselves, and I take some responsibility for what happened. Sophie was a child caught up in an adult maelstrom from when she was very young, and the people who should have saved her weren't there to save her. We were too busy saving ourselves.

So I'll continue to love, nurture and protect Sophie, and I will take her secret to the grave. Our daughter did a terrible thing, but the only people who know what happened that night are me, Sophie, and Simon – and none of us will ever tell.

A LETTER FROM SUE

I want to say a huge thank you for choosing to read *Our Little Lies*. If you enjoyed it, and want to keep up to date with all my latest releases, just sign up at the following link. I'll only send you an email when I have a new book out, your email address will never be shared and you can unsubscribe at any time.

www.bookouture.com/sue-watson

It's always been an ambition of mine to write a psychological thriller and *Our Little Lies* was borne out of the question – if you had to fight for everything you love, how far would you go? I'm fascinated by what makes people tick, how far our actions and characters are shaped by nature or nurture and by those we meet along the way. Writing this book has allowed me to explore some of these themes and it's been both exciting and fascinating.

I really hope you loved reading *Our Little Lies* as much as I loved writing it, and if you did I would be incredibly grateful if you could write a review. I really want to know what you think, and it makes such a difference helping new readers to discover one of my books for the first time.

Meanwhile, I'd love to see you on Facebook. Become a friend, like my page and please join me for a chat on Twitter.

Thanks,
Sue. x

    www.suewatsonbooks.com

    suewatsonbooks

    @suewatsonwriter

ACKNOWLEDGEMENTS

As someone who's written twelve humorous books, often involving love, laughter and cake, I have, at times had a little ache to write something darker. In my previous novels I've sometimes tried to 'kill off' a character or turn a summery romance into something a little darker, only to have my editor tactfully suggest that violent deaths and sinister leading men don't sit easily with love, laughter and cake. So when I offered the idea for this novel to my editor Isobel Akenhead, I was delighted that she loved it and wanted to publish it. Therefore I'd like to offer my eternal thanks to Isobel for her wonderful enthusiasm and for showing great faith in allowing this romcom writer with a cake obsession to unleash her dark side.

Big thanks to the Bookouture team, and as always Oliver Rhodes, who turned my writing dream into a career. Thanks to Claire Bord for listening, Jade Craddock for her forensic copy-editing and Kim Nash and Noelle Holten as always, for their amazing hard work in getting our stories out there. A special thank you to Kim for encouraging me to take the plunge into darkness and for helping me in her own rather magical way, to make it happen.

Huge thanks to my expert legal team, Glyn and Jan Newbold, who talked me through knotty plot twists, legal issues, and police procedures. They went above and beyond the call of duty providing invaluable guidance and performing a dramatic reconstruction of murder after several bottles of red late into the night. Any mistakes are all my own. Thanks also to Jackie Swift, who cast sharp eyes over an early version of the novel, and along with discovering many of my errors, provided extensive and valuable feedback. Her insight has benefitted the novel greatly. Thanks also to Sarah Robinson for reading an early version, spotting those mistakes and most importantly – not guessing the end! I am truly blessed to have such kind, supportive and clever friends.

Thanks also to my medical 'team', Dave Watson, for helping talk me through the appropriate diagnoses, drugs and dosages over beers and burgers – again, any mistakes are all my own.

Hugs and thanks to my girls Lesley Mcloughlin, Sharon Beswick, Louise Bagley, Alison Birch, and Kat Everett – you all rock.

Thanks to my mum, who always tells me 'you can do it,' and to my husband Nick, who came up with such brilliant, twisted ideas on how to commit a murder that I'll be cancelling my life insurance immediately!

And finally, thanks to my daughter Eve who shares my passion for trashy true crime TV, and serial killer thrillers, and inspired me to write my own.

Ingram Content Group UK Ltd.
Milton Keynes UK
UKHW021830250423
420770UK00011B/680

9 781786 817501